BY THE LIGHT OF A LIE

MARJORIE **ORR**

Horme Publishing
Suite 310, 176 Finchley Rd.,
London NW3 6BT

Cover design by Spiffing Covers

ISBN: 978-0-9562587-2-4

.

Marjorie Orr is a former print and television journalist, BBC documentary producer, psychotherapist and media astrologer with a global footprint. Political astrology is her main interest (www.star4cast.com) and her previous non-fiction book The Astrological History of the World was hailed as 'living proof of astrology.' This is her debut novel and she lives in the South of France.

CHAPTER 1

The rat crouched on top of the low wall, its nose twitching upwards with anticipation as it sniffed the early morning air. Long whiskers quivered as it searched for the source of the smell. Rank, sulphurous with a hint of sewage, the faint odour eddied and flowed in the riverside breeze. Two sets of yellowing, pronged tusks below its narrow snout were bared in preparation for a tasty morsel ahead. The beady eyes were intent, although flickering constantly on a radar sweep in the dim light for predators or rivals. Overhead the faint sliver of moon was abandoning its struggle against the polluted air to fade to nothing.

The rumble of a city that never slept grew louder as dawn broke, although it was muted in this enclave, which did not encourage passing traffic. The Thames was easing back from its height, the brown water rippling sluggishly away from the muddy banks. Low tide was still five hours away when the dank shoreline would be fully exposed, littered with rocks and accumulated detritus.

Minutes passed and the rat on the far side of the road was nibbling rapidly, its bucktooth prongs tugging at a small chunk of meat. Approaching voices from Blackstone Terrace, leading up to the underpass, caused it to tense then reverse into a space between stones where the low wall had collapsed.

'I don't know why we have to come here, Jaz. It's frigging freezing. That café was much warmer. I wanna go home.'

The younger of two teenagers shivered inside his grubby sweatshirt, the hood covering all but a few strands of his lank black hair. The sleeves were pulled down to act as gloves as he clutched a paper mug of coffee to his chest. He trailed after the older boy, scuffing his trainers on the ground, and sat on the near wall beside the broken section, hunching his back against the wind.

'Quit whining, will you, Petey. You got to toughen up. You know it ain't safe to go home till Pa's gone to work, especially since we got nothing to show for a night's sweat.' Jaz, across the road, faced out to the river, striking a pose with one skinny knee pulled up and his foot planted on the parapet wall. His hood billowed out as the gusts picked up. 'Anyways, you can sometimes find useful gaff here when the tide goes out.' He scanned the stretch of mud downstream as the river receded seawards.

'We're blaggers and not fuckin' scavengers, Jaz.' Petey stamped his foot on the ground with irritation, then half jumped up. 'Oh fuck, I think I put my foot in oil. Some bastard rear-ended this wall and must've done the sump. The shit's all over the place.' He shuffled further along, wiping his hand on his jeans, leaving dark smears. He sniffed his hand and shrugged. 'Doesn't smell like oil.' His back bent lower over his coffee. He wiped his nose on his sleeve and sighed miserably.

A yelp from across the road was followed by running footsteps. 'We're in business, my son. Lookie.' Jaz leaned excitedly over the wall, pointing to the half-hidden handbag with a gold lipstick case glinting in the grey light beside it and a leather wallet caught between stones two yards away. He swung one leg over, then stopped halfway. His shriek drifted out across the water. 'Holy Christ, there's a body.'

The two boys clung to each other as they looked towards the tide line ten feet away where a woman's foot was tangled in a loop of wire rope. Her body was floating face down in the moving water, the current pulling her white blouse round her auburn hair and her skirt up her exposed back. One arm was visible, the hand crushed with part of a finger missing.

'She got no knickers on, Jaz. You think she was raped?' Petey whispered hoarsely, clinging onto his brother's arm, his face lit up with appalled fascination.

'Don't know, don't care,' Jaz said after a few seconds. 'We need to get out of here before we get nicked. I'll just see what's in the wallet.' He swung his other leg across the wall and stood gingerly on a flat boulder, then stepping-stoned his way across to the wallet without leaving footprints in the mud. He averted his eyes from the body and twisted round to pull out a handkerchief that was protruding out of the handbag. He used it to pick up the wallet, search through the contents and remove a wad of notes. Then he threw the wallet towards the body without looking.

'No sense in takin' the credit cards. Not with a dead body. Even Sid wouldn't touch them. Jesus.' He reversed with difficulty over the rocks and sat down breathing heavily, sweat trickling down his acned forehead.

He turned with alarm when Petey started taking photographs of the body with his camera. 'Whatya doin? You nuts? We were never here, got it?' He punched his brother hard on the shoulder.

'Keep yer lid on. We can sell them to that dodgy photographer up Stanford Brook. He gets good money from newspapers and the telly. No questions asked. He'll say he bought them from someone passing by after the body was found. You got her name, yeah?'

The sound of a car on the far side of the Flying Duck pub a few hundred yards down the road cut their argument short and they ran back towards the underpass, their hoods pulled up. As they passed the caved-in section of wall, the morning light glinted on a pool of congealing blood. Petey reversed and took several shots of it, then sprinted after his brother.

The rat was huddled closer into the undergrowth of a bush, gnawing on its prize. It had cleaned the flesh off a small bone and was working its way steadily up to a varnished fingernail.

CHAPTER 2

Crimson ink slithered down the opera programme, curling round the grille of prison bars across the cover and splayed out to reveal the gothic font of Lady MacBeth of Mtsensk. Tire Thane sat frozen at her desk, consumed by the image as if her gaze was all that was holding her upright. Her mobile was still in her hand.

How the hell? Erica had left her at 11 pm last night outside the theatre in St Martin's Lane, taking a cab home to Hampstead to review case papers before court today. Killed in a hit and run near Hammersmith around 2 am this morning. That's what the secretary from her chambers had phoned to say, between bouts of tears.

Why would she be miles away in the opposite direction hours later? It made no sense.

A message ping from her laptop dragged her attention away from the gory artwork and she reached across the clutter on the desk to drop a folder on top of it. With a wince she remembered Erica's parting words. 'Can we try Gilbert and Sullivan next time? The screams of dying women. Ouch. Too much like work to be relaxing.' Then she had given a bright smile and disappeared into the taxi.

Still too stunned to be operating at her normal speed, Tire absently clicked on the email, which was from a newspaper features editor. 'Good stuff. Grateful for quick delivery.' A rush demand for an old travel piece as colour background to the recent flare-up in fighting in Ethiopia had kept her up till the early hours, tightening and revising. Holiday in sunny Yabelo, she had thought gloomily as she sent it, and get yourself butchered. But money was money and she was her only support system.

The tooting brass of Shostakovich's 'Festive Overture' was jangling her head, so she killed the sound on the speakers. The jumbled skyline of Soho on the other side of the glass wall of the office seemed to be advancing towards her. She blinked, stood up suddenly and knocked over the remnants of her coffee onto the grey carpet. With a curse she dropped a handful of paper tissues on it and tramped them into the puddle. 'What should I do, what should I do?' was running on a loop in her mind as shock started to give way to anger.

A thought struck her, so she sat back down and clicked through to the Standard news site. Under the headline 'Woman Killed in Riverside Accident' was a brief paragraph with the location. About to reach for another cigarette, she picked up her mobile instead and entered Blackstone Street, W6 into the GPS.

Five minutes later she was running out of her bedroom in a grey, sleeveless tank top, tight sweatpants, a mesh cap rammed over her cropped blonde hair, and a jogging belt containing phone, money, keys and a water bottle.

Did she really want to see where Erica had died? Her gut screamed no. Common sense said there was no point. But the impulse for action overrode both.

As her hand reached out to open the front door, a heavy knock from the other side made her head grate and her heart jolt. Who the hell? Her third-floor apartment was in a portered block so access was by street-level intercom only. She took a deep breath, forcing herself to shut down her feelings.

'Yeah?' she shouted through the door.

'Maintenance, ma'am. For the sink.'

Standing to the left of the door she clicked open the heavy security lock. She leaned round the frame, her left hand grasping a spiky bronze statuette that sat on the glass console table. She eyed the stocky, crew-cutted figure with a toolbox in the hallway suspiciously.

'Who are you? Where's Ali?'

'Had to go out for a couple of hours. I'm just standing in.'

'You could be anyone,' she exclaimed.

'Anyone's my middle name. Anyone and no one. That's me.'

They stared at each other. He was only slightly taller than her five foot seven, well built, with muscular, tattooed arms, a short neck and deep-set, tired blue eyes in a broad face. His jeans and grey T-shirt were crumpled, his desert boots scuffed and worn.

'And you can put down that weapon you're clutching. I'm no going to attack you,' he remarked with a faint smile, his Scottish burr lengthening vowels and dropping consonants. 'My name's Herk, if you're interested. Herk Calder. Handyman extraordinaire. I'll fix your tap and be away in five minutes.'

'Herk?' she asked slowly, still doubtful about letting him in.

He scratched his head. 'Well, I don't normally admit this. But since you're so antsy it's not a nickname, which is most often how I explain it. My sainted parents christened me Hercules.'

Tire laughed in spite of herself. 'Ouch. Your army mates must have loved that. You were army, weren't you? You have that look.'

'Aye, twenty years since I was sixteen. Just out a few months. But we're not here to talk about me. Lead the way to the tap and I'll be out of your hair before you know it.'

Seeing her standing firm, he took out his mobile, scrolled down and clicked a number, then handed it to her. Ali at the other end, the porter, assured her that Herk was more trustworthy than an archbishop and was his replacement for a few days, but please not to tell the landlord.

In the kitchen, Herk crawled under the sink and emerged saying gruffly: 'I was wrong. I'll need to go get another trap. That rubbish in there isn't holding and it's leaking into the flat down below.'

'Oh, to hell with it.' Her desperation spilled over into irritation and swept away any misgivings. 'You've got Ali's key. Just do it and I'll be back in a couple of hours.'

CHAPTER 3

Her trainers thudded mechanically onto the pavement. Past the Grill Shack, already wafting burger smells onto the street, with a wave for Sak, the Romanian cook smoking in the alleyway. Round the corner, she paused to smile and drop two pound coins in the begging bowl of a dishevelled youth sitting on the pavement with a scruffy mongrel. A motorcyclist on a bright blue Suzuki revved up beside her so she missed his mumbled 'thanks'. Then right onto Regent Street, crowded with shoppers.

Erica Smythson was one of the few friends she had made in recent years. A smart young barrister, stick thin from overwork and worry, she was a specialist in domestic abuse and human rights cases. They had met at the Frontline Club over drinks after a harrowing documentary about a Syrian torture victim, an escapee from Daesh, who had told his story and then committed suicide. A war correspondent friend of Tire's boyfriend introduced them and nudged Erica. 'Play your cards right and you'll get them read.'

Tire rolled her eyes upwards, managed a wry smile and said: 'Hi. I'm an investigative and travel writer. That attempt at wit was aimed at my astrology hobby. I roll it out at New Year as my party piece.'

'I don't think it's a joke.' Erica frowned and nodded to an empty table. She said confidentially after they sat down: 'My aunt was keen on astrology. She taught me a great deal about people.'

'But only to be whispered in corners.' Tire smiled, sensing Erica's protectiveness towards underdogs. 'I do use it, in-depth astrology I mean, not the flim-flam stuff, to get a handle on people I'm writing about.' She grinned. 'Not that I'd ever admit it in print. But my main interest is in geopolitical stuff – the astrology of the Iraq War, the financial crash, whither the USA.'

'Ooh, tell me more.'

Their friendship settled into a weekly night out over dinner and the theatre. Tire was pleased to have an intelligent and receptive ear for a subject she rarely discussed elsewhere. Erica shared concerns about the cases she was handling, without giving specifics, and asked occasionally for help in understanding tricky clients and colleagues. She did receive death threats but refused to take them seriously.

Tire tried not to imagine her body lying in a heap by the roadside. She screwed up her eyes, trying to blot out another image of a bloody corpse from long ago, then had to open them in a hurry as she cannoned into a heavily pierced teenager carrying a tray of paper coffee cups. Mouthing 'sorry', she sidestepped and nearly tripped over a news vendor. Ignoring the loud complaints she ran on, past Hamley's toyshop, round the curved grandeur of lower Regent Street.

Pounding along Piccadilly, keeping pace with a constant flow of cars and buses edging their way to Hyde Park Corner and giving the finger to wolf-whistling workmen, she racked her brain trying to remember the name of Erica's latest boyfriend, another barrister in the same chambers. Upper crust. Brideshead type name. Sebastian. That was it. Crumley.

Erica had turned up at her flat a month ago still in her dark city suit, looking embarrassed, clutching a bottle of expensive Bordeaux.

'We celebrating, then?' asked Tire.

'Well, nothing really. But there is someone new who might be...' she trailed off.

'Ah. A possibility?'

'Maybe,' she fidgeted. 'Um, I wondered if you could look him up?' she waved at Tire's PC.

Tire chuckled. 'Do you not think you might just enjoy him and see where it goes?'

She shrugged hopelessly and took a deep breath. 'What you told me about the married one let me see him clearly for the first time. The shit. So Jupiterian. He is just like Zeus, thinks rules don't apply to him. I don't know how I can have been so blind. I know you don't like being an agony aunt. But just this once. Please.'

How could she not have known Erica was at risk? Why hadn't she said something? Death never showed up on a chart, but danger did. One answer was her aversion to being dragged in as the all-knowing fixer of other people's problems. But it wasn't that simple. There had been dramatic changes and challenges in Erica's life, which she had noted and written off as career pressures in a job that thrived on crises.

Her feet were on automatic pilot so she had no recollection of getting from one side of the six-lane Hyde Park intersection, bowing under the weight of vehicles, to the other, although her nose retained a hint of a urine-soaked underpass. Then through the diaphanous kitsch of the Queen Mother Gates, she was into the green of the park.

What was Erica doing in Hammersmith when she should have been at home? She had a crucial day in court today in a difficult case defending a man she thought was innocent but would not help himself.

The clip-clop of horse hooves diverted Tire's attention briefly as a dozen Household Cavalry rode past, flashing red and gilt against the lush grass and leafy trees. In spite of herself she smiled. She jogged on, more relaxed with nature around and the Serpentine lake humming blue in the background. Her mind drifted off to Jin, imagining herself wrapped round his lanky frame.

What would he be doing? No, that wasn't a good thought. She frowned and yanked a strand of hair off her sweaty forehead. Sitting in some hellhole in Syria or Yemen getting blasted by grenade launchers or worse, his eye fixed to the aperture that would preserve the moment for posterity. Normally she shut down worries about his survival, but this time her sense of dread was ratcheted up to a constant background presence. Settling her stride twenty paces behind a tracksuited runner, she pulled her thoughts back to what Erica had told her of the trial she was about to start.

Accountant Jack Greengate was accused of murdering his wife by hitting her over the head with a hammer when he was drunk. He was not a heavy drinker, but remembered little of that night. There were incriminating emails to an office secretary suggesting an affair. He was so distraught Erica could get little out of him and had to lean hard to get him to plead not guilty.

'It's almost as if he wants to go to prison. But I know he didn't do it.'

Tire typed his birth details into her astrology software, pulled up his birth chart and said he seemed like a typical number-cruncher: dry, meticulous, hard-working, emotionally reticent, a backroom personality, not ego-driven and not aggressive. His immediate future looked grim.

So immersed was Tire in her thoughts that she nearly turned right to continue looping round Hyde Park. Forcing herself into a left onto Kensington Road, she lengthened her stride. Past the Italianate dome of the Albert Hall and the gaudy Indian temple memorial to Queen Victoria's lost love, she struggled to remember the detail of last night's conversation.

Greengate, Erica explained, had worked as an accountant for Cerigo, which ran high-end holiday resorts in several countries with nothing to suggest that it was anything other than sound and profitable.

'The boss is Harman Stone, son of Paul Stone, you know who does good work for the elderly.'

Tire looked up his birth date in Google and pulled up Harman Stone's chart. She took a minute to absorb what she saw. Venus Moon in Scorpio, badly aspected Jupiter Neptune and his Gemini Sun tied into Mars, Pluto and Uranus. She knew Erica did not want the detail so she simplified it to a thumbnail sketch: overly impulsive, chaotic, fond of the good life, insincerely charming, into sex of the sleazy variety, slippery, with a cruel father.

'No, I don't think that's right,' said Erica, 'The father is a saint. He organises holidays for poor children, raises millions for charity.'

Tire had given an enigmatic smile and shrugged. Erica had left shortly after, still anxious about how to approach her defence strategy but hoping sleep would clear her mind.

Six hours later she was dead. And in a place she wasn't supposed to be. Tire wracked her brain trying to remember other threats that Erica had mentioned. The Pakistani family of a girl rescued from a forced marriage. And there were others. What were they?

A wasp buzzed round her head so she swatted it with her cap, taking the chance to shake her damp hair loose. Checking her phone she saw she had three miles still to run, so she focused on holding to a steady pace down West Cromwell Road, trying not to breathe in the fumes of the cascade of buses, lorries and motorcyclists that were crawling alongside. Her heart was pounding and sweat trickling down her back, sticking her tank top to her skin. She sped past a Tesco supermarket and an airport terminal of an emporium, sheltering under a bulbous, high-rise block of apartments. Only when she reached MacDuff Road in Hammersmith did she start to slow down. Past the Hope and Sail pub, she saw signs for the underpass that ran under the A4 Great West Road. Nearly there. She almost stopped in the dimly lit tunnel, reeking of piss and beer, reluctant to face what was on the other side.

Blackstone Gardens came as a shock after the rumble and reek of urban flux. A handful of detached houses that had once been grand sat in a cul-de-sac that ran down to the river, where four men in a sculling shell were flowing along, with a lone kayaker further downstream.

Then she saw the spot. Police tape was looped round a small wall bordering the road that had collapsed in the middle, with a dark stain across it and several paint-flecked gouges where metal had collided with stone. Erica had been smashed against that. Tire's stomach heaved and her head seemed to be floating in mud. Collapsing onto the wooden bench, she bent forward, her elbows over her cap, arms blocking her eyes.

When she raised her head, a stout elderly woman walking past with a small fluffy terrier smiled at her. The normality of the scene made it worse. She had seen bruised and bloodied corpses before on her travels to remote places, tripping twice by mistake into war zones. But never a friend. And never on home territory. Except once. Maybe that was why she was so rattled. She drank heavily from her water bottle and reached into her jogging belt for a cigarette.

'That's what I like to see. A health freak with vices,' said a voice behind her. She jerked round to see a weedy youth in jeans and an anorak holding a camera and grinning at her. He focused on the wall and clicked several times.

About to remonstrate with him, she stopped herself and asked: 'Are you press?'

'Yeah,' he answered, about to walk away.

'What do you know about the… accident?' Her question came out more fiercely than she had intended.

He shrugged, 'Not much. It was early hours. No one about. The police have no idea.' He jerked his head towards two uniforms standing nearer the river. 'Though the papers and telly have got pics of the body from someone who was passing.' He paused and then emphasised with a grin, which made her want to punch him: 'After the corpse was found by a jogger.' He licked his fleshy lips and sighed. 'They won't use them all, mind you. Too gory even for the gutter journos. She might have been raped. No knickers on.'

He leered at Tire, who was standing rigid, her brain stalled, staring back at him. Everything had gone into slow motion, her eyes lost focus and she stopped breathing. She felt as if she was fragmenting and about to float away in the wind in tiny pieces. A hand on her arm made her jerk backwards and she gulped in air.

'Why are you interested? You knew the victim?' His expression livened at the prospect. A draft of curried breath made her move further away.

Her shake of the head was instantaneous. 'No.' The movement jerked her back into coping consciousness. Erica raped. She couldn't cope with that here, so shut it down. Erica murdered. Don't let it sink in. Wait till she was on her own. Concentrate on the here and now. Photographs, he had photographs. Through gritted teeth she said: 'Got a card?'

'Always pleased to do business.' He moved closer, looking her up and down suggestively, pressing a grubby card into her hand. 'I do all sorts of portraits. I'm just up the road in Stanford Brook.'

After he left, she sat staring at the rippling water. The effects of shock and not enough sleep were making her shiver but she had her mind under control, panic firmly battened down.

A coffee at one of the pubs might help. She stood up, flexed her leg muscles and started to walk. Within a few yards the wobble in her knees forced her to stop and aim for the riverside wall, where she sat down heavily on top of the white and blue Do Not Cross tape, leaning forward, her arms wrapped round her chest.

'Ma'am, you OK?'

The older, stockier of the two policeman was standing beside her, concern crinkling his eyes. The sympathy in his tone threatened to derail her again.

'Yeah, fine,' she croaked. Then before she could stop herself it tumbled out between gasps. 'I knew her. Erica. With her last night. At the opera before… this.'

He sat beside her and put his arm round her shoulders and she allowed herself to lean against his solid body, her eyes tightly shut.

The words of the photographer cannoned back to her.

'She was raped?' She turned and clutched at his arm. 'Tell me?'

His moustache quivered with disapproval. 'Now, Ma'am, we don't know anything yet. You don't want to be listening to that deadbeat. He makes things up and causes us a load of grief.' He patted her hand, then stood up, straightening his high visibility jacket. 'But we will need a statement from you later, down at the station.'

An awkward shuffle of his feet preceded a muttered, 'I'm truly sorry about your friend', before he turned away to speak into his phone.

A taxi pulling up outside The Raven, disgorging two passengers, jolted her back into gear. She found a business card in her belt, handed it to the younger policeman and ran for it. The driver looked askance at her outfit, but nodded when she pulled two twenties out of her belt. She slumped back on the seat and then had to hang onto the armrest as the cab swerved to avoid a lingering motorcyclist. Blue Suzukis, she thought, a plague of them.

Back at her apartment, she called 'hi' in the direction of the thumps from the kitchen and went straight to her bedroom. Having dragged on an oversize polo neck and jeans, she caught sight of herself in the mirror and winced. Her grey eyes looked haunted, the dark circles under them thrown into sharp relief by her blonde hair.

Don't think, she murmured to her reflection, don't feel. Just get the sink fixed and him out. She marched into the kitchen with what she hoped was a bland expression on her face. Once finished, he leant against the work surface drinking the mug of tea she had offered him. His feet moved restlessly, although his square face remained impassive. 'How d'you know I was army then? I'll need to sort my camouflage better.'

She forced a smile and strained to remember what she had said. 'Boots, straight back – and the eyes. Seen too much.'

He glared at her and said defensively: 'Aye, well, goes with the territory. But that's all behind me. On to better things. Anything else you want fixed, I'm around for a couple of days. Be down in the cellar if you need me. But don't tell the landlord, he wouldn't approve.'

Tire showed him to the door, where he paused and tapped the bronze statuette with solid arrowheads curving upwards. 'You could do a load of damage with that, if you stuck it in the right place,' he said. 'I'll remember next time to ring you in advance.'

In spite of herself, she grinned. Over his shoulder he added: 'And if you don't mind a personal comment you've got the loveliest smile I've ever seen. Don't let it get rusty.'

What came up as the door clicked shut was not the torrent of grief she had expected, but a spiral of visceral rage that gripped her belly and shot up through her chest. She'd get whoever did this and make them pay. Whatever it took. Her schedule was packed but she'd clear space. She owed Erica that much.

CHAPTER 4

In a second-floor council flat in Dowancross Street in Glasgow, south of Byres Road, a small, grey-haired woman in her sixties was laying two mugs of tea onto a small plastic floral tray, beside a cracked saucer with three tea biscuits on it. The cramped kitchen was painted blue on the walls, with green plastic handles on the cupboards matching the scuffed laminate surface. The window above the sink overlooked a strip of grass on either side of the road below, with a red sandstone, four-storey Victorian tenement facing.

'Jimmy, d'you want one biscuit or two?' she shouted.

'Aye, aye, don't yell, Elly, I'm only ten feet away,' answered a thin, white-haired man of similar age. He was sitting at a table by the window of the narrow sitting room. The room was crowded with two worn, dull red armchairs either side of a gas fire. One had a large basket filled with white knitting wool beside it and the other a side table with a reading lamp and a pile of books. On the opposite wall was an old-fashioned television set with an upright piano pushed down to the window end. Several watercolours in cheap frames hung on the walls, all variations of the same scene, with a bright blue sky and a row of conical cypresses running into the distance along a stone walkway.

Jimmy was pencilling a sketch with obsessive concentration, rubbing out mistakes every so often, muttering an irritated 'ach'. His grey flannels, a size too big for his frame and with the hem stitched up, had seen better days although they were clean. A green cable-knit sweater over a grey shirt did nothing to improve the pallor of his skin.

'What's up with you?' Elly asked anxiously, putting the tray on the low black plastic table in front of the fire. 'I hope you're not going peculiar again. We'll have to go to the doctor and maybe get you some better pills. He said to come back anytime.'

She came across to examine his drawing of a mongrel dog with elongated legs and said: 'Och, you're doing these awfy ugly animals again. They make me feel very odd.'

'Elly, I'm fine. Don't get so het up. I'm just kind of out of sorts for some reason.' He turned to pat her hand fondly as she leant against him.

'You only draw these things when you're getting real uptight. Is that man back inside your head?' she asked peering at him, her lined face and sagging jowls giving her a hangdog look. She fidgeted with the ties of the floral apron she wore over a dark tweed skirt and homemade jumper.

'Every time he pops up you get bad-tempered and faraway inside yourself. Just forget him. He's no real, a fiction of your imagination, that's what the doctor in the Hall said. You should paint one of your nice gardens instead. They settle you better.' She indicated a cheaply framed scene on the wall, with two rows of conical cypresses extending down a stone path with a fountain in the distance.

'There was someone on the television last night that reminded me of him, that's all.' He tried to smile reassuringly at her, standing up to get his tea.

They were a couple who could walk down to their local Spar supermarket and not be noticed, approaching old age and leaning on each other's arm. They often held hands outside, although more out of insecurity than affection as if one was scared the other would get lost. They switched parent-child roles constantly, so it was never clear who was looking after whom.

With tea drunk and cleared out of the way, Elly picked up her needles and ball of white wool, knitting a pair of baby's bootees.

'Why don't you play something? I like that when I'm knitting and it calms you down. That gymnastics piece is nice. Then we can go to the community centre. I've got four pairs of bootees finished and a wee jumper I want to give them. And you can talk to Len about your exhibition.'

Jimmy walked slowly over to the piano, lifted the lid and started to play, his eyes half-closed, rarely glancing down. His fingers moved fluidly, absent-mindedly, across the keys. The poignant strains of Erik Satie's 'Gymnopédies' filled the sitting room. Truth to tell, Elly was sick of listening to it, but this was his favourite. She had heard it so often in the last two decades it had become as familiar as wallpaper. But she had a lifetime's experience of accepting what she didn't like and told herself often that she should be grateful if this was all she had to bear.

He played on and she kept knitting steadily. She had just finished the second bootee when he stopped, looking, as he often did at the piano, sad and lost.

CHAPTER 5

Try as she might, Tire couldn't get her brain to focus. The rest of yesterday had passed in a jumble with a half-hearted attempt to write the penultimate chapter of her current book on a Mexican cartel hitman. But her concentration kept unravelling and she couldn't find the words. The bloodstained wall where Erica died came into her mind every time she thought about Sanchez, so she gave up trying.

Why hadn't she listened more attentively when Erica told her about difficult cases where threats had been made? They were brushed aside lightly as part of a criminal barrister's job. No sense in getting paranoid, she'd say with a smile, tossing her hair back and pressing her hands together as if in prayer. But not all threats are a belch of vengeance. Clearly, one had been carried through.

Her secretary, Susan, would know more and she had agreed to meet up for a coffee near her flat in Shepherd's Bush after Tire had given her police statement in Hammersmith.

The evening had passed in a blur of red wine and several episodes from a box set of 'Spiral', the gritty French police and law procedural, whose bleak view of degradation in low-life Paris with corruption in high places suited her savage mood.

A phone call at 5 am from Jin in Dubai reminding her they had a Skype chat booked was met with a groggy response.

'What the hell time is it there?'

'9 am sunshine, babe. Beautiful day here. I got a flight to catch at 11 so I'm rushing. We can do this when I come back, mebbe next week sometime.'

She had let him go without telling him about Erica, feeling guilty and irritated at herself. Wherever he was going it would be risky and she hated not having a proper conversation before he went. Normally she could push her fear for his safety aside and ignore it, but this time it was a constant, low-level dread.

The dawn light was making feeble inroads through heavy cloud when she made her way to her desk with a mug of coffee and lit a cigarette. Beethoven was playing quietly in the background. How do people listen to voices yattering at them in the morning on the radio or, even worse, television? She shuddered. Her entry into the day required at least two hours' gentle easing, preferably people-free.

Jin lingered on her conscience, so she turned her chair to look at his photographs, enlarged and unframed, black and white, hanging on the long wall. A deformed, leafless tree with amputated branches stood alone in a cratered desert. It had echoes of Paul Nash's 'Menin Road' without the puddles. A century on from the war to end all wars and here we are again. She pulled her black kimono tightly round her.

Next to it was a bomb-blasted building, its front wall ripped open to expose a family home reduced to pathetic chaos. On the ground floor, in the shadow of a few mud bricks left intact, squatted a small boy, his eyes wide and wary but also curious as he gazed up at the camera. Where would he be now?

These were what Jin cynically called his 'War as Art' series. They sold well. Normally they gave a chic look to the modernist room. Today she could barely cope with them.

A Korean American, he was well over six foot, with broad shoulders, a chiselled oriental face with heavy-lidded eyes, straight nose and full lips. They had bonded in a ditch under gunfire in Ethiopia eight years back. She had been writing a travel piece about wilderness backpacking in northern Kenya and had crossed into Ethiopia to look at the Yabelo Wildlife Sanctuary. Jin was a photojournalist on a break from the fighting on the northern Eritrean border, recovering from an injured shoulder.

A local tribal dispute had trapped them for three weeks in distinctly unsanitary conditions. By the time it blew over they were firm friends, showering together with relief when they reached a hotel.

The delight of Jin was they could be apart for six months and still feel instantly at ease when they came together. She never cared what he got up to when she wasn't there and he often related his funnier liaisons, which amused her.

Why was she so scared for him this time? Erica's death forcing her to face mortality? No, she'd been worried about him before that. She reached back to pull a book off the shelf beside her desk and flipped it open. Pages and pages of numbers and symbols like a railway timetable. Two months to a page. She found March/April and ran her finger across.

Merde, that's why. There were violently explosive aspects between Mars, Uranus and Pluto moving towards a peak in two weeks' time. They came round once in a while, but were worse than usual this year. For people living normal lives that would mean bad temper and minor accidents. But out in the world there would be major atrocities, disasters and plane crashes. Even more than the usual churning chaos that he was perpetually drawn to.

Her hand hovered over the desk drawer, where she kept a folder of personal charts. She stopped herself. Why bother? His astrology wouldn't tell her if he was going to die, just whether he would be in danger and that was a given.

By 8 am she was showered, dithered about what was suitable wear for a police interview and settled for a white T-shirt under a tailored pinstripe jacket with jeans and ankle boots. Her hair was cut short for easy management and blew dry in a few minutes, after which she ran her fingers through it. Make-up was also a minimum exercise with a dash of creme foundation and mascara; lipstick could wait till she was ready to go out.

She prowled. Christ, she hated being depressed. Work was her defence against falling into black holes. But there was nothing she wanted to tackle despite the pressure of an approaching deadline. If necessary, a couple of overnight stints when her brain had steadied would see the Sanchez book finished.

Her boot stubbed against a heavy cardboard box full of papers, financial data, court transcripts and press cuttings: background for a possible exposé of a pharmaceutical company. Maybe she could start on that? She bent down and picked it up, her jacket straining at the shoulders. Not a hope. It was a boring weekend's speed-read. She took three steps, then dropped it beside her desk and turned to head kitchen-wards for more coffee.

As she reached the door, a thud followed by a clattering slide made her spin to see the surface of her office desk cantilevering upwards. The box, having landed awkwardly on one corner, then righted itself to push into the end T-support. A fast dash grabbed her laptop before it concussed itself on the floor, as she muttered curses about the removers who had lost the bolts that fixed the desktop to its moorings. Force of gravity had kept the sturdy laminate surface in place for four years. But one-legged it stood no chance.

A laugh forced itself upwards as she surveyed books, papers, pens and ashtray deposited on the floor, festooned over boxes and a filing cabinet. Sod's law. Days that started badly usually got worse.

A knock on the front door followed by a voice made her jump. Neighbours, no doubt. She opened it, still clutching her laptop, to find Herk, toolbox in hand.

'Was next door. Heard a bang. You OK?' He rubbed a thumb up his nose leaving a smear of dust, his blue eyes red-rimmed and puffy.

'Just the man I need,' she said, waving him in. 'Minor mishap. A meteor demolished my desk and it's too heavy for me to lift back into place.'

'That right?' he said, standing at the office door, clicking his tongue. 'In the window and back out without leaving a trace. Your lucky day. Apart from…' He pointed a stubby finger at the pile-up in the corner and sniffed. 'Nothing to do with that box having fallen over, I s'pose, or the fact that the table was assembled by a gorilla.'

'Removers.'

'Nuff said.' His lips pursed in a soundless whistle. 'Don't suppose I could blag a tea?'

In the kitchen she laid down her laptop out of harm's way and switched on the kettle.

'Rough night?' she asked.

'Too little sleep. Was helping a mate out with a pick-up at Heathrow. His wife is sick so he couldn't go. Sodding plane was hours late. I didn't get back from Hampshire till five this morning.'

She stirred his mug with the teabag vigorously, assuming he liked it brewed black, switching on the Nespresso machine with her other hand to fill her own mug.

'Stars must be out of sorts then, today.' His deadpan tone managed to blur the line between question and statement.

Her hackles rose. 'You've been grubbing round in my office?'

'Keep your shirt on. I threw out the recycling yesterday and there was a paper on top that had zodiac whatsits. It was labelled Iraq, which is what caught my eye. I didn't know you could do astrology on countries.'

This wasn't a conversation she wanted, which must have registered on her face, since he started to move towards the door. She put a hand up. The table needed to be put back together.

'Sorry, sorry. No big deal. I just kind of like to keep my interest secret.'

He resumed his position leaning against the counter, blowing ripples across the surface of his tea. 'Why is that, then? You believe it, you should stick up for it.'

'Long story,' she said with a rueful grin, stretching out a foot to tap on the cooker. 'But you're right. Shitty day.'

There was silence. 'Tricky chat with my boyfriend,' she said, examining her boot. Might as well let him know she was spoken for. 'And I have to give a police statement later about a friend.' Her shoulders pulled back. 'Killed in a hit and run two nights ago.'

'You were there?'

'No, no. Gawd, no.' A tremor went down her spine, causing her arms to twitch and the coffee mug to lurch. She put it down. 'I was with her at the theatre just before and she shouldn't have been there – where she was killed, I mean. She said she was going straight home.' Why was she telling him this? A complete stranger.

On second thoughts, maybe a practice run wasn't a bad idea so she wouldn't disgrace herself at the police station by bursting into tears.

'You don't have to tell me,' he said, swilling down the rest of his tea.

'I'm going to get the bastard who did it.' She thumped the counter top with a closed fist and banged the tile floor with her heel.

'Calm down, now.' He walked past her and filled himself another mug. 'You can't charge into the police and tell them you're going to do their job. Best get it out of your system before you go.'

Taking a deep breath, she said: 'Erica was… a criminal barrister.' He rolled his eyes and nodded his head. 'There were always running threats. Domestic violence, child abuse, human rights cases. She never mentioned specifics.'

'And you think it might have been one of them? Where was the accident?'

'Hammersmith, by the river. I went to see it yesterday.' The bloody wall imprinted itself on the cabinet door opposite, shimmering like a laser image.

'I thought you looked as if you'd seen a ghost when you came back.' He slurped his tea noisily and scuffed his desert boot along a grout.

She continued in a rush, her panic rising, 'And she might have been raped. There was a news photographer there who…'

'C'mon, c'mon. You don't want to believe everything that lot say. They just like frightening people. Wait to see what the facts are.' For a moment his calmness disarmed her and she almost believed him.

CHAPTER 6

An hour later she was sitting in the hinterland of Hammersmith police station, corridors away from the classy Grade II-listed façade, in a bare, grey-walled room. Facing her across the desk was Sergeant Joe Roberts, her comforter of the day before. A young female constable, with an urchin cut so severe it was close-shaved, stood by the door. Without his visibility jacket, Roberts looked slighter than she expected. He offered his condolences again, but his crisp, white, short-sleeved shirt, black tie and formal manner suggested a short, sharp interview and out. Prising information out of him would not be easy.

After she'd given a brief statement, she asked if he had spoken to Sebastian Crumley, Erica's boyfriend. He looked surprised and said: 'Not personally. Another officer did, but he's got nothing to do with the accident. He was working overnight, as I understand it, with an important client.'

'Are you following up threats made against Erica because of her work?'

He shook his head and gave a bland smile. 'Not our department. That's another division. We just chase up immediate witnesses and try to trace the vehicle involved and, where necessary, hand it over.'

'And how many hit and runs do you solve every year?'

His mouth tightened and his moustache splayed out as he puffed out his cheeks. 'As many as we can,' he said firmly.

Bad tactic getting him on the defensive.

'But,' he added as an afterthought, 'You're right. I wouldn't like to get your hopes up.'

'Her mobile phone?'

After a hesitation, he said: 'No help there, I'm afraid. No calls on it that night.'

She lowered her eyes, half-turning her body towards the female constable. 'You won't know whether she was raped yet?'

'We won't know that for several days,' he said in an even tone. 'Once we have any information that can be divulged, Mary will be in touch.' He nodded towards the door and stood up. Interview over. His parting words were kindly meant, but conveyed a resigned acceptance that progress was likely to be slow. More likely non-existent, she thought.

At the front entrance, Tire turned to the young woman who was escorting her and said urgently: 'What do you think are the chances of finding the sod who did this?'

A quick glance over her shoulder to check no one was watching them, and the young constable leant forward with an embarrassed shrug and whispered: 'Not great to be honest. There's no CCTV down there. The vehicle will have been cleaned and repaired by this time. Unless the autopsy turns up anything.' She sighed. 'My cousin was raped two years back, got the full evidence kit and they still don't know who did it.'

***

By the time she had walked down Shepherd's Bush Road past the green, its trees and grass dusted brown with pollution from a trillion exhausts, Tire's conviction was growing that the police investigation was going to run into a dead end. They hadn't the resources and their will had been sapped by hundreds of similar cases that had never been closed. If they did stretch themselves to dig into Erica's cases, they'd meet a stonewall of polite disdain from her legal colleagues. Client confidentiality first, justice and truth poor seconds in their game.

Erica was her friend and she wasn't going to let her death hang like a plaintive ghost begging for an audience. She had the will in spades, wasn't limited by police regulations and could wheedle answers out of the antichrist, as Jin had once joked. She'd find the evidence and the authorities would have to follow up. Time was a problem since her schedule was packed. But there were twenty-four hours in the day and seven days in the week; she'd manage somehow. She always did.

The vast Westfield shopping centre was all echoing marble, chrome and garishly lit plate glass. A temple of commerce filled with wandering souls seeking salvation through the latest iPhones, glitter lipstick and designer handbags. Mercifully it also had a coffee shop with outside tables, which was why she had suggested it as a venue.

Erica's long-time secretary Susan was sitting huddled at a corner table in a tweed coat, with a plaid scarf bunched round her neck and chin and with a matching wool hat pulled down on her forehead, so only her swollen eyes and red nose were visible. A sodden handkerchief was clutched in one hand.

Ten minutes of commiserations and more tears followed before Tire could get any sense out of her and start asking questions.

'I'm not allowed to talk about cases,' she whispered, waving a feeble hand at teenagers chatting four tables away.

'Listen, Susan.' Tire pushed sympathy aside and adopted a commanding tone. 'I intend to find out why Erica was in Hammersmith and who did it, which means you need to tell me about the threats she received. You do want the person responsible caught, don't you?'

Two more coffees arrived and when Susan was blowing her nose discreetly away from the table, Tire dropped another two sachets of sugar into her cup. Waken her up.

She reached down to find a fresh handkerchief in her bag and emerged with a diary. Once she started talking, it all poured out.

'To be truthful,' she said, 'I'd been thinking the same thing. Though I didn't know who to tell. I wrote the worst of them down to tell Mr Crumley, though he didn't seem to be very interested. He was quite snappy with me. Maybe he was distracted because that was later the first day. He looked terrible.' She sniffed and twisted a ring round her finger nervously.

'Fire ahead. I'm interested.'

Susan's secretarial training kicked in and she read off the list with only a few gulps.

'There was the Pakistani father. Erica rescued his daughter from a forced marriage and found her a new identity. The father harassed Erica for months, trying to find out where their daughter was. The police had to be called eventually.'

Tire lit another cigarette, waving her on when she paused.

'A lawyer who had escaped from Kubekistan. He was an activist and they wanted him on fraud charges that Erica said were trumped up. She thought their secret police might be here looking for him. That one wasn't handled in the office. She worked pro bono in the evenings on human rights cases.'

The 'good die young' came into Tire's mind and her attention wandered for a few seconds before she pulled herself back.

'Then there was the brother of a man who had been killed by his wife. Erica got her off on self-defence. He'd beaten her for years so it was perfectly justified. The poor woman was completely broken down.' She looked up indignantly.

'The brother threatened Erica?'

'Yes, at the end of the trial. Said he'd get her.' Tire put a firm hand on Susan's arm when she threatened to dissolve into tears again.

'Keep going.'

The diary was snapped shut and Susan sat up straighter, attempting to smile. 'That's it.'

'No it isn't. There was another name at the bottom,' Tire said, pinning her with a straight look.

Susan shuffled uneasily on her chair, her hands twisting together. Gales of laughter from a faraway table made her flinch. Eventually, she said with a croak in her throat: 'It was very difficult. Delicate. A girl, a young woman, came to Erica saying she had been abused by her father. He was… is very important. Successful, a public figure.' Her face sagged, worry lines deepening making her look ten years older, and a blush reddened her cheeks.

'Erica supported the daughter,' Tire prompted.

'Yes. She wasn't sure at the start, but from what the girl said there was a case against her father. Medical evidence and she had told a teacher at school.' She lowered her eyes and fiddled with her coffee cup, then looked away across the mall. When she turned back she leant closer. 'The awful thing was the girl backed out, said it never happened and it left Erica in a terrible position.'

'She recanted?' Tire rolled her eyes and shrugged. 'It happens. She'd get scared.'

'But by this time the father knew and he was threatening to take legal action against Erica.'

'Unlikely. It would drag it into the open. No, I take that back. That sort are relentless. When was this?'

The diary opened and Susan bent over it. 'There was a meeting with his lawyer scheduled for next week.'

Tire sat back, eased a crick from her neck with one hand and took Susan's diary out of her hand. 'I need the contact details of all these people. And… ' she dropped her voice an octave, '…no argument. Email them to me from your home PC. Final question. Who was Erica's lover, the married one?'

'Oh, I wouldn't know that.'

'Yes, you would. You were her secretary. He was a lawyer. Spill.' Tire put an arm round her shoulders and gave a small tug.

'Justin Burgoyne. At Lowsdon Street Chambers.'

***

Back at her office, the desk had been reassembled, with, she noted, new brackets underneath holding it together. The spilled contents were neatly piled on top, the ashtray cleaned and cigarette ends swept up off the floor. The day wasn't turning out so badly after all.

Susan's list would be a start. Had she been too hard on her? Probably. But she wasn't a bereavement counsellor. Needs must if the end result was useful information.

With a pang of guilt, she absorbed how risky much of Erica's work had been, especially the pro bono cases. The version she had shared on their weekly meets over a bottle of wine had been heavily diluted and peppered with jokey comments.

A possible honour killing, a violent thug's brother, Kubek secret police, child abuse, and those were the only ones Susan had mentioned. There would be more. Drat! She'd forgotten to ask about the Greengate case. That would have to be picked up later.

For now she must push on with the Sanchez book and clear it off her plate. It wasn't her normal subject, but the publishers had leapt at it. The impulse had come through an encounter with a hitman she had met by chance in an isolated roadside motel in northern Mexico. Her rental car had broken down so she had to kick her heels overnight waiting for a replacement. She had heard groans from the next room and gone to investigate. A badly injured man lay on the bed, blood seeping through makeshift bandages across his chest and on one leg onto the grubby sheets. He shook his head vehemently when she said she'd go for a doctor, and the motel owner refused point blank to help.

His name, he said, was Jesus Ernesto Sanchez, a contract killer for one of the drug cartels. He'd been shot by an undercover US drug team and was wanted by a rival cartel so he couldn't be seen. The motel owner was a distant cousin but he was terrified of upsetting the local gang by calling in their doctor, the only one in the area. Sanchez knew he was dying and once he'd learned she was a writer said he wanted to tell his story.

For four days she listened with her tape recorder on as he told of a brutal abandoned childhood, living rough on the edges of a rubbish dump in the slums of Mexico City, his initiation into the local gang that gave him an identity and growing status as his tally of kills mounted. She hated what she heard, but wondered how she would have reacted in an environment where only the ruthless survived.

His explanations reflected no guilt about what he'd done, or self-pity, but he was reflective enough to wonder what kind of a life he might have had born into different circumstances.

By the fourth night his breathing had grown hoarser and weaker. The last thing he said to her was: 'You tell my story. I like that. I be remembered.' The motel owner had fled so Tire was alone when he finally died in the early hours. She sat in the darkness for a while until the overpowering stench from his body forced her to move.

Driving at speed afterwards towards the US border, she wondered whether she should have set fire to the motel to at least give him a funeral pyre. But it would have drawn too much attention. So she left his body to the rats, which she gloomily thought brought his life full circle back to where he started.

CHAPTER 7

At 8 am next morning Tire was at her desk, reading through her penultimate chapter on Sanchez, tightening and tidying up the punctuation. Nearly there. The phone rang.

'Calder here.'

'Who?'

'Herk.'

'Ah! Thanks for fixing my desk.'

'I'm at the Lavazza, down the road with a mate who can tell you about your friend.'

'Which friend?'

'The one who was killed.'

A scramble into jeans, boots and a jumper took three minutes and she grabbed her handbag and was downstairs and out the front entrance. Herk was sitting in jeans and an old combat jumper at one of the pavement tables with a ginger-haired man in a navy blue jacket. They nodded as she sat down, breathing heavily, on the spare chair with a coffee already on the table.

'This here's Momo. He was a medic in the army. Helped me out a bit at one point when I had a slight mishap.' Herk grinned. 'Works in pathology now. He can do less damage there.' He winked and both men laughed.

Tire offered round her packet of cigarettes and accepted a light from Momo, who thrust forward a hand with two missing fingertips. He had a squat nose and large ears that peered through the undergrowth of his fuzzy hair.

'Just to be clear,' he said, with a Welsh lilt, 'your friend Miss Smythson's body wasn't one I worked on, so I'm not... directly breaking any confidences. But Herk said you were anxious she might have been raped. She wasn't.'

'You sure?'

'Positive. I spoke to the orderly, the guy who assisted, and he said not.'

'Thank god.' Tire sat back, the relief unzipping knots of tension in her back. 'What else do you know?'

Momo frowned and waggled an ear. 'Sure you want to hear?'

'Yes.'

'Not much to be honest. Hard impact caused her death, crushed chest.' He watched Tire with concern. 'Vehicular death. Multiple fractures. She must have been caught against a wall. The water unfortunately had taken away quite a lot of traces. Tide there is strong and the body had a foot caught in a wire rope, so the water would have been pulling against it.'

A black taxi drew up four shops down and a cyclist behind swore loudly as he had to swerve, palming his helmet in annoyance once he had regained his balance. Tire ignored the distraction, mentally ticking off questions she could ask.

'But how?'

'Her underwear was caught round her foot. That's why it looked missing in those photographs some jackass took before the police arrived.'

Herk came back with three more coffees and she watched them joshing as they ladled in sugar. It was a curiously reassuring moment despite the oddity of the circumstances. Two mates comfortable in each other's company because they had faced death together. A hit and run would be small beer in their experience.

A mobile phone rang and Herk picked his off the table. After a muttered curse he said: 'Need to go. Water leaking in the basement. Thanks, Mo.' He clapped him on the shoulder and smiled at Tire. 'Hope that helped. I'll be up later to fix your window. Dodgy catch.'

They watched him lope along the street, hitching up his jeans as he went. 'Good lad, that,' Mo said, blowing a perfect smoke ring across the table. 'Heart in the right place. You known him long then?'

'Two days.' A brief laugh turned into a sigh. 'He tripped into my life the day it happened.'

'Ah well, that's Herk for you. Wrong place, right time. Always.' Mo's broad face creased into a smile. He was not attractive, but he had a warmth that was relaxing.

'Why is he squatting in my apartment cellar?'

'You'd have to ask him that.' The curt response was followed by a considered look. 'Sorry about that. He wouldn't tell you if you asked.'

She raised an eyebrow, cocked her head and put the hand nearest him on the table with the palm upwards in a placatory gesture. Why was she bothering? Did she really want to know? But people's lives always fascinated her even if she only got a cameo glimpse.

'Quite persuasive, are you?' He looked amused and rubbed a short finger against his nose, flattening it further. 'It's no big secret. But don't ask him about it.' He pursed his lips. 'He had a bad last mission. Lost three of his mates. Right mess it was. And he's like a lot of guys, feels guilty he survived and they didn't. He's just trying to find his feet, that's all. He'll wander for a while and then get settled,' a wide beam crossed his face, 'when he finds a good woman.'

He stood up and reddened in embarrassment when Tire threw her arms round him in a hug. 'It won't be me,' she assured him. 'I'm already as fixed up as I want to be.' Holding him on both shoulders, she added: 'Thank you for your help with Erica. I feel better that she wasn't... raped. Anything else you find out I'd be really grateful.'

CHAPTER 8

An email was waiting for her when she got back upstairs from Susan. 'I'm so glad we talked yesterday,' it said. 'Such a relief to know someone is looking into Erica's death. Everyone here is treating it like an accident.' Clearly she was back in the office, although it was from her private Gmail account.

There were no details, just four names and contact details. Hassan Chutani, Leeds. Bert Dugston, Hackney, London (dead brother Joe). Max Burkhanov (email contact Jean Malhuret, Paris). The fourth name made her blink. Rupert Wrighton, Eaton Square, London. Lord almighty, what persuaded Erica to take him on? She sighed, knowing full well that injustice would have been reason enough.

A quick Google confirmed what she already knew. Wrighton was second-generation money, his father's post-war scrap business hauling him up the social scale through a minor public school and Cambridge. Two failed commercial ventures in his twenties. Father dies and the inheritance funds him into politics. Indifferent Labour MP for twelve years, reputation as a loudmouth, not a team player. Deselected after argument with his local constituency party. Now television and newspaper pundit, chairman of a successful, cut-price DIY chain, run by his brother and son. A bully, from all she'd heard, in a Savile row suit.

Still, his ego fed on publicity so it would be easy enough to get an interview. He'd hardly be likely to confess to molesting his daughter, let alone getting rid of Erica, but she always liked to see the colour of people's eyes initially and then trust her gut if she thought they were worth pursuing.

If she checked his birth chart before she met him, it would give her a steer on the best way to handle him. She opened up the software, typed in his date of birth, sat back and sighed, staring at the screen. A bad-tempered windmill in a hurricane. Born into the chaos of the mid-1960s, when the Uranus Pluto conjunction was throwing everything up in the air globally with rebellions, revolutions and mayhem everywhere. It was tied into his Sun and Moon, so unstable, no impulse control. Thug of a father and a clinging wreck of a mother. She'd need to psyche herself up for that rendezvous.

Mentally she ticked off the leads, pondering how to follow through. Where to start? An honour-killer father, a violent thug, a refugee activist being harassed by secret police and a child-abusing millionaire. A lover and ex-lover – Crumley and Burgoyne – who might have information. And the Greengate case, although it seemed the least likely. Bumping off defence counsel in mid-trial would have been crass. Her grief and shock at Erica's death was receding as her research skills took over.

The names on Susan's list might all have had a motive, but that proved nothing. The enormity of what she had taken on rose like a cliff face in front of her. Her jaw tightened as she suppressed the voice inside telling her there was no point. To hell with it. If she found out nothing else she could make it a present to Erica to write about the threats she had faced. Even if none of them had killed her, they still deserved to be exposed.

Schubert helped her think, so she flipped through to find Symphony No. 5 and turned the volume up. An email zinged out to Jean Malhuret, the Kubek contact, suggesting a meeting when she was over in Paris in two days' time. Another went out to Matt, a disabled researcher she used occasionally to winkle out background information, who had good police contacts. That put an initial tick against Hassan Chutani and Bert Dugston.

The lover, or the ex-lover? Justin Burgoyne had been around longer, almost a year of an illicit affair, and might therefore be more amenable to pressure, especially if she landed on him unexpectedly. She looked up his details, checked through a couple of barristers' blogs for gossip and phoned his chamber's number, asking for his clerk.

'My name is Melanie Dabshaw. I'm a Newcastle solicitor, only in town for a day, and I'd like an urgent meeting with Mr Burgoyne.' It was a risk that he might be in, but no, he was in court all day and had a meeting and social engagements thereafter.

'What a shame. I'll have to try Robin Findston instead. He's our other possibility.'

The name of his chief rival for high-profile commercial cases was enough to soften up the clerk, who said Mr Burgoyne might have fifteen minutes before an NSPCC cocktail party he was attending with his wife at the Guildhall at 6.30 pm.

'What luck,' she said sweetly, 'I'm going as well. I'll catch up with him there.' She clicked off. Bastard. That's where he'd have met Erica. A call to Susan produced a panicky whisper at the other end.

'I can't talk now.'

'It's OK. Just wondered if there was an NSPCC invite for Erica tonight. If so, can I have it?' There was, and a courier was despatched to uplift it.

The juggernaut was starting to roll. Her excitement at the start of a new project gave her a pang of guilt. But she needed adrenaline to stay motivated and the end result would be her In Memoriam.

CHAPTER 9

A purple bruise on her thigh extended up across her hip bone as she examined herself in the bathroom mirror, having showered after a lunchtime jog. She towelled it gingerly and pulled on loose sweatpants and top. Dratted cyclist who couldn't look where he was going. She limped into her office, where Herk was up a ladder at the window.

He glanced over his shoulder. 'You injured, then?'

'Nah, just tripped over a lycra loon on a bike. Thanks, by the way, for Momo.'

After a final test of the new catch, he leapt nimbly off the stepladder, picked it up and moved towards the hall. 'That's OK. Luck, really. I had a drink with a few of the lads last night and he was there. You seemed worried so I asked him. Nothing to it.'

The ladder was stowed in the hall cupboard and a voice drifted through: 'I'll bring you a coffee. Just sit tight.'

With relief she landed heavily in her chair and winced. It took an effort to lift her legs onto the table, but it eased the throbbing when she leant back.

Herk emerged with her coffee and a mug of tea for himself, sitting opposite her on a grey, scallop-shaped chair with spindly aluminium legs, after giving it a shake to test its solidity. He put his tea on top of a low filing cabinet and leant his elbows on his knees, giving the impression he could leap up if the chair disappeared underneath him, and looked towards the window.

'Now, don't take this the wrong way. I've a suggestion for you. No obligation right. Bob, my mate with the car, he needs more work with his wife being ill and all, and he needs to keep up the hire purchase payments. So if you want a decent car any time, chauffeur driven, it's a BMW in good nick.' He laid a card on her desk.

'Sure.'

'Cash.'

She grinned, stretching down to hold one foot. 'You help each other out? You and your mates.'

'Well, if we don't, no one else will,' he said, biting his lower lip. 'And I've met a fair few since I moved round different units in my time. Those that are left, of course.' A look of sadness crossed his face, which shut down as he caught her glance.

'How did you meet up with Ali downstairs, then?' she asked to cover an awkward silence.

'I was dossing down with Charlie, another mate,' he grinned. 'He'd done a removal for one of Ali's family and sometimes helped here with odd jobs when he was needed.'

The doorbell rang and he waved her to stay still while he went to answer the intercom. Two minutes later he returned with an envelope.

'Courier,' he said, dropping it on her desk.

'So you'll go back to Charlie's when you're finished here?' she asked, shifting her position to reach for her cigarettes. When she swivelled to offer him one he was standing stiffly, his eyebrows raised, giving her a hard look and refusing a cigarette.

'OK, OK,' she laughed. 'None of my business. Bad habit of mine. Comes with the territory – asking questions. It's what I do for a living, especially the ones people don't want to answer. Sit down and finish your tea.'

He sniffed and sat down, holding the filing cabinet with one hand until he was sure the chair would hold his weight. 'On my territory, people who ask too many questions of the wrong sort get themselves shot, or at least banged up.' His blue eyes sparkled and he winked at her. A crumpled packet of unfiltered Camels emerged from a back pocket and he lit up. 'Now, I hope you're still not haring after the guys who killed your friend. Just leave it to the police.'

'The hell I will. They're getting nowhere and not looking.' She swung her legs off the desk and groaned as the bruise came into contact with the chair arm. 'I've already started. There's a list of suspects and I'm not stopping.' She tapped the envelope. 'Ex-lover, swanky barrister. I'll tackle him tonight at the Guildhall with his wife in attendance. He might know more and he'll talk, believe me, when I get him pinned against a pillar.'

Outside the window, gusts of wind were blowing leaves and a discarded chocolate wrapper up in the air. The sound of heavy drilling from roadworks round the corner broke through the constant traffic rumble, vying with the occasional horn blast for attention.

Lost in her thoughts, she didn't notice him stand up and thought he had left. A clatter in the kitchen indicated more tea was being brewed.

'Right,' he said, when he returned, banging down his mug and sitting down without pausing this time. 'These suspects, who are they?'

She rattled them off and he listened intently, running a hand round his chin, then through his bristly hair. When she finished, his cheeks ballooned as he blew out a long breath. He cleared his throat and scratched his upper lip.

'Reckon you can rub the Pakistani father off the list. Hit and runs not their style. And he'll still be trying to find his daughter.' He chewed the inside of his mouth. 'Brother of the dead man killed by his wife? Mebbe, but people say lots of things in the heat of the moment they don't mean.'

Why was she telling him all this, she wondered, let alone listening to his opinion? Still, a sounding board was always useful, helped clear her thinking. The sharp clang of his mug on the metal surface made her turn her head.

'Secret police,' he said with emphasis, 'from the old Soviet states are not people you want to tangle with. No pinning them against a wall. You'll end up in bits in a ditch.'

Despite herself she chuckled, although her brow wrinkled in irritated agreement. Before she could respond, he held up one hand with three fingers turned down and holding the fourth. 'Pervy millionaire. Hate that sort. Make me sick. If he was brought up in the scrap business, he'll know a few gangsters, no matter how respectable he is now. Might be a runner as a suspect or paid someone else to do it, but he'll never admit it in a million years.'

His pinkie was thrust at her. 'The case your friend was involved in. Also could be possible. But,' he thumped his knee, 'you'll get nowhere at all fronting these guys up. What do you expect them to say? You need hard evidence.'

A picture of her old headmistress ticking her off for being too impulsive flashed in front of her.

'Yes, Miss Archibald,' she said, one hand curling round her chin, her eyes widening. 'Could you tell me what I should be doing?' He ignored her sarcasm and sat thinking, twining his desert boots round each other.

'Well,' he started, when she stopped him.

'I wasn't looking for advice. I know what I'm doing.'

'You think?' His face screwed up with irritation.

Why had she started this conversation? Socrates didn't have ex-squaddies in mind when proclaiming the virtues of dialectical debate, although she had to admit his world-weary eyes gave off an air of battle-hardened resilience and common sense. On her estimation it would have been guerrilla fighting he'd been involved in. Her own work of probing and exposing was just a paler version, without the assault rifles.

'Right, what would you suggest?' The question emerged before she had time to reconsider.

'Get your intel nailed down, do recon and assess risk,' he said, as if reciting a mantra. 'Which means,' he added, steadying a twitch in one knee, 'only go in if you're half-sure of getting back out in one piece. And the end result is worth it.'

'Don't pick fights you can't win,' she responded with a rueful smile. 'I've had a few of those. Trouble is, I didn't find that out until I'd lifted a few stones. But hey, you win some, you lose some. This is for Erica. I've got to try.'

'You're feeling guilty you didn't save her.' His comment caught her off balance. She massaged her leg, sending pain shooting down to her ankle.

'You mean because I didn't know in advance from her astrology? It won't tell you. And wouldn't be helpful if it was. Do you want to know when you're going to die?'

'No way.' He shuddered. 'My old sergeant used to say fight today with an eye on tomorrow. I'm a tomorrow kind of guy.' He half-smiled, then looked down, rubbing the heel of one boot on his other foot. 'Mind you, so were the mates I lost.'

'And you're feeling guilty you're here and they aren't?' The words were no sooner out than she regretted them. She was intruding on his private life and trying to distract attention from her own muddled feelings. Before she could apologise, he stood up and walked towards the kitchen with his mug, saying over his shoulder: 'You'll be needing a car to get to this showdown with the posh barrister tonight.' It wasn't a question. 'What time?'

She shook her head in amusement, relieved he had brushed off her question without recrimination. Cornering London's top commercial barrister at a cocktail party wasn't going to be the most dangerous thing she'd ever done.

'6.30 pm there,' she called after him.

CHAPTER 10

The vaulted stone ceiling of the medieval crypt was tastefully illuminated by the best of modern technology at the head of each of the central pillars. The patches of stone nearest the uplighters dissolved into white nothingness, while shadows spread further afield tracing the branches of roof supports, giving the air of ghostly, fossilised trees.

Beneath was a sea of black, navy blue and pinstripe, through which glided waiters with trays of champagne and wine. Tire, in slate grey velvet trousers and jacket, stood beside the pillar nearest the door nursing a glass, trying to look inconspicuous. Conversation drifted over from the nearest group.

'You're quite wrong, Nicholas. He was taking the woodwind far too fast during the overture. I knew then it would be a disaster. And it was. If the tickets hadn't cost a fortune we would have left.'

Suppressing a groan, she slipped down the wall to her right, murmuring an apology as she squeezed past a trio of women, dressed identically in navy, their skirts extending a regulation two inches below their sturdy knees. They were discussing a recent Barnardo's report on child sex trafficking. Probably judges, she thought.

The invitees were substantially legal types with a sprinkling of City men and their wives, plus a couple of MPs she recognised. All about their charitable business of making themselves feel good while staying a million miles away from the poor, bruised, battered and unwashed kids who were the raison d'être of this elite gathering.

Then she spotted him, standing in the centre. Justin Burgoyne – grey hair slicked back, lightly tanned face, expensive dark suit, striped shirt and regimental tie. Next to him was an anxious woman, stick thin, in a silk maroon dress that did nothing for the pallor of her face despite layers of make-up.

That would be the wife Janice he was going to leave for Erica. Chance would be a fine thing. She was heiress to the Maxted money. No way he was ever going to bale, which was what she had told Erica having looked up the marital relationship chart. It was a match of convenience and commerce and would hold forever. She edged her way across.

'Mrs Burgoyne, isn't it? We met at a previous function.' Tire offered her free hand, to be met with a look of flustered alarm and a limp palm that barely made contact. After a few gushed sentiments about the good work of the NSPCC, which elicited panicky nods, Tire noticed out of the corner of her eye that Justin was taking the opportunity to move to another group.

Over the next ten minutes she tracked him across the room, pausing to attach herself with a bright smile and few words to whichever clutch of worthies was in her path. A familiar face off to her left tugged at her memory. Not someone she'd met. Seen a photograph of. Late sixties, well preserved, high cheekbones that accentuated deep-set eyes, aquiline nose, black eyebrows and white hair. Not handsome exactly, but striking. Paul Stone, that's who it was, father of Harman, who owned the company Greengate had worked for. He was talking to a ruddy-faced Tory MP and his blonde wife, who were both laughing with forced politeness at something he said. Sensing that he'd noticed her, she turned back to see Burgoyne walking back towards her so she made a move, hand extended.

'Justin Burgoyne, isn't it? Wonder if I could have a word?' She steered him by one elbow to an alcove with a stained glass window. His indulgent expression and appreciative glance down her body made it clear why he'd allowed himself to be shepherded.

'I'm a friend of Erica Smythson.' A flicker of alarm lit up his eyes and he stiffened. 'You had a long affair and promised to leave your wife for her.'

He practically hissed in her face.

'Cut the crap. I'm not here to blackmail you. I just want some information. Maybe outside would suit you better.' She indicated a door nearby, re-establishing her grip on his elbow.

Once out in the fresh air, he wrenched himself free and glanced over his shoulder before saying with a vicious edge in his voice: 'You're lying. There is not a shred of evidence of any such thing. I could sue you for slander.'

'Oh, please. I heard blow-by-blow accounts of the whole sordid episode for a year. I'm not interested in your love life. And don't worry, your wife isn't going to leave you. I've seen that type before. Martyrs to the end. I just want to know why Erica was in Hammersmith in the middle of the night.'

'How the fuck would I know?' He accepted a cigarette with ill grace, used his own gold-plated lighter and returned it to his pocket without offering, breathing heavily.

'Erica's old cases where threats were made. She discussed them with you?'

A look of puzzlement was accompanied by a gesture of incredulity. 'No. Yes. But so what? You can't possibly imagine it was deliberate?'

She nodded. 'Rupert Wrighton?'

'Now, look.' His face was three inches away from hers. 'You cannot go around alleging murder, for heaven's sake.'

'I'm not accusing anyone of anything,' she said, standing her ground. 'Yet.'

'I'm not putting up with this,' he said in a savage tone, dropping his cigarette and stamping on it.

'You can't have forgotten our deal this fast.' She inclined her head and gave a taut smile.

'Deal?'

'I keep my mouth shut and you help me with Erica's cases.'

He turned away and stared out across the yard, his shoulders pulling at the expensive fabric of his jacket.

'Human rights case?'

'That's more likely,' he answered, still with his back to her. 'I told her not to get involved with the Kubek activist. No hope of winning and it would put the hounds of hell on her tail.'

'Let's get back to Wrighton.'

'Why?' He spun round, his mouth extended in irritation, his white crowns catching the light from a nearby window, glowing like alabaster carvings. 'You think he'd risk his public reputation...'

She cut him off. 'Maybe to protect his image, given all I hear.' A dismissive hand nearly swiped her across the face, so she leant back without moving her feet.

'I always thought that allegation of his daughter was ridiculous. He's not the sort. He went to Cambridge.'

'Precisely.' She gave him a withering smile. His patience was clearly at snapping point but she thought she'd try one more. 'Harman Stone.'

'What?'

'The Greengate case.'

'You are completely insane.' One arm clamped across his chest, the other hand went up to protect his throat.

'Justin, you're wanted for photographs, old chap.' A voice floated across from the door. The fear in his eyes gave way to relief and he started to move. She thrust her card into his top pocket behind the silk handkerchief, leaning close enough to kiss him and whispered.

'A deal's a deal. If I find out you've been holding back, I'll spill. Phone me when you've had time to consider.'

The door banged shut behind him.

***

A phone call brought the car to the front entrance with Herk at the wheel, still dressed in T-shirt and jeans. She climbed in beside him.

'Any joy there?' he asked, pulling out onto Gresham Street.

'Rattled his tin. We'll see what falls out when he gets back to me.'

'Cooperative then?'

The elation of the spat began to recede and she ran her fingers along the seat belt.

'No. He's a self-righteous hypocrite. Worst sort of Sagittarius. But he's vulnerable and he knows more than he's saying.'

'So you do the simple stuff as well?'

She nudged the back of the driver's seat with her boot and laughed. 'Not too often. Otherwise I sound like Mystic Meg, but, hey, it works well enough. Lawyers are often Sagittarius or Gemini – know a little about a lot and can talk for England. Hot air balloons most of them, not much grounding in the real world.'

'Your friend Erica wasn't like that?'

'No. Libra with Saturn in Libra as well – fair-minded, meticulous about sticking to the rules. Although she had Venus and her Moon in Pisces so she was gullible, believed the best in people, which was a major difference between us. I don't.'

'Maybe that's what called her out that night. Someone leant on her sympathy.'

'For sure. She always said her emotions were her weak spot. My money would still be on Wrighton. His daughter would tug at her heart strings. No way she'd walk away from a situation like that, even if the girl backed out publicly. She'd never have left her trapped, no matter what she had to do.'

CHAPTER 11

Three men and a youngish woman sat on easy chairs round a low table looking at several drawings scattered across the surface. The room, glass-walled on three sides, was flooded with light, although the grey drizzle outside softened any glare. The older man had an abundance of untidy ginger hair above a ruddy complexion and was dressed in slacks and a coloured jumper. The dark-haired woman was more severely turned out in a white blouse over black pants. They smiled reassuringly at Jimmy, who sat hunched inside his coat, nervously playing with the end of his long, green scarf. Beside him in anorak and trainers was Len, his social worker, who once in a while put a supportive hand on his arm.

'It's great the gallery are putting on an exhibition for you,' Len said. 'Really great.'

'Aye, aye. But Elly was asking. Will it not affect my benefits?' Jimmy asked anxiously.

Len laughed and tapped his shoulder. 'Come on. You're going to be a success. It's just a paying hobby at the moment. If you do make more, then you won't need the benefits, will you? Just stop worrying about it.'

'You've no idea where you learned to draw, Jimmy?' The young woman cut in eagerly. Jimmy regarded her doubtfully and shook his head. 'Or play the piano? I gather you do that without music. I'd love to hear you play.'

Jimmy, feeling uncomfortable with the attention of more than one person, tried to steady his jittery knee with one hand and continued to look puzzled as the older man said: 'Len has explained to you what we're trying to do?'

Jimmy drew a deep breath and said softly: 'Find out who that man in my head is.' Then added sheepishly: 'I'm sorry, I forgot your names.'

'I'm Dr – well, John Donaghue. Call me John. And this is Janet Birch. I'm a psychiatrist and she's a psychologist.'

'Aye.' Jimmy didn't sound impressed. 'But my doctor is Dr McIntyre. Has he gone away, then?'

'No, not at all. He'll still be looking after you. We're just involved in a project trying to find out the background of people like you who were in Dunlothian Hall. But you must understand I can't promise that we'll be able to lay all your ghosts to rest.'

'And Elly,' Jimmy said insistently. 'You can't forget Elly. She was with me all these years.'

'That's very true, Jimmy.' Janet Birch leant forward with a tight smile that didn't quite reach her eyes. 'She knits, doesn't she? You live together. Do you know when you first met?'

A pause followed as Jimmy stared at his knees and John Donaghue raised a warning eyebrow at his colleague.

Jimmy was not sure when he had met Elly since he was hazy about his early years. He was told by the social workers that he had arrived in Dunlothian Hall in Lanarkshire at twelve years old, labelled mentally disturbed and was given ECT for several years, so he had gaps in his memory. The Hall was set up for mental defectives as they were called back then, but children with behavioural problems, classed as moral imbeciles, also ended up there, quarantined away from the world in a bleak Victorian asylum sitting in its own grounds and surrounded by a high wall.

Elly came in when she was seventeen suffering severe depression after the birth of a stillborn, illegitimate baby. Both had remained there for the next four decades, surviving the spartan regime of bad food, cruel staff and hard labour, living in vast, soulless dormitories, cleaning the Hall and the grounds. The final ten years saw huge improvements with better care, a nourishing diet and fun activities as well as kindly therapists keen to hear them talk.

As the effects of living in an institutional gulag gradually eased, they were slowly introduced to the frightening notion of moving back into the outside world. That they would stay together was never questioned, since they had been a couple for almost three decades. For the first twenty years only secretly, since liaisons were forbidden. But they found chances to sneak away to be together, clinging to each other like survivors on a life raft.

Many of the other inmates had learning difficulties but they were both smart, although badly educated and cowed into compliance by a system that robbed them of their identity. Jimmy had recognised a kindred spirit in Elly, helping her through her suicidal first few years.

In return, as she became more stable, she pulled him out of his periodic confusions and depression. With much trepidation, ten years ago they had moved into sheltered housing and were now living in their own council flat.

John Donaghue broke the silence. 'I know it will be difficult for you going back into memories of bad times. But it will help us – and you. Janet will spend time with you maybe once a week, just talking. And there's no rush over this at all. It's rather like peeling an onion, taking it layer by layer and finding out what's underneath. Then Janet can tell Dr McIntyre what she finds out, so he'll know how to treat you better.'

'He's treating me OK at the moment,' Jimmy said, wrinkling his brow, his eyes fixed on the floor.

'And in the meantime,' Len said hurriedly, 'you can keep drawing and painting. Ricky at the gallery said after they show your work he'd like to see some acrylics and maybe even oils as well as water colours.'

Jimmy stared unhappily out of the window, his eyes roaming across the neatly landscaped green space, trimmed grass curving round a central rockery, with plants spilling over half-buried chunks of granite and a few upright grasses waving in the wind. He would have liked to stay to sketch the garden, especially the lake beyond.

He loved watching the fallen leaves floating on the surface, then submerging in slow stages. The leafy branches of the trees at the edge reflected on the water, so often he couldn't tell what was a mirror image and what was not. Layer upon layer of copper-coloured shapes, lazily moving, changing places as the water rippled in the slight breeze. The cast-off leaves sank slowly out of sight to a muddy end while the trees continued to throw shadows, occasionally shrugging off another abandoned leaf to keep the pattern repeating.

But he had a stronger urge to get away. Years of imprisonment had taught him that invisibility was safer. Attention from doctors and staff usually meant trouble. He wrapped himself deeper into his coat. He did not want to relive those grey decades, to remind himself of what he had lost. Especially he did not like the woman, didn't trust her.

Len suddenly jumped up. 'Come on Jimmy, we'll off and leave the docs to it.' Jimmy smiled wanly at them and followed Len to the door.

'Now,' said Donaghue to the woman beside him who was looking thoughtfully at the departing figures, 'Janet, you must remember he's very fragile. So you need to build up his trust before you start digging. And you may never find out everything. He had ECT early on, which was a sin, frankly, quite inhumane. That will have wiped out some memories for good. So you'll need to tread warily. Are you clear on that?'

'Of course. I did my MPhil in trauma.'

'This isn't out of a textbook,' he said sharply. 'You have no idea what that place was like. It wouldn't have gone amiss in Soviet Russia. The doctors who oversaw it should have been shot in my opinion. But then it started life as an asylum for imbeciles, so what can you expect?'

'Like the Magdalene laundries.'

'Exactly. What would you remember if you'd been trapped in one of those places for decades? In the Hall Jimmy would have been starved, drugged, forcibly shocked, brutalised and stripped of his identity. The mind just shuts down in those circumstances, which is a mercy. The question is, what does he gain from you trying to open it up?'

She sat up straight and said with arched eyebrows: 'This study is enormously important. What we learn about memory will help countless others.'

'Yes,' he said, 'but will it help him? That's what you have to ask yourself every step of the way. The poor blighter has suffered quite enough. I know he's more interesting than some of them, but you need not to get too hooked into that.'

Shuffling the bulky folders in front of her, labelled D Hall patients, into a tidy pile, she pushed them with difficulty into her briefcase and stood up. 'But you must admit, he is intriguing. That talent doesn't spring out of nowhere. There's a family history that needs to be explored. And dilapidated as Jimmy is, he looks nothing like the photograph of his father in here.' She tapped her case and left.

CHAPTER 12

A sexy text from Jin started the day off well, reassuring her he hadn't run into trouble although there was no indication where he was. She relaxed for a moment at her desk, remembering the last time they had made love and her body tingled, making her shift around in the chair with a surge of longing.

Outside the window, two crows chased a pigeon across the roofs opposite, ignoring the morning drizzle and cawing loudly as they weaved and revolved, black feathers outspread, to harass their plaything.

Mentally chiding herself for getting distracted, she opened up an email from the researcher, Matt, headed 'first dibs'. There were two short paragraphs.

'*Hassan Chutani, Leeds, car-wash office worker, married to first cousin, one severely disabled son, one daughter, drives a ten-year-old Vauxhall, restraining order against him from Erica Smythson, otherwise clean record.*'

'*Bert Dugston, Hackney, sentenced to five years in Wakefield Prison for aggravated assault six weeks ago.*'

Did she want more?

No wonder Chutani wanted his daughter back and married in the faith, otherwise no grandchildren. At least of the variety he wanted. Didn't sound wealthy enough to have put out a contract.

Dugston was out of action although he probably had mates who would be amenable for a spot of damage if he had the money. No, less likely. He'd have wanted personal revenge.

'Not for the moment. Thanks,' she wrote back.

Deliberately shutting down the 'what next?' question, she switched her attention to finishing the Sanchez book. The final chapter was the most difficult since she was treading a fine line between explaining the hitman's motivations and not sounding as if she was excusing him. How do you cope if you're born into a hyena's lair, with even the pups tearing each other to pieces? Morality, empathy doesn't come into it, let alone sentimentality. The will to live is the only driving force. Making it to forty was a staggering achievement in the circumstances.

Her mind constantly flickered to an image of a filthy child, standing alone on a rubbish tip, scavenging for a life. Jin was right, she thought, I do feel a connection to this wreck of a psychopath who left a bloody trail behind him. Still, she had done what he had asked – remembered him – and she would no doubt be well rewarded by readers greedy for the details of his trade. Having written and rewritten, she finally left it as an open question.

She leant back in her seat, having put in the last dot and emailed it before she changed her mind to her agent. Completing a book usually left her feeling depressed and empty. This time her post-partum dip would have to wait, she thought, since she had a sudden one-day trip to Paris tomorrow to meet booksellers. Then she intended to get a grip of the Erica situation.

A fast forty-minute run might just be what she needed to clear her head and lungs and ease the stiffness out of her shoulders and her leg. In no mood to be whistled at, she threw on blue jogging pants and a loose, high-necked T-shirt with sleeves. Bored with Hyde Park, she headed north up Regent Street and had to concentrate to avoid the milling shoppers and stationary chatters who littered the pavement.

Only as she neared All Souls on Langham Place did she notice a black-clad motorcyclist keeping pace with her. What caught her attention was his slow pace, a contrast to his brethren who wended in and out of cars and taxis with careless disregard. Past Broadcasting House he dogged her steps, making her glance across more frequently. Suzuki was emblazoned in blue on the gleaming bike. Round the curve of Park Crescent she lost him momentarily at traffic lights, but within a minute he revved up even closer to her.

Probably the motorcyclist fancied her and had time to spare, so thought he'd chance his luck. Marylebone Road would fix him since he'd get locked into the traffic flow. Once across the lights on the busy thoroughfare groaning with the early evening build-up, she speeded up York Gate, with the Royal Academy of Music giving her shelter, and into Regent's Park.

Stretching out to a fast jog past the elongated Boating Lake, she was soon puffing and sweating. The outer circle was under four miles so she could easily do it at this pace, although too much sitting and smoking was taking its toll. Halfway round she collapsed onto the grass beside the canal and bent forward to rest her head on her knees, her hands curled round her trainers. The tendons down the back of her legs complained, although it eased her spine. Sitting up and arching back, she wriggled her shoulders, then scrambled to her feet. Looking left outside the park to Prince Albert Road, she saw him again. He was sitting motionless on his bike, one foot on the pavement, watching her through his tinted visor.

Whether he was a romantic stalker or a predatory watcher, he was beginning to get on her nerves. She started to jog on slowly, finding her mobile phone in her belt and keeping it ready in one hand. There was useful cover round the entrance to the zoo so she dodged behind the buildings nearest the road and waited, her back to a wall so he couldn't see her in advance. High-pitched monkey screams set off a squall in the nearby aviary, a hullabaloo pitching and rattling like a modern opera overture. She waited. The motorcyclist rode past slowly. Once the number plate was in view she clicked her phone several times. Then stepping back out of sight, she doubled back and retraced her steps for York Gate. There was no sight of him as she crossed over into the head of Regent Street and dog-legged home down the backstreets.

Once inside the front door, she grabbed a towel from the kitchen and rubbed her hair dry of sweat as she booted up her laptop, transferred the photo of the registration number across and emailed it to Matt, who would check out the owner.

CHAPTER 13

The yellow Post-it list stuck to the front of an African stone statuette on the far corner of her desk, supposedly a bringer of luck, stared back at her. She sent another email to Jean Malhuret asking about the Kubek lawyer. If she harassed him enough he'd have to reply. That left Wrighton and the Greengate case to excavate.

Googling Rupert Wrighton, she discovered his latest *cause célèbre* was campaigning on behalf of fathers accused of child abuse in divorce custody battles. No danger of him being excluded from the airwaves on that one. He had a reputation for sailing close to the wind and this was smart, she thought. Since he was a widower, no one could say he was grinding a personal axe. All altruistic public service.

While she was contemplating which excuse she could select to secure an interview, her mobile rang.

'Justin Burgoyne here.' The clipped, upper-class voice made her shoulders twitch. A pause. No doubt for effect. 'I may have been a little hasty last night. You did rather catch me off balance.'

She didn't respond.

'Look, Erica did discuss her cases with me. If you are determined on this idiotic idea then I'd start with the Alliance des Avocats pour les Droits de l'Homme in Paris.' His French was pitch-perfect and designed for show. 'That's...'

'I know what it means,' she interjected, cursing herself for not having made the connection.

'As to the others. Rupert Wrighton, what can I say? Child abuse cases are a nightmarish swamp. Commercial law is wholesome in comparison. But Erica was touched by the girl's story and on a mission to save her. Never a good idea in my experience to get personally invested in clients.'

'For sure,' she said and waited.

A cough and throat-clearing at the other end. Then silence.

'Greengate?' she prompted.

Finally, he said: 'I shouldn't talk about this at all. But in the circumstances...' He sighed. 'I pointed her towards the Greengate case since I had some dealings with the Stones, who really are nonpareil. Well, Paul Stone is. Utterly respectable.' Another pause. 'And it was an open and shut case as far as I could see. I thought it would give her useful experience.'

And maybe get it tidied away at high speed. How little you understood Erica. She doodled a dragon and a maid with a spear on her notepad, while she sensed him squirming at the end of the line.

'So are we square then?' he said eventually.

'For now,' she said briskly. 'I may be in touch if I need anything else.' She clicked off.

***

First stop, Wrighton. The deputy financial editor of *Der Spiegel*, the German news magazine, owed her a favour for handing over research that she could no longer use since they were about to blow a story she had spent three months on. She'd use their name to get an interview with Wrighton. A phone call to Wrighton's personal assistant – 'do just call me Felicity' – arranged a 9 am appointment two days hence.

She started to prowl round the office. Was this all a fool's errand, as Burgoyne suggested? Her common sense fought a battle with her gut instinct. Her leg still ached so she bent down to stretch her tendons. By the time she straightened up, her intuition – that the answer lay in these old cases – had won.

Her mind ran over what she remembered about Jack Greengate being accused of murdering his wife. An accountant with Cerigo, an upmarket holiday resort company, run by Harman Stone. The name Cerigo reeked of pretentious indulgence. The birthplace of Aphrodite, goddess of love and beauty, who rose from the foam created by Uranus's castrated genitals. She grinned. Bet they don't put that in the brochures.

Exclusive retreats on the Costa Brava, California, with more planned for Croatia and Goa. She skimmed through their website and scribbled 'Russell – Cerigo' on a yellow Post-it note. He was a freelance forensic accountant, her first port of call for financial gossip. There was nothing she could see on the net other than puff pieces, except on a travel writers' site on which was posted a notice for a press conference at 6 pm tonight chaired by Paul and Harman Stone for Cerigo and the Alzheimer's charity. Would it be worth it? They would have had little to do with a lowly accountant's private life and were hardly front-runners. Still, two Stones at one swoop. The coincidence of it happening that day made it too good an opportunity to miss. Might as well eyeball them and knock them off the list. Just as well she had checked.

A call to the travel editor on a newspaper she worked for occasionally produced an official invitation, which was gratefully proffered. She promised to send them a paragraph if there was anything interesting and promptly sent a courier round to pick it up.

Her adrenaline was starting to flow. Her hand hesitated over her phone as she pondered taxi or Herk? His irritation value was quite high, but on the other hand he did talk sense and put brakes on her wilder impulses. And, most importantly, she might need his pathologist friend again at some point. If she were honest she had also appreciated being able to bounce ideas of him. Being overly self-sufficient had its drawbacks.

Fifteen minutes after her text, he arrived wearing a camouflage jacket and holding a heavy canvas sports bag. His face was guarded, almost embarrassed. After an uncomfortable pause he said with a forced smile: 'You just caught me. I was off.'

'Off on your travels?' Tire said, surprised.

'Yeah, Ali's back, having banged a few heads together in his family and there's no room for two of us down in the cellar.'

'Where are you going?'

'Dunno really. Here and there, maybe. Charlie's got a new lady, so no room there.'

'Come on,' she said 'you've no idea. You can't just go wandering off into the twilight.'

'There's a hostel down at King's Cross. I'll stay there till I decide.'

'I need a car at 5.15 tonight.'

He thought for a moment. 'That's fine, but I'll need to go book into the hostel now and come back.'

The words came out before she had time to consider.

'You will sling your bag in the spare room. I'm away overnight tomorrow.'

Noticing his startled expression, she added: 'Don't worry I'm not going to seduce you.'

He laughed, although with a slight blush. 'I didn't think so. But you're intent on organising me and I don't take kindly to that.'

'You bloody need organising, so stop arguing. And I need help with tracking down what happened to Erica. So you'll be earning your board and lodging.'

His head hung down and he ran a hand round his lips, examining his boots with a frown. Just as she thought he was going to refuse he straightened up and said: 'OK. I'll stay as long as I can be of use. But no longer, mind.'

CHAPTER 14

Within half an hour she was showered and into tight pinstripe trousers over grey suede ankle boots, with a wide-collared, white blouse under a grey velvet jacket. Strings of gilt chains, gold hoop earrings and a white and yellow gold signet ring on her engagement finger added just the right touch of urban flashiness, she thought, nodding to herself in the mirror.

The car was waiting at the door when she answered Herk's summons. He stood to attention, holding the door open for her with a serious look on his face, dressed in a ill-fitting, dark grey suit with a white shirt and stained black tie. Inside, she said with a grin as he pulled away from the kerb with a satisfying surge of power: 'Chauffeurs are allowed to smile nowadays, you know.'

He took his time answering as he manoeuvred round a parked lorry and then roadworks barriers along Poland Street. Glancing in the mirror, he said: 'Yeah, well, I thought it might be sensible to cool it while the watchers were there.'

'Who?'

'Couple of guys who've been there today, lounging at the street corner trying to look inconspicuous. I thought I'd best look like a hired driver.'

'Wouldn't they have seen you go in and out?' she said, leaning forward.

'No, I always go out the back door, tradesman's entrance. They weren't watching there.'

'Shit. That's not good. I hope they are not from Cerigo, since that's where we're going.'

Herk shook his head. 'I can't see why a holiday company would be employing heavies.'

'They only turned up today, you said? You're sure they're not just louts out for an easy picking?'

'I know what surveillance looks like,' he said, waving a cab into the space in front. 'Even if they are rookies. Or trying to look like amateurs to warn you off.'

So that's why he'd agreed to stay. As a bodyguard. It was a surprisingly reassuring gesture. In the past she'd never given threats a second thought. They weren't uncommon when your business was poking into secrets people didn't want exposed. But then again, murder wasn't her usual terrain.

And she'd barely started raising flags. Jean Malhuret's emails could have been intercepted. Burgoyne could have alerted Wrighton, although it was unlikely from the way he spoke. Or Stone? Maybe Dugston had a tip-off from a dodgy policeman after Matt's inquiries. None rang bells. Maybe Herk was wrong.

He drove smoothly, with a cabbie's patience at the logjam in Oxford Street, and slowed into a near-gridlock in Regent Street full of early evening shoppers crowding and barging across red-lit intersections. Finally, they were swinging onto Marylebone Road heading, Tire noted edgily, for the Hammersmith flyover. In days gone by, she had enjoyed the swoop and curve of these aerial escapes from the stop-start clutter they left behind. She thought she'd never look on one with pleasure again.

'Drop me a text when you want picked up,' he said as he swung into the crowded entrance to the Kensington Hilton Hotel, which was milling with tourists, three cabs and a bus. 'I'll be round and about.'

***

Swinging her eye round the carpeted foyer, with its canopy of architectural ceiling lights over the mustard-fronted reception desk, she noticed a sign for Cerigo on an easel. Groups of excited American and Japanese tourists were scattered across the reception area so she had to wend a circuitous path to follow the arrow. A tall, smartly dressed, white-haired man caught her eye as she ducked and weaved round the chattering globetrotters. His back was to her when she paused at the far end, but one glance had confirmed it was Paul Stone. Even at this distance, his stance suggested authority. He was talking to what looked like a driver, dressed in a black suit and white shirt, who was nodding submissively to instructions.

Once in the meeting room she was welcomed by a receptionist in a low-cut, emerald sheath dress and signed in under the travel editor's name on her invitation. Then she settled herself at the back of a dozen rows of white and dark blue cushioned conference chairs, chosen to match a luridly patterned carpet. At the front was a huge screen towering over a small raised platform. With no one beside her, she texted Herk to look out for the driver with his description.

The room filled up rapidly with an assortment of travel writers and journalists, identifiable by their thrown-together outfits, some sleeker public relations and business types. All sat down expectantly, clearly keen for the meeting to start and finish and the drinking to begin.

Harman Stone arrived wearing a deep orange jacket over a white shirt and black trousers with slicked-back dark hair. He was short, only about five foot four, with a largish head and elongated chin. Surrounding him was an entourage of two young men who looked like male models, with beige rollneck sweaters under tailored camel jackets. And three women in their twenties, besheathed in various shades of blue on precipitous heels.

Stone spoke jerkily in a strangely mixed American-English accent from notes while one of his helpers cued in video excerpts of the renovations of Cerigo's holiday properties in Spain and California.

Tire stifled a yawn, glancing frequently at the shiny brochure on her knee that had all the information and pictures, neatly packaged. Her mind drifted off to what she could remember of his birth chart. The sleazy, over-indulgent Scorpio planets were certainly obvious. He was born in the mid-1960s, like Wrighton, so the same scattered, chaotic, restless temperament. Mars, Pluto, Uranus: trampled underfoot by a domineering and rejecting father in childhood. He could have stayed a doormat or, if he'd got out from under as he matured, he could have turned into a second-generation bully.

After twenty-five long minutes of saccharine guff he answered questions, only one of which raised Tire's interest. The question itself was standard enough, an accusation of failure to respond to a holidaymaker's complaint about a lost booking. But it was his reaction that seemed disproportionate. His tan reddened, turning his fleshy face an unpleasant shade of russet, and his eyes darted uncomfortably to where his father sat. Brushing aside the first question, he said sharply it was in the hands of his lawyers. When the question was repeated he started to bluster angrily, waving his arms around, mumbling about a new accountancy system giving problems.

'He's losing his grip,' she thought. A suave intervention from Paul Stone, who moved swiftly from his front-row seat to take over the microphone, closed the discussion.

'I am sure,' he said, in a slightly clipped accent, too precise to be his first language, 'that any oversight, if one has occurred...' He pinned the questioner with a hard stare, pausing long enough to make him squirm. '...It will be rectified without delay.' An engaging smile stayed on his face throughout although, Tire noted, the warmth did not extend to his eyes, which were unblinking and steady.

His charm moved attention smoothly onto his charities. 'Now I really am excited to tell you of progress we are making in linking up so many golden-agers through our Lifelong Friendship circle. Already we have half a million signed up round the globe, many of whom we have been able through kind donations to gift simple computers. Such a lovely feeling, knowing all these wonderful people no longer feeling isolated.'

He smiled warmly at the audience, moving his eyes expertly from one person to another. Good technique she thought, making everyone feel special. 'And Cerigo, of course, does sterling work giving holidays to deprived children and their grandparents.'

He turned to nod at his son, who was sitting with barely concealed ill grace at the end of the platform. Even a round of enthusiastic clapping did not bring a smile to Harman Stone's face.

'Maybe I should tell you,' he said, leaning forward confidentially, 'why these resorts are so special. They have been a dream of mine since I lived in a wonderful villa called La Mirabelle in Villefranche on the Côte d'Azur many years ago. I wanted to share that joyous experience with others.'

He's waffling to divert attention from the unpleasantness, she thought, watching his well-manicured hands reach out to his rapt audience. He lowered his voice and his smile widened, his glittering eyes continuing to roam and connect. She moved behind the person in front to block his view of her.

'I will let you into a secret. Our resorts all had the best feng shui experts involved in the design to lend harmony. And,' he raised a finger, 'I shouldn't admit this, but they were all opened officially on the most propitious time set by a world-famous astrologer.'

The front row dutifully clapped and the travel writers jotted on their pads. Neat manoeuvre, that'll be the headline, not a booking screw-up.

She scribbled a note to herself to look up his chart. After five minutes, the silky tones had moved onto his Alzheimer's drug research foundation and were beginning to irritate Tire, so she turned her attention to studying Harman and father together. Junior had bulging eyes, an exaggerated version of his father's aquiline nose perched above a bunched mouth, with a triangular jawbone that extended his conical chin below his Adam's apple. The face only a mother could love. Certainly no competition for father. Still, Paul Stone was sharing a platform with him and had financed his business so there must be a bond.

Could Harman be a loose cannon, letting his temper get the better of him? Trying to ignore his orange jacket, she imagined him setting up a murder and framing Greengate for it. The jacket won. He was too ludicrous a figure to be a mastermind and was anyway under the thumb of Pa Stone, whose reputation, she thought, had been too carefully crafted to allow for reckless behaviour. She was left with a niggling feeling that there was more to the relationship between father and son than met the eye.

Finally the meeting finished and, having been handed yet more glossy brochures about the charity, she was heading for the door. 'Miss Haddington,' a voice called behind her. Only the receptionist's alert smile reminded her of her name tag. She turned to find one of the rollnecked young aides behind her.

'Miss Haddington, what a pleasure, so good you could come,' he purred. 'Now, I know we have not had the privilege yet of welcoming the Sunday Chronicle to our truly splendid, luxurious Costa Brava resort. Might I inquire whether you might accept our invitation soon?'

Tire was about to brush him aside, when she stopped herself. Never write off even the most unlikely lead until you are certain. Accepting his business card, she assured him that it might be possible to come with a photographer for the magazine section, perhaps for a weekend. Overriding his protestations that Cerigo had its own photographers with the excuse that the paper preferred to use its own, she said she would email him with potential dates she might squeeze into her busy schedule.

An outstretched hand met her as she turned to leave. An attractive man in his early thirties with warm brown eyes and chestnut hair flopping across his forehead blocked her exit.

'I had rather hoped to meet you last night at the Guildhall,' he said, with a smile that veered between arrogance and condescension. 'But you were tied up with Justin Burgoyne and then you disappeared. Just my luck. I was hoping to wangle an introduction.' He laughed and swept his hair back. 'What did you say to him? He looked as if the dog had eaten his dinner when he came back in.'

Not even her killer stare diverted him. He winked, leaned forward to read her lapel badge and wagged a finger. 'Miss Haddington. Now I know how to contact you. Perhaps we might meet for a drink sometime. My name's Sebastian Crumley.'

Erica's boyfriend. Damn. Still in heavy mourning clearly. And she'd blow her cover with Cerigo if she admitted who she was. As she hesitated, he looked over her shoulder, obviously being summoned. 'Must go and have a word with Paul Stone.'

'You're a friend?' she asked.

'I'm a lawyer. One of our clients is a major donor to his charity so we like to touch base once in a while,' he said smoothly and walked away.

What a small pond London was. Everyone knew everyone else, at least among the tosserati.

***

Outside the conference room she texted Herk, who was waiting by the time she emerged at the entrance with the car, standing to attention at the open door as she climbed in. Once onto the slip road she said: 'Can you work a camera?'

'What?'

'There's a faint possibility we might be off to the Costa Brava to do a travel feature on Cerigo. Just for a few days. You can be the photographer. Might tell us more sniffing around onsite.'

'You reckon it's worth it?' he asked slowly.

'Maybe. Maybe not. We can decide later,' she answered. 'Nothing too specific there, although Harman Stone's an oddity, not entirely under control and his father's too unctuous for my liking.'

'Well, if I knew what that meant I'd probably agree. The old man's driver sat in the car all the time like he was cowering. I spoke to a couple of the other lads. They said he was kept on a very tight rein by the boss, with instructions not to speak. So he never does. That feels odd to me. The son's driver was from a limo company. First time with him, so no joy there.'

Herk suggested dropping her on Shaftesbury Avenue to avoid the watchers seeing him again, although she saw no sign of anyone loitering when she walked along Broadwick Street.

CHAPTER 15

That evening in her office, sitting in two armchairs round the glass coffee table over a few beers and a bottle of red wine to wash down a Chinese takeaway, they went over what they knew about Erica's death.

Herk's view, firmly stated, was that stumbling blindly after wisps of mist was not a good strategy, especially since they were persons without the protection of any authority. Her response, which came out more sharply than intended, was she was sure he'd often been in exactly such circumstances in the past.

For the first time since they'd met he gave her a hard look that dispensed with any pretence of being a broken ex-soldier on his uppers. She grinned mischievously, mouthing sorry.

'What do you do if you can't do a full recce?' she asked.

He rolled his tongue round his mouth and said thoughtfully: 'Get your intelligence nailed down best you can.'

'So, stage one plan of action.' She leant forward. 'I'll try to find time tomorrow in Paris to dig up Jean Malhuret, the human rights lawyer. I'm seeing Wrighton day after tomorrow, then it's Erica's funeral in the afternoon and I might catch up with her legal buddies. And I'll get a forensic accountant mate to dissect Cerigo's finances. Erica did look, but Russell can unearth what no one else would find.'

'And if all that meets a brick wall, what then?' His level stare earned a grimace.

'Keep beating your head against it till something falls out.'

He chortled.

'No, really. I've been at this a long time. Trust your gut and don't give up.'

'If you say so. I'll be off job-hunting while you're away in France.' She tensed. 'Round car repair shops and pubs near where she was killed. Lot of shifty characters down there. I'll fit in just fine. There might be local gossip that never reached the police.'

After an argument, he agreed to take payment at his standard workman's hourly rate. Becoming a full-time employee clearly did not suit him and it took her a while to persuade him that she hired freelances all the time who were partners for specific projects, not servants.

He crossed his legs, propping one boot across his knee, and looked at her. 'There's one condition to this and it's not negotiable. No secrets.' He emphasised the no with a finger pointed at her. 'You have to be straight with me about everything. What are you not telling me?'

Her tentative 'it might be nothing at all' got an angry glare.

'OK, I was followed today, out running, by a motorcyclist. But he could just have fancied his chances. It might not mean anything... ' she tailed off.

'Like the cyclist who knocked you down the other day, you mean?' he retorted.

She said defensively: 'I got his registration number and someone's checking it out.'

'Which could well be cloned – false plates. Might not tell us much. Still, worth finding out.' He sighed. 'It's a bodyguard you need. I'll have to dig out my running shoes. Must say it sounds like quite a pro set-up. I'm going off the slasher up in Wakefield as a suspect. My money might be on the Soviet lot. You'll have to watch your step.' Seeing her lips purse, he asked: 'You don't agree?'

Without answering, she stood up, refilled their glasses and took hers to the window. The city lights outside cast a gaudy aura upwards, blocking out the stars in the cloudless sky. A yearning for the islands and open sea tugged at her.

'Maybe,' she said. 'I still think Wrighton's up there. And there's something odd about Stone senior that doesn't square with him being a paragon of virtue. He's got a black soul.'

'That's an astrological thought, is it?' he asked with a grin, which earned him a withering look.

'I haven't looked. Just a feeling.'

With business out of the way, the evening mellowed. Knowing he disliked talking of his army days, she asked him about his childhood.

His father had been a regimental sergeant major and his father before him in a fighting line that traced back through every major conflict to the Peninsula Wars in the early 19th century. The family collection of medals over two centuries was jealously guarded and religiously polished by his mother, who still lived alone in a council house in East Dunbartonshire.

His father was a hard-drinking, hard-living man mainly away, he said, and his mother held the family of three boys under iron control.

All the brothers had escaped at sixteen into the army. One had been injured in the first Gulf War, dying a few years later from cancer. The other had died of alcoholism.

'Only me, ma and the bloody medals left. I might just toss them when she's gone. Though gawd knows ah reckon she'll see us all out. Built of cast iron, that woman', he remarked, helping himself to another glass of wine.

After a longish silence as he stared into his glass, she felt obliged to proffer a few details of her own. Taking a deep breath she said: 'What can I tell you? I grew up…' she hesitated, 'as an orphan, really, from five.' This was proving more difficult than she expected, given that it was a well-rehearsed story.

'Was shuffled around in the north of Scotland and eventually sent to boarding school in England. Though I went back on holidays to a courtesy aunt up in the islands in the north-west.' She looked at him with a wry smile. 'She wasn't a bundle of laughs either, like your ma. Cold as hell.'

'No brothers or sisters, then?' he asked.

'Nope, just me. Not too many friends at school since they all thought I was odd. On holiday my aunt made it clear the local kids were out of bounds. Not our sort, she'd say sniffily. Christ, she was a snob. So I went climbing, fishing, bird-watching on my own and read a lot. I enjoyed the freedom. So wasn't all a sweat.'

She fiddled with her pendant, feeling she was about to get emotional.

'Tell me,' Herk leant forward, breaking the awkward silence, 'how did you get into the stars? Seems odd for someone like you. A neighbour of my ma's read tea leaves, but she had her hair in a duster and could barely read.'

'Different skill,' Tire laughed, grateful to be away from her childhood. 'A Hong Kong astrologer read my chart years ago and understood my life, the past I mean, better than I did. The accepted wisdom said it was rubbish. But since I've spent my life fighting against the know-it-alls who are more often wrong than right, I dug in and learned how it works.'

'Just to stick two fingers up at them, you mean?' He rubbed his chest and beamed. 'Works for me. It's not like clairvoyance, then?'

'No, it's mathematical, all number-crunching, so suited to computers. There's no explanation for it. But that doesn't stop it working.' She lit another cigarette. 'In its own slightly peculiar way, admittedly.'

'And you can do the stars of countries? Like Iraq?'

'Yes. You have to find a date, which isn't always easy for old countries. Israel's easy since they cut the ribbon for the opening in 1948. Though most have significant moments of unification or independence. If you've got a time as well as a day you can tell about economic fortunes, rebellions and the like. You can do charts for events as well, like the launching of ships, movies, the Iraq War.'

He blew out a long sigh and reached for the wine bottle. 'You mean you knew it would be a disaster before it started?'

Her eye drifted off to Jin's photograph of a bomb-wrecked building on the wall across from her.

'Well, I wouldn't have started a war then. It was mainly Air and Water signs, which is unstable. Wholesale destruction from above, hopelessly unrealistic when it hit the ground. Run by armchair generals 6,000 miles away to send a message – like Hiroshima and Dresden. Not a clue about a practical follow-through.'

'Sounds about right.' He shifted uneasily in his chair, swirling his wine round the glass. Looking up with a forced smile, obviously keen to change the subject, he said: 'You've never asked what my star sign is? Normally with girlfriends it's practically the first thing they want to know. Not that you're...' He looked slightly flustered.

She grinned broadly, 'Nope. Absolute rule. Never mix work and play. Always ends in a mess. Your Sun sign is only a part of what you're about and often it's not what I look at first. There's another 2,500 pieces of information in your chart.'

'And you make all your decisions based on that, do you?' he asked cautiously.

'No,' she said. 'None of them.'

'Well, what's the point of it then? If it's no practical help?' He looked puzzled.

'It helps me understand what makes people tick. Who they are, what drives them. It's useful for books except I never say where my brilliant insights come from.' She smiled mischievously.

'And you never have a look if you're going somewhere dangerous?' he prompted.

'Well, maybe,' she admitted, wondering why he was so interested and decided against telling him about the astrology of the next couple of weeks. 'It's just not helpful to be constantly checking every time you need to make a decision otherwise your life would grind to a halt.'

That seemed to satisfy him as he gulped down his wine and stood up, saying cheerfully: 'Well, onwards and upwards, then. You'll have to be up early tomorrow.' He added over his shoulder: 'Since you didn't ask, I'm Taurus.'

CHAPTER 16

The plane bucked and shuddered as it droned through heavy cloud, the windows running with moisture. Flying back from Paris after what felt like a wasted day and a half, Tire was wound up and irritated. There had been a fruitless search to track down Malhuret, the French lawyer who might know about Erica's Kubek case. No one in his office would say where he was, or when he'd be back from a trip abroad.

Otherwise she had smiled through gritted teeth at constant questions from a stream of booksellers about a book she had written two years back, much of which she had forgotten, about a whistleblower in the pharmaceutical industry. He had died, so could not tell his own tale. It had been written in a hurry from his notes to catch a story that was still in the headlines, then been held up for a year by lawyers arguing over what could be printed and what was libellous. To her surprise, it was now going into paperback. Against her inclinations, she had also landed herself with another commission for a popular book on fraud in science.

Something had been niggling at the back of her mind all day, which only emerged as she reached Orly airport. Paul Stone had mentioned owning a Côte d'Azur house. She scrolled through her contacts. Michel le Lorier was a Paris financier she'd had a brief fling with two years ago, a firecracker month of passion that had fizzled out as quickly as it started, as she had expected from the volatile aspects in their relationship chart. She had been avoiding him since, although he had been slower to get the message. His father, if she remembered correctly, and she usually did, was senior partner in a firm of notaries on the Côte d'Azur. A flicker of embarrassment was suppressed as she clicked his number.

'Michel, this is Tire. So sorry not to have replied to your texts. I've been away a good deal and locked in the attic writing apart from that.'

An amused 'ouf' indicated what he thought of that excuse. Her flight flipped to boarding on the display. She winced and plunged on.

'Wonder if you could do something for me?'

'Huh. Ignore me, then you need me. *Absolument, non*, if it involves my firm or their clients.'

'Your father,' she said, starting to walk towards the gate. 'He has been a notary in Cannes for a long time?'

'*Oui.*' His tone was defensive.

'I just wondered if he'd come across a Paul Stone who bought a Villefranche house years ago.'

There was silence at the other end as she was waved through into the departure lounge.

'*Mam'selle*, you are asking for professional confidences to be broken. Again.' Another pause. 'I have heard him mention the name. He didn't like him, not at all. I am phoning him tonight so I will ask. But, I warn you, this will cost you a dinner next time I'm in London.'

'Bless you,' she said, blowing him kisses. 'Anything you can dig up, most grateful.'

***

A minicab driver was waiting for her at the Heathrow entrance, her name misspelt on his card as Thang. Refusing his offer to carry her case, she followed him to the ticket machine, then through foot tunnels to the car park.

An amiable Afghani, dressed neatly with a black jacket over a blue shirt and jeans, he answered her questions cheerfully on the forty-minute journey back, although not, she thought, truthfully. He had not been home for ten years, was settled into a new life in Harrow with his family, liked the way of life and the people. Since she was a single woman, she knew the cab firm never sent her the bearded drivers, one of whom had once tried to convert Jin with religious zeal. Many of the drivers she suspected disappeared back home frequently, having earned enough money in a few months to keep them in funds, when they reverted to being Taliban. It had crossed her mind as a responsible citizen she should really alert the security services. But she consoled herself with the thought that they must already know.

The M4 sped past with light traffic, but she found herself running out of conversation as the Hammersmith flyover approached. Normally, she would relax as the familiar bustle and busyness of central London welcomed her home. But now she found herself tense and almost tearful as the road swooped over the underpasses down into Knightsbridge. She pulled her cashmere jacket across her chest and twisted her scarf round her fingers.

It was a crawl from there, past Harrods and Harvey Nichols, the imposing architecture at odds with windows grasping for attention with a clutter of pert fashion on gawky dummies. A splash of green to her left brought Hyde Park Corner into view with the Wellington Arch marooned on a triangle of grass, the bronze Angel of Peace at its summit calming the frenzied horses of war. Piccadilly moved at snail's pace towards the garish Circus, flooded with neon adverts for Sanyo, TDK, Cola and several hundred smaller pleas for shoppers' money. Up Shaftesbury Avenue, left into Great Windmill Street, past the theatre and then she was home with a sigh of relief.

When she let herself in, she noticed the front door had been repainted and smiled. Herk was in the kitchen making himself tea, all the surfaces clutter-free and gleaming. To cover an awkward pause, she looked into the ceramic sink, which was cleaner than it had been for a while. Grinning, she said: 'Bed tidy to regulation, with hospital corners then?'

'You want to inspect it, ma'am?'

She reviewed him with mock superiority. 'I don't suppose you served under too many woman commanders?'

'Nope, none at all and I don't intend to start now, so you can get off your high horse.'

She laughed. 'Suppose that means I have to make my own coffee. God, it's good to be back. And to a clean house. Amazing.'

In the office she sat with her feet propped up on the desk while he moved an armchair into the opposite corner, his feet on the coffee table. He told her he had probably found an SUV that might have been the vehicle involved, but it had been stripped down and reassembled. The number plates were false and there were no serial numbers. The lock-up garage was about to ship the reconstructed version onto the continent and sell it there with false papers.

'So, right-hand drive?' she asked.

'Aye, and a very pro job,' he said, not meeting her eye.

'How do you know it was that SUV?'

'Because one of the guys who worked there said the bumper still had some traces of blood and ...' He trailed off, waving an apologetic hand.

'Bastards,' she said. 'Did you find out who dropped it in?'

'Maybe. I was only there for a few hours while they tested me out. I spun them a line about doing prison time.' He tugged one foot across his knee. 'I got Sam, the chattiest mechanic, drunk last night and he said it had been taken it in before he arrived. The boss was a mean bugger, so I didn't bother asking him. Sam did see a tall guy getting into a BMW round the corner when he was coming in. So could have been him. But no description.'

'And no way of finding out more?'

'Not a snowball's. This lock-up works with the dodgy trade so they don't invite questions and they cover their tracks. Anyway, the sod fired me. Said he didn't like my face. So no going back there.'

Tire swung her legs onto the floor, rapped on the desk several times with her knuckles. Then, jumping up, she started striding up and down across the grey carpet, humming tunelessly, a low-register monotone. Her heeled boots pounded up and down. She knocked on the door lintel with her fingernails, then disappeared into the kitchen and after more banging and crashing emerged with two glasses and a bottle of wine.

'Would you sit down, for god's sake. You're making me dizzy. If we're to work together there'll need to be some rules.'

'Rules? It's how I think,' she said, glaring at him.

'What? With your feet and knuckles? I thought that was my province,' he said evenly. 'Park your butt down and we'll discuss tomorrow's schedule.'

What had she landed herself with? A control freak and a bully. She waved a hand across her forehead in what could have been a salute.

'Rupert Wrighton first thing. That'll be a soft-pedal interview. No sense in ruffling his feathers too soon.'

'Bob'll drive you.'

'Who?'

'Owner of the BMW. He's a mate, handy sort. Best if I'm not seen too often with you.'

She was beginning to feel kettled. How many more mates did he have?

'Then I'll speak to Russell about Cerigo's finances. Erica's funeral is in the afternoon.'

'They organised that pretty quick,' he said, blowing his cheeks out. 'Must have yanked a few strings. Normally hit and runs lie in the morgue for weeks.'

'Never underestimate the pulling power of the great and the good,' she said, pouring herself another glass and pushing the bottle nearer him. 'What are you going to be doing?'

'Oh, this and that in the morning. Might be able to drive you in the afternoon. Will see.'

Her brows furrowed as she wondered whether it was worth pointing out that communication was a two-way flow. A sneak glance at him caught a bland smile. He was up to something.

Before she could demand an answer, he said: 'I've something to say.' Pursing his lips he continued: 'Your flat was nearly broken into when you were away.'

'What?'

'Aye, but they didn't get in. I was out, but luckily I'd set up a trip wire which alerted Ali. The two guys must have heard him and disappeared out the fire exit. They were in hoodies so he didn't catch their faces. Maybe just scruffs taking a chance with the backdoor open when Ali was taking the rubbish out.'

'You think?' she asked slowly.

He shrugged and scuffed his boots together. 'To be honest, that's the third incident within a few days, which would make me suspicious. Well, four if you count your friend's death. I've put a steel plate in your front door and bolts through the frame. So it'll stop any but the most determined.'

The bottle was pushed back in her direction and he stood up. 'I'm off for a drink with the lads. Might see Momo again.'

At the door, he paused. 'Don't let anyone in. I'll be back before 11.'

CHAPTER 17

Two magpies hopped across the grass, looking around intently, unconcerned by the two elderly figures approaching up the path to the ornate Victorian glasshouse. Jimmy and Elly had walked to the far end of Byres Road. The supermarket was more expensive there, but Elly knew he wanted to go into the Botanic Gardens across the Great Western Road. He had been muted, almost sullen, since he returned from his hospital visit, refusing to say much beyond having met new doctors.

His head was filled with a thick fog, obscuring any clear thought. His breathing was shallow and his heart pounded uncomfortably, echoing up into his ears.

Once through the doors of the Kibble Palace, an ornate nineteenth century glasshouse, passing the giant tree fern and ornamental pond, they headed slowly, as always, for the house of desert plants. The dry, hot air made Elly cough, but Jimmy brightened as soon as he saw the spiky, grey-blue aloe at the far end, its tough, fleshy leaves jutting out at odd angles. The leathery stems towered at least three feet above his head. He stood, as he always did, in rapt silence, a faint smile lighting his face, as if worshipping at a shrine of the Madonna.

'I'm sorry, Elly,' he finally said over his shoulder, 'this is boring for you.'

'Not at all, I quite like those wee flowers they've got down the other end. I just don't like the prickles on those cactus things.'

He laughed: 'They can be difficult to get out if you get one in your finger. C'mon, just a quick look in the Tropical House and then we're off. Maybe the passion flowers will still be out.'

Elly marvelled at his knowledge of the plants although she supposed they had been in the glasshouse often enough for him to memorise the labels.

'No for long then, I can't stand all that sweat in there. Maybe I'll just wait at the entrance for you. Just don't get lost. I'll expect you in five minutes.'

Jimmy smiled, walking on through into the rainforest section with its dense luxuriant foliage climbing way up to the domed glass roof. Even he found the humid eighty-degree temperature hard to tolerate for long, but, hurrying down the slippery pathway, he found what he'd been looking for.

Passion flowers were his favourite, with their cross-shaped stamen centres. He really preferred the blue or purple ones, but here in the South American climate house they were a striking red. He always chuckled to himself when remembering a gardener had told him they were named by the Jesuits who first discovered them. The passion was of Jesus and his crucifixion, not of earthly lust. The priests saw great symbolism in their structure, with the stamens representing the nails and wounds of Christ on the cross; until they found other varieties that had a different flower centre, but by that time the name had stuck.

He stood gazing at the splashes of iridescent scarlet against the sombre green foliage, dotted at intervals as the stems clambered upwards over the neighbouring plants. His heart had settled to an even pace and his shoulders dropped. Luminous primary colours made him feel alive, gave him a moment's space, his head not rattled by anxious thoughts.

His mind could not hold steady for long. The red led to thoughts of the passion of Christ, which led to an image of a bloody crucifix with the tortured face of Jesus looking down. He turned away in revulsion to find a gardener standing behind him. For an agonised instant he thought it was the man who tormented his dreams. Those cold, dark eyes, tight, cruel lips and sharp cheekbones. He froze.

'You all right there?'

'Aye, sorry,' Jimmy replied. 'Fine. Just fine. My mind was somewhere else.' He let out a long breath and said: 'Is there somewhere I can sit down?'

Now he was in a state again and needed to settle before he went back to Elly, otherwise she'd fuss. He had tried talking to therapists and social workers about the bogeyman who had haunted him as long as he could remember. All had assured him the tall, dark-haired man in the smart suit did not exist. Nothing he could say would alter their kindly dismissal. Nothing they said could shift his conviction that he existed.

His present social worker, Len, had produced photographs of all the previous doctors in the Hall, but none looked like this man, although he did have a bad turn seeing Dr Brand, now dead, whose special patient he had been in the early days. That gave him several wretchedly sleepless nights when he had trouble breathing.

Len had found his birth certificate and tried to trace his family, but they were dead or disappeared. Cirrhosis had seen off his Irish father, a construction worker, thirty years ago and his mother had followed ten years after that from a stroke. Neither had visited him, ever, as far as he could recollect. There had been four other siblings, but they had all moved away.

He knew Elly worried when he became obsessed with the face in his head so he needed to clear him back into a box, as one therapist had suggested, with the lid padlocked shut, before he rejoined her.

There was only one occasion he had disappeared, just after they had been let out of Dunlothian, when Elly had been in hospital having a hysterectomy. He had seen a newspaper picture that resembled the face in his head at a London society function in a Park Lane hotel. So on impulse he had borrowed money from another resident, plus an old army greatcoat, taken the bus to London and slept rough across the road from the expensive hotel where the photograph had been taken.

By the sixth night he was running out of money, was chilled and frightened. That's when he saw the man again, dressed in a dinner suit and black tie. He had stared from across the road, unsure whether he did recognise him. Even in his muddled state, he knew that fifty years was a long time so the face etched in his mind wouldn't be the same.

If the photographers had not been there causing the man and his elegant lady friend to pause at the entrance for several minutes he would have stood where he was in indecision. But it was almost as if a hand behind was pushing so he crossed the road walked up to the man, looked up at him from the bottom step and said loudly: 'You're tessoro'. He had no idea where the word came from or what it meant.

The silver-haired man with the dark eyes had looked at him for what seemed to Jimmy an eternity of frozen time. Then he had summoned a policeman standing nearby, who had removed Jimmy into a police van and off to the cells for the night. He had been pleased enough of a dry bed and some food, although his mind was in such a turmoil he barely knew what he thought. He wasn't sure of anything.

Next morning the police, having found his return ticket and identity, phoned his social worker, drove him to Victoria bus station after a hearty breakfast and saw him back on his journey up north, with a kindly warning not to return.

'You're looking awfy pale,' Elly said anxiously, when he rejoined her at the entrance.

'I'm OK, just jangled at the thought of having to go back over those years in the Hall.' His shoulders dropped so she gave his arm a squeeze.

'There were some good times as well. The friends we both made.'

'It's that woman, Dr Birch. She makes me nervous. Why is she so interested in me?'

The attendant at the door nodded to Elly and looked questioningly at Jimmy, who hadn't offered his normal greeting. She shrugged an apology. Outside they bent into the wind, aiming downhill for Byres Road. Elly glanced at his crumpled face.

'Maybe, it doesn't matter why she's so keen. What's important is you get settled about that man in your head. If she can help, then she's worth putting up with.'

They stood at the traffic lights and he leant against her. 'You're right. And about the good times as well. I was just thinking about Lachie this morning. He was a good mate.' The green walker lit up and they moved across Great Western Road. 'But I don't want to talk about him to her.' He sniffed, his eyes reddening. 'I did think I might paint his grave. It's a beautiful setting there above Greenock.'

'Which you organised for him. You were the best friend he could have had, even if he didn't get to enjoy his freedom.'

'I still can't believe it. All that time in the Hall and he gets killed when he's just out. It was a crying sin.'

CHAPTER 18

Next morning at 7 am, Tire was awakened by the front door closing softly. Expecting Herk to be gone she wandered through to the kitchen, pulling her robe over her nightdress.

'What the hell?' she exclaimed, as she came face to face with a bright yellow workman's jacket above orange waterproof trousers. A white hardhat sat on the counter.

'I'm just going about my lawful business, that's what,' he remarked cheerfully.

'Digging up roads?'

'Nah. Checking out these watchers outside. Nobody ever notices workmen. Better than a burka for disguise. Workmen are always standing around, so won't raise any suspicion.'

'Soooo…' she said, stifling a yawn as she made herself a coffee, 'you're going to watch the watchers. What then?'

'Well, follow them back where they came from, of course,' he said.

'In that rig-out?'

'Never you mind, I have my methods.'

'Which are?' she demanded.

'None of your business,' he replied smartly. 'Though on second thoughts, maybe you do need to know. I have a helper and he'll need paid.'

'Who?'

'You don't need to know that.'

'Herk, it's too early in the morning for pussyfooting around,' she snapped.

He smiled, making her more irritated, and said, draining his tea: 'Your life would not be enriched knowing his name. He's a mate with a white van. That's all. If you could sub me maybe a hundred quid I'll let you know how much he cost and give you the change tonight.'

'Don't do anything stupid,' she said, handing him five twenty-pound notes from her handbag, suddenly anxious.

'Do I look dumb?' the door slammed behind him with a solid clunk.

What would Rupert Wrighton expect a sympathetic interviewer to be wearing? Standing in front of her wardrobe, she ruffled through possibilities. Nothing too masculine, otherwise he'd think she was a subversive lesbian. Frilly and feminine were in short supply, but she might make do with a long scarf tied in a bow. She shuddered.

What would 'just call me Felicity' wear? Short, tight skirt, stilettos and a figure-hugging blouse probably. No, if he really was into underage, he'd appreciate a hint of schoolgirl mischief. She didn't possess a short, pleated skirt. What she did have were loose, blue, pleated trousers that were a tragic mistake and had been hanging unworn in the spare room wardrobe since. They would do with a white shirt, tie, blazer-type jacket and flat shoes. The image that stared back at her from the mirror made her glad Herk was out.

Downstairs, Bob was waiting inside the BMW. He was roly-poly with a cheerful, ruddy face and thinning black hair, combed in a slick over his scalp. She averted her eyes from a workman leaning against a road drill at the corner with three road cones at his feet. Classic FM on the radio was turned up, indicating that conversation would not be invited, so she checked messages on her phone. Michel's from Paris said simply: 'Call me lunchtime.' Jin had sent a picture of himself smiling, with a sand dune behind him and three Xs underneath. Long-distance love affairs with adventurers had their pluses and minuses. Instead of suffocating boredom, there was anxiety about whether he'd come back in one piece.

***

Lost in her thoughts, she came to as the car slowed in front of the cream-stuccoed columns of Eaton Square.

Drat, she really should have been concentrating on her strategy for the interview. He'd have a high-wire temperament, from what she remembered of his chart, hair-trigger impatience, spraying off in all directions at once like a sackful of fighting ferrets. She sighed. Sweet smiles would have to do until she sensed which way the wind was blowing.

The front door was opened by a short, motherly woman in a mauve cardigan and floral skirt, who gave her a welcoming beam and said in a squeaky voice: 'I'm Felicity. How nice to meet you.' Got that one wrong.

She was ushered across a white marble floor flanked by white walls, thrown into relief by yards of black ornamental ironwork on doorways and up the imposing staircase. It looked dusted and polished to within an inch of its existence, camera-ready and unlived in.

Inside the vast sitting, no, most certainly drawing room, framed on both sides by three floor-length windows looking out onto greenery, there was a hushed calm. The beige, taupe and slate grey furniture was designer-placed in neat groups on a cream carpet with polished parquet surrounds.

Standing in front of an impressive stone fireplace and a glinting pewter fire basket was a vision in pale blue. Slighter than she expected – he was only five foot nine at most – in freshly ironed jeans and a cashmere V-neck over a striped shirt, with casual, tasselled moccasins on his feet. Friendly, man next door, common touch. I'm not the only one who dressed to fit a role.

What spoiled the illusion were his eyes, shifting constantly, not meeting hers when he offered a perfunctory hand. She was waved to a seat on a long, uncomfortable couch and he ordered Felicity to bring tea. At the opposite end was a full-length oil painting of a young girl, dressed in red, in an embossed gilt frame.

'Your daughter?' she said, with what she hoped was an interested look, tucking the pleats behind her legs.

'No. It's an Annigoni.' His tone dripped condescension. 'My mother.'

'Of course. Silly me.' As big a prat as everyone said, although not quite the bruiser she had expected.

In answer to his questions, she explained her credentials from *Der Spiegel* again, praying he hadn't checked since there had been no confirmation from her contact there. Then she launched into a half-thought-out spiel about wanting to write a balanced piece that gave accused fathers fighting for custody a chance to have their say.

'Balanced?' he said sharply. 'You'll be talking to the other side?'

The smile she gave him stretched her cheekbones back to her ears. 'Oh no,' she purred. 'They've had a great deal of coverage. This will be just for you. Your campaign, I mean.'

The door opened and Felicity entered, carrying a tray with a silver teapot, milk jug, sugar bowl and fine porcelain teacups sitting on a linen cloth. He extended his head forward. 'There's no lemon, Felicity. Our guest might like some.' She flinched and milk slopped out as she laid the tray down.

'No, I don't take lemon.' Tire jumped up and moved to block his view of the tray, winking at Felicity with the eye he couldn't see. 'Why don't I pour?'

The older woman hesitated, whispering that he liked a dash of milk and one sugar stirred in, then sidled off towards the door.

When she carried his cup across to him, he gestured to the occasional table beside the fireplace and started talking at high speed. The iniquities of a court system biased towards mothers, willing to believe any lies that money-grubbing wives wanted to tell. The pain suffered by fathers cut off from their children.

'*Their* children,' he emphasised with an outraged expression.

She might have been persuaded that in some instances what he said held a kernel of truth, were it not for the fact that he clearly regarded children as a possession. He could probably work up the same level of hostility if a business rival tried to poach on his territory. She let him rave on, writing occasional notes on her pad, with the recorder sitting on the table in front of her.

When he finally drew breath, she said: 'What is your view of the lawyers who become involved in these abuse allegation cases?'

His cup, halfway to his mouth, froze and tilted as his hand shook. 'What do you mean?' His eyes could have lasered holes across the carpet.

She looked down and rearranged the pleats on her knee before replying with as much faux sympathy as she could dredge up.

'They facilitate these allegations. How do you feel about them?'

'I'd string them up. Bury them in a landfill. They spread lies and cause immense damage.' He spat the words out and then turned away from her to face the fireplace, putting both hands on the lintel, his knuckles clenched white.

Suppressing an instinct to get up and kick him, she remembered something an old therapist had once said about how to get people to talk. Through gritted teeth, she echoed his sentiments. 'Those who do damage should certainly be brought to justice. What you say is so true. They should be named and shamed.'

When he didn't answer, she prodded: 'Do you have any plans to expose lawyers who support these wicked allegations and stop them destroying lives?'

'Oh, yes.' He swivelled, not to face her, but to look out of the window, with an unpleasant smirk on his face. 'We have plans. But none you are going to print. Don't want to give them forewarning.' That was an order, she thought with grim satisfaction. Getting him rattled. But don't push too hard.

'Tell me about your father.'

'Why? What's he to do with this.'

'You're supporting fathers. I thought you must hold him in high esteem.'

A quiet knock on the door diverted his attention. It opened to reveal a thin, pale-faced girl of around twenty with long blonde hair, clutching a violin case. She stood in the doorway, nodding a polite smile at Tire and a tentative glance at him.

'I'm back, Papa.'

'Well, give me a kiss, Miranda, and sit down till I'm finished with this interview. Where were we?'

She dropped her eyes and walked across to put her violin carefully on a chair and walked back towards him with her head hung down. Then she stood dutifully as he pecked her on both cheeks and retreated to perch on the furthest end of the couch, putting Tire between herself and her father.

His stance at the fireplace became more exaggerated, his chest puffing out.

'My father. Never really knew him. My mother brought me up. But since you ask, quite a hard man, very successful. Did what he had to in a tight corner.' And apples never fall far from the tree.

The presence of his daughter was freezing Tire's brain as she sensed the nervous tension beside her. What a nightmare situation to be trapped in. Having found the courage to accuse her father, she was back here trapped in Bluebeard's cave, being brainwashed into saying it had all been Erica's doing.

'You look just like your grandmother,' she said, half-turning towards Miranda, who blushed and shook her head.

'Hardly.' The sardonic tone made the girl jump. 'She's much more like her mother.' Tears filled Miranda's eyes and rolled down her cheeks and she jumped to her feet, running towards the door, pausing only to grab her violin case.

'I'm sorry, did I say something wrong?' Tire said as evenly as she could, wanting to plunge a dagger into his chest.

'No.' He shook his head irritably. 'She's still not got over her mother dying and that was eighteen months ago.'

'Poor soul. Miranda must have felt abandoned.' She was pushing the limits of her tolerance for this asshole. Her fingernails ground into her palm.

'Don't know about that. Her mother spent most of her time malingering in bed. And then took the easy... ' He stopped and frowned at himself. Tire jotted down 'check mother's death', flipped over to a clean page and looked up, smiling expectantly.

He checked his watch. 'Perhaps you'd let me see the first draft of what you're writing, so I can check it. Just for factual inaccuracies, I mean. Never good to be tripped up.' No indeed. 'Then if you need more time with me I'm sure it can be arranged.'

A sheaf of brochures and photocopied articles was waved at her. Dismissed. There was no handshake. By the time she had reached the door she no longer existed in his universe.

In the hall, Felicity was fussing in the alcove below the curving stairs over a giant vase of flowers the size of a small Christmas tree. She stepped forward to open the front door with a well-prepared smile. Tire put a hand on her arm and whispered: 'Look after Miranda. She needs it.' The look of consternation, hopelessness and fear that evoked stayed with her all the way back home.

CHAPTER 19

Her front door was ajar when she returned, giving her a flutter of apprehension. Ali hadn't been at his desk when she let herself in downstairs and gusts of damp chill were blowing in from the rear entrance, which was open. Footsteps inside from the left made her curse; she had left her illegal but useful pepper spray in her bedroom.

'You gonna stand there all day, then?'

Thank god. Herk. She summoned up a laid-back smile.

'How did you know it was me?'

'How do you think? Bob phoned me. Coffee?'

In the kitchen they compared notes about their morning's work. Herk had lost the watcher, who had left his post just after Tire. He had been picked up by a red Citroen minivan, which they tailed onto the M4 spur but were stymied by traffic lights and lost him heading up Holland Park Avenue towards Ladbroke Grove.

'I've got someone checking out the number plate. Hope that tells us something.' He didn't look hopeful. 'How was Wrighton?'

She scratched her head, tugged her hair, lit another cigarette and said with a long sigh: 'Depressing. A five-star, tin-plated shit. Guarantee he abused his daughter. She looks totally beaten. He's a bully with a mother complex. Wife dead. From what he said that sounded like suicide though it isn't written up that way in his biog.'

A nervous twitch like an electrical discharge spun along the wires from the memory of the girl on the couch. She turned to him with an anguished look. 'That poor kid, you should have seen her.'

'We're not social services. Keep your focus.'

'Not much given to sentiment, are you?'

He sighed. 'You can't solve all the problems of the universe at once. One at a time.'

'OK, you're right.' She dragged her attention away from Miranda. 'He does loathe lawyers.'

'Enough to kill one?' His bald question rattled her head and she banged her foot down, scraping a heel along the tiles. 'And put the heavy mob out to menace the lawyer's friend?'

'He might have bumped off his wife and made it look like suicide.'

'You're clutching at straws. And we're not investigating the wife's death. Only Erica's. For which we have no hard evidence of any variety. I'll just have to keep tracking these watchers. They're the best lead we have.'

Failure was never an option in Tire's book. The way to tackle no results was to redouble effort. But where Wrighton was concerned she had no sense of what else she could do. Keep concentrating. Even if the answers didn't come, new questions might. And Herk was right. Getting dragged into Miranda's dire situation, however tempting, would be a mistake and a distraction. Which didn't stop her wanting to throw Wrighton into a slurry pit.

Her head shot up. 'Landfill. He mentioned disposing of bodies there. Well... ' she wriggled her fingers, 'maybe that's stretching a point. But I wonder if his father's old scrap business was sold and moved into wholesale rubbish disposal.'

'Which would tell us what, precisely?'

She strode into the office, sat down, fired off an email to Russell asking about Wrighton Senior's old business and then remembered Michel. She glanced at the time: 11.15 am. So 12.15 am in Paris. Too early for him to be at lunch? No, he'd probably been in since six that morning.

His precise, clipped tone with a murmur of voices in the background when he answered the call indicated he was in professional gear for the day.

'*Le Lorier. Un moment, s'il vous plaît, mam'selle.*'

Half a minute later he'd obviously walked into a quieter room.

'*Cherie*, I have to be quick, we are about to close a deal. I spoke with my father last night. He remembered Paul Stone well and thoroughly disliked him. Imperious and arrogant, he said, and something he did not trust. There was a problem over a son from his first marriage.'

'Yes?' she said, her interest sparked.

'You know, French succession laws are very particular about children. They cannot be cut out of inheritances. And it is the *notaire*'s responsibility to check that they are all itemised in the paperwork. Stone was very evasive about the boy, kept saying he wasn't important, just a stepson. But if the boy had been adopted by Stone in Italy, then he would have the same rights. He became quite nasty about it and threatened to take his business elsewhere, so my father caved in. And has had a conscience ever since.'

'Italy?'

A voice in the distance summoned Michel. '*Ma belle*, I must go. My father is sending me the sale documents that will have the name of Monsieur Stone's first wife and his second listed. I will email you them. It's not really appropriate, but he would be grateful if you find out anything about the son. He has worried about him all these years. *Bisous*.' The call ended.

***

Keeping an open mind was like living inside a kaleidoscope with fragments flying around, none of them sticking long enough to form a solid mass. The favourite had to be whoever was after the Kubek activist, although Harman Stone and Wrighton were a close-run second. Maybe she should go up to Wakefield Prison to interview Dugston, just to be sure she wasn't overlooking the obvious.

Her usual modus operandi wasn't any help in this situation: an archaeological dig through archives and paperwork and finding bystanders happy to lift the lid on misdeeds. But a murder? No one would keep records or confess. Anyone in the vicinity would be too scared to open up. Felicity? She had enough on her plate looking after Miranda, and Wrighton would have contracted the job out anyway. She sighed. Herk was right. The watchers were the best bet and that was his department. Being superfluous to requirements did not feel good.

The slow, pulsing strings and lamenting soprano of Gorecki's 'Symphony of Sorrowful Songs' echoed through the apartment, doing little to calm her impatience. The morning's outfit had been tossed in favour of slim-cut black trousers and jacket, with a wide-collared, white shirt underneath. A long, emerald green scarf hanging loose gave her a Parisian look, although she was feeling anything but coolly chic.

At Herk's suggestion she left by the back door and met him two streets away for the drive to the north London crematorium. Throughout the thirty-minute drive he said nothing, but constantly checked the mirror to monitor vehicles behind. Through the archway into the parking area, she could see there was a large turnout.

'Text me when you're ready to leave,' he said, as he held the door open for her.

There was a smartly dressed turnout of legal and City types, who were chatting avidly and viewing with disdain the few of Erica's poorer ex-clients who had turned up to pay their respects. Several men eyed Tire appreciatively, which earned them a steely glare before she turned away.

Her hackles were up before she moved into the crematorium, sitting deliberately far back, away from the thrusters in their Gieves & Hawkes suits and the icily severe women in their Louboutin spiky heels. Like a bloody school uniform, she thought. Clones who don't have the guts to be themselves, if they even know who that is.

The eulogies were standard fare, with the usual overworked poems badly delivered and limp personal stories about contact with Erica. The only reading that stuck in Tire's head was given by Erica's boyfriend, Sebastian Crumley. There was no hint of nervousness from him as he read without notes in perfectly enunciated tones, with the occasional flick of a hand to brush back his hair. 'Abiit nemine salutato,' he intoned as he finished. Then he paused and, with a nod to the less-educated among the congregation, added: 'She went away without bidding farewell.' A mannered performance from a consummate Leo.

You'd have made Erica very unhappy, she thought morosely. Why didn't she have any sense about men? A first-class mind, super-competent, would probably have made judge and yet zero instinct about the opposite sex.

It took her half an hour after the service ended to drag him away from the jostle of sympathetic pats, some awkward back-slapping and a few faux-teary kisses from the ladies whose mascara, Tire noted, slid not a centimetre. Cards were exchanged surreptitiously as professionals caught up with each other's career moves.

She finally lost her cool with the glad-handing and grabbed him by the elbow, steering him across to the crematorium garden, oddly exotic with traditional Greek and Japanese gravestones. His eyes lit up when he saw her and he put up no resistance to being manhandled.

'Miss Haddington, what a pleasure.' His brown eyes widened and he clasped one of her hands in both of his.

'I'm Tire Thane, a close friend of Erica's,' she said flatly.

He stepped back, the smile intact but less friendly. 'An imposter, huh?'

'The name tag at the press conference was for the travel editor.'

Before she could continue, he clapped a hand dramatically to his forehead.

'You're the astrologer, aren't you? Erica told me about you,' he smirked and stood back to run his eye over her. 'Rather classier than I expected.'

'Not so classy I can't slap you if you don't stop flirting with me at your girlfriend's funeral,' Tire snapped back. 'I'm a journalist and writer anyway. Astrology is just a hobby.'

Her silk scarf half slid off as she tugged one end and for a moment she wondered what it would feel like to strangle him.

'What I want to know is why was Erica in Hammersmith that night down by the river?'

Was that a flicker of alarm or shame in his eyes? He raised an eyebrow and put on a practised look of puzzlement. 'Why do you think I would know?'

'You were in the same chambers and close friends. That's why,' Tire said.

Ten more minutes of banter, as he parried every question about Jack Greengate's trial with a polite deflection, produced no more information.

Finally, he said: 'You're right. I'm sorry. I was fond of her. But funerals, y'know, require a degree of detachment.'

'Acting, you mean?' she replied.

'I can't help you. Really, I can't. I was gutted, we all were. But it's in the police's hands now and they think it was just an accident. The chambers are in constant touch with them.' He looked away from her over the Japanese shrine, staring at the yew tree beyond.

With a slight break in his voice, he said: 'Try Simon Dunstan, he's taken over Greengate's defence. In the rumpled black suit, by the entrance. As to the other threats? Frankly, your guess is as good as mine. She never discussed them with me.'

As she turned to leave, he put a hand on her arm. 'You have a card? If I think of anything I could let you know. Perhaps we might meet for a drink?' He moved closer to give her a cologne-doused kiss on the cheek. Slapping him was one option. Spitting in his eye another. Never slam the door on a lead won; she handed him her card.

CHAPTER 20

By the time she reached the Tudor-slatted opening that led out of the crematorium, Dunstan was just stepping into a taxi on his own. So she followed him in.

A harassed-looking thirty-year-old with a receding hairline and slight paunch, he was not an inspiring figure. Clearly nervous around women, he edged closer to the end of the seat, holding the door handle tightly.

'Terribly sorry, I'm not going to the City. Greenwich, well, Woolwich, Belmarsh in fact. One client to see and then back to the office in a rush. God, it's all too much at the moment. Can I drop you somewhere?'

'No, Belmarsh Prison will suit me fine,' Tire said, trying to suppress her eagerness. Taking a deep breath fuelled by prayers, she said: 'Are you going to see Jack Greengate?' As he nodded, she added: 'Sorry, I'm Tiresa Thane, a close friend of Erica's. A professional friend and colleague.'

'Oh god, so awful, so sorry,' he stumbled out with a stutter.

Great barrister he'll be, thought Tire but usefully pliable. She stretched out the leg nearest him to touch the facing seat of the cab, moving one hand across the seat. This so unsettled him that when she announced she had a personal message from Erica to give to Jack Greengate in prison he barely argued.

'Well, I suppose he's pleading guilty, so not much more to be done. Not sure it's very appropriate mind you, taking you in. But seeing as you're a colleague... What chambers do you say you were with?'

Ignoring his question, she murmured: 'An act of mercy, really. Erica was quite fond of him and it will help him settle to what's ahead.'

'Yeah, ten years minimum and not in a comfortable prison either. Not what he's used to. But what can y'do? Hit your wife over the head, you have to expect to pay the penalty.'

'Erica didn't discuss the case with you?'

'No, I was just dragged in after – y'know – and he'd changed his plea to guilty. They don't normally let me lead on defence.'

Tire managed to sound surprised at this, thinking he'd come in handy later if she ever had to revisit Greengate or get access to the papers.

'What chambers did you say you were with again?'

She avoided the question again by raising her phone to her ear and then texting a message to Herk saying to pick her up at Belmarsh.

The rest of the journey from Hendon to Thamesmead was taken up with constant calls on his mobile, at which he looked increasingly harassed.

'I can't stay long here, y'know. Too much on. They're piling the work on me at the moment. Others taking on Erica's cases and leaving me with what they don't want.'

She leant across and patted him sympathetically on the arm, which evoked such a sharp intake of breath she decided not to repeat it.

Within twenty minutes they had reached the Blackwall Tunnel. Slowed by heavy traffic, Tire started to tense. She had been in several prisons in her adult life, visiting subjects for her books, but they always depressed her. A living grave was how one long-term inmate once described them and she knew exactly what he had meant. Even the modern versions with their tidy brick exteriors were soulless, designed to depersonalise all who entered. The architecture had changed from the old Victorian criminal warehouse she had once visited as a child, but not the spirit.

***

The formalities at Belmarsh Prison were cursory, with bored, indifferent staff at the reception, who, having looked at Dunstan's credentials, waved them through. Tire walked behind him in what she hoped was a suitably submissive way, through endless locked doors into a large interview room with barred windows and an overweight warder by the door.

Greengate was already sitting behind a table, his eyes fixed on the scratched surface, hardly lifting his head to nod at them. They had just sat down when Dunstan excused himself to answer another phone call on his mobile. Tire sat quietly looking at the crumpled figure across from her. Now in his late fifties, he looked ten years older with sagging jowls and wrinkles of dark flesh below his red-rimmed eyes. His scalp underneath his wispy grey hair was flaking and he put his hand up every so often to scratch and then thought better of it.

Looking at her, he said apologetically: 'Psoriasis. I keep asking for some ointment. But it hasn't come yet. There's only one thing ever works for me.'

'Had it long?' Tire asked.

He sighed. 'All my adult life. My wife... ' His eyes filled with tears and he had to breathe in before he continued: 'She said it was too much worry that brought it on.' He grimaced, his eyes downcast.

Tire heard over her shoulder Dunstan saying agitatedly he'd be at his next appointment in half an hour. He was so pressured he did not raise any objection when Tire said she'd stay.

Having got Greengate to herself, she explained she was a friend of Erica's and asked why he had changed his plea. A look of flustered alarm came over his face, the reddening on his cheeks and forehead becoming almost puce, shining with sweat.

He said finally, in a hoarse voice: 'I'm pleading guilty and that's that. That's the end of it.' His knuckles were white as he held the edge of the table.

'We both know that isn't true,' Tire said, tapping a finger on the table. 'Why was Erica in Hammersmith that night?'

'I've no idea, really I haven't. I don't know what you want from me. There's absolutely nothing I can do for you.' His tone was becoming desperate.

'What I want is justice for Erica and, if her accident was connected to your case, I want to know.'

'Guard,' he shouted with surprising vigour. Then he looked at Tire with fear in his eyes. 'Just leave it. Understand me. There's nothing more to be said.'

After he left, she paced up and down the barren room for a minute or two, cursing herself for mishandling the interview, before turning for the door.

'Miss, your papers. You forgot them.' The warder standing guard pointed to a chair at the head of the table. She walked back and picked up a thick folder, flicking it open to see Erica's handwriting on the first page.

'Many thanks. It's the case notes. Mr Dunstan must have left it there. I'll take it for him.' She smiled warmly.

'Seems a bit scatty, that one,' the warder remarked with a wink. 'Not like that poor Miss Smythson. Crying shame, that was. She was doing her best for him.' He stood back, holding the door open for her, although showing no signs of wanting to end the conversation. 'And she was much nicer than that first lawyer he had. Unpleasant sort and he really upset Greengate. He was sweating and shaking after that meeting the first day he was here.' A podgy hand went up to scratch his ear. 'Suppose that's why he changed.'

***

Don't drive and talk appeared to be Herk's rule, so she slumped in the backseat running over what if anything she had learned and what came next. This was still the string-pulling stage when hope and instinct were all that kept forward momentum afloat.

Greengate was clearly scared and willing to take the fall of a long prison sentence, which meant the alternative was worse. He'd be killed? More likely someone close to him had been threatened. Who? She patted the file on the seat beside her.

Crumley wasn't saying everything he knew about the night Erica had been killed, she was sure of it. That flicker in his eye had been guilt about something. So drinks or perhaps a dinner – more time to get him to loosen up – would be in order. Wrighton fogged her thinking, since all she could see was his wretched child, shaking at the end of the couch. But there was no obvious next step with him. Even if his father's scrap business had been sold on, what would it tell her?

'What are you doing about the stalkers?' she said, as they passed through Tower Hill.

'Motorcycle followed you to Belmarsh. I lost him on the way back.'

'Another blue Suzuki? Pity you couldn't have squashed him against the tunnel,' she said, flicking the door panel with a fingernail. 'Get his number?'

'Yes, but that won't tell us much. He'll just be scum for hire and until we know what's behind all this there'll be no sense in picking him or them up. We just have to look dumb for now and be careful.'

'Sod it,' she said with feeling and picked up Erica's case notes on Greengate.

She skimmed through the fifty pages of official documents and handwritten notes. Greengate said he remembered nothing after taking the train home that night, only coming to when the police found him slumped, drunk in an armchair with an empty bottle of vodka at his side in his house, his wife lying dead in the back garden, her skull smashed in by one blow. He said he drank infrequently, mainly sherry and wine, never spirits.

He had described his marriage as old-fashioned and ordinarily happy against which Erica had jotted 'faithful and boring'. He denied the affair with the Brazilian secretary, whom he said had been over-friendly towards him since she arrived, which he had found embarrassing. The emails on his office desktop to her made no sense, he said, and had not been sent by him.

When Erica had quizzed him about problems with the company accounts he had said they were in good order and had been signed off by one of the big four accountancy firms in the City. But there were several question marks in the notes so she had clearly felt the need to check. His son, an Oxford student, had not visited him in prison, she had also written in the margin.

Maybe he had flipped in a moment of crazed rebellion against years, probably decades, of a dull marriage, Tire wondered. His only child had left home, so he was facing a grey future stretching ahead. A late, explosive mid-life crisis. But his astrology chart had indicated nothing about a hidden urge to be free. He had a battened-down life, which suited his methodical temperament.

His memory blank could be traumatic or could be a spiked drink on the train. The blood tests only showed his alcohol level, but they had probably not checked for other substances. She scribbled 'Momo pathology' on a Post-it note. The blood sample would have been held for the trial, although getting them to run further tests in the face of a guilty plea would not be easy.

'I'll drop you at the front door. No sense in acting out of the ordinary. You in tonight?'

Was that a question? Too drained to argue, she said: 'Yeah. There's lasagne in the freezer and a box set of Better Call Saul. I feel like a laugh and other peoples' problems I don't have to fix will be relaxing.'

CHAPTER 21

Running away was beginning to feel tempting. Away from the grey confines of London, the tunnel vision of city life, the relentless grumble of traffic noise. Away from Herk? Probably. She wasn't used to having a constant presence round the flat. Away from her guilt about having to solve Erica's death or save Miranda. Repeat after me, 'I am not God. I don't have to fix everything.'

Escape. Sitting on a cliff top staring out to sea with only fulmars, terns and a bracing wind for company. She felt the tension in her body melt away.

'Coffee.' Herk's voice outside her door jarred her head. 'You've got emails.' Dammit, he was taking over her life. She levitated out of bed, splashed her face with cold water, threw on jeans and a jumper and was into the office at speed.

His back was to her. 'It's OK, I didn't read anything. Just noticed it when I came to check the window catch.' A likely story.

Among the twenty messages in her inbox, half of them spam, was yet another from a solicitor who had been pestering her recently, she'd no idea about what. It could wait. She homed in on Le Lorier. M with *compte de vente* in the subject line. She clicked open the attachment, which was the first page of a French sale document for a villa in Villefranche bought in 1966 by Paul Eric Stone. It listed his past address, date of birth, present and previous marriages.

Her eyes widened. Obsessive bureaucracy and the Napoleonic succession laws had their uses. Born 16 July 1939 in Cairo, current address in Beirut, 1962 married Alessia Neroni, widowed 1965, 1966 married Souri Javadi, born Lebanon. Harman, she knew, had been born in 1967, so presumably after the purchase.

She emailed Matt to see if he could start initial net searches for Alessia Neroni's son and added as an afterthought to check her cause of death and any info on Souri Javadi.

'Useful, then?'

'Maybe,' she said cautiously, 'if I'm writing Paul Stone's unauthorised biography. Not necessarily connected to Erica.'

'So it's classified, until you decide what's relevant and what's not?' His sarcastic tone made her grin and she turned to offer him a cigarette.

'Sorry, I'm not used to discussing as I go, well, not outside my head anyway. You read French?' To her surprise he nodded, so she printed off the document and handed it to him.

The inbox also listed a response from Jean Malhuret's email address. There was no message, only a shortened URL. It clicked through to a French news website where a three-week-old story related briefly that Max Karimov, a Kubek lawyer, had been found dead in Marseilles. It was not thought to be a suspicious death since he had been in poor health with advanced cancer.

She clicked print, gestured to Herk and slumped back in her seat. Was Karimov's death natural? Unprovable at this distance and late stage. Would his death suggest it was less likely her stalkers were connected to his situation? They might still be worried that Erica held incriminating papers that she might have access to? Too many mights, maybes and uncertainties were stirring a headache into gear. The only way to draw them, whoever they were, into the open would be to stay a visible target, which was not an enticing prospect.

'Hm. If you were asking my opinion, which I notice you were not, strikes me the Kubek connection is a dead end. With him being deceased. That would be all they wanted and natural causes so much the better.'

'They?'

'State security.'

'You're familiar with such?' She turned towards him and swung her feet on the desk.

His eyes narrowed and he stared steadily at her.

'Well,' she said, 'that's makes two of us not so great at sharing.'

For a moment she thought he was about to march out, but he walked up the office to collect an oak dining room chair from the far end, carried it back and after nudging the flimsy one aside, dropped it and sat down.

'That's better. Now, what's today's game plan? Are you going out? That seems to get the surveillance on the move, which means I can follow them.'

'Like a moving target?' she said, scratching her cheek. 'Lovely.'

'Bob can drive you. Charlie has borrowed a couple of bikes, so we can be hanging around behind, with helmets and gear on, so unrecognisable. I want to find out where they come from.'

'Give me a moment.' She held up one hand as her mobile rang, scrabbling on the desk with the other and unearthed a business card. Sebastian Crumley. She winked at Herk.

'Mr Crumley, I'm in a meeting, I'm afraid.'

He prattled on, apologising for being offhand at the funeral. Could they meet for a drink to allow him to make up for his behaviour? She bared her teeth at Herk.

'I'm pretty jammed this week, apart from tonight. What about a week on Thursday? It would be nice to reminisce about Erica.'

'Caprice? Tonight? Well,' she paused for ten seconds, 'I suppose since you're practically a friend, why not? 7.30 would be OK.'

Herk picked up her coffee mug and chuckled quietly towards the kitchen.

'What a prize jerk.' She followed him through. 'I cannot believe Erica fell for that smartass. Still, he may know more about Paul Stone and he's got a twinge of guilt about something. I'll prise it out of him before he discovers he's not getting me into bed.'

'Not Mata Hari, then?'

She poked him hard in the ribs. 'I have never sold my body for information, I'll have you know.' She cocked her head to one side as he washed the mugs at the sink. 'Well, unless I fancied him.'

His expression was serious when he turned round, which she thought for a moment was disapproval. But he had switched back to his question. 'What else today?'

'Publishers' meeting in Holborn at 3 pm and I might just rouse Dunstan to give him back Erica's case notes. I'll see if I can fit him in after. Give me an excuse to get away. This morning is desk tidying.'

'Don't go out unless you ring me first.' Her salute went unnoticed as he left.

Back at her desk she gloomily contemplated the afternoon rendezvous with the book editor who wanted, according to her agent, minor rewrites on the Sanchez Killing for a Living story. Her hackles had risen at the thought. She was used enough as a journalist to have her material worked over by sub-editors. Since she never read the end result, she was unfussed if they changed the punctuation or cut out chunks to fit the space available. In this case, however, she feared a fight ahead if the publishers were trying to change the slant of the book, to make it, in their favourite phrase, more reader-friendly.

She had no time, and less inclination, to add or subtract bloody details according to their whim. They could like it or lump it, she thought crossly, although no doubt her agent's diplomatic skills would be brought to bear on her uncompromising 'No', which would mutate through a reluctant maybe to a grumpy acceptance of the bare minimum of alterations. Team work was not her forte.

The landline rang, with a London number showing. She laid her cigarette in the ashtray and answered it.

'Miss Thane?' a softly spoken voice asked.

'Yeah.'

'I'm David Lewis from Harper & James, solicitors. I have sent you several emails. It's about your father's estate.'

She stiffened and picked up her cigarette, answering cautiously, her breathing shallow.

'What about it?' she said slowly.

'I should explain,' he continued briskly. 'Eighteen months ago we took over Fennington & Fulsome after the sole surviving partner died. We have been clearing out their archives and came across papers pertaining to yourself and your family. I wondered whether you would like us to keep them or you would prefer to have them.'

Her brain froze and her heart punched back into her chest. The old feeling of shame trickled down her spine. Outside the window, a grey heron slowly flapped its way from a morning's foraging in the pond at Buckingham Palace, heading north to its nesting colony in Regents Park. She watched the powerful wing beats, drumming through the grey sky.

'Miss Thane?'

Taking a deep breath, she forced the words out: 'Why don't you send them over.' He checked the address and rang off.

A voice in her head screamed 'NO'. She did not want anything connected to her father. More than three decades of her life had been spent trying to blot him out. He had murdered her mother, spent ten years in prison, tainted her childhood. The money that paid for her boarding school and clothes, and later came as income from shares, she had accepted grudgingly. It was just money left over from a useless life, a feeble attempt to make up for the damage he had caused. She had persuaded herself that accepting it was an act of revenge since she had no intention of ever forgiving him. In recent years she had refused to spend the income on herself, immediately handing it on to Médecins Sans Frontières.

When the bulky packet of papers arrived by courier an hour later, she threw it unopened into the bottom of an office cupboard and shut the door.

Her morning unsettled, she found a Whitney Houston album that had sustained her through bleak moments in her teens, although her attempt to fuse the pop lyrics of 'I Have Nothing' with Jean-Paul Sartre and Nietzsche in one holiday essay had so infuriated the English teacher she had been forced to write another. She had reproduced her bird-watching diary in sixty densely packed pages, one for each day of the two-month vacation.

'Didn't you see anyone or go anywhere?' Miss Potts had demanded, her long nose and thin lips twitching with incredulity and concern.

'No, Miss. I walked three miles to the cliffs every day. Saw maybe two hundred thousand birds,' Tire answered with a defiant glare, omitting to mention the evenings spent with Donny on his fishing boat. She smiled at the memory. Half a lifetime ago.

The brick wall of the building across the road, rising blankly up to the level of her window, was more oppressive than usual. Why do I live in a city, she thought, for the umpteenth time? It was an old dilemma, but was getting more pressing since she had stopped travelling so much. Work and theatres was her flip answer. The reality was that city life gave her the pretence of being among people, even if she connected with very few. Going to live on an island was a comforting dream, but she'd knew the isolation would consume her.

Her depression was kept at bay by packing her schedule with several running projects, ensuring she was always moving forward. But she hadn't felt the panic the phone call threatened to set loose in a long time. It made her feel as if she was falling through an empty universe and about to explode at the same time. Clamping her jaw, she forced the unwanted feelings down and slammed the trapdoor shut.

Go somewhere, do something. But she was trapped inside the apartment till Herk returned. Cursing herself for being weak-minded, she heard his rough Scottish voice in her head. 'Keep your focus steady.' A thought struck her and she phoned Trevor at Cerigo. He was surprised but delighted when she suggested she come with a photographer to their Emporda resort on the Costa Brava.

'I'll have to check obviously with Mr Harman, but there will be room in about three weeks' time.' Her heart sank.

'Nothing sooner?' she said, trying to keep the desperation out of her voice.

His response was cautious. 'We close for two weeks from next Wednesday for the poor children's holiday. Mr Harman likes them to be left undisturbed. I know, since journalists have asked in the past.'

'Before next Wednesday might be possible? It would suit me better.' Why was she pushing and pleading?

'Let me ask Mr H. I'm sure it'll be fine. Then I will need your passport details to fix plane tickets and a car to pick you up from Barcelona. What a pleasure it will be to welcome you, Ms Haddington.'

Is this going to be a mistake or at least a waste of time she wondered, aware that her decision had more to do with running away from what she didn't want to face, than any pressing reason to check out Harman Stone on home ground.

CHAPTER 22

The meeting with her new book editor had been easier than she expected, with only a few points raised that could be tidied up in a morning's work. She had dispensed with driver Bob's services against his resistance. So the mile walk from Holborn across to Farringdon Road to meet Simon Dunstan filled in the half an hour she had to spare. Arriving first at the coffee shop, she ordered an espresso and watched the passers-by without really seeing them: a moving wallpaper of anonymous people going about their business. Dunstan arrived fifteen minutes late, his collar awry, ginger hair plastered with sweat above an unpleasantly shiny face. Tire managed a reassuring smile, and didn't offer her hand, as he stammered out a nervous apology.

'Sorry, no time to stay. I must be back in the office in twenty minutes,' he said.

She hesitated, not sure how to extract information out of him over what was clearly going to be a rapid cup of coffee.

He continued: 'But I did want to contact you. Erica left you her jewellery, books and paintings.'

'She did?' Tire's eyes filled with tears.

'Her money is going to various charities. Very thoughtful of her,' he remarked, not meeting her eye. 'But there are her possessions. Her flat was rented and the owner has agreed to break the contract if it's cleared by the end of this week. No furniture, obviously, just clothes and... things... ' He tailed off, looking at her sideways. 'Wondered if you could manage? Know it's a distasteful business. But has to be done. Sorry for the short notice. Keep anything you find, it won't matter for the estate.'

For once, Tire was almost speechless, as the prospect of getting access to Erica's papers fought a battle with her sense of loss.

He slid a set of keys across the table with an address label attached. 'Just above Belsize village, you know. Easy to find. My cousin lives there,' he added inconsequentially. Then looked flustered and muttered, 'but of course you'd know being a close friend, sorry.' Not that close or that long a friend, she thought with a stab of sadness, to be the only one to get a mention in her will.. She tightened her jaw to keep her face expressionless and handed him Erica's Greengate folder from the prison.

'Aah, I wondered where that had got to,' he said, brushing his hair back anxiously and reversing away from her as if he was scared she might embrace him. 'No harm done. He's gone down for a long stretch and that's all closed now.' Then he shambled off.

Her inclination was to find a cab and go immediately until she noticed Bob's BMW sitting across the road. Her phone rang, displaying Herk's number.

'We had an arrangement. Having security means you do as they tell you. We had to follow you on foot, which is not ideal. Now get in the car. You'll need time to change for dinner.' He rang off.

The walls were closing in again, but he was right. She gave Bob an apologetic smile and climbed in.

Back at the flat, Herk was hoovering the kitchen floor, an open bottle of beer on the counter top. He grunted when she walked in, so she collected a can from the fridge and waited till he had finished and switched the machine off. His expression when he turned round was inquiring, but not angry. Bless him, she thought, he doesn't go in for recriminations.

Erica's keys dangled from her finger. 'Tomorrow first thing I'll... we'll go through Erica's flat. There might be documents there.'

'No,' he said. 'You're not going anywhere until I've had a recce. You've no idea who might be watching.'

'Am I to spend my life getting paranoid about stalkers?' She looked at him exasperated, nearly slopping diet Coke on the floor.

'If you're intent on hurtling into hornets' nests, always best in my experience to check how big the beasts are in advance,' he responded with an offhand wave. 'What else from today?'

She took a deep breath. 'I've agreed we'll go to Spain to the Cerigo resort maybe in three days to check it out.'

'And this is worth it why?' It wasn't a criticism, more a straight query for information. She couldn't, wouldn't tell him the real reason she'd made the instant decision.

'It'll only take a couple of days. They'll pay for flights and pick us up.' She rotated one shoulder blade. 'I just think there's something odd about the Stones. Giving deprived kids a free holiday doesn't square with the feeling I get from either of them.'

He looked doubtful, but surprised her by saying: 'Why are they fixing transport?'

'Just standard. I do a write-up and it gives them publicity. So they sort out a free trip. Though I'll have to explain I'm not Ms Haddington since they want passports, which is a pain.'

'No chance,' he said, decisively. 'We'll drive.'

'To the Costa Brava? That's a helluva stretch.'

'It's only fourteen hours. You rely on them and you're trapped. If we go, we're going to have an escape route. Bob's wife is going into hospital so the BMW will be free. You can make an excuse about doing another job on the way back. Toulouse or Montpellier or somewhere. And you keep your name to yourself – and mine.'

CHAPTER 23

Stepping out of the shower, she realised she had forgotten to ask if Herk had made progress with tracking the motorcycles to source, or whether Momo had come up with any information on Greengate's case. No doubt he'd tell her when he was good and ready. Leave it till tomorrow and concentrate on nailing Crumley tonight.

Black suited her mood, so she pulled on velvet pants and jacket with a black silk blouse, polished silver earrings and a long, matching, heavy chain and art deco pendant. The car was at the front entrance when she left at 7.30 pm for the five-minute drive to Caprice, with Herk behind the wheel in a suit.

Sebastian Crumley was already seated when she arrived, with a glass of white wine in front of him. He kissed her lightly on the cheek and said: 'Very smart, and you've dressed to match the décor, I see.'

Tire looked around at the black and chrome art deco interior and laughed. 'Promise I'm not turning into a chameleon. Just what first came to hand.'

Accepting a glass of Macon, she viewed him across the table. He was undoubtedly handsome with dark eyes the colour of melted chocolate, a classical nose, full lips and abundant blondish-brown hair worn long enough to brush his collar. Pity he wasn't her type. His lightly mocking smile was honed to break the ice of conversations. She expected he wore it fifteen hours a day. They skirted and danced through a non-conversation about the David Bailey photographs on the wall, which he pronounced 'just impeccable' while she murmured a grudging 'talented, just the wrong subjects'.

He looked astonished. 'They're all famous celebrities,' he said.

She raised an eyebrow. 'Not too fond of portraits myself. I prefer my shots without anyone in them.'

'Not people-friendly, then?' he said, leaning towards her coquettishly as she gritted her teeth.

Over the first course of seared scallops she brought up the subject of Erica. He looked at his plate and shrugged with a look of what could have passed for wistfulness on his face. Plunging in, she asked if he had thought more about what she had been doing in Hammersmith in the early hours of the morning.

'Beats me. No idea, I'm afraid.'

'Was she having problems from any of her other cases?'

'Trouble?'

'For heaven's sake. She wasn't where she was supposed to be, tucked up in bed. She's dead, there must be something behind it. A vengeful client, disgruntled relative, a human rights case that trampled on the wrong corns?'

'You do have an active imagination,' he drawled. 'I told you before, she never mentioned any threats to me and her human rights work was out of chambers, so off my radar. Anyway, the police clearly think... well, I don't know whether think is too strong a word for them. But they're not pursuing any leads at all, as far as I've heard.'

She stared at her remaining scallop marooned on an algae-green sauce on the square plate, wondering what the best tactic to use on him was. The distressed feminine. How did actresses turn on tears? And he was Leo, so ladle in a few compliments.

'It's just,' she said, putting a hand on his arm, 'I thought you would be the best person to turn to. I feel so guilty.' She sniffed, hoping it wasn't too melodramatic. 'Maybe if I had asked her to stay that night she would still be here. Or if she'd been with you.'

His wine glass clinked against the side plate as his hand jerked. There was a spasm of what on his face? Guilt? Shame? His eyes hooded over as he stared at the damp patch on the tablecloth. Then the moment passed. His recovery was seamless as he smiled and reached across to pat her hand.

'Sorry. I didn't mean to jibe at you. I have no idea is the honest truth. We all have cases that go wrong, but mostly we survive to retirement. Sounds implausible, frankly, that it'd be deliberate.'

'So what was she doing out there at that time of night?'

'Hmm, got me there.'

'You were out overnight with a client.'

His brows furrowed. 'How do you know that?'

The shadow was back in his eyes. What was he ashamed of?

'Police told me,' she said, snapping a bread stick.

'Yeah, not that it matters. A surprise late meeting, too much excellent cognac consumed. Not a client directly and not even sure what the purpose of it was. Had a terrible head next morning, was late in the office and then heard about Erica. It wasn't a good day.'

He sat back as her chicken Milanese and his calf's liver were set down and a bottle of red Bourgogne Pinot Noir appeared.

'Dunstan,' he said. 'He got hold of you, I gather. She obviously thought highly of you. No one else got a mention in her will.' His eyes drifted off to a neighbouring table, his lips drawn tight.

She nodded and sighed. 'And I hadn't known her that long. But there are no relatives as far as she told me. Her father died a year ago and Erica had said she was the only one to attend his funeral.'

Both sat uncomfortably, eating to avoid talking. Finally she said on impulse: 'Tell me about Harman Stone.'

He put a bland smile and was about to bat her question back when she pinned him with a straight look. He laughed wryly. 'What can I tell you? Runs a successful business, though how much that's down to his father I don't know. Not a towering intellect. Drinks too much, going to seed a bit. Surrounds himself with pretty boys and passable women.'

'Samples both?' she asked, munching a cherry tomato.

'Don't know about that,' he said, frowning in mock disapproval. 'More he likes to cater for all tastes.'

Seeing her raised eyebrow: 'No, not that. The boys would be there to entice older single ladies. Or married ones with golfing husbands. It's all cosmetics and pampering in these kinds of places. Very pricey as well, to safeguard the exclusive brand.'

'Except,' she murmured, 'for the poor kids who get free hols. That doesn't quite fit.'

'Being charitable makes the rich feel less guilty,' he answered shortly. 'And the brats won't go when any of their standard clientele are around, I guarantee, and they'll fumigate the place thoroughly afterwards.'

She continued to push the last remaining piece of chicken round her plate. 'They don't quite fit together; father and son, I mean.'

His eyebrows arched. 'You're very interested.'

Tire raised her fork to her mouth and replied: 'I'm just an observer of human nature. I like to know how people tick.'

The waiter hovered with the remains of the bottle of red. Tire shook her head, indicating her half-full glass, so Sebastian's empty glass was refilled. She reckoned he'd now drunk almost a bottle and a half and was mellowing. A couple of liqueurs might just get him to spill any information he had.

The quiet hum of the restaurant was occasionally punctuated by spurts of laughter from a nearby group of eight, although the tables were far enough apart and the acoustics well designed to keep individual conversations from drifting too far. He leant back in his chair, waving to the waiter to remove the finished plates.

Over the course of the next hour, he ate contentedly through a coconut rice pudding with caramelised mango, of which Tire, under pressure, tasted a teaspoonful, and drank two glasses of Muscat followed by a sizeable cognac. She ordered coffee and, after hesitation, a single malt.

Paul Stone, he said, had made his millions in mining, construction and chemicals in the Far East and South America, then sold up twenty years ago to concentrate on philanthropy and investment.

'Not English by birth?' she interjected.

'He lived in Lebanon for years early on, was my impression. Though he's not Lebanese. He's fairly close-mouthed, not the sort to indulge in reminiscences.' Leaning across, he clasped her hand. 'There must be more interesting things we can talk about. You for one.'

Tire withdrew her hand abruptly then, seeing his irritated expression, added hastily: 'It just keeps my mind off Erica, talking about someone else. I know she thought highly of the Stones, both of them.' Not entirely a lie, she excused to herself.

The second glass of Muscat soothed his sulks and he gave in to Tire's prompts. Paul Stone had been married, he thought, to a wealthy Iranian who had produced Harman and then been killed when he was months old in a car crash in the Alps. After that, Paul Stone settled in England with his mother, who had died only a few years back.

'Never remarried?' Tire asked, mentally storing a note to check out the car crash.

'Too grief-stricken was the story, I gather. Though Lord knows I wouldn't have thought he was much given to emotional attachments.'

'With the exception of his mother,' she said, as warmly as she could manage. 'Presumably that's why the Alzheimer's research and the Lifelong Friends.'

By this time he was starting to slur his words and leaning on her arm, breathing into her face.

'Actually, mother was a great mystery,' he confided. 'A colleague used to visit their house in Holland Park for business meetings. Said he never understood a word she said. Spoke very thick French or Spanish, he could never work out which. Bit of a peasant and a flirt, which was quite grotesque given her age. He said if she'd been his mother he'd have hidden her away in a sanatorium. But Stone Senior insisted on having her there with carers.' His lips were beginning to drool.

Tire decided it was time to wind the evening up, nodded at the waiter for the bill and ordered two cabs. He paid up meekly, fumbling in his wallet for his black credit card and muddling the pin code twice before it went through. When he objected to her going home alone, she patted his shoulder and said briskly: 'Too soon Sebastian, too soon.' Then swept out as the first cab arrived.

She was sure he didn't know anything about Erica's death, but he was bothered about something from that night. Was it worth pursuing? Might have been a sex tryst gone too far. With a client? The rich at play. Russian hookers swinging from the chandeliers more than likely.

CHAPTER 24

The gallery in Bothwell Place, just below the Glasgow School of Art, was already crowded when Jimmy and Elly stepped nervously out of the cab. Jimmy's new shoes were rubbing his heels and the stiff corduroy trousers felt strange against his legs. Not only had Ricky, the gallery owner, sent them a car for the evening opening, he had also instructed his assistant to ensure they were dressed for the occasion.

She had arrived at their flat bearing a long bright red tartan scarf for Jimmy. He viewed it doubtfully, but was assured it would set off his olive green jacket, bought from the charity shop, perfectly. Elly was handed a black cashmere wrap, which she stroked wide-eyed, saying it was far too good. But she happily discarded her old and only tweed coat, wrapping the fine wool shawl round her skirt and jumper.

Three of Jimmy's watercolours were on small easels in the window. Two were of Italian gardens with towering cypresses and the third was a meticulously observed, grey-blue aloe flanked by white marble male nudes. Elly had fussed about their genitalia on display, but Jimmy had shrugged and said: 'I just paint what I see. They're no obscene if they're art.'

Inside, expectant faces turned to Jimmy as he entered very slowly, blinking in the light. Clutching Elly by the hand, he tried to find a familiar face and was much relieved to see Len, his social worker, among the blur of people. A round of applause brought a blush to his face and, to his discomfit, tears to his eyes. He stared embarrassedly at his feet, unsure how to respond.

After a minute, Elly took one elbow and Len the other to walk him round his sketches and watercolours hanging inside. There were thirty in all, some fine details of plants, the others the ones Elly disliked: a woman's face shattered into bubbles, a fish sitting on a television set, a huge ornate key melting over the side of a carved box, two striped dogs with elongated, stilt-like legs unable to reach their food, a tree floating in the sky, its roots dangling into clouds.

'It is extraordinary,' a clear-cut voice from the crowd carried across the room, 'how someone from that background would even begin to know how to paint subjects like these and with such talent and no tuition.' Jimmy shivered, twisting his borrowed scarf in his fingers.

'Well, Jimmy, this must be quite a new experience for you.' Dr Donaghue's kindly tones behind him made the effort of turning round to face the room easier.

Jimmy smiled shyly. 'Aye, well, I've had a couple of showings at the community centre. But I knew most of the people there. No as posh as this.' He looked round warily, stiffening slightly as he noticed Janet Birch beside Donaghue.

'I think it is absolutely marvellous,' she gushed, 'You must be so pleased. Where do you get your ideas?'

'Same as most artists,' he answered after a short pause. 'I just paint what's in my head. Don't really think about it. Just comes out that way.'

'So it's almost like a photographic memory?' she asked, moving closer than he liked. He shifted back a pace, knocking his shoulder on a frame.

'Nah,' he frowned, 'can't be a memory since I never seen it before. It's just in my head, that's all.'

An arm round his shoulder caused him to flinch and a breeze of tangy aftershave tickled the back of his throat. Bunching a hand to his mouth, he half-turned to see Ricky, in a beige jacket over midnight blue trousers and shirt, with a vivid green, silk cravat, beaming at him. 'Needed for photographs, my love. Do excuse us.'

Sweeping back a ribbon of black hair off his forehead, he whispered: 'Buyers love to see photographs out in the media. You're going to be a star by the time I've finished. And I've found you a studio, near where you live, so you can start doing oils. They make much more money.'

Jimmy's head was spinning so he didn't respond, allowing himself to be moved among the crowd, doing his best to smile or look thoughtful when asked. After fifteen minutes he was getting irritable, so the photographer took him into a large back office. A print of the painting in the front window of the giant aloe and two nudes was sitting framed on an easel.

'They're making copies, then?' he said, puzzled.

'No. Well, I've no idea to be honest,' the photographer replied. 'Just makes it easier to photograph without the glass. This one will go out to

London magazines and papers. But a good idea. You can make a lot of money from prints.'

He had to take a deep breath before going back into the main gallery, wishing fervently he could go home. He looked down to avoid the blur of interested faces smiling at him. He spotted Elly's sensible laced shoes among the mass of feet on the far side. Only when he reached her side did he realise she was talking to Janet Birch. He forced a smile.

'Jimmy, I was just asking Elly about your friend Lachie. This is his gravestone, isn't it?' She indicated the watercolour behind them of a solitary tombstone with sea and hills beyond. The inscription 'Lachie Nichols, 1955–2004' was clearly visible.

'Aye,' he said slowly, 'I wanted to remember him.' He blinked back a tear.

Elly patted his arm. 'Jimmy collected money from all the people who knew him to pay for the stone to give him a send-off. Well, a marker, like. And he wrote the words on the stone as well,' she added proudly.

Jimmy laughed embarrassed. 'Nah, I didn't make them up. They were just words I knew.'

Janet Birch peered at the painting where the first lines of the epitaph were faintly visible, reading aloud: 'We pray for you, Our Lady, star of the sea.' She sniffed. 'How touching.'

Jimmy stared fixedly at the painting over her shoulder, then said quietly: 'Shine upon us in our distress on the sea of life and lead us to the joys of eternity.'

She turned to face him, her eyes widening: 'You learned that from someone at the Hall, did you Jimmy?'

He glared irritably at her, wishing she would stop asking questions. 'I've no idea. I just know it, that's all.'

On the way home in the cab half an hour later, Elly nagged Jimmy about his lack of manners. 'She's only trying to be interested. No need to snap her head off.'

'She just never stops poking and prodding. It gets kind of tiring after a while. If I don't remember, I don't remember and there's no amount of pushing will make me.'

Elly patted him on the knee. 'Ach well, the evening went well. You must be pleased with seeing all your pictures so well laid out.'

He didn't answer, staring out at a rain-swept Sauchiehall Street, the crammed tenements giving way to the damp green space below the gothic spires of the university on the hill. His eye switched across the road to the

Kelvingrove Art Gallery, the red sandstone dulled to a deep rust by the constant downpour.

'D'you know. It's an odd thing to say, but I sometimes miss the Hall. Outside at least. It was open with green fields, no as cramped and lumped all together as this place is.'

'Can't say as I do,' she murmured doubtfully. 'All I think of is being freezing cold and no enough to eat. And having to work all the time.'

As the cab turned into the bottom of Byres Road, he sat up straight and said: 'I'd like to go and see Mary. You remember, she was one of the nicer nurses and there right from the start.'

'Mary? For heaven's sake. Is she still alive? She'll be ancient. What d'you want to see her for?'

'She was only about nineteen when she went to work there, so seven years older than me. She'd remember Lachie. I'd like to talk to her. Len found her. She's living in Largs. We could take the train down.'

Elly look astonished and then quizzical. She smiled.

'So Dr Birch is getting you moving, is she?' Then, hastily before he could respond: 'That would be nice. A day out for us. We deserve it.'

CHAPTER 25

Next morning the aroma of sizzling bacon met Tire before she reached the kitchen. Herk pointed a questioning hand at the frying pan crammed with four fatty rashers and two eggs. Wincing a refusal, she wordlessly made herself a coffee and carried it through to her office.

Five minutes later he came through carrying a mug of tea in one hand, his breakfast plate in the other and a bulky packet under his arm, which he offered to her. Between munches that she attempted not to see or smell, he said the surveillance on the watchers yesterday had been useful since he'd managed to get a photograph of one without his helmet. But since they were on foot, he glared at her, they couldn't follow them.

She filled him in on the evening with Sebastian Crumley. 'More wisps of mist. There's nothing solid. Harman Stone is a playboy, none too bright. Senior is an icon of respectability. His mother was a complete fruitcake. And that was pre-dementia.'

Herk fiddled with his mug of tea and said slowly: 'Well, you can always give up, there's no pressure on you to sort this out.'

She put her feet on the desk and looked over the clouded rooftops. With a break in her voice, she said: 'But Erica didn't have anyone else. Sebastian said she was the only one at her father's funeral a year ago and no one came to hers except colleagues. And they sure as hell are going to do nothing. And the police are stalled.' A feeling of enveloping loneliness pulled her perilously close to frustrated tears, so she banged her fist on the desk.

'My vote would be to keep going for the time being,' she said, her voice still husky.

'That's OK by me,' Herk answered calmly, 'but it's equally OK if you decide to call it off and get on with your life.'

Her eyes lit up. 'Drat, I forgot. Paul Stone's second wife died as well. I'll get Matt to check cause of death if he can track down where.' She scribbled a note. 'Or ask Harman when we're in Spain. Simpler.'

'That's still on, then? You've given up on Wrighton?'

'Not exactly. I'm just waiting on inspiration to see how to get further into him.'

'That usually works?' He wiped his mouth with the back of his hand.

'You'd be surprised. If I think hard enough, something usually pops out. In the meantime follow what's available, which is a trip to the Costa Brava.'

She sat up straight, her energy and mood rising. Travel always made her feel better even if this one was on the slimmest of pretexts. If she were to be honest it was really displacement activity. Still, she could always write a newspaper piece on Paul Stone even if he had nothing to do with Erica's death. That at least would pay for the research expenses and the Spanish trip. Her eye fell on the packet on the desk. 'That'll be from Russell,' she said. 'His initial report on Stone's finances.'

'No. It's from Harper & James, it says on the back. Ali downstairs said sorry, by the way. Came in yesterday lunch time. He was in the midst of another family panic so somehow it got forgot.'

A lead weight thumped in her heart and she clenched her jaw, staring at the packet as if it was about to explode. Jumping up, she went to the filing cabinet and pulled out the package she had thrown in yesterday. Ripping it open, she found Russell's papers. She sat down heavily.

'And what's that, then?' he looked closely at her, his eyes alert. 'Who're Harper & James?'

'I don't want to talk about it,' she said tersely.

'Aye you do. If it's trouble, you're best to open it and see the worst. Otherwise it sits there like a lump of undigested food.'

'I can't,' she said miserably. 'It's legal papers from my father's estate and I really don't want to know.'

'You'll never get on with your life if half of you is stuck in the past. Just bite the bullet, preferably before we go to Spain. I want your mind on the job, not wandering around somewhere else.'

They stared at each other for a minute, then she sighed and smiled wryly. 'Who's organising who now?'

He grinned and got to his feet, saying he was off to check Erica's flat.

The Harper & James package sat on the side table, lowering at her. She racked her brain trying to find a pressing task to divert her attention, sent several emails, made herself another coffee, smoked another four cigarettes, flipped open Russell's balance sheets and closed them again. Sibelius's 'Finlandia' was brooding and threatening, in the background, an icy protest against oppression that suited her mood. Finally, with her stomach churning, she reached across and opened it.

Her father's will sat on top, a short document leaving all his money to her, to be held in a trust till she was twenty-five administered by Albert Fennington of Fennington & Fulsome. Jackson St Clair, of Albany Mansions, London, was named as guardian and executor. There were reams of papers below about payments for her schooling and clothes and, she noted with a grim chuckle, sizeable annual payments to Euphemia Dougall, Isle of Harris, whom she'd thought was a courtesy aunt offering her school holidays out of the goodness of her stony heart. Now she turned out to be a paid retainer.

Her mother's death certificate was included, which she patted softly as well as the marriage certificate. Herk was right, she thought, best get it all laid out and then file it away for good. Her mother's maiden name she saw was St Clair, which sent her rifling back through the papers. Same as the guardian she never knew she had. Perhaps a relative? Her heart jumped momentarily until she clamped it firmly back down. He'd probably be dead.

She had lived as an orphan for so long the prospect of living relatives was unsettling. Probably just a coincidence. Otherwise they would have taken her in over the holidays, given her a home to go back to.

There were dozens of letters from Jackson St Clair to Fennington indicating agreement for payments and investments over twenty years. The final one, from nine years ago, was from a different address near Sandhurst, Berkshire. In it he confirmed the winding up of the trust, mentioning he had now retired.

That was the point Tire remembered guiltily she had instructed her lawyer to handle all the paperwork and leave the remaining £650,000 in shares with the stockbroker, which brought in a small additional income every year. Thumbing back through the old receipts, she reckoned there must have been a considerable sum of money to start with. She had known almost nothing about her father, wanted to know nothing, except he had been described, in the one old newspaper report of his trial that she had geared herself up to read, as an aircraft engineer. Maybe it had been her mother's money. That would make it easier to stomach.

She did feel different, not in any way she could put her finger on, but lighter in spirit and more solid. Collecting all the papers into a neat heap, she found an empty box file on the shelf and dropped them in, clanging the lockspring on top and shutting the lid. Then she dropped the box at the far end of the office. It could go into the spare room once Herk had left.

There was a morning stretching ahead with nothing pressing. Rewrites for the Sanchez book were wanted by the month's end and there was no sense in delivering ahead of the deadline. Russell's financial background on Paul Stone would need to be read before they left for Spain. Her hand reached across the desk then stopped. She was focusing too much on Stone when there were still question marks over Rupert Wrighton. Reluctant though she was, making friends with his secretary Felicity was the only option she could see.

She lifted the phone. 'Felicity. Good morning. This is Tiresa Thane. I met Mr Wrighton the other day. How are you? I was so interested to read the articles and papers he gave me and wondered if you had more?'

The sound of a door clicking shut at the other end filled a pause before Felicity said in a shaky whisper: 'How nice to hear from you. Can I phone you back in five minutes?' Her voice resumed its normal high-volume squeak. 'Ah, no, he's left.'

'Left?'

'He's gone to a conference in Leeds for two days.' The relief in her voice echoed down the line as well as her desperation. She sounded exhausted and near cracking point.

'How's Miranda?'

'She's gone to stay with a college friend. Her father doesn't like her to be in the house by herself.'

Better and better. Felicity was on her own. But she couldn't go out. Herk would shoot her if she went walkabout without him. Having established there were other papers, she took a deep breath and ladled out apologies for being presumptuous, but could Felicity possibly bring them over to Soho since she was up against time pressures?

Half an hour later they were sitting at a corner table in Lavazzo, just round the corner. A quick glance as Tire left her front entrance did not spot any suspicious lurkers or motorcycles. Felicity was wearing a shapeless camel jacket over a billowing russet skirt, with a faux fur scarf round her neck and matching hat, giving her the air of a badly stuffed teddy bear. She sat with her handbag on her lap, her small, bird-like hands constantly moving.

As Tire pondered the best way into the conversation, she noticed tears filling the older woman's eyes and spilling down her cheeks. She pushed a paper napkin towards her and put a hand on her arm.

'I'm so sorry. I just can't cope any longer. Miranda is so unhappy and I'm scared she'll go the way her mother did.' Her desperation and despair were palpable.

'Get her away from her father.' The words came out before Tire had time to consider. 'Is there no one she can stay with? An aunt, grandmother, boyfriend?'

Felicity shook her head, scrunching the napkin against her nose. 'She's run away a couple of times to stay with other students and he always found her and brought her back. She has no close relatives. There was a nice lawyer who was helping her. But now she's gone.' She put both hands across her face and sobbed.

'How…?'

Felicity stopped her and said with an anguished look, 'You won't print any of this?'

'Lord, no. Absolutely. I promise.' She felt like moving round to give her a hug.

'She is finishing her music studies next week and I had hoped she would go away to a three-month course in Cornwall, but he refused to pay for it.'

Trying to keep her mind off Miranda, Tire said: 'Tell me, this lawyer, how did Wrighton react to her?'

'He hated her. He used to go off on rants about what he'd do to her. How he knew people who would sort her out. It was dreadful.'

'What sort of people?' Tire moved closer.

A frown crossed Felicity's face and she shuffled in her seat. 'Are you sure you won't write about this?'

'Believe me, I won't do anything that makes this worse for Miranda. She needs to be away somewhere safe. Publicity wouldn't do her any good. You have my word on that.'

The hairs on the back of her neck prickled and she half-turned to see Herk standing at the corner. They exchanged glances and he checked his watch as if waiting for someone and leant against the wall.

'I should leave.' Felicity made to stand up, sniffing noisily.

'Not before you tell me where Miranda can go. That's one. Second is what sort of people did Wrighton know? And how did he react when he heard Erica Smythson was dead?'

'You knew her?' The question came out in a breathless squeal as an accusation.

No sense in lying at this stage. 'Yes, she was a good friend. I'm trying to find out what happened to her.'

This brought on a fresh round of sobs and Felicity buried her face in her scarf, pulling it half over her head, as if wishing she could disappear.

Sally, the café manager, arrived with two more cups of coffee and winked sympathetically at Tire.

Eventually, Felicity's face reappeared and she pulled down her jacket, sitting up straight. 'What am I going to do?' It was a straight request for help, Tire knew, but Herk's words about not being social services were echoing in her head.

'Take the questions backwards,' she said firmly. 'How did he react?'

The twitch across her forehead had turned into a tic that made one eye blink. 'Surprised, really. And pleased. He said a friend must have been listening to him.'

'Which friend?'

'I don't know, really I don't. There were some rough types he knew from childhood. They were never invited to the house. Eddie, the driver, told me he went occasionally to a pub near Tower Bridge to meet them.'

That's one for Herk.

'Any others?'

'A few of the men in the fathers' organisation were really unpleasant.' Her brow creased. 'Though some were nice and had been badly done by.'

'Unpleasant?'

'Angry, vengeful. Horrible. I got the impression they hated women.'

That was not an enticing prospect, having to infiltrate a group of misogynist neanderthals. Felicity's eyes appealed to her across the table. The gazelle in the conversation. Miranda.

A loud scrape as a van misjudged the kerb, followed by a stream of curses out of an open window, provided a moment's grace.

'Right,' she said, more authoritatively than she felt. 'You'll need to stay till she finishes next week. Will she go on this residential course without her father's permission? I can probably rustle up a patron who would pay.' Tire thought, what am I doing? This is terrible stupidity.

Felicity nodded, putting one hand up to stop her eyelid twitching. 'She's desperate to go. I really think she's at the end of her tether.'

A loud cough from Herk carried across the traffic noise, indicating he was getting impatient.

'Email the details and your personal mobile number. I'm away for two or three days, but I'll let you know before I go.'

After a heartfelt hug from Felicity, she walked back to the apartment. Expensive or not, it would give three months' breathing space with Miranda off her conscience. Perhaps her absence might rattle Papa into... quite what she didn't know. But getting people off balance usually helped.

CHAPTER 26

In the kitchen Herk was brewing up in a large white teapot with 'Where There's Tea There's Hope' on it in red lettering. Despite herself she laughed, as she opened the fridge to find a bottle of water.

He stirred the tea with a large spoon. 'Now, tell me, I see from your desk you've opened these papers about your father. Is that all sorted in your head?'

'And this is your business?' she snapped, wondering where his sensitivity about intruding on personal matters had gone.

'We're partners, right? Whatever gets in the way of the job interests me,' he replied, turning round with a level stare. 'I've had to work with guys whose marriages were falling to bits or their mothers had died and there were some near disasters. There's too much confusion about as it is, and risk, so I need you focused.'

'OK, OK,' she admitted. 'Sort of.'

She explained about the money and her courtesy aunt who had been paid to look after her and the old executor, now living near Sandhurst, who had her mother's maiden name. He leant back against the counter with both hands wrapped round a red mug with a crown motif and 'Keep Calm and Carry On' written down one side.

'Are you restocking my kitchen with market tat?' she asked.

'Nah, just making myself feel at home. Your mugs are too thin and delicate. It's not important,' he said irritably. 'You're inclined to go off in all directions, aren't you? Focus.' He tapped one toe down on the tiled floor and sniffed. 'Sounds quite a set-up, the St Clair chap having lived in Albany Mansions. Very exclusive that, as I recollect.'

She frowned uneasily. 'Odd. I had this notion of my father as a kind of car mechanic, well of aeroplanes. I assumed the money came from my mother.'

'And what's your intention now?' he said, looking out of the window.

She answered promptly with some emphasis: 'Focus. Remember? Erica's flat. Ancient family history can wait.'

He chuckled. 'Touché. OK. We'll leave in thirty minutes.'

Back at her desk, on impulse she googled Jackson St Clair. There were only two brief mentions of his name, referring to him as government civil service pensions, and no photographs.

'Here, put these on.' Herk was standing behind her, holding a blue workman's overall and a baseball hat. 'We're the cleaning and removal people.'

'For heaven's sake. Are there people watching?'

'Don't think so. But the only way in is through the front door. So best be on the safe side.'

The uniform smelt faintly sweaty, which made her wrinkle her nose, was too large and slightly too short, so she pulled out her heavy walking boots with thick socks to cover the gap round her ankles. Stuffing her hair under the cap and pulling down the brow, she thought she looked suitably unattractive and anonymous.

Outside the tradesman's entrance at the back of her apartment was parked a small white van with 'Charlie's Speedy Clean and Move' labelled on the side.

'You're a constant source of wonder, Herk,' she said, having climbed in. 'Where do you magic up all these... accessories?' He grinned and didn't reply.

Neither said much on the twenty-minute drive to Belsize. The closer they got, the heavier Tire felt. Even the exotic golden dome of the Regent's Park mosque, which usually lifted her spirits, passed by unnoticed. The Swiss Cottage traffic lights, for once, sailed them through on green. She found herself clinging to the door handle as they turned right off Fitzjohn's Avenue past the Tavistock Clinic and Freud's statue.

Herk fished a parking permit out of the glove compartment, indicating she should prop it against the window as they pulled into Wedderburn Road. The long row of converted Victorian mansion houses, set back from the road with small, well-kept front gardens, gave off an air of genteel solidity. The plane trees lining the pavement cast shade well beyond the second floors.

Following instructions, Tire retrieved a large pail full of cleaning materials and several rolls of plastic rubbish bags. Herk grunted slightly under the weight of a large cardboard box. Tire unlocked the front door, which clicked shut behind them. They avoided the lift and walked up to Erica's first-floor apartment.

Once inside, she looked around. The interior hall was exceptionally tidy with white walls, a glass console table and fitted beige carpets. In the spacious sitting room, taupe armchairs and a long sofa were positioned precisely on three sides of a square coffee table, neatly piled with design, garden and fashion magazines. The high, corniced Victorian ceilings should have given it character, but it felt soulless.

An image she had been trying to block out for days of Erica's body, bloodied, torn and dumped in a muddy river, surfaced with a jolt. A friendly hand on her shoulder made her open her eyes and Herk nudged her towards an open door.

In a matter-of-fact tone, he said he'd clear the bedroom into suitcases, which surprised her, but he said it would be easier for him since he had never met Erica. She should concentrate, he said, on finding any bills, documents or diaries that might be useful.

The spare room, which she walked into with reluctance, overlooked the gardens at the back and had been turned into an office with a white desk by the window, two small, matching filing cabinets and the single bed pushed back into a far corner. There were shelves of books up one wall, mainly spy thrillers, biographies and political memoirs.

On the wall to the left of the window, which the desk faced, was a framed, coloured copy of Erica's birth chart. She smiled wanly, remembering her saying: 'If it's good enough for Teddy Roosevelt to hang his in the Oval Office, then it's good enough for me.'

'Yeah, but that was to remind him of his tendency to lose his temper. You never do,' Tire replied.

'No, but I do procrastinate. I think things round and round till I'm dizzy. My Libran failing.'

The cordless phone was flashing on its stand. She picked it up, ignored the twenty-five messages and fiddled to find the call list. The night of Erica's death there were four calls just before midnight, when she must have been home after the theatre. The first three were from blocked numbers and were logged as missed calls, which may well have been because Erica never answered unless she knew the caller. The fourth was from an 07 mobile number, which had been taken.

Tire's finger hovered over the screen, wondering whether to call. Then hearing Herk's voice in her head urging caution, she found her own phone and noted down the number. The prospect of finding who had lured Erica out to kill her brought on an attack of shakes so she sat down. She buried her head in her hands, with panic threatening to surface.

With an effort of will, she forced her feelings into a corner in her mind. Drawing a trembling breath, she looked around the room. Do something. Get moving.

The laptop in front of her on the desk looked inviting, but almost certainly needed a password so that would have to wait. One filing cabinet held house and car insurance, income tax forms, bank statements, stockbrokers' reports, a family personal folder. The other had tabs labelled with the names of different Middle and Far Eastern countries and foreign names. That must be her human rights papers.

'Right,' Herk's voice cut in behind her, 'that's me finished and packed. Nothing in the bedroom of interest. I've kept the jewel box separate.' Her anguished expression had no effect on him although he touched her lightly on the shoulder, which was strangely reassuring. He continued briskly: 'We'd best start packing the documents into the fold-up cases I brought. And you can look through them later at your leisure.'

In half an hour he had the office contents stowed into cases. By 3.30 pm they were on their way back with the van piled up with cases, boxes and bags. The books, Herk, said, could be picked up in the morning by Speedy Charlie and kept in store if she wanted.

'You mean he actually exists?' Tire asked, surprised.

'Of course. You didn't think I rattled this up out of nowhere, did you?'

On his insistence, she delayed testing the number on the phone until he had it checked by a mate who worked in telecoms. Tire was beginning to doubt whether his sources were as straightforward as he made out. But she didn't care, as long as they found a name.

She stepped with relief out of the sweaty overalls and busied herself stowing Erica's clothes in the box room and the document boxes in the office. The jewel box lay on the desk and she took a deep breath before lifting the carved wooden lid. Probably her mother's, she thought, feeling tearful and uncomfortable about prying. Neat boxes with rings, brooches and necklaces lay on one side with velvet pouches piled up on the other. Tucked in the pleated silk at the back was a memory stick. That would contain family photographs. And now there was no one to remember or hand them onto. Her head drooped.

'Well, not a huge amount out of that,' Herk came in with two mugs of coffee. 'It was a sim card bought for cash in Notting Hill five months back, topped up by pay-as-you-go, so no contract and no name, which is what the police would have found. Assuming they bothered, of course. I got someone to try the number.' Tire tensed.

'Foreign-sounding geezer. Started by saying something like 'anjep'. Then switched into English, but with an accent. And cut it rapidly when he found it was a cold call.'

'Anjep,' she repeated, rolling it round her mouth. 'Could be Russian for hi or could be a name.'

'Which is no help since London is full of Russkies, Albanians, you name it. You want something nasty done, they're up for hire.'

She stared disconsolately at the file boxes on the floor. Her shoulders flinched as a cold draught ran down her spine. Her teeth gnawed at her lip.

'I don't know what the hell's wrong with me, Herk,' she said, sitting up straight suddenly. 'I spend my life chasing nasty people on faint trails and hunches and dig up shit till it all gets tied together. With this I feel... scared isn't quite the word, but edgy, erratic. One moment firing ahead, the next thinking it's all nonsense and wanting to chuck it in.'

He rubbed one boot against his blue overalls, considering his answer. 'I'm no wanting to push you either way,' he said slowly, 'but if you want my honest opinion this thing is bigger than you think. Not because you're being watched. Just my guts, I suppose. It feels,' he hesitated, 'like the kind of thing that could prove you more right than you ever wanted to be.' He looked at her calmly and kindly. 'But you're in the driving seat. Your choice.'

She sighed. 'I keep hearing this voice saying in my head – what am I going to do, what am I going to do? I had that all through my childhood. Suppose it was being on my own too much. But normally when I'm working I'm like a terrier after a rat.'

He grinned. 'You strike me as bigger than a terrier, given the people you've tangled with in the past. But maybe here, I don't know the circumstances, but maybe it's because your mother was killed, much like Erica was. It's got you rattled.'

Outside a police siren wailed, vying with an errant car alarm and a circling helicopter for attention. For an instant, Tire wished desperately for the peace and wildness of the islands. London's anonymity and busyness was normally a comfort. Only occasionally did it threaten to crowd in on her. She swung her chair round to stare out of the window.

Across the street two crows were at their usual game of harassing a pigeon, chasing it round rooftops. Suddenly all three birds scattered, as a small hawk came into view. It circled purposefully scanning the ground below for prey.

'You don't often see these here,' she said, her interest diverted. 'It's a sparrowhawk.' She laughed. 'Mrs Mac, who looked after me up in

Inverness when I was young, always said they were lucky, the messengers of God because they flew the highest.'

'She was good to you, was she?' he asked.

'Yeah, that was very early on. She baked great pancakes and tucked me in at night. Must have been after my mother died.' Smiling at the memory, she felt warmer.

'Superstitious, was she? The Highlanders often are. I fought with a number of the lads from up there, always looking for omens they were. And sometimes they were right, too.'

The hawk dived out of sight behind a row of buildings, then emerged a moment later, its wings pushing it rapidly upwards. Herk moved close to the window.

'D'you know, ah think it might have got a mouse.'

Tire pushed his arm. 'You can't possibly see at this distance. Even your miraculous talents don't give you the eyesight of an eagle.' He nodded mischievously and went off to the kitchen to find a bottle of wine.

'Now,' he said, handing her a glass, 'I think you need to sort out your family stuff before you go any further, even just a bit. Otherwise you'll be in a muddle.' He raised a hand to stop her protest and said firmly: 'On the way down to Dover on Sunday you can drop in and see this St Clair guy and it might put your mind at rest before we get to Spain.'

'He might be dead!' she exclaimed.

'No, he's not. I checked,' he said with a satisfied grin. 'And I'm not taking no for an answer on this. You'll go and see him and I'll drop in on a mate at Sandhurst when you're there.'

It was a strange feeling having the decision made for her. Normally she objected strenuously to outside interference, but she found herself relaxing into the inevitable. Her shoulders dropped and the tension in her spine unwound.

'Now what do they mean?' Herk pointed out the window as a pair of large-winged grey birds with trailing feet made their way with slow, powerful wing beats across to the east.

'Herons. The Egyptians thought they were a sign of new beginnings.' She watched them make their unhurried, rhythmic way out of sight.

'Ah. Kind of storks, are they? Saw a lot of them in the Middle East, smaller mind you, and white. Can't say they brought us much luck, but maybe the grey ones are better.'

'It's all in the eye of the beholder, I think, when it comes to omens,' she replied with a faint smile.

CHAPTER 27

Unusually, Tire lay in bed next morning staring at the ceiling with daylight streaming through the blinds, reluctant to emerge into the day. As far back as she could remember, she had blocked out her father's existence, reducing him in her mind as far as she thought about him at all to a degenerate. It was shocking to be faced with evidence of his money and his connections. The insatiable curiosity that drove her career had run into a complete blank where he was concerned. She was not at all sure she wanted to lift the veil at this late stage.

The day was overcast when she got up, with sporadic thunderclouds casting a pall over the morning. The office uplighters were on full as Tire waded her way through Erica's documents and notebook. After two hours, having come up with no names relating to Anjep and nothing else significant, she admitted defeat. What she needed was Erica's old case files. They would be under lock and key in the chambers. Not even Dumbo Dunstan would be gullible enough to give her access to them.

Her long experience of research was that persistence paid off. Keep wading through mountains of confusing or irrelevant information, up cul-de-sacs, round circular tracks and at some point it all began to fit together. Like a mole, she thought, burrowing its way through the darkness until it hit daylight. The key was not to give up and stay buried along with the secrets someone didn't want known.

A clap of thunder followed by a jagged fork of lightning brought the rain sheeting down and some relief from the slight headache that had dogged her since she got up. The rest of the day stretched ahead of her with nothing she could sink her teeth into. No work made her uneasy, to add to the already edgy feeling she had about the days ahead. Her discomfort was largely about being dragged into her father's past rather than the Spanish resort visit, which she reckoned was probably going to be a waste of several days.

A phone call to Jackson St Clair, her father's executor, had fixed a Sunday morning meeting at his house. The elderly voice on the other end sounded surprised and wary when she phoned. 'How had she got his number?' he asked. She said shortly it had been on his letter to the lawyer. There were longish pauses between his answers, but finally he said if she felt it worthwhile then to come, but there was little he could tell her and it would have to be brief since he had a lunch engagement.

She knew Herk was right about sorting out her family situation since it was fogging her brain and preventing her intuition working. An old therapist had once said that she coped with her ruptured childhood by overinvesting in her mind and pushing her emotions out of sight. What had she called it? The regressed self. A swamp of unarticulated feelings that had to be kept firmly closed off to prevent it drowning her coping self.

How bad could it be? St Clair probably knew nothing and had only been put in place by the court as a safe pair of hands to oversee her father's money. He may not even have met her father. Get the meeting over and then get on with pursuing Erica's killer.

Whitney Houston's 'The Bodyguard' soundtrack, which she hadn't listened to in years, was back on for a second time. Tears prickled behind her eyelids as she remembered how her teenage self had clung onto the soulful lyrics of loss and fear, needing someone who would keep her safe. Twenty years on, she had lost that hormonal anguish. Only occasionally did the ache of aloneness surface to beat against the resilience she had built up. Grow up, she told herself crossly, and reached for Russell's financial report on Paul Stone.

'Company accounts – multiple private companies, byzantine structure, impossible to unpick. Donations listed for tax relief – Alzheimer Drug Research – £15 million to California University laboratory. Memory drug research £10 million Paul Stone to Vana Clinical Laboratory in Mexico City (first of these kosher, heavily regulated. Second????) Will pursue via sources in HMRC and SFA.'

What would Revenue and Customs know about a Mexican research facility, she wondered? The Fraud Office would be keeping an eye on money laundering, but that was normally money going in the other direction into legit UK banks. She racked her brain trying to think of who in her contacts book might know about the Mexican pharmaceutical scene. If Russell was pursuing, it had obviously raised flags in his mind.

The phone rang, with the name Sibyl on the screen. A pang of guilt made Tire frown. It was months since they had spoken.

'My dear, how are you?' The voice was quavery, but still clear. She must be in her mid-eighties now. The conversation moved through pleasantries about Sibyl's move to Brighton, her walks by the sea with her recently acquired shih tzu from the rescue pound, the new clientele she was building up, while Tire wracked her brain trying to find excuses for not having been in contact.

'I know you've been very busy, but I just had the impulse to call you. I never ignore these feelings, so tell me – what is going on with you?'

There was a time years ago when Tire had clung onto Sibyl, needing someone to calm her anxiety and hold back the blackness that was threatening to drown her. The justification had been for Sibyl to expand her knowledge of astrology, since self-teaching only went so far. The trust that built up through their weekly telephone calls and occasional visits had prompted Tire to be honest for the first time about her story and vulnerabilities. And Sibyl provided an alternative perspective, a structure, albeit fragile and imperfectly understood, to stave off the random chaos of the world.

Two sentences collided in Tire's head and she couldn't decide which was more important. Taking a deep breath, she said: 'My friend was murdered in a hit and run. I'm trying to find who was responsible. And I'm going to see my old guardian, the executor of my father's estate tomorrow, whom I've never met.' She gulped down a mouthful of cold coffee and reached for a cigarette.

Long silences were normal with Sibyl, so she waited. Papers rustled at the other end and the voice, when it came, was stronger.

'A challenging time emotionally, that is certainly clear. Uranus is over-strong in your chart as it is. You will have to curb your impulsiveness. You cannot find your friend's killer on your own, my dear. And a family matter on top will put you off balance.'

'I have Hercules.' Tire chuckled. 'He crossed the River Styx into the underworld and made it back, didn't he?' Then she added: 'Herk's an ex-squaddie, much more sensible and cautious than I am and handy in a tight spot.'

'Good. But you must be careful. In the next two weeks there will be surprises, unexpected turns, some danger from accidents and unpleasant people. What sign is Herk?'

'Taurus.'

'Solid, unflappable, practical. Doesn't like being pushed around. You'll get on well with him since you're Virgo, both earth signs. If you can stop arguing, that is. He's very stubborn.'

'Too true.' Tire laughed, then stopped. 'Are you really worried?' Sibyl wasn't prone to phoning up with warnings.

'Well, as you know, my dear, it's never possible to say literally what will happen. It is symbolic information and we can only see the potential, not necessarily the outcome. But I did have a client this week who was born two days before you. She had been mugged and was in a terrible state. It reminded me and I looked up your chart. You obviously haven't checked it recently.'

Staring at the computer screen with her chart displayed after the call ended, Tire knew exactly why she hadn't been paying attention. She was scared it would show up losses that might mean Jin would be killed. Her own safety had never crossed her mind.

'Just checking that we're not about to fall off a cliff, are you?' Herk's voice made her jump and she swore. She scrabbled to find the volume command and turned the music down.

'It's nothing.' She pulled down the cover of her laptop. 'Just idling the day away. What have you been doing?'

'Sorted out the car, all the documents in order.' He slurped a mouthful of tea and gazed at her with that irritating question in his eyes. 'And I got word from Momo about Greengate.'

'What did he say?' she said, suddenly back in focus.

'First off, he said if his drink had been spiked on the train he'd never have driven home. So we can forget that. He'd have had to have taken something when he got home. There were faint traces of – I can't mind what he called it – but a slight question mark from the test. But they only took his blood later that day and most of these GHB and date rape kind of drugs clear quickly. He said you really need to test the hair since it lingers there much longer. He was also on heart medication. Frankly, he said it was a miracle he survived, having had a bucket of vodka on top.'

'Trying to make it look like a murder-suicide, then?' she nodded.

He lifted one foot off the floor, rolled it in a circle and said evenly: 'Well, we need to go cautious. It could very well have been a murder-suicide.' He put up a hand in response to her glare. 'I'm just saying, keep an open mind. There's no more than a grain of sand of solid evidence pointing in any direction at the moment.'

She looked intently at him. 'What does your gut tell you?'

He sniffed, rubbed a fingernail across his teeth, then chewed the inside of one cheek and finally blew out a breath. 'Well,' he said dragging out the vowel, his eyes narrowed, 'I'd have to say I do think there's something not right been going on. There's just too many loose ends and oddities. But,' he emphasised with a hand slapping onto the window ledge, 'that doesn't mean all the loose ends join together. We just need to follow them all through separately.'

He glanced down at her laptop as an email pinged in. She turned back round, minimised the astrology software and opened her inbox. The research from Matt on Paul Stone's wives was there on an attachment. She printed off a copy of the one page report and handed one to Herk.

First wife – Alessia Baglia, born 23 February 1936, married 1953 Constantino Neroni, Rome, one son Louis Claude born 1955, widowed 1957, husband killed skiing accident. Married 1962 Paul Stone, deceased 1965. Accidental death in cliff fall, Amalfi.

Second wife – Souri Javadi, born 1 January 1940 Tehran, married Paul Stone in Beirut 1966, deceased 1972, car crash in Stelvio Pass, Italian Alps, body not found for two weeks in heavy snow.

'My, isn't he the unlucky one with wives?' Herk remarked.

'I'll say,' she said, 'and both with no way of proving foul play, dammit.' She stared at the paper. 'I'll set Matt off to see if he can dig up the first wife's son, Louis Neroni. He'd have been eleven when she died. Might just be worth pursuing.'

'D'you think?' Herk looked askance. 'I've known some very unlucky guys, people dropped dead all around them and it wasn't because they tried.'

'Believe me, just by looking you can tell there's something dark at the heart of that Stone family. Senior may be the perfect English gentleman, but he has handed a toxic legacy down to his son. If one generation doesn't live out the nastiness, the next one down gets a double dose.'

'But the death of his wives, maybe his stepson, would have nothing to do with Harman since he hadn't been born.'

She jerked her head up, cricking her neck and swung round in her chair to glare at him. 'You keep telling me to focus on Erica and I really cannot see Paul Stone getting involved in anything so crass as a hit and run.' The African statuette on the desk wobbled as she banged one clenched fist up and down. He smiled calmly, infuriating her more.

'You're in a muddle, careering from one theory to the opposite. Just try to stick with what we know. Is the astrology no help?'

'You don't believe it.' She turned back to stare moodily out of the window and muttered: 'Anyway, you really don't want to know what the next ten days is like.'

'Well, you obviously do and you're not stupid so there must be something in it. What's up with the next two weeks?'

His edgy question made her half-choke on a laugh and she said: 'For us, probably just evilly bad-tempered. Out in the world there'll be more accidents and disasters. With luck, we won't be in the middle of them. No sense in both of us getting neurotic.'

Herk shook out another Camel from the packet with one hand, steadying a twitch in his knee with the other.

'Sensible caution isn't the same as imagining horrors that will never happen. Tell me more about how it works. Just a crash course. I pick up things quick and I'll try to be open-minded,' he grinned.

She gave him a weary look. Collapsing a decade of learning into a handful of soundbites wasn't going to tell him much. Straightening her back, she plunged in. 'Day-to-day predictions are based on how the planets aspect each other up in the heavens, plotted onto a two-dimensional plane. So, for instance, Uranus is square Pluto at the moment, square being a ninety-degree angle. That's what has been causing all the global chaos in the past few years – rebellions and old structures collapsing. It was around before in the mid-1960s when Mao's red revolution was raging, anti-Vietnam War and civil rights demos in the US and other stuff elsewhere. And before that the European year of revolutions in the nineteenth century.'

'By causing, you mean the planets send down death rays, like?'

'No, it's just an easier, sloppier way of saying they accompany such happenings. Coincidence, synchronicity, whatever you like to call it. Historically, we know when these aspects come round; so do certain types of events. No one actually believes the planets have any direct physical effect.'

'Fancy.' He rubbed his chin. 'Keep going.'

'Personal charts are drawn up for the time and location of birth with the planetary positions for that moment. That tells you a huge amount about temperament and potential. And,' she said forcefully, 'don't even ask the why question. We've no idea. The personal chart will also react to the present movements of planets, for even less explainable reasons.'

His cupped hand gestured for more, his face intent.

'Examples are easier even if there's no birth time.'

She pulled up Harman Stone's chart from files, typed in Paul Stone's details and printed both pages with a zodiac circle dotted with symbols and degree numbers and handed them to him.

'It looks mystical, but in reality it's all mathematical. It's a shorthand way of encoding the huge amount of information. Think of a car mechanic reading off a computer engine diagnostic which looks like gobbledegook to most people, but means something to a specialist technician.'

'I can understand that. Indeed,' he smiled condescendingly, 'I can even understand a diagnostic printout. Keep going.'

She gave him a friendly finger and pointed to the screen. 'You look at which planets are in which signs, where they stand in relation to the horizon at the moment of birth and the geometric angles between them. Each of the variables has an effect on how the energy of the planet operates. It's a bit like baking a cake, seeing how the ingredients mix.'

'Eh?' He leant forward frowning and shaking his head.

She smiled. 'Take Paul Stone, for example, though frankly I think his son Harman is more in the frame. He's got one sleazy chart.'

'Can we take one at a time?'

'OK, OK. Just to explain. Good god!' She paused, staring at her computer screen. 'Would you look at that.'

'What?'

'Paul Stone. Ouch. He has Pluto close to a Cancer Sun so it merges the two energies. The Sun is his identity and Pluto is controlling, power-hungry, secretive. That is opposite –a hundred and eighty degrees across the zodiac – from Mars in Capricorn, so he's not only ambitious for money, he's ruthless, do-or-die determined. And worse, Sun Pluto Mars all square – ninety degrees – onto Saturn in Taurus. So he's cruel, money-minded, mean, stubborn to the nth degree. No wonder his son is a train-wreck.'

Herk sat back, looking puzzled. He scratched his head. 'You lost me back there with the baking cake bit. Do you not mean like a chemistry experiment? Making crystal meth or explosives. Chuck it all together and you get something different.'

She nodded. 'Yup, that would be the more masculine analogy.'

'Well, I don't see you baking too many scones.' He half-smiled and sat back staring doubtfully at the screen, his eyes intent. 'So what can you tell from all this stuff then? It'd save the criminal courts a load of trouble and expense to just get a read-off and bung the bad guys straight inside.'

She chuckled. 'Not that simple. It tells you the potential of the chart, but not necessarily how the person is going to live it out. An underworld thug will have much the same chart as a criminal barrister. They both work in the same criminal environment, but approach it in different ways.'

'So Paul Stone could be a sweetheart, then?'

'Not a chance with that chart,' she replied. 'He had a really tough life early on that made him cold and hard, not afraid to cut corners to get what he wanted. Getting sentimental about lonely old-age pensioners isn't what he's about, I guarantee. He was born a day before Ayatollah Khamenei of Iran with virtually the same chart and temperament. So he's a tough bastard. What doesn't kill you makes you stronger, I suppose. Though not usually in a good way. Huh. I'll have to think about this.'

Herk moved his chair back. 'Before we leave it, can you tell when Stone senior and junior are going to get their comeuppance?'

'Die, you mean? No,' she said, 'it won't tell you about death. It will pinpoint the timing of major difficulties and danger. But Paul Stone is pretty unbreakable. What would floor most people would slide off him.'

'Aye well, best to know what you're up against,' Herk remarked cheerfully picking up both coffee mugs and heading for the kitchen. He added over his shoulder: 'If we are up against him, which isn't that clear yet. Remember, we leave sharpish tomorrow morning.'

CHAPTER 28

Elly sat in the window seat on the train down to Largs, entranced. Jimmy had insisted they take a minicab to Central Station since this was to be a treat. He seemed in a jovial mood, so despite her reservations about wasting money she said nothing. The train left promptly at 10 am and the grimy urban track soon gave way to the open Renfrewshire countryside, with rolling hills and small villages dotting the green on either side. Within half an hour, they were skirting the borders of Muirshiel Park.

'Odd, isn't it,' Jimmy remarked, 'the grass is greener here than it was around the Hall. Seemed almost grey there. As if the soil was bad or something.' He breathed in deeply. 'And you can smell the sea from here.'

'Can you? I didn't know the sea had a smell,' Elly replied.

He smiled softly. 'Aye. Fresh, makes your head clearer. And it can be brilliant blue, really lovely.'

Elly had never been to the coast in her life, having been moved from her village home as a teenager into the Hall and then to Glasgow, so could only nod expectantly. She puzzled for a moment about how Jimmy could be so certain since he had never mentioned any seaside trips to her, apart from their visits to Lachie's grave on the river.

When the shore finally came into view, she said in disappointment: 'That's no blue. It's grey.'

Jimmy, lost in thought, did not reply.

They asked for directions at the station for the address on Waterside Road that Len had given them. Twenty minutes later they were knocking on the door of the ground-floor flat with Mary Duncannon's name under the bell.

A hunched, elderly figure shuffled slowly to open the frosted glass door. She greeted them warmly, apologising for her arthritis, and led them through to the small sitting room. Elly handed her a box of chocolates they had brought and insisted she go off to make tea for them.

'I can't believe you're here,' Mary whispered. 'Come all this way just to see me.' She looked overcome.

'No get many visitors from the Hall, then?' he asked.

She laughed grimly. 'Naw, they were all that pleased to be away they didn't need reminding, especially of the early years.'

'Ach, you were OK Mary, better than most, well all really. You left when? About the mid-1980s or thereabouts? It got much better after that.'

The conversation over tea was stilted since Mary was embarrassed and Elly had no idea why they had come. Jimmy finally put his cup down and said: 'Really, what I wanted to know was what you remembered about the early days and about Lachie. He came in about the same time I did. You knew he'd been killed in a mugging?'

Mary blinked hard, kneading the swollen knuckles on her hands, her slippered feet twitching involuntarily. Her face contorted with frowns and grimaces as she tried to cast her mind back. After a few minutes silence she said: 'I remember his face, I think. Kind of rough, dark hair, stocky. That right?' She looked at Jimmy for confirmation and then continued: 'We always used to think it was odd you being pals since you were so different. You were more refined, like, and had your reading and writing. He was kind of stupid.'

She looked straight at Jimmy with tears in her eyes. 'We always, well some of us, thought it was just awful what Dr Brand did to you. All those electric shocks, wasn't good. You were terrified of that man. He was much worse to you than the others, for no reason we could see.'

Jimmy crumpled, hunching his shoulders to hold in a shudder. He shut his eyes in an attempt not to see that room, the contraption with the wires, the leer on the doctor's face as he held him down. The hard voice that always said the same thing. 'Little boys who make up stories need to learn to keep their mouths shut.'

He was going to die. It was going to happen again. Fear started to mount, his shoulders shook and his teeth were clamped so tightly it sent spikes of pain up his jaw. He could hardly breathe. His mind seemed to be detached from his body, floating away into a fog. He heard Lachie's voice in the distance. 'Are you alright there, pal?' Then a pat on his shoulder brought him a good feeling. Lachie would look after him, keep Dr Brand away from him.

Elly shook him gently and sat on the edge of his chair with one arm round his shoulders, the other rubbing his forehead. 'Come on now. You're not there anymore. You're safe here with us.' His breathing returning to a calmer rhythm, although his heart continued to pound and he looked embarrassedly at the older woman sitting across from him. She waved a crippled hand at him.

'There, there I shouldn't have brought that up, I'm sorry.' She stared over his shoulder out of the window.

'It's OK. I came to ask. My memory is so mashed up about what happened back then. But I do remember Lachie was strong. He protected me, when he could.'

'There was something else about...' She shook her head, as if trying to clear a jumble. A low, rasping hoot from a boat in the distance, repeated at intervals, filled the silence. She shifted uneasily, and obviously painfully, in her seat until Jimmy leant forward and said softly: 'Don't worry, Mary. Anything you can tell me will help.'

'I feel stupid saying this,' she whispered, 'but I cannae get it out of my head that I want to be calling you Lachie, no him.'

'What?' Jimmy looked aghast.

She apologised immediately, saying she was old and her memory got muddled, then tried to take it back.

He sat back in the armchair, his eyes fixed on a gaudily painted print of a whitewashed cottage on the edge of a turquoise sea. Eventually he said, his voice trembling slightly: 'Lachie doesn't sit right with me somehow. But d'you know, Mary, I think you're onto something. I think we did swap names. I can't remember why. It didn't make any difference since we were just numbers there. Maybe after Dr Brand died. And I've been Jimmy for so long I forgot all about it.'

'Oh Jimmy,' Elly leant forward anxiously, 'and you put that name on his tombstone.'

'Och, for god's sake, what a muddle,' he replied. 'This'll take some unpicking. I got given his birth certificate when we got out and he had mine.' He chewed on a fingernail, then seeing Mary's stricken expression leant across and patted her knee.

'Don't upset yourself,' he said kindly. 'I came because I wanted to know. I knew there was something ticking away at the back of my mind and that was it. Poor, poor Lachie.' He shook his head sadly. 'Now is there anything else you remember, Mary? This is very helpful. When we first came in to the Hall, that is.'

'Oh dear,' she said, 'my head's spinning now.' She sat up straighter, wincing as her spine complained. 'You came in and were different, better dressed as I remember, not the rags that the others had. Though they took your clothes away. You hid in corners, crying for your mother for a long time. I think she'd died. Lachie – Jimmy – the other one, he was more cocky like, except he acted dumb for the doctors since he didn't want to go home. That's all I can think of, I'm sorry, Jimmy.'

Afterwards, Jimmy and Elly walked arm in arm along the promenade, the Atlantic wind whipping the glaucous blue sea into frothing breakers that occasionally lashed spray onto them. She knew better than to ask questions when he was sunk in himself. The cold, seeping through her coat, eventually made her say that lunch in a café might be nice.

Over fish and chips served with a large pot of tea, he munched silently, staring out at the grey haar coming in from the sea. Eventually she put her hand across the table to hold his. 'Are you going to tell Dr Birch, then? I think you should. She's not as bad as you make out. And she's trying to be helpful.'

'Maybe,' he said cautiously. 'It's just I can't work out why she's so interested in me, as if she thought I was someone special. I don't like to be special.'

Elly thought for a moment, wiping her mouth on a paper napkin. 'Perhaps it doesn't matter why she's interested in you. What matters is she's pushing you to find out what you want to know anyway.'

'S'pose you're right. I'd never have come down to see Mary if she hadn't been prodding me. But it's kind of scary finding out things I've forgotten. I just can't get my head round Lachie being my name. Doesn't feel right.'

The train journey back was as sombre as Jimmy's mood, with rain lashing against the windows obscuring the view.

As they neared Central Station, he gripped Elly's hand and said with a fearful look in his eye: 'Maybe it was me they were trying to kill, not Lachie, when he got beaten up.'

CHAPTER 29

A bark of 'Reveille!' and a repeated loud knock on Tire's door ended a broken night's sleep. What the hell?

'OK, OK,' she shouted, trying to see the clock as the banging on the door continued. 'What's up?'

'Nothing. Just making sure you're awake. It's 6.30. We leave at 9 prompt.'

Oh god, marching orders. For a moment she considered going back to sleep then decided it wasn't worth raising more arguments this early, when her head felt fragile. She stumbled out of bed into the shower, blow-dried her hair, put on minimal make-up, threw on tight jeans with short cowboy boots and a light wool sweater. Thirty minutes later she walked into the kitchen, dropping her travel bag – packed the night before – at the door with a thud.

'Right,' she said briskly, heading for the coffee machine. 'Reporting for duty, sir. What's the schedule for the next two hours before ETD?'

Herk leant against the long kitchen counter, both hands wrapped round a tea mug. He was dressed in desert combat trousers with deep pockets, squad boots and a green T-shirt with an eagle printed on it. With a satisfied grin he said: 'Pre-op briefing.'

Lighting a cigarette, she said: 'And that couldn't have fitted into the fourteen-hour drive?'

He chuckled. 'To be honest, I thought you'd take longer to get ready. I'd forgot you weren't like other women.'

'So,' she continued crisply. 'Leave at 9, Sandhurst at 11. I meet St Clair and you skive off for a buddy's tea party, then Channel, France, then the Costa Brava. Anything else I should know?'

The hand holding her coffee mug, she noticed, was trembling slightly so she put it down.

'Have ye thought about what you're going to ask St Clair, then?' Herk looked directly at her.

She flinched and shook her head, her chest caving in as her shoulders drooped. Eventually, she said: 'I don't know that this is such a great idea. St Clair, I mean. You think it'll clear my head. I'm scared it'll muddy it more. Not that it terribly matters, I suppose. Spain's probably going to be a waste of time.'

Herk fidgeted with his feet and ran his stubby fingers along the counter, then he cleared his throat and said: 'Look, you've gotta sort out your family stuff. I'm not going to be around forever and you won't do it unless I push. So you might as well get it over and done with.' He hesitated and continued slowly: 'And I'm not so sure Spain's going to be a walkover. I don't have a great feeling about it, to be honest. So we need to be on our toes down there. Which is why I've arranged to swap the car in Barcelona for a decent cross-country four-wheel.'

'God almighty, do you think so?' Tire looked incredulously at him, then blew out a long puff of smoke. 'It would fit the astrology. Christ. I do need to get my shit together.' She straightened her spine and took a deep breath.

Over a breakfast of scrambled eggs and smoked salmon, which Herk regarded with suspicion and Tire insisted was good protein and lighter than a fry-up for a long journey, they discussed strategy for St Clair and the holiday resort.

The wind was blustery as they slipped out of the apartment backdoor. Herk was carrying a canvas holdall and didn't offer, she was pleased to notice, to take her bag. The streets were quiet with only a few passers-by out for the Sunday papers and little traffic as they walked along Beak Street, with Herk constantly glancing around.

'Crying shame, that,' he remarked, as they passed a contemporary art gallery with 'Riflemaker' above the window. 'Used to be a good gunsmith long ago and now it's full of all that crap'. He glared at three abstract paintings with blotches of colour spread unevenly across the canvas. 'I can't understand why anyone would buy that stuff.'

'It's known as culture,' she replied sweetly. He walked on ahead.

Two streets further on, he nodded to a black BMW parked by a meter and bleeped the boot open. Bags stowed, they climbed in, Tire after an argument settling into the back seat. Regent Street sped by into Haymarket and then onto the tree-lined open space of Pall Mall. Tire found she was gripping the door handle as they drew nearer the flyover onto the M4. Why do all roads lead this way? She registered little of the hour's drive thereafter, along the M25 motorway then south on the M3 towards Sandhurst, feeling morose and not a little jittery.

What was she going to ask St Clair? Herk had tried to make her think about what she really wanted to know over breakfast. The answer was not much. Did she really want it confirmed that her father was the sod she had always thought? Maybe St Clair had known her mother, was related? She drew a shuddering breath, irritated at her nervousness. Interviewing some evil thug of a murderous warlord, which she had done on several occasions, was easier than this. Maybe she could treat it as if it wasn't about her at all. This was just another research interview.

By the time Herk had looped off the M3 and was driving in open countryside towards Sandhurst she had started to relax. He seemed to know the route off by heart and had the GPS switched off. Once through several small villages, he turned left into a small road signposted Owlstone. High hawthorn and briar bushes either side blocked the view of fields beyond. Finally, he stopped at imposing, grilled, metal gates at the end of a curving, gravelled drive up to a house whose chimneys were just visible. 'The Manor' was etched in white ironwork on the wall beside a video entryphone.

'Right,' he said shortly, 'I'll drop you here and wait to see you get in. Give me a ring on the mobile when you're finished. I'm only ten minutes away.'

Surprised, she said: 'You're not coming in?'

'No need. He'd just have to let me out again. And you'll be safe enough there.'

The video entryphone lit up several minutes after she pressed the button. A distorted voice crackling with static said 'Yes?' She answered: 'Tiresa Thane' then wondered, as the gates swung open and she started to walk up the long drive, why she had used her full name.

Once the house came into view she raised an eyebrow at the elegant and imposing two-storey villa. Five chimney stacks stood proud on the red-tiled roof above a long row of windows. Must be six or eight bedrooms, she thought. Heavens, maybe he has a family. She hadn't known what to expect, but nothing this ostentatious. The front garden was meticulously manicured with clipped bushes either side of the entrance and apple trees growing out of well-trimmed grass.

An elderly, white-haired man in a tweed suit and waistcoat, which hung off his frame, was standing at the front door. He nodded courteously although distantly at her. There was an awkward moment when she wondered whether to shake his hand, then noticed he was holding the door with one hand and had a walking stick in the other.

'Perhaps you would be kind enough to go into the dining room, third door on the left,' he said, with a tremulous though authoritative voice. She walked ahead of him across the marble tiled hall with a vase of fresh flowers on an antique table. She paused at the door of a large room with extensive windows looking out on the back garden. The soft beige walls matched the fitted carpet and in the centre was a highly polished, oak rectory table. A grandfather clock stood in one corner with an elaborate Edwardian walnut desk on the far wall, with two highly polished astrolabes on top. The effect should have been calm and tasteful, yet it seemed cold and impersonal.

She hesitated before sitting down, but, since he was taking his time, she chose a chair facing towards the windows. On the table was a jug of water and two glasses. After he had manoeuvred himself with difficulty into the carver chair at the head of the table, hooking his stick over one of the arms, he cleared his throat.

'Now, how can I assist you?' he asked, in a curiously aloof manner. She was about to snap at him and then remembered her resolve to treat it like any other interview. He wanted to play hard ball, she could do it better.

She smiled, softened her tone and replied: 'Well…' looking down at her hands, 'I just wondered…' raising her head to look directly at him, 'since you were my guardian why I've never met you before? Indeed never heard of you.'

They stared at each other. His expression was surprised, then thoughtful, as if he was working out what to say. Hers was unflinching. He coughed several times, his body shaking with the effort. He waved at her to pour a glass of water.

Right, she thought, distraction manoeuvre. You're not getting away with this. She watched intently as he put both hands round the glass and raised it shakily to his mouth. He set it down and took a coloured handkerchief out of his pocket with a trembling hand to wipe his mouth.

Eventually he said: 'I realise it must seem strange, but I was put in place in a professional capacity as guardian and executor because there was no one else. There was never any suggestion that I take a…' he hesitated, '…a participatory role. I was there to oversee the monies and ensure everything was properly executed.'

'So you're not related to my mother, then? And where did the money come from? There was a fair amount and as far as I knew my father was a mechanic,' Tire pressed on, not about to let him off the hook.

He considered her questions before replying, giving nothing away. Typical bloody civil servant, she thought.

He nodded. 'It is true I was distantly related to your mother. A third cousin, I believe. But I never knew her.' He ran a hand across his mouth, the gnarled knuckles making it a clumsy movement.

His breath was rasping more heavily as he continued: 'The monies were partly an inheritance from your maternal grandmother your mother received before she died. Plus your father's savings. He was rather more than a mechanic.'

'What was he then?' she asked, her interest sparked.

St Clair shook his head, clearly tiring. 'I'm sorry, I really have no idea. I only met him once. I was a court appointee for his estate. His profession was not relevant.'

The hairs on the back of her neck prickled. That was a whopping lie.

Another paroxysm of coughing had him holding his red handkerchief to his mouth. There might have been blood on it, but she couldn't tell. She should have been sympathetic, but instead her anger was bubbling up. To stop herself telling him what she thought of him she said: 'Would a brandy help?'

He leant back in the chair and nodded towards the cabinet behind him. She poured him a sizeable tot from a cognac bottle into a wine glass and put it in front of him.

He sipped at it several times and eventually smiled ruefully and said: 'I'm not really allowed. But at this stage it hardly matters. One day my housekeeper will find me on the floor and that will be that.'

In spite of herself, she smiled back. 'You've no family, then?' she asked.

'No,' he whispered. 'I never married. This was my parents' home. Far too big for me, of course, but I could never bear to let it go.'

Outside the window a wisteria-covered pergola provided a shaded seating area facing down an expansive, trimmed lawn flanked by flower beds.

'It is beautiful,' she said, wondering how to get the conversation back on track.

He sighed. 'The brandy really does help, thank you my dear. Now I can't talk much more. So why don't you tell me what you're doing at the moment? I've read all your books and many of your magazine articles and very much enjoyed them.'

To her surprise, she found herself telling him about Erica and her suspicions about Rupert Wrighton and Paul Stone. Then after a while she stopped since he seemed not to be listening, his eyes cast down onto his thin, bent fingers curled round the wine glass.

The doorbell rang in the distance and he came to and croaked hoarsely: 'That will be my lunch guest. I wonder if you could answer it for me?'

She waited at the front door after pressing the entry button and watched as an Audi swept up the drive. A well-dressed man in his thirties in a blazer, white shirt and flannels emerged with a briefcase. His smile was pleasant, although formal, and he clearly was not surprised to see her.

'Is he alright?' he asked as he came up the steps. Tire shook her head and shrugged. 'Not really. He's coughing a lot and tired, I think.'

His brown eyes looked concerned and he added: 'He really can't do meetings any more, I'm afraid.' Then he offered his hand. 'I'm Jake Harrister and you're T.A. Thane, I know. He told me you were coming.'

He was handsome enough and fit, she thought, but there was no zing from him. Possibly gay, she reckoned.

'You're his lawyer?' she said pleasantly as she shut the door behind him.

'No, indeed. A colleague, well ex-colleague, much junior obviously,' he replied smoothly over his shoulder, clearly keen to see Jackson St Clair for himself. Inside the dining room his manner towards the older man, sitting slumped in his chair, was respectful and solicitous.

Tire picked up her scarf and bag, saying: 'I'd best be off. Thank you for seeing me.' She nodded uncertainly at St Clair, unsure what she had to be grateful for since she was sure he hadn't told her all he knew.

He wheezed and said with a struggle: 'There is one thing I should say.'

She tensed in anticipation.

He looked at her, his watery eyes glistening. 'I would be careful what you write about Paul Stone. He is well connected. Has many powerful friends. And has made it clear in the past that his son is untouchable. Remember the old saying, my dear. If you're going to attack a giant, kill him.' He sank back, his breath rasping.

'And Wrighton?'

He shook his head, holding his handkerchief against his mouth. 'Unsavoury, an ass. Vengeful. But not in Stone's league.'

Harrister pulled lightly on her arm and escorted her out of the room. At the front door he said quietly: 'I'm sorry if he was not as helpful as you wanted. He is pretty far gone nowadays.'

'What did he mean about Stone?' she asked.

He stood with his hand on the open door. 'Exactly what he said. If you're going to attack an influential figure you have to know you can bring them down. Otherwise they'll do you damage.' A bout of coughing sounded behind them and he leant closer. 'There was a journalist some years ago sniffing around Paul Stone who ended up in an unfortunate car crash.'

'Another one? His life is littered with them.'

He put up his hands in a non-committal gesture and replied: 'I know nothing. It may just have been a coincidence. Go carefully.'

Then he put his hand out firmly to close the conversation. Instead of shaking it she held it in both her hands, aware that he disliked her touch. 'What paper?'

This earned her a look of heavy disapproval. 'I believe it was one of the Scottish popular papers. Now I must go to him. Your driver will find you, I'm sure, at the gate. Goodbye.' The door shut with a soft clunk.

CHAPTER 30

There was little conversation on the long drive to Barcelona. Tire mulled over her meeting with St Clair and stared moodily out of the car window, daydreaming about Jin and about sea birds crying, shrieking and squawking on wind-blown cliffs. Herk seemed preoccupied with his own thoughts. A compilation of classical music, copied from her iPod, played for hour after hour. He had snoozed on the Channel crossing and stopped every three hours for a twenty-minute nap, refusing her offers to take over the wheel.

He swung round the busy Paris Périphérique and on down through multiple junctions till they were safely onto the A75 motorway heading south. At his insistence, she had brought cash to feed the péage tolls. 'Don't want to leave a credit card trail,' he had explained tersely. For a moment she had wondered just how paranoid he was and whether she should be worried about being stuck with someone she barely knew, then smiled at herself for being neurotic.

A French radio newsflash cut through the music to announce two hundred dead in a mental hospital fire in eastern Russia.

'Ugh,' she said, 'probably chained to their beds, poor sods.'

He retuned the player to BBC news as the presenter ran through stock prices and cricket scores. On the hour, the headlines droned through a gloomy IMF economic report on global debt, multiple bombings in Turkey, Iraq and Jordan, devastating floods in Timor with hundreds killed and a junior Tory minister's resignation over an affair with a transgender hooker. At the end, breaking news came of a water skiing accident that had left international footballer Martin Diegolu in a coma. The radio cut back to music as he stubbed a finger on the screen with the volume turned down.

'Tell me how much of that is due to these cranky influences you were talking about yesterday.'

The chuckle came out before she could stop it. 'You're getting to be like Erica. She always asked questions like that.'

She eased her back and stretched out one leg to prop it against the footrest.

'There's always murder, mayhem and catastrophe somewhere in the world, three hundred and sixty-five days a year. But they are worse around hard influences. Usually there are two or three headline-grabbers which seem to soak up the energy. Like Diegolu and back last year Michael Schumacher's accident, plus road rage and major traffic disasters. Then there are the longer-scale ones. Are you really interested in this?'

'I wouldn't have asked if I wasn't.' He took a hand off the wheel to gesture her to continue.

'Uranus Pluto over five years provoked the underdogs to rise up, which is why the Arab Spring happened and freedom fighters, or anarchists, clashed with the forces of suppression and the status quo. And then it was joined by Neptune in Pisces, which stokes up the religious loony-tunes brigade – fanatics and the like.'

Another péage broke her flow as they slowed behind a queue of three cars. She leant out of the window to slot a twenty-euro note into the machine and retrieve the change.

'Don't suppose you're interested in the economic stuff?' she said, as he accelerated away into the fast lane.

'I earn money, don't I? Keep spilling.'

'Pluto moved into Capricorn in 2008, bang on cue for the financial meltdown. It only comes round every 250 years or so and you could write a history of economic theory on the times it's been around. The effect is to deconstruct outworn financial and government systems and rebuild sounder ones. It always starts by reducing to ashes.'

'When do we get to the better bit?'

'The million-dollar question. Once lessons have been learned. There's another eight years to run and the Uranus square has been creating an unwanted distraction. That's nearly out of the way, though there's a Saturn-Pluto coming up in 2019. That might just drive it home – painfully.'

'I'd best concentrate on driving carefully, then,' he said equably.

'And avoid locked rooms and risky sports.'

They settled back into companionable silence and St Clair's words echoed back at her. 'Kill the giant.' Was that hyperbole or a considered warning? Maybe caution was advisable. Once they'd passed the turn-off for Toulouse he slowed from 130 kilometres an hour down to a steady

100, saying: 'We're early since I don't pick up the four-wheel in Barcelona till later. We'll stop for lunch and take the mountain road across. It'll get us off these bleeding motorways.'

And away from prying eyes and cameras at the main border crossing into Spain, Tire thought but didn't say. She checked her phone, scrolled through a long message from Russell and swore softly.

'What?' His question was repeated several times with increasing irritation.

'I'm thinking. Don't bully me.' She rolled down the window to light a cigarette as they exited at Perpignan Sud, took the Argelès-sur-Mer sign and headed for the coast. 'Wrighton and Harman Stone were involved in two business ventures together, both of which went toes up. A chain of travel agencies collapsed with major debt in the 1990s. And an online pharmacy in 2001 was shut down after suspicions it was selling counterfeit drugs from India, but no charges were brought. I don't remember reading anything about those. How did they manage to keep their involvement quiet?'

'Well, how?'

'St Clair told me that Stone senior protects his son. Maybe he had it shut down.' She turned to shoot him an exasperated look. 'But what it does mean is that Harman and Wrighton know each other. Christ, it's so incestuous that world. Burgoyne and Crumley trail after Paul Stone like grovelling courtiers, and now these two jackasses are in each other's pocket. Which means they'll all cover for each other.'

'Bit of a spider's web, then. Doesn't make it easier for us with Erica being connected to both.'

'Erica was as straight as a die.' She felt like punching him on the arm.

'Keep your hair on. I wasn't suggesting she was anything other than unlucky.' He blew out a long sigh and rotated his shoulders. 'It'll make more sense after we've had lunch.'

The dual carriageway, dotted with coloured bridges over underpasses and rivers, was flanked on the right by a small mountain range and on the left by cherry orchards with the sea beyond. The signs welcomed them to the Côte Vermeille.

'You know this area?' she asked, making an effort to sound interested.

'Aye, the French marine commandos train down here for diving. We were stationed with them for a while, back a few years.'

That's why he can read French, thought Tire.

'You dive, then?'

'Not now. Too old,' he answered with a shrug. 'Your heart and head won't take the pressure for ever. Well, no the kind of things we were doing. It wasn't scuba diving for pleasure.'

The modern red-tiled bungalows with ochre walls of Argelès sped past. Even the outlying commercial centre with aluminium warehouses looked clean and tidy. Signs for beaches and the marina made clear its function as a seaside resort. Round a wide curve the village of Collioure came into view below them, tucked into a bowl in the bay, the blue sea lapping up to an ancient fort standing proud of the surrounding houses.

'Too touristy,' Herk said shortly, when she looked questioningly at him. 'We'll go into Port-Vendres, next one along.'

Within five minutes he had driven down a narrow winding road, past houses with palms and aloes in their front gardens and blue plumbago and purple bougainvillea spilling over their fences, into the village and parked the car against the harbour wall. Small fishing boats were moored, their orange nets piled on deck. Glistening white pleasure yachts lined one side of the inlet, overlooked by a row of cafes and restaurants. An incongruously large, five-tiered cruise ship sat on the other side.

'It's a very deep sea port,' Herk remarked, marching ahead of her past the yachts clunking gently against their moorings. 'All the military transport for the Algerian War left from here. They bring fruit, veg and fish in now from all over the world for transport north.'

Looking around with a smile, she breathed in the faint whiff of tar, ozone and exhaust fumes. 'Reminds me of Scottish fishing villages when I was a child, except they only had trawlers and no sunshine.'

They settled at a corner table outside a restaurant, Herk sitting with his back against the wall.

'Old habits die hard?' she asked.

He ignored her and said: '*Moules frites* are good.'

Tire laughed. 'Almost fish and chips but not quite.'

Over lunch, as they happily fingered their way through a mountainous bowl of mussels, he quizzed her about her meeting with St Clair.

'Not much to tell,' she said, munching on a chip. 'Said he was a court appointee, only met my father once, was a third cousin of my mother and had never met her. The money came from my maternal grandmother's estate and my mother's life insurance.' She sighed. 'And my father's savings. Though I did think he lied about my father. Said he wasn't a mechanic, but didn't know what he did.'

'Why did you think he was a mechanic?' Herk asked absently, looking around the busy street.

'One of the newspaper reports of the trial described him as an aeronautical engineer.'

He turned to her, exasperated, and said: 'Engineer covers everything from the guy who designed the aeroplane to the guy who checks the screws. He could have been an overseer, or an inventor, for all you know.'

'OK, OK,' she replied. 'That can get investigated later.' Or not, she thought to herself. 'I've got my father back in his box for the time being. The more important matter is Paul Stone. St Clair warned me against going in too heavy, unless I had enough to topple him. And the young guy who turned up before I left...'

'That was the Audi?' he interrupted.

'You were watching?' she asked, intrigued.

'Not really, but I saw it go down the road.'

She looked at him suspiciously.

'Well, what did he say? Who was he?'

'Said he was an ex-colleague, Jake Harrister, mid-thirties, possibly gay. He said, when he was showing me out, that a Scottish journalist investigating Stone had been killed in a car crash.'

'Help my god, they tumble like nine pins around that guy. Reckon St Clair is right. Best tread very softly or,' he gave her a straight look, 'give up all together.'

'No chance,' she said firmly, 'I've been up against some hard nuts before. I'm not letting this one go, given what he might have done to Erica. Or paid a goon to do.'

She scowled at a passing woman, who flinched and looked away discomfited. Two mopeds roared past, dodging in and out of the lingering tourist cars. Coffee came and after the waiter had cleared away the empty mussel shells and plates, he said thoughtfully: 'The mate I went to see in Sandhurst, a sergeant I served with at one point, he said they kept a special look out for St Clair's house.'

'Why?'

'He didn't know. But he's clearly not just a retired paper-pusher. There must be security implications. Smells like MI5. And Harrister is a name that rings a bell with me somewhere.' He scratched his head and rubbed his lips, then raised a hand for the bill. 'I can't place him. I did work for an intelligence officer at one point, maybe he had contacts with him. It'll come to me.'

Back in the car they circled back round the bay, back onto the main route and through a short tunnel hewn out of the mountain.

'That's Cap Bear,' Herk pointed to their left where a white lighthouse glinted in the sunlight on a promontory. 'Hellish weather out there sometimes when it's blowing. Worse than the north of Scotland.'

'You served up there as well?' she asked.

He didn't answer, but kept his eyes on the curving road, dipping and weaving its way round the mountain edge above the sea. At the next village, turning right on the stony seafront, the road straightened out. They passed wineries that wafted their pungent scent into the open car windows.

Once under a railway bridge, it narrowed to a winding country road through vineyards and olive groves, with a rising mountain directly ahead. The BMW, sitting low on the tarmac, negotiated the hairpin bends smoothly. The road zigzagged, clinging to the edge of steep drops and passing almond trees planted in neat lines on a perilous slope, hedged by wild figs and scraggy cork oaks.

At the top, Herk waved a hand at the valley below. 'There you are. Spain. And not a gendarme in sight.'

'There's no border controls at all?' Tire asked, amazed.

'Nuh. And there are roads like this all the way across. They wouldn't take an articulated lorry, but it saves all that fuss at the main crossing after Le Boulou. You can get held up for hours there in summer. The customs guys and the policía

poking their noses into car boots. Right pain. Mind you, after the Madrid bombing it wasn't surprising and the Basque terrorists used to be a worry as well.'

A huge brown bird hung lazily in the sky in the distance, circling so slowly it was almost at a standstill. Tire peered and said: 'Perhaps an eagle. Might even be a lammergeyer. They've got broader tails, but I can't see at this angle.'

'Which would mean what exactly?' he asked.

She chuckled. 'Off on your omens again? Eagles are majestic and a good sign. Lammergeyers? They're vultures, scavenging after dead carcasses, cleaning up decay. The Egyptians and Romans thought they were lucky. Sacred to the mother goddess. Protective. All about renewal, death and rebirth.'

'You're a walking encyclopaedia,' he replied, admiringly.

The bird disappeared slowly over the hill into the next valley. She wound down the window and lit a cigarette, blowing the smoke into the passing breeze. Feeling suddenly self-conscious, she said: 'I grew up with birds, on holiday anyway in the Western Isles. There were thousands of them, hundreds of thousands. I felt connected to them and later I read them up.'

'But you don't believe in omens; apart from astrology, I mean?'

She nudged his arm and laughed. 'Not that I'd admit to publicly. Though if I was honest, and I don't know why I'm telling you this...' He grinned. '...I have seen birds and dead animals at times that fitted with what the astrology was saying. Tiresias, the old Greek seer, had the gift of prophecy by the birds. There's a whole mysterious world out there that isn't talked about. Astrology is just a touch more respectable.'

The well-surfaced single track descended quickly, crossing a ford, passed a farm with Charolais cows grazing on the river pasture, then through several rustic Spanish villages sitting amid acres of vines. Tire could feel her tension rising again. Once onto the main drag for Figueres, the signs for the Dali Museum flashed past. She checked her phone for emails.

'No joy on Louis Neroni yet from Matt,' she said. 'Paul Stone's stepson. He's traced his birth certificate to Orvieto in Italy, which was a lucky guess from a cutting about his father's death. They evidently don't do central registers out there, so you have to search village by village. He'll try immigration into France and UK after his mother's death, on both the Stone and Neroni names, and see if he can turn up anything.'

'Bit of a long shot, that,' Herk remarked sourly.

She gave him an amused glance. 'Hey, I've been researching for two decades. You just keep pursuing every angle till you get lucky.'

Another email caught her attention and she flicked up and down it, reading it several times. 'That is strange,' she said thoughtfully.

'What?'

Her hesitation caused him to look at her irritably. 'OK, OK, I'm just trying to work it out. Paul Stone funds research into Alzheimer's drugs, presumably to improve memory or at least stop it deteriorating. Perhaps because of his dear old ma. But he also funds research in Mexico into drugs to suppress memory. Why would he do that?'

Herk shrugged. 'Sounds quite sensible. Some of the lads who were suffering from PTSD after Kosovo and Afghanistan used to get medication to make the memories less overwhelming.'

'According to this, from a Mexican doctor, these drugs they are testing aren't just about dampening down the emotional affect, they are aimed at obliterating memories altogether. A bit like a chemical cosh, he says. He doesn't approve.'

The car swerved sharply to the left and Herk swore at an articulated container lorry that had pulled out in front of them with no indication.

'Fucking idiot. No discipline on Spanish roads. They're a bleeding nightmare.' He accelerated past a tailgating series of lorries and pulled into the inside lane. 'I've two questions for you. Do all these research people not cost you a fortune?'

'They're tax-deductible,' she said shortly. 'And this one came free, anyway. Next?'

'What's wrong with deleting bad memories? Some things I've seen, I never want to remember.'

After a long pause, she said: 'Your memory is your biography, your life story. If you destroy that, you aren't you any longer. Your sense of identity would be damaged.'

Herk absorbed what she said and replied: 'I don't see that. I'd be who I was before and I knew who I was back then.'

She searched for an explanation without wishing to probe too deeply. 'The point is you aren't who you were before. Your experiences have moulded you and being able to digest the memories of what happened allows you to move on as a whole person. Deleting memories would be a bit like amputating a limb, and maybe worse, since messing with the brain has all sorts of unforeseen consequences.'

'Well, I don't know about digest, speaking personally. More like vomit them out and get rid of them,' he said cheerfully. 'But, as you say, it begs the question of why Stone is so interested. And I could see how it could be misused. There's a lot of the top brass would be happy if some of us forgot quite a few things they threw us into.'

The three-lane motorway hurtled south, flashing past pine forests and rivers, with occasional old-style, stone Spanish houses on either side, their rural idyll rudely interrupted by modern progress. The traffic started to thicken as the approaches to Barcelona drew near.

Tire was searching for an elusive piece of information that was staying irritatingly hidden. Finally she said, banging her boot on the floor: 'That's it.'

'What?'

She waved a hand above the dashboard and said: 'I'll need to take this slowly since I don't remember it too well. Wiping the past clean means you can start with a pristine new world of your own creation. It's the classic sign of a megalomaniac. It's all about control. No guilt, no responsibility for what has been. And no situations in which you were powerless. You can step across a threshold shining white and start again. Think about Tony Blair.'

'I'd rather no, thank you,' Herk replied smartly.

She could feel her heart racing as another piece of the jigsaw fell into place. This made sense. What was in Paul Stone's past that he was trying to hide?

CHAPTER 31

Underpass after underpass, the maze of subterranean tunnels that was Barcelona's answer to surface clutter kept the rush-hour traffic moving quickly. Fume-filled darkness gave way to regular patches of blue sky over roads lined with palm trees. Then back into the concrete subways burrowing across the Catalonian capital.

Out the other side into open country, they drove along the Ronda ring road following the signs for the El Prat de Lobregat airport. The arterial entrance led directly onto massive multi-tiered car parks, perched on banks of grass. They swung into the one marked C and spiralled upwards through almost-empty floors to the top level.

At the far end, a car park attendant in a visibility waistcoat was smoking a cigarette, leaning against a mud-splattered black Range Rover. Herk pulled into the bay beside and jumped out. He nodded curtly to the attendant, handed the BMW keys and gate ticket to him and gestured towards the boot. The travel bags were brought across to the Range Rover as Tire frantically scrabbled in the front for her scattered belongings. Within five minutes Herk had checked over their new transport, handed the impassive Spaniard three hundred euros in notes from the stash Tire had given him and they were on their way back down.

'That was quick,' she remarked. 'Is there anything you can't brew up?'

He grinned and said: 'It's not difficult. You just need to know the right people to contact, grease their palms and it all happens. With luck we'll swap back in four days. You needn't worry. It's got insurance for the maximum. Now for the port.'

'Why are we going there?' she asked, getting edgy about not being kept in the loop.

'I've a meeting with a guy there,' Herk answered nonchalantly. He stopped the car just before the airport exit, set the GPS and within fifteen minutes they were heading into the Port of Barcelona and passing the dock entrance. The ticket and embarkation office was crowded with milling tourists, security guards and two policía outside. Herk drove past and found a parking space, then flipped open his mobile. He found a number in his contacts and when that answered said simply: 'Black Range Rover, Spanish plates, ten cars down.' Then he lit a cigarette and waited.

Tire stared resignedly at passers-by heading for the Majorca ferry, dragging wheeled cases behind them, then jumped when Herk rolled his window down further, leant out and roared at a couple approaching them. 'Watch out, pickpockets.' The wife turned to find two skinny teenagers in dirty jeans and hooded jackets jostling them from behind and she let out an ear-splitting yell. The youths turned tail and ran, and the flustered couple gave Herk a grateful smile.

'Your good deed for the day?' Tire asked, then she jumped again when the passenger door clunked shut behind her.

'*Buenas tardes, senora*,' a deep voice said, his garlicky breath reaching over her shoulder. '*Como estas hoy, Senor Smith*?'

'Stow it, Fred. Ye can cut the pleasantries. Have you got what I asked for? Both of them?' Herk said brusquely, turning to look at him.

'Nice to see you again, Herk,' the voice replied. 'Yup, they're tucked under the seat. See you.' The door clunked again and he disappeared without Tire having seen his face.

'What the hell was that about?' she asked, bending round to try to see what had been left and failing.

'Just a bit of backup, in case we run into trouble,' he replied cheerfully, negotiating across a busy roundabout.

'You don't mean guns, do you?' she screeched. 'What the hell do you think we're going into. It's a holiday resort, for chrissakes. Do you not think you're getting a bit paranoid?'

He swung onto the Ronda Littoral, then settled at a steady 110, before replying: 'I'd rather be hyper-cautious than caught out, that's all. Don't get your knickers in a twist. If I don't need them, then they'll go back and no worries. I just didn't want to bring them across the border, that's all.'

Her claustrophobia was making her brain fog over and she cursed herself for deciding to come on this idiotic jaunt. The road signs for the A7, direction Girona and France, came up. For a moment she almost suggested going home. How had Herk managed to morph from helper to control freak in charge? She had always operated alone in the past. Now she was being ordered about like a squaddie and ferried around as if she was a submissive wife. Her sense of humour got the better of her and she giggled at the irony. She was a sucker for new experiences so she might as well enjoy this one.

Eventually she said weakly: 'Where are we going now? We're not expected till tomorrow morning.'

'Begur,' he replied. 'Fred knows a decent hostelry and he booked us in. Then we can do a recce first thing before we get to Castell Pajol. It's only fifteen kilometres away. I need to know where the roads are in and out. In case we need a fast exit.'

What was Herk's gut telling him? Her head grated. She was not going to allow herself to get infected by his pumped-up anxiety. If she worried about threats round every corner she couldn't function. The worst that could happen was a wasted trip.

CHAPTER 32

The sheen on the bronze statue of a reclining man, exaggerated by an overhead spotlight, gave the impression of a heavily oiled body. Although nude, one muscled thigh was drawn up to cover his genitals and his face, buried between his arms, was also hidden. The gallery was empty of people so the ten statuettes, each on their own display stand, were all visible.

Jimmy, having examined the sleeping figure minutely, moved on to view a kneeling woman, her breasts bare, the warm brown of the bronze thrown into sharp relief by the gold-coloured blindfold and gilt cloth draped discreetly just above her pubic bone. He wrinkled his nose and frowned. Loud laughter from the office at the far end made him jump.

'My dear chap,' Ricky's voice echoed round the gallery. 'I didn't realise you were here. Examining my treasures, are you? Aren't they wonderful? My cousin sent them over. They're by an Italian sculptor.'

He strode across, his camel jacket open over a black polo neck and black trousers, tossing his hair out of his eyes. He put a friendly hand on Jimmy's shoulder, smiling widely, then looked concerned.

'You don't like it?' he said.

Jimmy shook his head. 'It's that yellow brass on it, that look's too modern, I suppose. For my taste anyway.'

'Wally, what do you think?' Ricky called over his shoulder.

A stocky, ginger-haired man emerged through the door with a cigar in his hand. He had a rough, reddened face that sat uncomfortably with the loud check of his tan suit and waistcoat. Unaware or uncaring about his appearance, he carried himself with confidence and a hint of aggression.

His voice was brusque and gravelly. 'No sense in asking me, Ricky. I don't like your sculptures. At least this one's a woman. No like that obscenity.' He waved his cigar at another male nude standing erect on a marble plinth, his arm outstretched.

Jimmy moved across and leant closer to the offending statuette. 'That's Apollo,' he said quietly. 'See – he's holding a lyre.'

Wally snorted as Ricky winked at Jimmy, then moved forward with his hand outstretched. 'I'm Wally Strang. I like your paintings. Ricky here said you'd do me one specially.' It wasn't a question, so Jimmy nodded politely, moving back a step.

'What's more,' Wally said, advancing towards him and putting an arm round his shoulders, 'I think we could be related.'

Jimmy's body crumpled slightly, his mind spiked with alarm then diffused into a jumble of panic. He let out an audible moan.

'There, there,' Wally patted him awkwardly on the back. 'No need to get upset. One of my sisters married a drunk called Black and I think one of their kids ended up in the Hall for being dumb, like. Bunch of no-hopers that family, total losers the lot of them. That could be you.'

Jimmy turned away, his head swimming and barely able to focus, holding onto the corner of one of the display stands to keep him from falling over. A cacophony of bagpipes and drums blared up, jarring him further. It stopped after a few seconds as Wally started shouting into his mobile phone.

'It's alright,' Ricky whispered in his ear, 'he's not very tactful, Wally, but he's OK. He's rich and he likes your work.'

The paintings on the wall in front of him seemed to be pulsating, from light to shade, the images distorting and blurring. After a minute of heavy breathing, he began to see more clearly. His eye flickered down the wall only to see his watercolour of Lachie's grave. Wincing, he looked away towards the bronzes further up the gallery. Hesitantly, as if he feared his legs wouldn't hold him, he moved from one display stand to the next, putting a hand out to steady himself.

A badly executed statuette of a female warrior with sword, shield and a large bird perched behind her helmet, was multicoloured in different patinas, looking more like a videogame toy than a work of art. He shook his head and walked more certainly on to the furthest corner, where a small, mottled-green bronze of a heavy horse bearing a barelegged man in a toga made him smile.

'One of my kids wanted that one,' Wally's voice grated behind him. 'She said it reminded her of Princess Zena from the television.'

'No,' Jimmy said calmly, turning back round, 'It's Athena, the goddess. See – you can tell from the owl and the snakes on her shield.'

'My, my, aren't you the knowledgeable one? Doesn't sound like the Black family at all,' Wally said grudgingly, giving him a doubtful look.

'Where did you learn all this, Jimmy?' Ricky asked, with a placatory smile.

Jimmy stood silent, his mouth twitching as he tried to think what to say, then he blurted out: 'Truth is, I don't think I am Jimmy Black.'

Elly, who had been sitting unnoticed in a chair by the front window, came across to put a steadying hand on his elbow. With a catch in his voice, he said: 'I think I'm him, Lachie, down there.' He pointed to the painting of the tombstone.

Wally growled an exasperated 'What?' while Ricky blinked several times before saying with forced cheerfulness: 'I think we all need a cup of tea.'

In the office, Elly took over the explanations as Jimmy sat huddled miserably beside her. Wally's cigar smoke swirled and eddied as he listened intently, with narrowed and occasionally flashing eyes. His anger reddened his cheeks and he leant towards Jimmy with a look of naked hostility.

Jimmy cowered back, muttering: 'I'm sorry. I didn't mean to mislead anyone. It's all just come to light recently.'

'That's not the problem, son,' Wally spat out, jabbing his cigar uncomfortably close to his face. 'The problem is someone bumped off one of my family. And I did nothing about it. It's bad for my reputation, that.' He sat back, a deep frown creasing his forehead, his mouth pulled tight and rubbing his chin with a stubby, calloused hand.

He gave an unpleasant smile and said: 'No worries. I'll find out who did this and see to him. I've got ears on the ground and contacts in the polis. Someone will know. You reckon it might be this man in your head had something to do with it, or was it just a random mugging?'

Jimmy shrugged and said cautiously: 'I dunno. Maybe.'

Suddenly, Wally jumped to his feet saying he had to go, stubbing his cigar out carelessly in the copper ashtray on the office desk. He put a firm hand on Jimmy's shoulder and said: 'I don't care you're not a relative. Frankly, I'm relieved. I couldn't believe that lot would produce any talent. I still want a painting from you, the bigger the better. Ricky says you'll do me an oil. He's got the keys to one of my flats you can use as a studio. If you need any protection, just give me a shout.'

He strode out of the door without a backwards glance. The atmosphere in the office relaxed as he left and Ricky slumped back in his seat, fanning a brochure rather dramatically in front of his face.

'What the hell do we do about your name, then?' he asked, his eyes wide in mock puzzlement. 'It's all over the publicity. We got great coverage, by the way, for your exhibition, and a buyer for this one.' A clutch of cuttings and printouts from several websites was thrust across the desk. On top was a photograph of Jimmy beside the painting of the giant aloe and two nude statues from an online London arts magazine.

Jimmy shrank back, half-turning away from his success as if embarrassed, and fiddled with his scarf.

'What's better, they want the copyright as well as the painting. In one way that's a pain, since it means we can't make prints. But I tripled the price since he wanted a total buyout. That will be shipped to London this week. And there'll be nothing to stop you doing another similar in oils in future.'

The sound of small steel balls bouncing off each other filled the silence as Ricky's finger strummed the strings on a desk ornament.

'Your name?' He sighed. 'Too late to change it now. We'll just have to regard Jimmy Black as a stage name. And the real Lachie stays out of sight in the background.' He sipped at his tea and put the cup down with a clatter. His hair was pushed back off his forehead with an excited gesture. 'But what a story you've got to tell. It'd be a pity to keep it quiet.'

'I'm saying nothing.'

Jimmy's emphatic response brought a flinch, then a placatory smile across the desk. The metal balls clanked more loudly as they ricocheted off one another.

Eventually Ricky said: 'You're right. Your decision entirely. But as my old granny from Umbria used to say, *mal comune, mezzo gaudio*. A shared trouble is half joy. We'll catch up this afternoon and I'll show you your new studio.'

As they retraced their steps home past the blackened walls of the Art School, Jimmy kept his head steadily down, murmuring under his breath, '*mal commune, mezzo gaudio*' over and over again until Elly yanked at his arm.

CHAPTER 33

Next morning Tire was wakened at 5.30 am by a knock on her bedroom door. A tepid shower woke her fully and she dressed quickly in clean jeans and a glittery white T-shirt she had bought specially for the occasion, with a lightweight, navy velvet jacket on top. She fished in her travel bag for gilt chains and bangles and a huge navy cotton sunhat, which had to be yanked into shape.

Herk was waiting with a cup of coffee, which was all that was on offer. They spent the next two hours driving up and down the coast, along the only surfaced road leading to the motorway, and then along three heavily pitted tracks marked on his ordnance survey map. Two of them ended abruptly inland, collapsed into giant craters by the previous winter's floods. Eventually he pronounced himself satisfied and they stopped at a roadside café for a breakfast of coffee, so strong it made Tire blink, and sweet pastries.

'Now, let's run over the story one more time, just to check we're on the same page,' he said half an hour later, as they sat outside the impressive locked gates of Castell Pajol, waiting for an answer to the entryphone. The name was discreetly painted on a board half-hidden by a sprawling clump of bougainvillea, so clearly not intended to attract passing trade. A huge *privado* sign was on the opposite wall.

'I'll do the chat,' she said firmly. 'Photographers follow along behind and do as they're told. You'll have to get back into humility mode.' She beamed at him, pleased to see him grimace, and continued as the gates swung open. 'We've taken the chance since we're in the vicinity to photograph part of one of the pilgrim routes to Santiago di Compostela. Not all the way. Just Olot to the shrine of the Black Madonna of Montserrat. Which is why we have an off-road vehicle. Got that?'

He touched his forehead, 'Yes, ma'am.'

'Both of us are freelances, so work for various magazines. What's your name, by the way? I'm supposedly Patricia Haddington.'

The long, gravelled drive curved and wound through heavily wooded land until the castle came into view, an enormous rectangle of ancient, red, stone blocks, with its lower reaches fanned outwards like a skirt to give a firm grip on the ground. Tall, elegant cypresses grew to one side on clipped grass intermingled with giant pots with red flowering plants. The extensive lawn on the other side ran down to the cliff edge, with a few parasol pine trees leaning exuberantly over the drop above a glittering blue sea below. Just visible behind the castle was a large swimming pool and beyond that several whitewashed villas.

'Harry Connor,' Herk whispered in her ear as a trim young man with slicked-back hair, and dressed in black trousers and a neat black waistcoat over a white shirt, approached the car. He offered to carry their travel bags in but Herk refused curtly, saying his camera equipment was breakable and he'd manage himself, after he had parked the car. The bellboy looked flustered, but after a moment shrugged and indicated to the left of the castle, where the gravel path led into a sunken parking area.

Tire put on her brightest smile and walked ahead through the open door, a massive, varnished oak affair heavily studded with black iron straps and knobs. You wouldn't hack through that in a hurry, she thought. She was ushered through to a large interior sitting room, designer-furnished with white sofas and chairs, antique chests and bow-legged coffee tables with tiled tops. An archway up steps led out into a glass-covered, sunlit sitting area looking out to sea. The heavy, dark terracotta tiles on the floor, combined with the bleached walls and furniture, gave it a luxuriously restful feel. Flamenco guitar music was playing softly.

Another young man glided in to greet her, introducing himself as the assistant manager. He apologised, saying Mr Harman Stone and Javier Manresa, the manager, had been called away to Barcelona and would be back late in the afternoon. In the meantime, her bags had been put into an upstairs room and she should feel free to wander at will round the castle and grounds although respecting the privacy of the guests at villas two, five and nine. The other eleven villas were empty this week.

Accepting his offer of a coffee, she indicated the sun room, which she noted had ashtrays on the tables, and moved through. Five minutes later Herk joined her, carrying a large camera case with an expensive-looking Nikon with zoom lenses hanging round his neck. He laid it carefully on an adjoining chair along with another small digital camera he took from his pocket.

'I can't see this as the place for poor kids and their impoverished grandparents, myself,' Herk said. 'Maybe they have a barn out back they stick them in when he's doing his charity weeks.'

'Me neither. It just gets odder and odder,' she remarked quietly, although there were no other guests around. 'Still, where there's a mystery there's usually a good story. So we'd best go explore. Lunch as per Spanish style is at least four hours away.'

The property was extensive, ranging along the cliff top for almost a third of a mile, with fourteen hacienda-style villas, each with a pool discreetly shaded from the others by shrubs, pergolas covered in flowering climbers and small trees. There was another large, brick-built building tucked out of sight behind the car park, which seemed to be staff quarters. Herk raised and lowered his camera every so often. At the far end the trees thickened into a wood, well pruned but less manicured, with a rutted track leading away from the villas. The remnants of a ruined tower were just visible through a gap.

'That might give me a decent shot,' he said, 'if I can climb up it.'

'Is that necessary?' she whispered.

'It's an excuse, like?' he whispered back giving her a withering look. 'I want to see where that track goes.'

She turned to walk back towards the cliff, shaking her head at his constant need to find escape routes wherever he went. A paunchy jogger in white T-shirt and blue shorts came pounding towards her round the perimeter of the grass, breathing heavily. Nodding politely, she was about to walk on when he stopped, said hello hoarsely and then bent to lean his hands on his knees.

Smiling sympathetically, she said: 'How far is that?'

'Gawd, eight miles I think, been going round so often I'm dizzy.' An American drawl petered out as he heaved and puffed. Finally he straightened up, wiped his hand on his shorts and extended it. 'Hi, I'm Chip Nathon. You're new here and clearly not going running just yet.' He looked at her appreciatively and smiled.

'No, I'm a travel writer, here to do a puff. My name is T… Trez, really. That's my nickname anyway.' Why the hell did I do that? she wondered, irritated at herself. Great undercover I'd make.

'I just love English nicknames. Everyone over your way has them.' He gave her a boyish grin, which sat oddly on his fleshy middle-aged face. 'Might see you over lunch, Trez. Best keep going before I collapse.' Off he panted.

Herk joined her ten minutes later, a slight grin on his face, saying the track ran close to the road outside with only a flimsy wooden fence at the far end and no ditches either side.

Lunch came not a moment too soon at 2 pm in a high-ceilinged dining room with wooden beams straddling overhead. The overall effect was sombre, despite the white walls, with the antique tables and sideboards in carved dark walnut. The gilt-framed portraits and still lifes spread liberally around had pitch black backgrounds. Tire and Herk sat opposite a forbidding Spanish matriarch of long ago. Herk murmured something uncomplimentary about his mother while Tire waved to Chip Nathon, who was dining on his own several tables away near the window, the only other occupant.

The menu was substantial and pages long, so Tire ordered from the shorter specialities card, with asparagus for starters and sardines for the main course. Herk said dinner would be a long way off, probably not till 10 pm, so best to fill up when there was a chance. He proceeded to munch his way happily through shellfish soup, and a hefty sausage and bean casserole followed by a custard flan with caramel sauce.

She was about to order her second coffee when Chip Nathon stood up and gestured to the outside terrace. Leaving Herk to finish his family-sized dessert, she followed, lighting a cigarette with relief when she walked through the open glass doors onto the stone patio, which was scattered with expensive, wickerwork chairs and with two alabaster statues of classical male nudes at either end.

'Now, that's what I like to see,' Chip Nathon boomed, reaching into the top pocket of his flowery beach shirt for a packet of cigarillos.

Initial questions to him about his business and knowledge about Castell Pajol were met with a friendly stonewall. He worked vaguely in IT, but too boring to discuss on vacation. He'd been before, but no specifics. He certainly didn't want mentioned in her puff piece. Not as bluff and dumb as he looks, she thought.

So she changed tack and gushed about walking and photographing the old pilgrim route to Santiago in bite-sized pieces. The Black Virgin at Montserrat, the magnificent scenery, the visit she hoped to make to the Cathar fortress at Montsegur across the border in France on the way back. Within ten minutes, he was relaxing and flirting with her in a rather clumsy way.

'Ever come across our way?' he asked with a glint in his eye, moving his knee closer.

She knew it was a risk, but she took a deep breath and said: 'Yeah, sometimes. I have a friend in the film business and he's having a wrap party for his latest movie in Big Sur sometime soon.'

'You don't say! What's his name?' he said, looking impressed, and moved his chair closer.

'Tom Bateson.'

'Isn't that a coincidence? I know him too.'

Oh shit, she thought. I'll have to phone Tom and get him to lie about me.

'Well, when I say I know him,' Chip waved his cigar in the air. 'Have met him a couple of times. Throws a great party. There must have been three hundred at the last one.'

Ah, an American best friend, that's easier.

The waiter hovered with more coffee and Nathon ordered himself a chocolate tequila liqueur, after which he started to open up. He was a major player, he informed her, in IT, with a software company in Santa Cruz and a biotechnology business nearby.

She flattered him, playing girlish ignorance about biotechnology. It always appalled her how well it worked. Was he helping Paul Stone with his wonderful work for Alzheimer's drugs, she asked ingenuously. He gave her a considered look and said no, different field altogether. Then he clammed up.

Had he vacationed in any of the other Cerigo resorts, she twittered. She had heard they were wonderful. Sure, he said slowly, the Big Sur resort was one of his favourite weekend breaks. The Scottish one, too, in Wester Ross, great for shooting, he slurred, then paused uneasily before adding, although not for the weather.

'Truly international,' she twittered. 'But then Harman is half-Iranian. It'll give him a global perspective. And Paul Stone came from the Middle East as well, didn't he?'

'Don't know about that,' he frowned into his drink. 'His mother was French, across the border from here. Arles something or other. At least that's where he buried her a few years back.' He shot her a suspicious look. 'Hasn't his office given you his bio?'

'Yes, indeed. I just haven't absorbed it all,' she said hastily, with an ingratiating smile. 'It is so kind of Harman Stone to give poor children holidays here. He and his father do so much good, it's touching.'

Nathon looked out to sea, yawned and replied: 'The charity comes mainly from pa. Kind of an obsession with him. Junior isn't quite a chip off the old block.' He blinked several times and yawned again. 'Think I'm sagging. Must go and grab a nap.'

He stood up unsteadily, hitched up his trousers, promising to meet over dinner, then hesitated before he left, saying with an edge of sarcasm: 'My ole daddy used to say a hard-boiled egg has a heart of gold as well. Ha ha! Not always easy to tell the difference.' And he stumbled off.

Now there goes a troubled man, she thought.

***

'We're outta here,' Herk said urgently behind her. He put a hand on her shoulder to stop her reacting. 'Stone Junior is back and he's got two heavies with him who were the ones watching your flat. They don't know me but they'll know you. I collected your bag without being seen so we need to get to the car and leave. Here's your sunhat. Ram it down over your face.'

They left the sun room by the garden door and walked quickly round the front of the castle with Tire keeping her head low, past the giant pots and cypresses down into the car park. She fished in the glove compartment and found her spare, oversized sunglasses. Then turned up her collar.

Dammit, Herk had been right all along, she thought, her stomach tight with tension as they bumped out of the car park into the wood and onto the muddy track with gouged-out ruts that even the Range Rover strained to plough across. The surfaced road outside was visible through a few scraggy bushes and a dilapidated wooden fence. He turned sharply left to crash through it.

'Don't think it's worth the risk taking time to put that back,' he said. 'We'd best take that farm track across to the motorway. It's just along here. And get off the main roads in case they come looking since they'll have heard the noise.'

Shit, shit, shit, she thought. We've blown it. Now they'll know we're after them. Only after ten minutes of being thrown around as the vehicle bounced through potholes, ruts and craters at speed on a muddy trail heading inland did the penny drop. There was now no doubt that it had been Harman Stone.

CHAPTER 34

Huddled in the back of Janet Birch's car, Elly was looking miserable, not bothering to clear the mist from the inside of the window. Jimmy fidgeted restlessly in the front passenger seat, tense with anticipation and dread. Inner Glasgow merged into outer Glasgow as they sped down the M8, houses and industrial buildings giving way finally to dull, damp, green countryside as their route veered off onto the M74 heading south. He barely registered the surroundings as they pulled off the motorway, heading for the village of Carston. Half a mile beyond, the grilled gates of Dunlothian Hall, set in a high wall with broken glass cemented on top, came into view. Janet Birch kept driving, which made Jimmy look sharply at her.

She indicated ahead. Within two minutes they were at the back entrance where the wall was broken down and one rusty gate, detached from its hinges, had been thrown to one side. The other was missing. Driving slowly along a potholed track, with overgrown, twisted rhododendrons encroaching on either side, it took fully five minutes of bumping and scraping to clear the dismal tunnel of shrubs.

Elly had her eyes shut and Jimmy was staring fixedly at the dashboard as the car stopped. With an effort, his jaw clenched, he looked up and blinked. The massive crenellated central portion of the Hall, rising three floors above the weed-strewn ground, was crumbling, with broken windows and one turret leaning at a perilous angle. The lower wings were even more dilapidated, with sandstone cornices weathered to nothing in patches and glass littered among the debris below.

'We'll need to watch,' Janet Birch remarked briskly, 'and stand well back, since the structure isn't safe anymore.'

She took Elly's arm, walked down a few steps and left her sitting on a low stone wall facing determinedly away from the Hall. Jimmy was standing rigid, with one hand leaning on the car bonnet and looking up at the cumbersome structure, a complicated jigsaw of blocks, his eyes running up the square columns and across the heavy Neo-Gothic detail. It should have been ornate, soaring upwards in grandeur. Instead it looked leaden, as if it pressed heavily on a ground struggling to bear its weight.

Eventually he said: 'It's just so... I dunno, nothing really.'

Janet leant towards him expectantly.

'I'd expected to be scared and it was a scary place. An awful place. But it's lost whatever it had. Can't be its soul, since it didn't have one, but there's just nothing here...' He petered out, sounding puzzled and almost disappointed.

'Do you remember the first day you came here?' Janet's voice cut into his thoughts.

He turned angrily. 'Now, don't you be pushing be your questions. I need time.'

The easterly wind blew a gust of leaves across the long-derelict frontage and up onto their clothes. He brushed one off his face and started to walk towards the far wing with an arched entrance at the end. Then he turned right down the main drive, stepping round puddles of muddy water on the pitted surface and over piles of stones uprooted by weather and neglect. Almost as if he was counting the steps he marched on, then he turned suddenly round to face the towering asylum, distance allowing him to see it in its entirety. Janet Birch, who had been following, moved quickly behind him.

'It's odd,' he remarked, 'when you think about it, that me and Elly spent most of our lives in a castle. Not quite aristos, but still.' He chuckled grimly, his eyes roving constantly and rhythmically back and forth from one end to the other.

After a minute or two his head jerked involuntarily, as if the plates inside were grating. A fencepost gave him an anchor, as his lightheaded feeling of several days back in Largs returned. Sunlight and blue skies broke through the drabness, flooding the ground with warmth. The chill, hostile grey of the Hall, for a moment, shone ochre with the turrets rounding into a more amiable cluster. Lush vegetation grew on the steep slope below.

Then the vision was gone just as suddenly, as if one side of his mind had shut down. The dank surroundings returned and the pervasive smell of stagnant water and rotting vegetation enveloped him in a cloud of shame. To his embarrassment, tears started to roll down his face.

Janet Birch stood ten feet away, not moving to comfort him, waiting.

He sniffed, wiping his nose on the back of his free hand and muttered: 'I don't know how any of us survived, honest to god I don't. It was like living in a labour camp. Nothing to cheer you. No family, no enough food ever and freezing cold most of the time, since they didn't give us decent clothes.'

'No one to hug you,' she said tentatively.

His chest convulsed and his cheeks streamed with tears. His head hung down and he clung to the fencepost as it were a life raft.

'Your mother hugged you before you came here, didn't she?' she said softly, fishing in her pocket for a handkerchief.

Drawing a shuddering deep breath and then blowing his nose noisily, he looked across to where Elly was sitting patiently.

'She did that,' he said slowly, 'often.' A look of wonder gradually crossed his face. 'Do you know, I haven't been able to see her all these years. Yet here she is in my mind, clear as day. She was very beautiful with long dark hair. And she lived where there was sunshine, not dreary like here.'

'Can you remember where that was, Lachie?' Janet's eager tone made him shudder. Her use of the name Lachie jangled his head and his mounting confusion threatened to push him into a full-blown panic. When she repeated the question, he clenched his fist and stamped his foot like a frustrated child.

'But it is really important, Lachie,' she said in a wheedling voice.

'My name isn't Lachie,' he shouted. 'Don't call me that.'

'What did your mother call you?'

'Lookay,' he said, forcing the words out.

Her face was three feet away, a hazy image flickering in and out of focus. He wanted to back away, but without the post for support he was scared he would fall over.

'She was Italian, like the gardens you paint?' He nodded dumbly. 'Do you mean Luce, like *luce del sole* – sunlight?'

Tears were streaming down his cheeks and his breath was ragged, causing him to gasp for air.

'Was Luce your real name, or a nickname?'

His head started to shake from side to side, the spasms outside his control. The rough wooden post was sending splinters into his hand.

'Take a deep breath. You're nearly there. How did she introduce you? Do you remember her name, or your father's? Where you lived?'

A spurt of anger began to force through his confusion. 'Leave me alone.' He drew himself up straight and glared at her. 'I can't be doing with all your prodding.'

'This is important.'

'Maybe to you, but it's not going to help me. I'm not doing this anymore.'

As he steadied himself against the post, ready to walk off, the sunshine came back. He was about five years old, dressed in a dark suit, with a white shirt and bow tie, standing beside a tall man he didn't like, his mother close by in a long cream dress with a veil.

The words that came to his mind he had no intention of speaking, but they came out before he could stop himself. 'Signora Neroni. Alessia from Orvieto. And I'm Louis.' His tone was flat, his expression detached. 'And now I'm going. That's enough.'

An insistent tug at his arm nearly pulled him off balance.

'You can't stop here. This is hugely significant and exciting. You must see that.'

'What I see is Elly over there getting cold. We need to take her home. That's what's important. Not your meddling.'

He pulled himself angrily away from the fencepost, catching the edge of his palm on a rusty nail. The pain made him pause and he watched the blood flow down into the sleeve of his coat. Then he saw his mother again, blood running down her face, her head twisted to one side as she lay crumpled on a stone path. He sank to his knees, covering his head with both hands, his body shaking with racking sobs.

Elly came rushing across and pushed Janet Birch, who was standing over him, to one side. She knelt beside him on the rough ground, put an arm round his shoulders and held him tightly. It took several minutes for his tears to subside and his rasping breaths to slow down. He remained bent double, his head hidden in his coat, his arms wrapped tightly round his chest.

Eventually Elly, with some difficulty, persuaded him onto his feet. He sat speechless and miserable for the forty-minute drive back to Glasgow. Not even the nurse's kindly questions in the hospital accident wing provoked any response as she cleaned and bandaged his hand, mopped the blood from his face and gave him a tetanus shot.

One phrase ran insistently through his head that his mother had said to him on her wedding day, *'Chia ama, crede'*, and had made him translate it into English for his new life ahead. He who loves, trusts.

CHAPTER 35

The track twisted and turned round giant boulders and dipped through rain-gouged craters. In places it disappeared under soil washed down from above, then started to climb in serpentine bends uphill. Herk kept checking the mirror as he held onto the bucking wheel. The ground fell steeply away on Tire's side the higher they went and the muddy surface narrowed, barely clinging to the mountain edge. She shut her eyes several times as disaster seemed inevitable. The vehicle felt wider than the track holding them up. At least twice she thought the outer wheels had gone off into space.

Nearing the top they came round a bend, shielded by trees, to find a bulky jeep blocking their way. Herk swerved to the left onto rock-strewn terrain, muttering curses. They slid rather than drove down precipitous slopes, skidding across mud and rubble. The roar behind indicated the jeep was keeping pace with their descent.

'Get the guns out from under the back seat,' he said. Tire loosened her seat belt and wriggled round with difficulty, trying to jam one leg against the footrest to keep from being thrown around. Her fingers were just reaching for the canvas bags when there was a crash. It was the last thing she remembered as she was flung backwards towards the windscreen. Everything went black.

A foul taste of muddy saltwater in her mouth confused her, as her senses gradually returned. Her nose seemed to be filled with sand. How much time had passed she had no idea, but everything hurt. Her left shoulder was searing pain down her arm. Her body was bent across a hard, uneven surface and her head, echoing like a drum, was hanging face down off the edge. Struggling to breathe and clear her vision, she heard a murmur of voices and heavy breathing. Old instincts kicked in and she lay still. Gradually she recalled the car and the crash. But she was clearly no longer there. The air smelt musty and acrid. The taste in her mouth, she worked out, was blood. Opening one eye she saw a rough wall two feet away, its plaster smeared with animal muck. Below her was a filthy stone floor with a few handfuls of greying straw and a broken farm plough, rusty and disintegrating.

A harsh, roared curse from Herk behind her and a smell of burning made her tense, which sent waves of agony down her back.

A guttural voice was speaking. 'Why were you at the Castell?'

A sharp thud of a hand hitting flesh and another curse.

She needed to keep her head clear and think. Her eyes searched the floor for a loose brick, any kind of weapon. Footsteps behind her brought the warmth and smell of a body standing over her, so she shut her eyes again. A prod in her back was almost unbearable, but she didn't react. The voice said: 'She is still out of it. We wait till she wakens up. Then we have fun'. A laugh was followed by the footsteps moving away. Then she heard two men speaking in the distance in what sounded like Russian or one of the Slavic languages.

Making a supreme effort, she levered herself up with her right hand, pulling on the decaying bags of hardened cement onto which she had been thrown. She swung her legs over the edge and turned round. Herk was lying shirtless, face up on a narrow table, his arms pulled back underneath, his hands tied with cable. His chest was smeared with blood and dirt, the flesh reddened in patches. Wondering whether she was capable of standing up she looked at him and, unbelievably, he smiled and whispered: 'Just take it calmly now. Come over her and untie me. Now.'

Gritting her teeth, she obeyed. Her legs trembled as she moved across and knelt down to tug at the cable with her one good hand. She pulled feverishly at the knot, but the wire cable would not budge. It was too tightly entwined. Sweat was pouring down her face and one broken fingernail, torn away at the root, was dripping blood. She needed a lever. Searching around, she saw a rusty nail sticking out of the wall, but it was firmly stuck.

'Over there. That implement.' Herk's eyes swivelled across to the far wall. She limped across to the sacks of cement, sat down awkwardly and pulled hard at one narrow shard of metal on the plough which, after several yanks, came away with a loud grating sound. Wiping the blood and sweat from her hand on her jeans, she stood up and swayed, as dizziness threatened to topple her over. She sat back down, breathing in to clear her head. Crawling seemed easier, so she hauled herself across on her hands and knees. Ignoring his stifled grunts, she inserted the metal spike into the cable knot and with several desperate wrenches pulled it apart. He sat up quickly and untied his feet.

He grabbed his T-shirt, which was lying on the floor, put it on and whispered calmly: 'Now we're halfway there.' He picked up a short, metal fencepost from the floor and handed it to her, then walked to a corner where a rusty pickaxe was leaning against the wall. 'Stay behind me at all times. Got it?' He nodded to her, his eyes glinting. He gestured her to a position behind the door.

The two men were laughing outside, then the sound of scraping on the ground and panting brought them closer to the outhouse. Herk stood with the pickaxe, blunt side up, ready to swing. The first man reversed in the door dragging a heavy battery. He was nearly inside when Herk brought the rusty iron down hard on the back of his neck with a terrible crack. Then he stepped into the doorway and threw it forcefully at the second man, the pointed end catching him mid-chest.

Tire thought she was going to throw up as waves of nausea spiralled up into her head. She shut her eyes, clinging onto a metal hook on the wall. A gurgling, croaking sound from outside seemed to fill the air.

'C'mon now,' Herk's voice was kindly and controlled. 'Why don't you go and sit outside over there, while I sort out this mess.'

He put a hand under her elbow and led her across the doorway. She kept her eyes firmly averted from the growing pool of blood outside and leant gratefully against him till they reached a flat stone with a grassy bank behind, facing away from the bodies. She sank down and leant back against the soft green.

Herk returned with a can of Coke and a chocolate bar from the Range Rover and said with a wry chuckle: 'Caffeine and sugar, that's what you need. I won't be long.'

She sat weakly, hurting in so many places it all seemed to merge into one overpowering ache. Time drifted past. A loud crunch of metal made her wince, but the effort of turning round was too great. Then an engine started, stuttered and then powered up again.

'Right, here's what's happening.' Herk sat down beside her. 'Can you drive the Range Rover with that arm? Not far, just up the hill a bit. If you can't, I'll do it and walk back.'

'And leave me with them? I don't think so,' she exclaimed, coming back to life. 'What's the plan?'

'Well, they're both dead so they won't harm you and I'll take them with me,' he said, putting a hand lightly on her good shoulder. 'I thought best to make it look like an accident. I can push the jeep off that steep slope up there and with luck they won't be found for days and the injuries could just be their vehicle somersaulting down the hill. The policía here don't tend to be over fussy.'

He walked her over to the Range Rover, giving her a hand up. She sat for a moment waiting for the throbs to subside. He leant in and said: 'Just take it very slow and first gear all the way so you won't have to change. Keep both hands on the wheel. But wait till I'm ready behind you with the jeep.'

Her sense of time had slowed to a dreamy trance so she waited, only glancing once in the mirror to see Herk drag a body to the jeep. After his shout, she started cautiously up the steep slope, keeping a tight grip on the wheel with her right hand and praying her left would not give way. She drove at a torturous snail's pace for what seemed like an eternity, then joined the original track, pointing upwards in the direction they had intended to take and stopped.

Herk, driving behind her, turned right and disappeared. Ten minutes later he returned on foot and she slid with difficulty across into the passenger seat.

'Well, that was good and bad,' he remarked as he accelerated, waving a hand behind him. She looked back with a wince, to see a plume of smoke rising up above the trees.

'Went down a good hundred feet, turned over a few times and then caught fire. They won't get much in the way of forensics out of that, especially if they're not looking. I just hope it doesn't alert anyone too soon.'

'Or set off a forest fire?' she said uneasily. 'It's dry as tinder around here.'

'As long as we're not caught in it, that'll be fine. Even less evidence.' He laughed grimly. 'But we need away from here as fast as possible and back to France.'

'What about this car?' she asked.

'Ach, Fred'll bring the other one up from Barcelona and take this one back. It'll be no bother. I just don't fancy tangling with the Spanish policía.'

She laughed and then wished she hadn't. 'The gendarmes are cuddlier, are they?' she said. He didn't answer, merely giving a snort.

The track finally ended, much to her relief, meeting a small surfaced road with signs for Garriguella, Llança and Figueres.

'How's your head?' he asked glancing at her. 'You'll have been concussed and that needs seen to. There's a good doctor in Port-Vendres who knows how to keep his mouth shut. I'll text him in a minute.'

'Bit woozy, but OK,' she answered. 'Are we going back over the mountain?' She suddenly wished for an uncomplicated motorway.

'Nah,' he said slowly, 'never like going the same way twice and it's kind of isolated, that road. Not that anyone's coming after us. If you can stand it, I'll go by the coast, though it is very winding.'

She groaned and waved a limp hand, saying, 'Whatever you think best,' then adding: 'Sir.'

A road so straight it could have been built by the Romans sped them in the twilight towards Llança. There the sea glowed deep blue in the dusk, throwing into contrast the stumpy, whitewashed apartment blocks. Not throwing up was her principle concern, so she had to take continuous deep breaths to steady her stomach. Thereafter, she was so intent on wedging herself into a position where she wouldn't be jarred by the twisting and turning of the cliff route that she paid little attention to the scenery flashing by.

Finally, Herk said: 'This is the border coming up. Portbou.'

'Thank god,' she murmured, 'and we don't have to go far beyond that? Please.'

'You're doing great. Just hang on. Only Cerbère after that and we're sort of there. About thirty minutes.' He grinned at her and she suddenly felt a fraud for making a fuss, given what he'd been through.

Portbou was an eerie village sandwiched between the dark sea and even darker sheer cliffs of the mountain towering behind. A few umbrellas on the pavements with café tables outside attempted to set a holiday mood and failed.

'Blood in the walls,' she murmured.

'What?'

She waved a hand around. 'These kind of places. You can feel a savage history seeping out of the stone.'

The car throttled up a curving rise, with a sheer rockface inches away, out into open road again. He said: 'Aye well, I suppose Portbou has had its moments. Spanish Civil War wasn't great or what came after.'

'Was I dreaming or did we actually go through a village called Colera? And there's Cerbère coming up. It's like something out of Dante's Inferno.' She stared out into the darkness beyond the headlights, remembering the phone call with Sibyl and her joke about Hercules and the River Styx. Cerbère? She tried to clear her head. No it was Cerberus, the hound of Hades that guarded the route into the underworld. He had to be paid before allowing entry. Two dead bodies. Was that high enough a price? Her stomach heaved again.

He chuckled: 'Heaven and hell is what a mate of mine called it. Beautiful and cursed. Suits the Catalans, he always used to say. They've got dark souls.'

The pain slowly started to subside in her shoulder so she wriggled her fingers on that hand, pleased to know they still worked. Her head felt less fog-bound, with fresh air blowing in the partly opened window. A wave of guilt swept over her.

'Herk, I am truly sorry I got you into this mess. Jin was right. I do go flying in and don't stop to think. You must be hurting.' She took a shuddering breath. 'And you killed two men because of me.'

A series of s-bends took up his concentration, then he took one hand off the wheel to scratch his ear.

'Och, I've had worse. It just stings a bit. The doctor'll sort that. As to the other, I'm not five years old. I came in with my eyes open. You didn't force me. And killing them? It was us or them, and in those circumstances there's no choice. So just forget it. It never happened. But we'll have to think carefully about what comes next.'

'Too bleeding true,' she said, wondering whether he could really brush aside the killings so lightly. 'We're up a gum tree since they'll now know exactly who we are.'

Cerbère came and went, the sparse lights giving way to the open, empty, dark road, before he replied slowly. 'Well, not necessarily. I had a brief look at their mobiles, which are in the back by the way. There was a couple of angry texts asking where they were. And no responses from them. In fact, no texts or calls from them for several hours. So they weren't in touch with base since they took off after us.'

Tire bent back with an effort, fishing with her right hand for the plastic bag on the back seat that held phones, wallets and keys, some smeared with blood. Flinching, she fired up both mobiles and searched through messages. There were eight increasingly irritable texts from the same Spanish number demanding their immediate return and no responses had been sent. A feeling of relief flooded over her.

On the unbloodied phone there was also a text from a blocked number, which she contemplated before saying: 'Wonder what that means?' She read out: 'LN, 34 Dowancross Street, Apt 6, Glasgow. Name Jimmy Black. Get it right this time.'

'Never mind that for the time being. Just switch them off and take out the batteries in case they're tracking them,' Herk responded curtly. 'As long as they didn't click that our disappearance had anything to do with theirs, then we might just be OK. Though we'll need to spin a story about why we're not there anymore. I'll get Maria, the doctor's wife, to phone up. She's Spanish. She can say you were taken ill and I had to get you to hospital in a hurry. They were all in a bit of a scurry with the bosses back and no one saw me coming out with the bags. So they might just swallow it.'

A tunnel ahead heralded the entrance to Port-Vendres with the Cap Bear lighthouse flashing off to their right. Herk took the second exit and, having come down to the harbour, drove on back up the hill towards Collioure. At the top, he drew into the entrance of a substantial villa facing out across the cliffs to the sea.

They were clearly expected and Tire allowed herself to be fussed over, prodded and manipulated by the doctor, who pronounced her bruised but unbroken, although concussed. She was ushered off to bed with painkillers to help her sleep. He said he would check in on her every hour. Before she drifted off she could hear gales of laughter from the sitting room.

CHAPTER 36

A gusting wind drummed and roared against the windows, rattling the wooden shutters outside, bringing Tire to a painful wakening. She lay motionless, peering above the duvet to the daylight flickering through the thin curtains. Rolling slowly onto her back with an effort, she felt a sharp twinge in her left shoulder. She wriggled her toes and fingers to check they were still working, then pulled back the covers with her right hand and slowly brought up her left arm.

A soft knock on the door was followed by Herk's face looking questioningly at her. She grinned and pulled the duvet back up to her chin.

'Breakfast's on the table if you're up to it,' he said cheerfully. 'Jean-Claude and Maria are away for the day to the surgery.'

She waved him out of the room and, clenching her teeth, moved to the side of the bed to stand up. A hot shower sparked up tender spots on her back but she felt more flexible and relieved to be clean when she emerged. Downstairs, Herk was sitting in an open-plan kitchen diner at the French windows, which faced out to the back garden that was sheltered from the blasts of the wind. He poured her coffee from a large jug into a cup the size of a soup bowl and indicated a pile of croissants.

Neither spoke for several minutes as they munched through the flaky pastries smeared with butter and jam. Her left hand was back in operation as long as she didn't move her shoulder too much. The silence, she realised, was a strangely comfortable feeling.

'You've got diabetes,' he remarked, as she lit up her first cigarette.

'Really?' she said, licking jam off her lower lip. 'Serious, is it?'

'Not now that you got to the hospital and they changed your medication. Maria phoned them last night and they were concerned about you disappearing. But the lad she spoke with seemed relieved to know it wasn't anything too serious. He said just to tell them when it was convenient for you to return. She got the impression there was a flap on. Lots of shouting in the background in English and Spanish.'

Herk rubbed his chin and looked thoughtfully out to the garden, where the water from a small fountain was being swirled and splayed by the wind. Her mood of elation and relief switched suddenly to dread and guilt as she remembered the dead bodies and the blood. She put a hand on his arm.

'Herk, we need to talk about yesterday...' she started, only to be interrupted by a stubby muscular hand going up instantly, warning her to stop.

'No, we don't,' he said firmly. 'I've been in these situations before. If I know one thing, it is you never look back. Be grateful you got out in one piece and keep moving forward. We've tidied up the loose ends and with luck there's nothing connecting us to them. So leave it.' He gave her a sharp look.

Two black and white swallowtail butterflies chased each other around a sprawling bush of blue plumbago, their flight unfazed by the strong gusts of sea breeze. Tire followed their dancing path, feeling steadily more depressed. She had bitten off more than she could chew and had failed. Her eyes were sad and defeated when she finally said, looking away from him: 'I think we should give up. I can't see what else we can do.'

Herk ground a thumbnail between his front teeth, clicking repetitively, his eyes narrowed, gazing upwards at the sky. His lack of response started to irritate her.

'Well? Are you looking for omens up there? What do you think?' She banged on the table, making the coffeepot wobble.

He sniffed. 'You're rattled.' He raised a hand: 'Perfectly understandable. But it's not the best state of mind for making decisions.' He stretched his legs under the table, leant back and continued: 'I've always thought this was bigger than you... it seemed. Which just means moving cautiously. We know more than we did before. Sometimes you have to wait. And as you said once, keep following every lead till it makes sense.'

Her shoulders slumped and a twinge of dizziness made her draw several deep breaths. A bleep from a mobile got Herk to his feet. He walked over to a corner table where several phones sat and opened one to read a message.

'Fred can't make it till tomorrow to swap cars. Just as well. Your concussion could do with another day.'

'Who is Fred?' she said, her old exasperation coming back.

Herk sighed, 'He's a mate from the old days. He owed me a few favours. There's nothing mysterious about him.' He nodded over his shoulder, 'He'll also check over these mobiles we picked up yesterday. I took out the tracking devices but there's other ways to make them untraceable. The batteries are out for the time being.'

A light bulb went on in her head and her mood lifted as she remembered the text from yesterday about LN with the Glasgow address. Could that have been from Wrighton? Maybe the business partnership with Harman Stone had continued with shared security. That should be followed up.

She stubbed out her cigarette and lit another one, her mind running over the information trails that were still in play. Russell, the accountant, digging into Stone's and Wrighton's finances. Juarez, the doctor in Mexico, had promised to find out more about the memory drug tests. And the researcher Matt was still checking out Paul Stone's stepson from his first marriage, Louis Neroni. He would be stepbrother to Harman, so perhaps a financial threat if he were owed an inheritance from his mother. They were no further forward in finding out who had killed Erica; if anything the spider's web was getting more complicated. But they still had leads to follow.

Reinvigorated, she beamed at Herk who stared evenly back at her. 'I know,' she said, waving an excited hand, 'I'm getting manic. But that text about LN in Glasgow, it could be Louis Neroni.'

'Aye,' he said cautiously, 'but I'm not driving from here to Scotland.' She frowned and he added: 'So we'll get the car back to London and fly up.'

'So you're OK to keep going?' she said slowly, pulled between guilt at involving him and knowing she needed his help.

He looked down with a wry smile and said: 'It's not the best motive. But to be truthful I've got a vengeful streak. I hate being messed about.'

She chuckled in spite of herself, trying not to think about yesterday's ordeal. Herk cleared the breakfast table and announced he was going to look over the Range Rover. A dull ache across the back of her skull was crowding into her thinking space. To clear her head she walked twice round the small back garden, moving stiffly up the stone steps, easing her shoulder as she went. A striped and mottled cat swished its tail at her from a neighbouring fence, ears flattened back, then was distracted to its feet by two herring gulls chasing and squawking overhead. Best of luck there, mate, she thought.

A spiky pyracanthus bush, weighted with white flowers, snagged through her jeans, causing her to wince. The wind swung strands of hair constantly over her face, which became irritating so she turned round and walked back down, testing every step, and was pleased to feel more sound.

Back inside, Herk was scrubbing oil off his hands in the sink. A thought struck her.

'Can you look up how far Arles is from here? We might nip across there since we've time today?'

'What for?' He frowned irritably, dried his hands and checked his phone. 'Three hours there and three hours back. No chance.'

'It must be closer than that. The American Nathon said Paul Stone's mother was born and buried near here. Arles something.'

He checked again. 'Arles-sur-Tech. Fifty minutes inland, past Amelie-les-Bains. Why are we interested in Harman's grandma? You could just sit still and let your head recover.'

'We're here. We might as well. The more you know about the broader background, the more you know. Wheels within wheels.' She held her head up and forced her shoulders back, attempting not to let the twinges show.

He shook his head. 'Unknown knowns and all that. If you insist.'

***

An hour later they were driving up the Vallespir valley, deep into the eastern Pyrenees, with snow-tipped mountains crowding around. Despite the sunshine it felt cold and the small, historic commune uninviting. Tire knew she was winging it, but past experience indicated that luck plus persistence sometimes paid off. The *mairie* was unhelpful but the *office de tourisme* came up with the name of a retired school teacher who would be the same age as Paul Stone and had always lived in Arles-sur-Tech. They also gave her a map to the local cemetery.

After collecting a boxful of pastries at the local *boulangerie* and a bottle of wine from the *cellier* next door, she climbed back into the car and handed Herk the address. Twenty minutes of driving round the outskirts, circling back on themselves after incomprehensible directions from an aged peasant who was out walking his dog, they found the cottage at the end of an unsigned track.

The elderly, white-haired owner, dressed in jeans and a fleece waistcoat, came out, leaning on a walking stick to greet them. His manner was civil but disinterested, since he clearly thought they were lost tourists. Once he heard that Tire was researching a biography of a person who had been in Arles during the war and after, and was offered the bottle of wine, his eyes twinkled.

His English was excellent and he volunteered that he was always pleased to get the chance to use it. At first, sitting round a wooden kitchen table with wine glasses in front of them, he disavowed all knowledge of Paul Stone. Tire persisted, saying his mother was local and had been buried here. Crumbs from a cheese pastry stuck to his moustache and clung to his waistcoat. Finishing it, he brushed a shaky, veined hand across his mouth and down his front.

Not another dead end. Maybe Nathon had the place name wrong and it wasn't Arles-sur-Tech. A stray thought struck her about Paul Stone's Cote D'Azur house. 'Would La Mirabelle mean anything?'

His shaggy eyebrows shot up and he looked sideways at her, suddenly defensive. He said slowly: 'You wouldn't mean Lilou Pedra? Mirabelle was the name on her cottage.'

Tire sipped her wine, giving him an encouraging look.

'Pedra means stone in Catalan.' The old man looked puzzled, almost furtive and rubbed his hands together uneasily. 'And yes, she did have a son, about my age. I was at school with him for several years.' He shuddered. 'An unpleasant child. Not that it was his fault. He had a terrible life.'

He gave her an uncomfortable look and said: 'I don't think he would want this printed. If it is him. Which it may be. The child's name was Pol. Pol Pedra. Paul Stone.' He gave a sour laugh and shook his head. 'I loathed him, all of the children did. But I should say no more.'

'When did he leave here?'

'About eleven, I think. He certainly did not come to senior school. They went to Barcelona, he and his mother.'

'His father was Spanish?'

The old man gave a heavy sigh as Herk poured him another glass, and he stroked a mottled cat that had jumped onto the table. 'No one knew who his father was.' He paused as if embarrassed, then said: 'His mother was a prostitute and was illegitimate herself, not quite right in the head.' He tapped his skull. 'They were outcasts and he was bullied because of it. It turned him nasty, very nasty. He hurt animals and the smaller children. Everyone was pleased when they left. It was thought she went to ply her trade where there was more money. They speak Catalan in Barcelona, so she would fit in easily. It was a real tragedy because he was bright. In different circumstances he could have done well.'

'Well,' she said cautiously, 'we don't absolutely know Pol Pedra and Paul Stone are the same person. So best to keep it quiet for the time being. Do you remember Lilou's funeral?'

He shook his head. 'No, and I attend most of them. I doubt he'd have dared to bury her in the cemetery. People have long memories around here. Maybe he just brought her ashes back and scattered them where no one could see.'

As they left, she assured him she would write when she knew more, and once back in the car, switched off her pocket recorder. The Range Rover bumped back along the track and turned, to her relief, onto a smoother, metalled road.

'This helps does it, knowing Harman's grandma was a whore?' Herk's tone was brusque.

'If I can nail it all down, it fleshes out a background. The police only need the evidence. I need colour, the whole three-act family drama, to write a decent piece. Which will, I may point out, pay the expenses for all of this.'

'None of which is going to happen unless we get the evidence as well,' he retorted.

'The proof's all there in the astrology,' she said, wagging a finger at him. 'Father was bred in hell's kitchen and managed somehow to claw his way onto a pedestal of respectability. But genes will out, at least the psychological ones. His unlived rage all got bundled down a generation, so became doubly toxic in Harman. Pity there's no birth times, that'd help to anchor down more detail.'

'Which would be as much use as illegally obtained evidence. The courts would slap any prosecutor daft enough to raise it into a straitjacket. And you already said you never use it in your books.'

'Sod off. All I meant was it was interesting.'

'Try thinking useful, not whimsical.'

CHAPTER 37

The rest of the day Tire spent in bed, her headache pounding even through Jean-Claude's painkillers, although his sleeping pill gave her an uninterrupted night's sleep. In the morning he insisted on checking her over again. No sickness or dizziness, he asked? She lied and assured him she was fine. He issued strict instructions about going to a hospital immediately if she had any symptoms and then shrugged with a smile and left.

While she waited for Herk to finish the handover with Fred, who had arrived from Barcelona with the BMW, she checked her messages. Matt, the researcher, had found a passenger list with a Louis Neroni entering the UK by ship in 1966, but there was no Stone mentioned. Thereafter, there was no record under passports, social security, or citizenship.

She emailed him back, saying could he check out the Dowancross Street, Glasgow address under J. Black? Also find a copy birth certificate for a Pol Pedra born 16 July 1939 in Arles-sur-Tech with full details of time of birth. Also find any people who had been given charity holidays at Cerigo resorts in Spain. There was something that just didn't square about poor kids in that plush setting.

The ten-hour drive up to Calais was tedious but curiously restful. She alternately dozed and stared mindlessly out of the window at the countryside flashing past. They caught a late-night ferry and were on the outskirts of London before she allowed herself to start planning again. Her brain was whirring when Herk dropped her at the back entrance with the bags, having rung the bell for Ali, the porter, to help.

Once inside, she booted up her laptop and sat down with Stravinsky's 'Rite of Spring' hammering out dissonant rhythms. Despite her renewed confidence, she knew they had precious little to go on. Felicity had emailed to thank her for finding a sponsor for Miranda's residential violin course and said she would go directly from her friend's at the end of the week. Wrighton himself had gone from Leeds to a further conference in Amsterdam so wouldn't be back till she was gone.

Tire had no sense of strategy about how to tackle him as a suspect so she pushed it to one side. That would have to wait until after the Glasgow trip. And she was not sanguine about Russell finding enough about Paul or Harman Stone's finances to be a real breakthrough. What the old school teacher had told them didn't amount to more than a salacious gossip paragraph.

Then she remembered the Scottish journalist Harrister had mentioned, who had been investigating Stone and ended up dead. That would have to be tracked down and looked into when they were up north. She flicked through her address book idly, wondering who she knew who might be useful. A crime reporter who had helped her years ago on a story about money-laundering syndicates that had fizzled out. What was his name? She racked her brains. Murdo Scott, that was it. She faintly recollected he had taken to the bottle badly and been fired, but his paper might tell her his whereabouts.

A few minutes sweet-talking to the news editor on the pretext that she owed Murdo money produced his email address, but not his phone number. She dashed off a vague message to him saying she was trying to track down the name of an investigative journalist who had been killed in a car crash years ago. It sounded weak but she didn't want to be too open at this stage, especially if he was drinking heavily.

The front door banged shut and there was a clatter in the kitchen as Herk brewed himself a mug.

'Problem?' she asked, when he came through to the office.

He sat down heavily and said: 'Ali said there was a couple of guys hanging about when we were away. Different ones, obviously. Which is good in one way since it means they didn't connect us to the Spanish trip. But it's a pain in the ass all the same.'

At his insistence she booked a flight to Glasgow first thing in the morning.

'Might as well tie up this loose end and then see if there's anything else,' he said, chipping the toe of his boot on the tiles. 'If it's nothing, then maybe we should back off for a while. Go about our normal business. They might get bored and go away, whoever they are. Have you another project you could be seen to be working on?'

The rain drenched the window, running in rivulets down the glass. Tire swung one way and another on the office chair, her heels tapping on the floor.

'The bonking Buddha,' she said brightly. 'It's an idea my agent was pushing, but I reckoned it was too tedious. Sex and money-mad, a total fraud. He's down in Hampshire somewhere.'

'That sounds just fine. You can immerse yourself in that and…'

'Not a hope, sunshine,' she smiled sweetly. 'If I'm doing it, you're coming too.'

'Oh, hallelujah,' he said wearily but, she thought, not unhappily.

An email from Matt arrived, she noticed over her shoulder, so she swung back round to her laptop. Dowancross Street in Glasgow, he wrote, was a low-rent housing association property. No specific information on the electoral roll. But he wondered if a diary piece about a James Black, artist, in the local paper, was the same? She thought it unlikely, but clicked on the URL. The headline read: 'Local painter makes a splash. Ex-Dunlothian Hall inmate has first exhibition.'

'Oh, fuck,' she said after a startled moment, staring at the photograph of a greying, nondescript man with a long red scarf standing nervously beside a painting of two male nude statues either side of an exotic spiky plant.

'What?' Herk jumped up to peer over her shoulder.

Her hand was trembling when she pointed. 'Those…,' tugging at her hair, '… statues are on the patio at Castell Pajol.'

'They probably churn them out by the hundreds at Homebase.'

She shook her head. 'No, they were alabaster originals, hand-carved.'

'They could still have made copies,' he said, less certainly. Blowing out his cheeks, he wrinkled his nose and tapped the back of her seat. 'Mind you, it's odd, there's no doubt.' He scratched the back of his head, 'If they are the only statues like that, then maybe Stone saw that photograph as well and it set a few bells ringing.'

'Great minds,' she said typing in a Google search. 'Voila,' she said triumphantly, as an art magazine website featured the same photograph. 'That's a London site. More likely he saw it down here.'

His hand went down onto her shoulder as she started to rise out of her seat. 'No, you don't. We're going to Glasgow tomorrow, not today. The instruction about getting Jimmy Black went out to the guy who's down the bottom of a Spanish gully. So there's no great rush.'

She looked again at the photograph and shook her head, frowning. 'That poor soul doesn't look up to coping with Stone's heavies.'

CHAPTER 38

The morning plane to Glasgow was taking an interminable time to move away from the stand at Heathrow. Tire glared at the stewardesses, the tarmac, the closed cockpit door and finally at Herk, sitting beside her reading the sports section of the morning paper. Her heeled boots were propped hard and kneading against the seat in front, until a cough alerted her to their pressure being an irritant. Mumbling sorry, she whispered forcefully to Herk: 'I think we should have come yesterday. We may be too late.'

'Nice perfume that you've got on,' he replied after turning the page, which earned him a sharp elbow that pushed his arm off the rest.

The engines roared and the plane started to taxi so she tensed in anticipation.

'Now, look,' he said quietly. 'We'll get there when we get there so you may as well relax. There haven't been any more texts from the number that sent the muscle to Glasgow. So whoever sent it will reckon they're on their way.'

'But it was sent from the UK so it couldn't have been Harman,' she said, frowning as the thought struck her.

'Could have been Wrighton, if we're assuming they're still in league. Or might be a security boss who gets his orders from god knows where. Fred got one of his guys to check and it was pay-as-you-go, so no way of checking. Leave it.'

He folded the paper noisily and immersed himself in a football commentary. She twisted away from him, staring morosely out of the window as they rose above the urban sprawl into cloud. Her night had been jarred, not by images of blood, but by suffocating smells of decaying cement dust and rotting manure, which woke her up several times scared to breathe in. And that croaking, wheezing sound that returned again and again. Even now, it leeched through the rattle and throb of the plane to echo in her ears.

With a sigh, she pulled up her bag and found a paperback titled *Living through Loving, Learn from the Masters*, which had a chapter on Shri Tantaalum, the Hampshire guru. After flicking through the disingenuous gush, she sighed again. Even as a camouflage project it was going to be tough going.

Glasgow was drizzling with a fine grey mist, the sky low and threatening heavier rain as they emerged from the terminal building into the car park to pick up the hire car. Herk set the GPS and raced along the motorway. Heading riverwards past the Southern General Hospital complex, they shot through an empty Clyde Tunnel and into the red sandstone territory of the west end and on into the city centre.

The first port of call was the gallery that sold James Black's paintings, since she reckoned a few preliminary soundings would help to see how the land lay. The plate glass window of Marinello Arts displayed three small watercolours on easels, with a gilt card carrying the name James Black. Visible beyond, was an open exhibition space with more paintings and stands with small bronze sculptures. Two policemen were standing talking to an excitable, dark-haired man in his forties who was gesticulating wildly.

Tire's stomach churned. They pushed open the door to hear him say hysterically: 'I know nothing was stolen. The security system here is the best there is, but some bawbag tried to break in last night and it's now nearly one o'clock.' He screeched irritably, brandishing his watch. 'There is CCTV footage. I want you to catch them.' He glared at the larger of the two policemen.

'Difficult, sir,' the policeman remarked stolidly. 'He had his face covered. But we'll do our best.' He put away his notebook, nodded to his companion and left.

Wafts of spicy aftershave flowed off the man as he ran his fingers agitatedly through his thick hair. Then he forced a smile, adjusted his turquoise silk tie and said silkily: 'Just want to look around, do you? We're shutting shortly but do feel free. I do apologise. A slight mishap last night. I'm Ricky Marinello.'

'No, actually.' Tire stepped forward and put out her hand confidently. 'I'm from the Sunday Chronicle and this is my photographer. We want to interview James Black.'

His expression froze and he stamped his foot. 'Really, this is too much. You can't turn up with no notice. It just isn't possible today. Come back tomorrow.' He turned away with a dismissive wave of his hand.

'No,' said Tire sharply. At the same time, Herk stepped forward to say brightly: 'It'd mean more sales for you.'

Ricky turned with an exaggerated gesture, thrusting a leg, tightly encased in flannel trousers, forward and pulling his open jacket back to put his hands on his hips. His eyes were wide open and he looked from one to the other. He spoke with dramatic slowness: 'If I were to tell you exactly what I thought...' He broke off and peered doubtfully at Herk. 'You don't look like any photographer I've ever seen, mate. More at home in a boxing ring, frankly.'

Tire moved forward to face him directly and said softly: 'Look, we really need to see him. I can't explain why, but it is very important.' She gave her final words extra emphasis.

Indecision and suspicion spread across his face. 'Why?' he exclaimed. Clapping a hand dramatically to his forehead, he continued: 'I quite forgot he's gone off on a painting trip with his wife and he won't be back for a couple of weeks. At least. Mull of Galloway, I think he said. We could perhaps fix a meeting when he returns? He doesn't have a mobile.'

'You're sure he's away?' Tire said doubtfully, handing over a plain business card with only her name, email and mobile number on it.

'Absolutely certain, dear lady. He wanted to sketch some sea scenes and landscapes in preparation for his next exhibition. I promise I'll be in touch,' he said, ushering them determinedly to the door with a fixed smile.

'One last question. Did he ever talk about his early childhood in Italy?'

Ricky's hand tightened round the door handle, his expression rigid.

'Jimmy Black sounds Italian to you, does it? Last time I looked Govan was south of the River Clyde. You're up a gum tree. Now go.' The door slammed and locked behind them.

'Did you believe him?' she asked Herk outside.

'Difficult to tell with all that gesticulating he does,' he answered with a sniff. 'He hardly looks as if he's in league with the devil. But if Black is off elsewhere for two weeks and uncontactable, it might just be safer for him.'

She scuffed the sole of her boot against the pavement, then shrugged. 'Best get on. Pity there's no phone number.'

Inside the car she stared moodily out of the window as the rain lashed down. They stopped for a lunch of tagliatelle al pesto at a small Italian restaurant and delicatessen on Hyndland Road, and then retraced their steps and drove back through the Clyde Tunnel, heading for the south side. Following the signs for Ibrox Stadium, they exited onto Shieldhall Road and, after overshooting the turning on the duel carriageway, finally made a dog leg back into a street of drab terraced houses with dark slate roofs, black-framed windows and dull khaki walls. The gutters were hanging loose in places and the flaking paint had not been renewed in years. The only concession to care was the polished television dishes attached at first-floor level, their cables running down the wall.

'Now, what's the story here?' Herk said, drawing up outside number 68, which had an ironwork fence and gate with patches of rust showing through, and a patch of grimy, unkempt grass in front of the house.

'I'm writing a piece about Cerigo charity holidays and you're taking photographs. The kid is probably at school but best bring your camera in with you.'

The interior, in contrast, was neat and bright with a strong smell of lavender freshener, Tire noted, as they were welcomed in the door by Mrs Kinley. She was a white-haired woman in her sixties with a surprisingly unlined face and kindly brown eyes, and wearing slippers and a tartan apron. She led them through to the small sitting room, which was cheaply but comfortably furnished.

Within half an hour they had learned about her family's woes with a daughter dead from breast cancer, leaving her only son in the care of her mother, his father having disappeared before his birth. She had been on Cerigo holidays in Spain two years running with her grandson Rory, organised through her Lifelong Friends membership, and had enjoyed the sunshine and free food. The boy had also enjoyed swimming in the pool and playing with the other children.

She spoke carefully and was keen to emphasise how grateful she was. They had been well looked after, staying in the block behind the main house, which had small rooms but was clean and the staff were polite, she said.

Tire pondered on her options since Mrs Kinley was clearly keen to return to Spain.

'Has Rory kept up with any of the other children?' she asked. 'He must have made new friends.'

'No, they had been asked not to keep up contact afterwards,' she replied. 'The man said they should make friends locally, not on the internet. And they came from all over. There were no other Scottish children there. Well, except one.' She hesitated.

'Perhaps we could interview him and his grandmother?' Tire asked sweetly, her antennae up.

Mrs McKinley frowned and shook her head. 'I don't know their address. He was very muddled, quite aggressive, that boy when he came. Then he got ill and they took him away to the big house. We didn't see him again.'

After considerable coaxing, she admitted she had chatted to the boy's grandmother from Dundee, who said she had adopted him after he'd been taken into care as a toddler. Her son and the boy's mother had been drug addicts and he'd been starved and beaten as a baby.

'She had a big heart taking all that on,' she said admiringly. 'You could see that his background had affected him badly. He had a real nasty look in his eye the first time we met him. But Rory saw him just before we left and said he was much nicer and calmer. Though maybe they had him doped up.'

'This was the last holiday you went on?' Tire asked smoothly. 'Were any of the kids ill the previous time?'

The old lady rubbed one wrist with a knobbly hand and thought for a moment. 'To be honest, and I wouldn't like this to go in your article, they were all sick the previous time. Not vomiting or anything, just not right in the head like. It took Rory a while to feel normal again. They said it was a virus. He couldn't remember his sums for weeks after. At times I wondered if he knew who I was. I was worried, but the manager assured me it would wear off and it did. They sent a young doctor round to check on him here, which was very kind. Saved me going down the health centre.'

There was little else she could tell them, but they lingered till her grandson came home. Herk took a few shots of both of them sitting on the couch, Rory holding his favourite signed football.

Outside, Tire said: 'What did you make of that?'

'More questions, no answers, lots of maybes,' he replied, manoeuvring back out into the rush-hour traffic.

CHAPTER 39

Their next port of call was a rendezvous with the reporter Murdo Scott, with the hope that he might shed light on the journalist who had been killed in a car crash while investigating Paul Stone's business. Back through the tunnel again, more slowly than before, crawling along Anniesland Road into the leafy suburbs of Great Western Road, past Gartnavel Hospital and then heading north over the River Kelvin at Queen Margaret's Bridge into tenement country.

The Maryhill pub was noisy inside and out, with smokers hanging around beside the litter bins, pulling their jackets tight against the wind and clutching glasses of beer, the smoke wreathed across the heavily grilled doorway. Inside, the din was louder with piped pop music and the raucous chat and laughter of customers winding up for a long night ahead. The brass-railed bar stretched the length of the long, low-ceilinged room, with spirit bottles stacked up to the ceiling on shelves in front of the mirrored wall. The décor was muddy brown.

Herk pushed ahead of her, clearing a way through the jostling crowd of men still in their grimy work clothes, until she tapped him on the shoulder. She was praying that Murdo Scott would still be sober enough to make the meeting worthwhile.

He was sitting crouched over a corner table, the collar of his raincoat turned up, a few strands of lank, greying hair lying across his bald scalp. When he raised his head, the deeply lined skin on his face seemed to slide downwards, pulling at the pouches under his reddened eyes. A feeble wave acknowledged her presence. In front of him was a wine glass half-full of clear liquid, with bubbles rising to the surface.

She patted him on the hand and introduced Herk.

'Not too great at the moment, I'm afraid,' he wheezed. 'Docs have got me on this cat's piss,' waving at the spritzer. Now that she was closer, she could see tinges of yellow jaundice on his skin and in the whites of his eyes.

Deciding this was no time for a full medical rundown, she charged in and asked whether he'd found out anything. His rheumy eyes regarded her blankly, blinked several times as if he was trying to stay awake, then he grasped her hand.

'Joe said you owe me money,' he said intensely, leaning towards her. She attempted not to breathe in too deeply, as his musty odour spread across the table.

'Sure, Murdo, sure,' she said brightly. 'Loose ends from the last gig. I'll settle up. But I need to know about this reporter.'

To her surprise, tears filled his eyes and, having blown his nose loudly into a filthy red handkerchief, he said: 'Aye, Davey Campbell. I knew him well. I helped with his last investigation into some London bigwig. But after he'd gone I didn't have the heart to keep going. Or the money to be honest.'

Roy Orbison's Only the Lonely was blaring out with the volume turned up full and several voices joining in on the dum dum doo-wahs and oh yay yay yay, yeahs. A plump, blonde woman in her fifties at the next table, still in her supermarket overalls, was belting out of tune for all she was worth. Herk, returning with two beer tumblers full of coca cola, raised one in greeting to her.

When the next track, a Barry Manilow, came on to the accompaniment of boos, the volume was turned back down. Hardly daring to hope, she said quietly to Murdo: 'I don't suppose you have any of his notes from that investigation, do you?'

He regarded her with mock superiority and smiled, for the first time looking in focus. 'Of course I do. What do you take me for? No, don't answer that,' he said, sighing heavily. Bending down with difficulty, he brought a tattered briefcase up from the floor. It took her all her time not to grab the case, but she stopped herself and rescued his wine glass instead, which was in danger of being knocked over.

The effort seemed to have exhausted him so he sat for a moment breathing heavily, clutching the scuffed leather to his chest.

'Tell me about the car crash,' Tire said, when he looked less stressed.

'Don't know much about that, to be honest. Up in Wester Ross somewhere. And before you ask, his death certificate's in here, well, a copy I got at the time.'

'You thought it was suspicious?' She fingered the condensation on her glass, trying not to sound too eager.

He half-laughed, which turned into a choking cough, so she pushed the glass of Coke towards him. He nodded and took a sip, dribbling the brown liquid down his chin.

'Don't we always?' he replied. 'But truthfully I was pretty far gone when he died, so I couldn't even go up and check. Felt bad about that. I owed him.' His face was anguished.

She gave him a sympathetic smile and said: 'Maybe me and Herk can go check and let you know.'

He shook his head. 'Nah, I won't be here long enough. My number's pretty much up. To be honest, I wasn't sure I'd make it here tonight. Doc says maybe a month, maybe not.'

'No mountain high enough,' roared the blonde at the next table as the Manilow track finished. 'Just call me and I'll be there.' This earned her an enthusiastic round of applause. Murdo pulled at Tire's shoulder bag to bring her closer, and croaked in her ear: 'But I do need money to give to my son. Could you do me five hundred. Please, Tris?'

She nodded to him as 'Listen baby' started up at full pitch, and gestured outside. They left as 'Ain't no river wide enough' boomed out across the street. Even the rumbling evening traffic sounded muted in contrast, as they walked slowly towards the traffic lights. Herk flagged down a passing cab for Murdo as Tire found ten fifty-pound notes in her bag, tucked them into his jacket pocket and then paid the cab driver for his journey home to Dennistoun. He collapsed onto the seat and as she leaned in to blow him a kiss from the open door he rasped, saliva trickling down his chin: 'See Davey right, will ye? He was one of the good guys.'

A sense of bleak despondency kept her quiet on the way to their hotel. Drink, she thought, the Celtic curse. Filling the black hole of nameless pain and galactic loneliness out of the bottom of a bottle. A communal habit, but really a solitary vice of souls crying out for a connection they could never quite make.

She turned to Herk as he was parking and said: 'What did your father die of?'

'Cirrhosis,' he answered, staring ahead. 'And his father before him, and one of my brothers and two uncles. I know what it looks like and that guy'll be lucky if he sees the end of the week.'

Later, over a bottle of wine in a quiet corner of the hotel bar, they reviewed what they knew and what came next. The Stone family history, involvement in illegal drug testing and perhaps a journalist's death covering up whatever he'd found out about their finances. The reporter Davey Campbell's notes could be added to Russell's research list. And who was Jimmy Black? That would mean another Glasgow trip.

Tire could feel herself getting drawn into a distracting curiosity about the Stones, which might lead to a sensational exposé – and a libel nightmare – but was not getting them any closer to nailing down Erica's killer.

She slumped back in her seat. And Wrighton? Where did he fit in? Buddies with Harman. Two shits together. Scratching each other's back when they had problems.

'Want to know what I think?' Herk's voice broke into her thoughts. 'Only chance we have of getting the evidence we need is to track the watchers and motorcyclists back to base. We have to know whether they were mercenaries freelancing for several employers or working for one. The text on the phone in Spain suggested they might have several different gigs running at once. I could put a team together. Two men and a dog aren't enough. It'd cost, mind you. How are you doing on money?'

'Kind of OK.' She gave him a distracted look. 'There's cash in from the Sanchez book and another advance for the next one. I can write chunks of expenses off against tax as a development project. And I'll write a travel piece about the Costa Brava, and California, which'll pay a bit.'

'What about California? Did I miss something? You never mentioned that before.' He drummed his fingers on the table. 'I thought we were backing off for a while. Neither of the Stones will be there or Wrighton, will they? So what's the point?'

'Calm down,' she said more loudly than she had intended, causing the couple two tables away to turn round.

Lowering her tone, she said: 'Plane tickets are free off airmiles. It's only an in-and-out trip so we'll be back in three days and you can set up your counter-surveillance gig before then. My gut says Harman Stone's the answer, so the more I know, the more...' she trailed off. Then giving herself a shake, she said firmly: 'And Chip Nathon is the best source I've got so far.'

'For Paul Stone's biography, maybe, but I can't see how he helps with our main priority, which is Erica.'

'And Greengate and Jimmy Black,' she said, absent-mindedly peeling the gilt edge off a table mat, exhaustion making her head spin.

'Hey, hey. Hold hard. No mission creep. We can't save the world. Keep your focus steady.'

CHAPTER 40

'Calm down man, for god's sake. I don't know what you're saying.' Wally's rough accent roared down the speakerphone on Ricky's desk. 'What fire?'

'It's where Jimmy lived,' Ricky screeched hysterically. 'And there's three dead. The whole building went up at three this morning. It's on the TV news.'

There was silence from the other end, then a long growl of anger, followed by an echoing bellow to get the car. 'I'll meet you there in ten,' he said tersely and rang off.

Ricky tried to drink his coffee, but was shaking so much he had to put the mug down. He sat stunned, with his secretary and assistant hovering wide-eyed in front of his desk. 'I should have done something,' he wailed. 'I knew he might be in danger. And I didn't do anything.'

He sank his head in his hands and gave two heaving sobs. Eventually Priscilla collected his coat and handed it to him while Alex went off to flag down a cab.

The area was cordoned off when he got there, with three fire engines still tending to the smouldering ruins of what had been a tenement building. The soot-blackened windows on the second and third floors, the glass blown out and the frames scorched, gave testament to the heat of the blaze.

A claret-coloured Bentley was parked in the middle of the road at the far end of the police barriers. A stocky figure in a sheepskin coat with a yellow construction hard hat was inside the cordon talking animatedly to a policeman. Seeing Ricky, he beckoned to him and after a moment, when he got no response from the figure clinging onto a lamp post, sent a policewoman across to collect him. He clapped Ricky hard on the shoulder, more to jolt him into coping than out of sympathy.

'It's too soon to tell,' he said gruffly. 'Too hot to get in, according to Joe here.' He nodded at the uniformed man beside him. 'One body's been recovered, an old woman, from the first floor, smoke inhalation. But that second floor is in a real mess. So they reckon at least two more dead. If not more. They've no idea what started it.'

An ambulance siren was wailing and car horns blaring as the traffic seized up behind the roadblocks. Two fireman, covered in dust and wet soot, clambered over debris with a stretcher carrying a closed body bag. Ricky leant against Wally and sobbed.

'Listen up.' Wally shook him upright. 'You're sure he couldn't be anywhere else? My flat he's using as a studio?'

Ricky looked wildly at him, hope flaring and then instantly dashed. He shook his head miserably, tears running down his cheeks. 'They wouldn't stay there. It was too grubby.'

'Well, nothing to do here. Joe'll keep me informed about what they find. Best go take a look. Just in case.' He grabbed Ricky's arm and manhandled him towards the Bentley.

The mountainous driver with a bald head and tattoos on the back of his neck cursed and honked regularly as cars got in his way. They had to take a long route round to Castleton Street and approach it through a rat run of narrow streets that were a tight fit for the Bentley. Ricky cowered in a corner of the back seat, saying over and over: 'It's all my fault. I should have done something.'

'No sense in crying over spilt milk,' Wally admonished him, with an irritated look. 'What's done is done. But I'll get the bastards who did this, if it was arson. They'll be the same ones who did for my nephew Jimmy. I found out yesterday they were foreign cunts. Dorry finally tracked down a kid who saw it. A contract job for sure, and someone is going to pay, you can take my word on it.' He drummed on the armrest with one stubby hand, glancing occasionally out of the window to frown as they slid past parked cars only inches away.

They walked up the stairs of the tenement with Wally puffing, and prodding Ricky from behind every time he threatened to collapse. At the top they looked at each other, then Wally hammered hard on the door with a clenched fist. There was an echoing silence for almost a minute, which brought more tears and a rumble of aggravation.

Then the door opened suddenly to reveal Elly wiping her hands on a dish cloth. 'What's all the noise about?' she asked indignantly.

Ricky rushed past her into the main room to see Jimmy standing brush in hand, looking puzzled, and threw his arms round him in a passionate embrace.

'We thought you were dead,' Wally remarked tonelessly. 'You stayed here last night, then?'

'I hope that was alright,' Jimmy answered, looking bewildered and embarrassed. 'It was just I painted till late and then there was a garden programme on television I wanted to see.' He shuffled nervously. 'And the set here's better than the one at our place. We got fish and chips round the corner. After it was over, we thought we might as well stay. The bed's very comfortable.'

'Thank Christ.' Ricky tottered unsteadily to the sofa and sank into it, burying his head in his arms.

'Hey missus, any chance of a cup of tea?' Wally gave a tight smile to Elly, who obediently went off to the kitchen. He walked to the window and looked out, came back and stood viewing Jimmy's half-finished painting of a stone path in a garden with an ancient wall to one side and a blank space in the middle.

'What's going in there?' he pointed a finger at the canvas.

Jimmy came across hesitantly, barely able to take his eyes off the huddled, tear-stained figure on the sofa. 'It's where my mother was killed, I think,' he said faintly. 'I wanted to do one last painting about the past and then leave it for good.'

'Your flat was torched last night,' Wally replied abruptly after he was handed a mug of tea.

A squeal from Elly was followed by a clatter as she dropped the tray of mugs onto the table, slopping tea and milk across the surface. It brought Jimmy to her side and they clung together, listening with horrified expressions to Wally's blunt description of their burnt-out tenement and the dead neighbour.

'Poor Mrs McDonald,' Elly whispered through tears.

'Stop snivelling, man.' Wally growled in disgust at Ricky's blotchy face and reddened eyes. Then he turned to Jimmy and said with a dismissive sneer: 'He thought you were dead and he hadn't protected you.' He searched in his pocket for a cigar and added through pursed lips: 'Mind you, there but for the grace and all that.'

Jimmy stood rooted to the spot, staring as the cigar was lit, drawn in rapid puffs and smoke spiralled into the room. His eyes drifted off to the half-finished painting with its grey stone, green plants and blue sky. The patch of raw canvas in the centre he'd been reluctant to fill in stared back at him. With a considerable effort he brought his gaze back to the barrel-chested figure standing impassively beside him.

'You don't mean it was deliberate?' he said, his voice breaking. 'To get me?' His eyes were anguished as he searched vainly for reassurance. 'I was the reason my neighbours got killed?'

Wally shrugged. 'Don't know yet. Could just have been an accident. These things do happen.' He sniffed and furrowed his brow into a scowl. 'But I do know that my nephew was bumped off, deliberate like. So it's not a stretch to think they might have come back to get the right person this time.'

The room shrank to a dot, then expanded rapidly, almost explosively, in Jimmy's vision. His head felt as if metal plates inside were grinding against each other, sending off sparks like a welder's torch. He blinked rapidly then had to sit down on the sofa in a hurry, Elly pushing Ricky over to sit between them.

He desperately didn't want to go forward in his search and now he clearly couldn't go back. A numb terror tightened his chest, his shoulders twitched. His memory jerked him back to the Hall, sitting outside Dr Brand's room waiting in abject fear for the terrible jolts that always followed.

'Now, here's what's going to happen.' Wally's abrasive voice sounded far away. 'You two can stay here till I hear more about the fire. If you're reckoned as dead no one's going to come looking. But I'll put a couple of lads outside to keep an eye out just in case. They'll bring you up any food you need. That'll cover us for a couple of days anyway.'

CHAPTER 41

Back in London, the effects of days of constant pressure and dashing around were flagging even Tire's energy. Her shoulder still ached and her head was muzzy, although whether from the concussion or just too much information flying round her brain she couldn't decide. Two days to wind down and recoup was an inviting prospect.

The information Murdo Scott had given her about the investigation into Stone's finances could wait for another day, she decided, until she could think straight although she texted Matt and asked him to dig around the car crash that had killed Davey Campbell, the journalist, in the north of Scotland.

The watchers had disappeared, according to Ali, which Herk suggested was probably something to do with their colleagues having gone AWOL in Spain.

'Getting short-handed,' he remarked. 'Bit of a pain since it stymies any tracking. Maybe they'll come back.' He sounded almost hopeful.

Her mobile rang at the same time as the entry bell, so she answered the phone walking towards the door and collided with Herk emerging from the kitchen, a tea towel in hand. She swore as pain twinged down her arm to her elbow, then had to apologise to her caller.

'Tom, how great to hear from you,' she said with as much enthusiasm as she could muster.

'Drinks tonight, sweetie, at the Langsdale Hotel, 7 pm. Hope you can make it. I've put your name on the list, with a partner, since I won't have time to give you much attention. We've got the film backers in and they need all my love and adoration. But great to see you. Lots of celebs coming, so you'll enjoy yourself. Hope you're not forgetting the wrap party in Big Sur this week. It's gonna be great. And we're all banking on your predictions being right for a stratospheric roller.'

He rattled on without pausing for any responses, breaking off occasionally to shout instructions at his PA, in a curiously hybrid English-American accent.

'Ah, nearly forgot, angel. Acquaintance of yours will be there. Chip Nathon – you met him in Spain, he said. He got your name wrong, said it was Tres. But his description was spot on. See ya.'

She laid her head on the desk and said weakly: 'I just want the world to stop turning. Please.'

Tom Bateson had been a light-hearted fling in Morocco years ago. She had been riding one of the old camel routes for a travel magazine and he had been producing a movie at Ouarzazate. They had nearly collided in the desert when his jeep planed off the rough track at speed and skidded sideways towards her. A week of grit, sand and seasickness from the erratic gait of her elderly mount had begun to pall, so she accepted his offer of a bath and a comfortable bed with alacrity.

His shoot of a biblical blockbuster had been plagued with problems and had claimed the lives of two crew members in accidents, so he had listened intently when she said that starting principal photography on risky influences wasn't a help. Ever since he'd kept in touch with requests for propitious start dates and been impressed by the string of successes that followed. Now he was paying back with a connection to Chip Nathon.

A thump made her wince as a heavy package landed on a side table.

'That'll be from Russell,' Herk said. 'And I'm off. You need a day in bed. We'll pick up tomorrow.'

'No, we won't,' she said. 'Drinks at the Langsdale tonight. Tom Bateson, a film producer friend.'

'You don't need me there. And I don't have a tux.' Herk stood in the doorway, with a canvas bag in one hand, his cheek muscles pulled tight.

She drew in a deep breath. 'Chip Nathon will be there. I need to prise more info out of him. He's the only decent link at the moment to the Stones. It's a film party. Distressed jeans and a T-shirt will be de rigeur.'

There was silence from the hall then a thud as Herk's bag hit the floor. He came in chewing his bottom lip. 'Right,' he said. 'What time? I've got to hand back the French car and pick up Bob's.' As he turned to leave, he added: 'Does this mean we can skip the USA?'

***

An afternoon's sleep revived her spirits and she slipped into slim, black velvet trousers, a low-cut, black silk camisole with a silver shawl on top to disguise the bruises on her upper arm. She climbed into the passenger seat, noting Herk's ironed jeans and black T-shirt with a screaming eagle on the front.

The Mayfair hotel was only a short drive, although the early evening theatre traffic was heavy. Hyde Park Corner was brightly illuminated, with the Wellington Arch standing proudly at the centre, its columns and intricate cornices glowing a radiant beige. Into Belgravia the streets emptied, although nearer the hotel several stretch limousines, Bentleys and Rolls-Royces were blocking the drive into the Langsdale.

'Do you really need me in there?'

'What do you think? And that's a straight question.'

After a moment's hesitation he climbed out and handed the keys to a valet. The liveried doorman nodded them in through a discreet black door held open by a junior flunkey. In the sumptuously decorated foyer, a vast, multicoloured floral display on a circular table sat on a red and green patterned carpet. Cumbersome art deco standard lamps marched down either side of the long room, with enormous circular pendant lampshades hanging overhead. Both of them blinked.

'Man,' she murmured, 'Downton Abbey meets Ivana Trump. Lord save us.' Herk stared around, saying nothing.

The large reception room was humming with excited conversation, and three-quarters full, when they walked in unnoticed, except for a few fleeting glances that quickly wrote them off as nonentities. Dominating the scene were seven mammoth chandeliers, suspended above the hubbub, shaped like hollowed-out drums, with vertical glass slats and a cascade of crystal hanging from the centre.

She grabbed two glasses of champagne from a passing waiter and whispered in his ear: 'My optic nerves are going to shatter. This is worse than Gaddafi's palace.'

Tom Bateson was across the room so she waved. In his fifties and fitter than the last time she'd seen him, his grey hair was crew-cut and he was dressed entirely in denim with tan cowboy boots. He was holding an enthusiastic discussion with two short, fat men in evening suits whose pencil-slim wives, in expensive evening dresses, were standing bored in the background.

'Great to see you,' Tom said as they passed, leaning out to kiss Tire on the cheek, gave Herk a sharp appraisal, and said with a nod of dismissal. 'Chip's down in the smoking lounge. Catch up later.'

'Or not,' Tire muttered as they moved away. A waiter pointed down a long corridor panelled in dark wood with olive green fabric on the walls and a brown carpet. After the ostentation of the earlier scene, it was a considerable relief. At the far end, double mahogany doors opened into a large space dotted with green pot plants, leather armchairs in groups and dimly lit by a few Moroccan style lanterns.

Adjusting her eyes to the dusky ambience, she searched for Nathon while Herk walked across to stand at the corner of the bar. All the seating areas were occupied by men in smart suits with exceptionally beautiful girls sitting close in tight dresses and towering heels. Russian hookers, she thought, giving one a cursory glance. A hand, waving from a corner, caught her eye and she smiled in return, suddenly feeling tense.

'Tres, great to see you. Hope you're recovered.' The portly figure in the armchair, in a black suit with black shirt, levered himself to his feet. He gave her a cursory kiss on the cheek, enveloping her in wafts of cognac, and sank back down. A girl who had been hovering just behind him raised an eyebrow and glided away.

'Oh, sure,' she said, 'just new medication gone wrong. All fine now.'

'Yeah, we were worried about you. But there was an almighty flap going on, so I didn't hear till next day that you were OK.' He peered at her groggily and patted her knee.

'Oh,' she said, putting a concerned hand to her face. 'I hope nothing was wrong.'

He shook his head with a grimace, 'Two staff did a runner. Harman was kicking up hell about it. Don't know why. Workers are always going missing in my experience.'

She chuckled politely and turned to accept a glass of cognac from a waiter and a cigarillo.

'Did they find them?' she asked, hoping the question sounded casual.

'Yeah, three days later at the bottom of a ravine. Motor burnt out. Just a bad accident. Two of their best security guys. Don't think Harman was too keen to tell the old man.' He laughed harshly. 'Pa would have blamed him for being careless.'

'Does Harman share his security team with other people than his father, I mean?'

He gave her a straight look. 'Do you mean does he go off the reservation? I'd think all the time. He's a loose cannon, but he's also terrified of his old man, so he'll keep it below the radar.'

'They don't get on well?' she asked, putting on a surprised expression.

'Tell me who does? Senior is not easy,' he answered sourly, waving to the waiter for another cognac. 'Now, tell me about you.'

She dodged and parried his questions, prattling at length about her new book on the sex-mad guru and saying she hoped to go back to Cerigo to finish her write-up soon and talk to Harman Stone. Maybe she should interview Paul Stone as well? Would that be a good idea, did he think?

Nathon shot her a hard, although bleary stare, blew a smoke ring from his cigar and stared across the room. Eventually he said: 'Now, look. You seem a nice lady. If I were you, I'd avoid both the Stones. I'm thinking of backing off myself.'

An anguished smile crossed her face. 'What a shame,' she purred, putting a hand on his arm. 'And you were such good friends.'

'Don't know about friends. We did some business together. My wife hated him, and especially Harman. She's gone now. So too late to tell her she was right. You know, you remind me of her. Thought that first time I saw you.' He slurped noisily out of his brandy goblet and slid further into the armchair, his fleshy face crumpling in misery.

'Can you keep this to yourself?' he said slowly. 'I always discussed everything with Maybelle, but can't now. I just got ta have someone to share with and you have so got her eyes. Warm and deep.'

'Of course,' she said, running her fingers down his arm to hold his hand.

Over the next fifteen minutes he blurted out his concerns about Paul Stone. He was, he said, involved in developing dodgy drugs at a Mexican research laboratory and testing them on human guinea pigs, poor kids, in Europe and the USA. Harman was in it up to his neck as well. The old man nearly went through the roof when he discovered Harman was marketing these drugs with an English partner. They weren't safe. Tire couldn't prise out of him, in his drunken state, precisely what he thought. He was slurring his words and repeating himself.

'The name of this English partner? Do you remember it?' She tugged his arm.

'Hmm, Teddy something.' He frowned blearily and then raised one arm and made a vague gesture with his thumb and index finger pressed together.

Charades were not her strong point. What was he doing? Writing.

'You don't mean Wrighton? Do you?' She leaned forward and put a hand on his cheek, resisting a temptation to pinch. 'Rupert Wrighton?'

'Thass right. Harman called him a teddy bear. I met him once. A real jerk.'

Shit, so they were all in it together. She realised her hand was still on his face and sat back in her chair.

'So Harman and Wrighton operate without Paul Stone's knowledge?'

'Dunno about that. Scrape off that surface charm and Paul's not that different. Plus, I reckon he's gone *tonto*. Harman always was, but the old man has lost his self- control. I really need to back away once this deal we've got is through.'

She pulled her hand away and watched him for a minute to see if he was properly asleep. As she was picking up her bag from the floor, he came to and grabbed her arm clumsily.

'Really enjoyed our chat. Good to unload. Must do it again. You coming to Big Sur day this week? Be great. I can show you round Cerigo there if you like.' He subsided again.

'Useful schmooze?' Herk asked, when she moved across to the bar, his eyebrows raised. He downed the rest of his fizzy water.

'If I had a conscience,' she replied as they exited, 'it would be kicking me. But I don't. This is too important. He reckons the Stones are dangerous and getting more unstable. Even Senior. America is definitely on. I need more.'

The main reception room was even more jam-packed with beautiful, skinny women, a few beautiful men and more who were not. Tire couldn't see Tom, so they left quietly and quickly.

CHAPTER 42

Tire's mobile jerked her out of a deep sleep. Blearily she looked at the clock. 10 am. Heavens, she must have slept for nearly eleven hours. She ignored it and turned over, pulling the duvet over her head. The phone rang again, so she swung her legs out of bed and rotated her shoulder, pleased to find the stiffness had almost disappeared.

'Miss Thane,' a well-bred voice she faintly remembered but couldn't place, apologised for disturbing her. 'It's Jake Harrister. I don't know if you remember?'

Fully awake, she rang a hand through her tousled hair and cautiously said yes.

'I'm sorry to tell you that Jackson St Clair is failing fast, but he was anxious to see you before he… dies. I'm afraid by the look of it that would mean today.'

'Ah,' she said, wracking her brains for a sensible excuse. There was no way she wanted more clutter in her head.

'It's about your father,' Harrister said gently. 'I really think you should come.'

Struggling into her kaftan, she walked out of the bedroom to see the front door opening and Herk walking in. 'Sandhurst today?' she mouthed to him with a weary look. He nodded.

'Sure,' she said to Harrister, 'be there soon as,' and clicked the phone off.

The hour's drive gave her a chance to skim through the notes Murdo Scott had given her about the investigation into Paul Stone's business and background. Most of it was clippings from old financial articles with incomprehensible jottings on the margins, plus some balance sheets and old company reports. Her heart sank and she decided that sending it to Russell was the best idea. He might make sense of it.

The St Clair manor looked bleaker than before with grey clouds overhead and a chilly wind blowing leaves across the gravel as they drove up. Harrister opened the front door and raised an eyebrow when Herk followed her in, but didn't argue. A nurse was coming out of a room at the right-hand end of the hall and he indicated to Tire that she should go in.

A hospital bed had been installed in a small library, sitting at an angle to the shelves behind to give a view of the garden. The frail figure propped up on pillows had a drip connected to one exposed, shrivelled arm. His eyes were shut and his breathing was rough and stuttering. The sheet tucked under his chin had a towel on top with a few red spatters on it.

She sat uncomfortably on the chair beside him, her mind jerking back to a blood-stained Jesus Sanchez in the Mexican motel.

After several minutes he opened his eyes with difficulty, saw her and then shifted his gaze to the window. He swallowed painfully and still without looking at her said: 'I'm glad you could come, my dear.' The words came out one at a time with hoarse rasping in between, his thin chest heaving under the covers. 'Your father. I'm sorry.' His voice faded and his eyes closed.

She leant forward and put a gentle hand on his arm. A feeling of sadness brought a tear to her eye as she thought, this man was my guardian and I never knew him.

A thud at the window made her jump and she looked out to see a stunned pigeon standing groggily on the terrace, having left a smudged feather on the window. After a couple of ineffectual flaps, it finally made it into the air to fly low to a birch tree, where it clung to a lower branch. Higher up, a single magpie peered down intently. She shivered.

His hand twitched under hers and he looked beseechingly at her. She moved an ear close to his mouth to hear his whisper. 'I only learned years after his death. The crash that killed your mother was not his fault.' He sank deeper into the pillow, a trail of saliva bubbling out of the corner of his mouth, stained red. You can't die now, damn you, she thought fiercely, feeling tempted to shake him back into consciousness.

After a minute or two of stuttering breaths, he rallied. 'He was set up, of that I am sure. I was suspicious at the time but could never prove anything, although I did gather some evidence. It's too late to right the wrong now, but I thought you'd like to know. Jake has all my papers.'

A hand on her shoulder pulled her reluctantly to her feet. She glared at Harrister, who shook his head with a weary expression on his face. Pulling her out of the room by her arm, he beckoned to the nurse standing in the hall beside Herk. He almost pushed Tire into the dining room, said he would organise coffee and left. Walking to the window, she stared down the lawn, which was glistening in a passing shower. The trees were swaying in the stiffening breeze, with blossom from nearby bushes fluttering to the ground.

'There's a magpie,' Herk remarked casually, behind her. 'On its own.'

She turned to grab him tightly by the shoulders and said desperately: 'He says my father wasn't guilty. He died in prison for nothing. What am I going to do?'

Her anguished tone caused him to blink. Releasing him, she started to stride up and down the room, frowning to herself. Herk perched in a corner of the window seat.

Fifteen minutes later Harrister came in with a tray of coffee mugs. He put it on the table and said quietly: 'That's it, I'm afraid. He's gone.'

Only a considerable effort stopped Tire swearing. Standing with her back to him, she replied through gritted teeth, her voice crackling between anger and forced politeness. 'Did you know what he was going to say to me?'

'No,' he said, drawing out the vowel. He hesitated. 'But I may be able to find out more when I get into his papers.'

'Could you?' she said agitatedly.

He nodded. 'It'll take a few weeks. I have a good deal to clear up first.'

'So have we,' Herk remarked abruptly, standing up.

'You're not still after Stone, are you?' Harrister asked distractedly, his eyes narrowing. 'I really would watch your step there.'

'Tell me about it,' Herk muttered sourly, scuffing one boot on top of the other.

'You found out about that reporter?' Harrister's interested tone caught Tire's attention.

'Yup, got his notebooks,' she said, examining his face for a reaction. 'And two of Harman Stone's heavies nearly wiped us out in Spain,' she added for good measure.

'Now, look,' he said, swinging round to face her directly, 'you really ought to leave this to the professionals.'

'Fat lot of good they've done,' she exclaimed. 'The Stones have clearly been running amok for years and no one's done bugger all about them.'

He had the grace to look shamefaced, saying: 'Paul Stone has always cultivated the right people, politicians and business leaders. He's been very astute. He protects his son, who is much more questionable.'

Herk grunted. She pursed her lips, reflecting on what to say next. 'My information is that Senior is descending into madness.'

'That's not good.' Harrister laid down his coffee mug, looking concerned. 'You really can't go up against them on your own.' He tilted his head and added: 'Hens always lose against a fox.'

Herk chortled and Tire smiled acidly. 'So what are you going to do to help? Bring in the hounds?'

'I really don't have time for this,' he said edgily. 'There's too much else going on. But you've got ten minutes to tell me what you've found out before the doctor comes.'

They sat round the table while Tire outlined what she knew. Erica's death, Greengate in prison, her flat under surveillance, their near miss in Spain, Nathon's worries about Stone's drug testing, suspicions about Harman trying to kill off his half-brother Louis, his birth name in France. Harrister listened attentively, running his hand occasionally through his hair and stroking his cheek thoughtfully.

When she had finished, he said: 'Well, we could get Paul Stone for falsifying information on his passport if that last bit is true. And that's about it, unless we get proof about the drug testing or any of the deaths. What are you doing next?'

'Nathon's the best bet for information at the moment,' she said. 'I remind him of his wife and he drinks, so I should get more out of him. We're on a flying visit to California this week to a party where he'll be.'

Harrister frowned. 'This must be costing you a fortune.'

She shrugged. 'I'll get it back and more if I can expose him. Anyway, I'm doing this for Erica.' She threw one end of her scarf over her shoulder and looked at him sideways. 'We've got some info on his business finances from years back but haven't gone into it yet. Is that angle worth pursuing?'

'Maybe,' he said noncommittally, and stopped as the doorbell rang. Standing up, he said in a more definite tone: 'Probably.'

For a moment he looked flustered, and she could see his grief surfacing. 'Look,' he said, 'I'll have to go. Here's my card with my private mobile on it. Keep in touch and if I find out anything about your father I'll let you know. Can you let yourselves out?'

Suddenly desperate for a cigarette, she grabbed her bag and was heading out of the door when Herk said: 'What's that?'

She turned to see him staring out of the window. Heaving a noisy sigh she walked over to him, followed his eye line and said snappily: 'You and your bloody birds. It's another magpie.'

'No, it's not,' he said, tugging at her elbow to hold her beside him. 'There's red on its neck and under its tail.'

The bird, perched on the trunk of a tall beech tree at the far end of the lawn, obligingly spread its wings, displaying horizontal black and white stripes with a flash of scarlet underneath.

'Fancy,' she said, 'you're right. It's a greater spotted woodpecker. And before you ask – it's a bird of prophecy. Peck. Peck. It warns you about what's coming soon. Now let's go.'

CHAPTER 43

A day to recuperate, catch up on sleep, read, research, sort out office clutter and slow the world to a more manageable pace was not working. Tire's dreams were filled with dead bodies being thrown around a circular room, propelled outwards as the entire edifice spun at speed. She was on a motorbike, riding fast round the vertical metal perimeter, ducking and weaving to avoid the random debris, only the momentum of forward movement preventing her from careering down into a bottomless pit.

These were old nightmares that only surfaced when she was seriously overstretched. In odd panicked moments she considered giving up her hunt of Paul Stone. She knew it was turning into an obsession and clouding her judgement. Maybe Harrister was right. Don't pick fights you can't win. Getting herself or Herk killed wouldn't help bring justice for Erica. The world was full of jerks who never got their comeuppance. Or were only exposed when they were dead.

Not having company was normally a comfort, since she had always prized having space to herself. Now she realised she was missing Herk's straightforward, can-do presence. Nothing seemed to faze him. She felt safe when he was around.

The dead reporter Davey Campbell's shorthand notebooks and clippings about Stone's early business dealings had gone off to Russell. Matt was chasing up Stone's Pol Pedra birth in south-western France. She made lists of leads to follow, if she decided to keep going. Automatic pilot was her way of coping. The decision dangled above her head like the sword of Damocles.

'Well, made up your mind yet?' Herk's gruff bark behind her made her jump. She spun round in her chair, then half-turned back to switch off the raucous fanfares of Shostakovich's 'Fifth Symphony'. She stared at him, one hand foraging behind her on the desk for her cigarettes. Lighting up and blowing out a long stream of smoke, she contemplated the yes/no question. Go on or give up. His gaze was steady, non-committal. We actually understand each other, she thought with surprise. It was an odd feeling.

'Yes and no,' she said decisively.

'Feminine logic, is that?' He raised an eyebrow.

'Nope. We go to Big Sur because it's booked. If nothing definite comes out of that, or if it's too big to cope with, then we cut out. Or at least I wait till the bastard's dead before I fillet him in print.'

'You need less evidence that way, then?'

She chuckled. 'No, just no libel risk and,' she added, her jaw tightening, 'less risk of us getting killed.'

Only later, as Herk went off to shower, having had a sweaty morning acting as Speedy Charlie's helper in a removal, did she remember about Jimmy Black in Glasgow. Her heart sank. She might have the luxury of giving up, but he was almost certainly still in danger. But at least he was away for another ten days, according to the gallery owner. Filing that one in her think-about-later folder, she went off to pack for the three-day in and out trip to California.

An empty afternoon stretched ahead. On impulse, she phoned Felicity on her personal mobile. To her surprise, she answered instantly and brightly.

'You can talk?'

'Oh yes, I'm at home. Mr Wrighton fired me.'

'Tell me.'

'He was furious when he came back and discovered Miranda had gone off to the residential course. I said it was on a scholarship and he accused me of setting it up and betraying him. He was quite horrible to me. But I don't care. My old job at a cancer charity has become vacant and I'm going back there.'

'And Miranda?'

'She'll stay in Cornwall for three months. By then, she'll be twenty-one and her grandmother's trust – that's her mother's mother – will be hers. It isn't a huge amount, but it means she'll be independent. And she might even win a place in a music college in Ohio.'

'Lord, that will put his nose out of joint.'

'Oh, he doesn't know all that. He thinks she'll come home. But he seems to have business worries that are keeping him distracted, which is a blessing.'

'Do you know what they are?'

'Some pharmaceutical investment that a lot of people in the fathers' organisation had put money into. I was not supposed to know about it, but I used to check his emails when he was out. He was hopeless with computers and I found his password written down one day. All the money went to an offshore account in Belize. Then it was switched to somewhere else in South America and he was most unhappy. I overheard a really angry phone conversation about it.'

'Do you know who with?'

'Just Harry. I never knew his surname. They used nicknames on email addresses. He came round one day and Mr Wrighton insisted I stay in my office. But I peeked through. He was very peculiar-looking.'

'Short, long chin, big nose?'

'That's right.'

'Felicity, I don't suppose you kept any copies of these emails?'

There was a long pause and a bout of nervous coughing before she whispered: 'Yes. I put them all onto a flash drive and gave it to Miss Smythson. She was angry with me, said obtaining them was illegal and they couldn't be used.'

Not in court maybe, but in an exposé, for sure. Where would Erica have kept it?

'Did you copy more recent ones?'

'Yes, I have a memory stick here. I was going to delete it, now that Miranda's away from him and safe.'

'Don't do that,' Tire yelped. 'I'll send a courier round to pick it up. No one will know you took the emails.'

Could Erica have wiped the original flash drive? Pure, straight-up, middle-of-the-road, stick-to-the-rules Erica, always playing the legal game according to the book? A bead of sweat trickled down Tire's forehead as she remembered being teased about her own slippery methods of extorting the truth.

'What kind of memory stick was it, Felicity?'

'Oh, large. Well, you know what I mean, 64 gigabyte, since there were several years of emails and documents. It was black.'

Erica's jewellery box. They weren't family photographs. She scrabbled in a dish on the desk among the paperclips for a key, unlocked the bottom drawer, opened the carved wooden box, pulled out the black flash drive and plugged it in. While her laptop found the driver, she scribbled down Felicity's address and phoned a courier, then settled down to read. Gotcha, you bastard.

CHAPTER 44

The schedule was tight, arriving San Francisco early afternoon, driving down to Big Sur, dinner with Chip Nathon, next day with luck visiting the Cerigo holiday resort, attending Tom's film party and back to San Fran to fly back the morning after.

They both slept remarkably easily on the ten-hour flight from Heathrow, arriving just after lunch to sunny skies. After a lengthy queue at immigration, they picked up the bulky Jeep Renegade, which Herk had insisted on renting, and set off on the hundred and fifty-mile drive to Big Sur. The suburbs of San Francisco disappeared quickly as they headed for San Jose on the 101.

'You gonna tell me what all that Wrighton stuff was about, then?' Herk's tone was even, but didn't brook argument. She stared out at the flat countryside speeding past, trying to impose order on the blitz of emails and documents she had waded through until the early hours.

'Was there anything about Erica?'

'No smoking gun,' she answered slowly. 'Lots of hate. Some of the neanderthal friends he had confided in wanted her raped and mutilated, but no direct indication of a plot to kill her.'

'Weren't these encrypted?' He turned off for Monterey, heading towards the coast.

'Very amateur. Easy enough to access. What was more interesting were the emails from Lord Adonis, who I assume is Harman Stone. Adonis was one of Aphrodite's lovers – the Cerigo connection.'

He snorted.

'They weren't too detailed, but he and Wrighton were selling an energy-boosting drug, called ZZZWipeOut, mailed from Mexico and not just sent to the UK, but all over the world. Monies collected by credit card abroad, deposited in Belize. Until Adonis decided there was a risk of too much transparency in the bank there and switched the funds, several millions, to Ecuador, he said, although Wrighton clearly didn't believe him and was livid. Especially since some of his buddies had invested heavily.'

'Which tells us what, exactly?'

She swivelled in her seat towards him and said: 'What does wipeout suggest to you?'

'Video war game, destruction.'

'What about a memory cosh drug?'

'S'pose,' he said slowly.

'Think about it. You'd hardly need the darknet to market a pick-me-up.'

'Could be steroids.'

'More likely it's the drugs they were paying to be developed in Mexico to wipe out memory. The ones that screwed up the kids at Cerigo.'

'How do we prove it?'

'I got Russell to order some, sent to a PO box he's got set up. There's a forty-eight hour service at extra cost. Then get them analysed and we'll see. Selling illegal drugs will put them inside for a fair stretch.'

'And Erica?'

There were times she felt like taping up his mouth. His relentless, single-minded focus was never her way of working. Keep battling through the hurricane, grabbing at whatever papers or information floated past and never give up. At the end there was usually a narrative that could be pulled together. But there again, she didn't usually set out to prove a murder. Just to shake down the shady, with whatever weapons came to hand.

Eventually, she said weakly: 'We'll catch a break if we just keep plodding on. At least we might get Greengate out of prison, if the illegal drugs were what got him stitched up.'

***

The sea was dashing in foamy breakers against rocky escarpments and stony beaches, with grey architectural bridges crossing canyons along the shore-hugging Highway One, which was the only route south. She always felt at home here since it reminded her of the Scottish islands.

'Is that a hawk or one of the Spanish vultures?' Herk pointed ahead, where a large bird circled in the distance above the rising mountain.

She fished out a small pair of binoculars, focused them and then wondered whether to answer. Finally, she said: 'It's maybe a turkey vulture or a condor. Can't see at this distance. The flight path is wobbly, so probably a vulture.'

'Hallelujah,' he said gloomily. 'I just don't fancy a rerun of the last time.'

'Oh, for heaven's sake. People live under them fifty-two weeks a year and manage to stay upright.'

A slow-moving Winnebago in front with a 'God Bless America' sticker in the rear window held his attention for several minutes as he willed it to move into a lay-by to allow them to pass.

'You haven't mentioned our stars for a day or so. According to the news, Diegolu is still in a coma and there was a bus crash in a Swiss tunnel that killed thirty-five. It's all piling up, as you said.'

'Same as, same as. It's got a few more days to run. High stress, irritable, blocked.'

'You mean risky and trapped?' he said, giving her a sideways glance.

'For some, not necessarily us. Don't worry, the world isn't going to implode. It'll pass. Look.' She diverted his attention out to sea where a flock of large brown birds with extended beaks were massing just above the waves, some plummeting straight down into the water and rising up with their pouches sagging under the weight of fish. 'Pelicans. They're cute.'

'What do they mean?'

She twisted in her seat to see if he was joking or serious and couldn't decide, until she noticed his lips twitching.

'They bring their young back from the dead, feed them on their own blood.'

There was a silence and then they both laughed out loud. Shit. She'd forgotten. Rummaging in her briefcase she found the full astrology chart of Paul Stone, aka Pol Pedra, which she had printed out before she left but had not had time to absorb.

'Matt found Stone's original birth certificate and it has his time of birth.'

'Huh. Makes a difference?'

'Yeah. It gives you more information. Too complicated to explain why. But what it headlines is he's running into a brick wall about now – loss of reputation, trapped, enraged. Complete devastation, major confusion.'

'Like a cornered tiger, you mean? Not sure that sounds so great. Desperate men can do very stupid things,' he answered.

'No, you miss the point. If he melts down, and it may be nothing we're doing that causes it, then he's no longer in a position to protect Harman.'

She punched his arm with a grin and settled back in her seat with a relieved smile on her face, her motivation and morale restored.

The highway snaked round the mountain edge above the choppy sea, dipping inland at one point as the terrain fell away into a valley, then twisted back to cling once more to the cliff edge, with the Pacific crashing against rocks below.

Once through Big Sur Valley, they headed for Nepenthe, with Herk straining to read the occasional, small, painted signs off to the right, with tracks to wooden houses perched on the edge above the ocean.

'Coordinates would have helped,' he muttered.

'Just before the Los Santos Inn, Tom said. They're doing the food. Not well signposted. The owners he rented from don't like passing trade dropping in.'

He swerved onto a track suddenly, causing the car and caravan behind to brake sharply and honk in complaint. The surfaced road looped left and right round tall, bushy conifers blocking the view from the track until it splayed out in front of a two-storey wood and glass ranch house of considerable size, sitting within yards of the drop down to the sea.

A dark-haired woman with a white apron came out to welcome them in broken English, telling a youth in jeans and white shirt in Mexican Spanish to take their luggage. They had been allocated adjoining rooms on the first floor, both with heart-stopping views from plate glass windows across the Pacific. Herk said he'd go off to recce the route to the Cerigo resort, while she stayed to sort out emails and shower.

Her room was a calming beige with one wall of pale, sandstone blocks, a rustic contrast to the ultra-modern king-sized bed and open bathroom at the end. This is heaven, she thought. Seven-star accommodation in the middle of a wilderness with a moving swell of water of the Pacific Ocean stretching beyond the horizon for five thousand miles. Comfort and isolation.

For the first time, the prospect of success seemed a real possibility. She collected a bottle of water from the fridge and went out contentedly to the small terrace to smoke. She contemplated a pine tree, rooted a yard from the precipitous hundred-foot drop, whose parasol branches framed the ruggedly beautiful coastline beyond.

After a leisurely bath, she put on white jeans, a red, low-cut, cotton top and flip-flops and went downstairs. Outside on the patio, comfortable armchairs and sofas were arranged round a roaring log fire set into a massive stone surround. Chip Nathon, leaning against a pillar of a wooden pergola laden with purple bougainvillea, raised a martini glass in greeting. She requested a spritzer from the youth, now attired in a white waistcoat for his evening duties as waiter.

Two other couples arrived, film executive friends of Tom Bateson's from LA, so the conversation skimmed and skittered until the sunset brought all chatter to a halt. Tire moved across to stand beside Herk as the giant ball of red turned orange and moved slowly down towards the sea. Faintly in the distance the sound of drums marked the passage of day's closure.

'Let's eat out here. We can smoke.' Chip's voice broke into her reverie, his tension betrayed in a hard undertone. He indicated a table set for two near the fire. Herk stayed where he was staring out into the darkness, stars appearing singly and in shoals overhead.

'Is he a bodyguard?' Chip whispered loudly enough to be heard across the room.

She shrugged and mouthed: 'Photographer.'

Another vodka martini appeared and he ordered a Chardonnay for Tire without asking, with a bottle of Cabernet to follow. He smiled tightly, made fulsome compliments about her appearance in a half-hearted manner, and then said in a rush: 'What a relief to see you, can't tell you. Look, sorry to dump this on you, but I got no one else I can talk to. That thing we were talking about last time. Paul Stone. It's worse, much worse.'

Tire put on her most sympathetic smile, stopped moving her leg to avoid his knee and put a hand across the table. The words tumbled and burbled out, at times without much connection, but she gathered the gist – that both he and Stone had lost heavily in a joint investment in South America. 'Can't tell you how many tens of millions,' he mumbled, adding viciously: 'His fault since he must have known it was dodgy from the get-go. I took him at his word since I thought he knew what he was doing. And on top of losing, I think there'll be repercussions here, which I seriously don't need.'

She toyed with her chicory salad and pushed a piece of quince round her plate, before saying, with a perplexed look: 'I thought he was a near genius with money.'

A lump of risotto with a mushroom on top slid onto the table as Nathon angrily banged his fork down. 'Huh, like my great-uncle Sam who went bust in '29. That shit hot. Took my family three generations to catch up again.' He slurped at his wine and wiped his chin on the back of his hand.

Her brain was racing as she pondered her response. Speaking carefully and hoping she sounded naïve, she said: 'Was he desperate for money in taking that kind of a risk?'

'How do you know that?' His eyes, buried in folds of reddened flesh, sparked with suspicion. When she returned a placatory smile and a graceful hand gesture that would have done credit to a Thai temple dancer, he nodded with tears forming in his eyes. 'Female intuition. You are so like my Maybelle, I can't tell you,' he sniffed.

There was a tense pause while plates were removed and the red wine poured. Lost in his irritation and anguish, he held her hand in his increasingly sweaty grip, which made her stomach and conscience churn, and she fervently hoped Herk wasn't watching. With relief she saw the main course being brought across and he started to talk again.

'I reckon he might be completely bust,' he said, pushing a forkful of duck breast smeared with butternut squash into his mouth. 'Lost a bucketload on oil and some central African deal went tits up. His own fault, mind you. Asking for it, doing business with these kind of places. Plus he was hit badly with Swiss and Venezuelan currencies going *bronco*.'

She lifted the quail leg from her plate, holding it delicately between her finger and thumb, dipped it into ginger sauce and munched on the tempura batter.

'You thought he was losing the plot last time we spoke. Mentally, I mean. And getting involved in some kind of drug testing.'

Wondering whether she was pushing too hard, she concentrated on eating for a moment. When she looked up, he was focused on his plate shovelling food into his mouth as if his life depended on it. Wiping his mouth on his napkin and waving to the waiter, he said: 'Yeah.' He lit a cigar and leant back.

'Some damn fool notion about blotting out memories. I could never make head nor tail of it, though I know the medics didn't like it. One of them told me it would roll psychiatry back to the bad old days of lobotomies. That's when I began to think his circuit board was seriously overloading. If he gets the Drug Admin boys on his back he's got trouble.'

A movement to her right made her glance over to where Herk was standing on the sea terrace, gesturing he was going upstairs. She nodded imperceptibly and suddenly felt sick of this charade with Nathon. But needs must.

'But you'll be alright, won't you?' she said, not entirely insincerely.

He smiled grudgingly and sighed. 'Kind of.'

'And what about Paul Stone? Is he coming to the party tomorrow?'

'Christ, no,' Nathon guffawed. 'Not his scene at the best of times since he's not in charge. Anyway, Harman tells me he went to ground in the lodge in the north of Scotland days back and refused to take any security with him. Said he had work for them elsewhere. Baby boy sounded edgy. Not that he cares about his father, but he was clearly worried about him going off the rails. I had the impression the cash flow had stopped. These resorts can't be too profitable the way he runs them, so he needs his old Pa.'

The evening dragged on with two mountainous portions of chocolate mousse with whipped cream being presented, then cognac and more cognac. She manoeuvred herself into a position where her seat was beside a palm tree. She hoped it liked the alcohol she poured surreptitiously into its roots every time he looked away.

Finally she excused herself, arranging to meet next morning to see round the holiday resort complex ten miles down the road, and fled upstairs. There was silence from Herk's room but she banged around just to let him know she was back and on her own. As she lay down to sleep the words 'needed elsewhere' ran round her head.

CHAPTER 45

There was a gentle, rhythmic splash of waves breaking against the shore and a perfect blue sky overhead. Tire stretched and climbed slowly out of bed, made herself a coffee and wandered out to the balcony to see if she could spot any sea otters swimming among the tangled bed of brown kelp floating offshore.

The thought nagging at the back of her mind from Chip's conversation at dinner took three cigarettes before it clicked into focus. 'Security guys needed elsewhere.' Doing what? Or more to the point whom? The hair on the back of her neck prickled and a chill rippled down her spine. She walked across the balcony to look into Herk's room, which was empty with the bed tidy but clearly slept in.

Chewing her lip, she leant over the balcony to look down onto a patio table below where a blue jay with a dark, peaked hood of feathers was searching for crumbs. Turning on her heel, she went into her room to find her mobile phone; flicking through her contacts she found the Marinello Gallery and rang the number. An assistant told her that the owner was not available and wouldn't be for several days.

In a quandary she pushed for his personal number, only to be politely rebuffed. After a moment's hesitation she asked about Jimmy Black, their artist. Was he still away? There was a long silence and the voice finally said, in a stilted tone as if reading from a script: 'I'm very sorry to tell you his tenement was burnt down yesterday and several people are dead.' The connection was ended.

Holy Christ. A stab of guilt was followed by a choking cloud of dread and then pure rage ran through her body, tingling down to her fingertips and toes. She'd get the bastard if it was the last thing she did. Fifteen minutes prowling, stamping and banging her fist on the stone wall did little to clear her head. The mobile rang as she was aiming for a cold shower. Thinking it was Herk, she didn't read the incoming number.

Before she could speak, a harsh Scottish voice snarled: 'Who the hell are you?'

'What?'

'You were asking about Jimmy Black.'

'Who are you?

'Never mind that. What's your interest in him?'

'Is he OK?' she said, her heart taking a jump.

'I'm saying nothing till you tell me why you're asking about him.'

Thinking rapidly, she decided to take a chance. 'Who I am isn't important. But I think he's in danger.'

'You don't say.' The voice oozed contempt.

She didn't reply, wondering if he was one of Stone's heavies. Maybe not, if he had connections to the art gallery. There was an impatient growl at the other end. A different approach was clearly needed, so she softened her tone.

'I'm a writer and I just came across some information that suggested he might be at risk.' She took a deep breath.

'More.' The roar did not brook argument.

'How do I know you're not one of the ones threatening him?' she said.

'Because,' the menacing voice said slowly, as if talking to an idiot, 'I'm a friend of Ricky's and the bastards that tried to get Jimmy killed my nephew. So if you've got information I want it. Now. And I'll sort them, never you fear.'

'Is he alright, Jimmy?'

'He's fine and under my protection. So anyone coming for him will have me to deal with. My name is Wally Strang, by the way. I'm kind of well known round these parts.'

'Oh, thank god,' she said, sagging onto the bed. Jimmy safe and a heavyweight ally.

In the ten-minute conversation following, she was circumspect in what she told him, since there was little substantive proof implicating Harman Stone directly and Wally sounded arrogant and reckless. He might be a force to be reckoned with in Glasgow, but that wouldn't mean much outside. Only an agreement to meet up with him in Glasgow in two days' time stopped his insistent questions. In return, he said he intended to move Jimmy completely out of harm's way into a safer house tomorrow.

Glancing at her watch, she dashed for a shower and was out of the door and downstairs to meet a waiting Chip at the front door. He was standing beside a sleek black Chrysler with a chauffeur behind the wheel.

He motioned her into the back seat and she waved to Herk, who was behind in the jeep.

The fifteen-minute drive north was uneasy with Chip constantly glancing at her, almost speaking at points and then looking embarrassedly out of the window as his nerve failed him. Tire's head was buzzing with too much excitement for small talk to be easy. When his hand slid across the seat several times, she diverted his attention by pointing out to sea at otters she thought she had seen, even whales spouting south, until the driver said flatly it was the wrong season for whales going to Baja.

Why were they going to this damned resort, she wondered? It would be a waste of time except for Herk to take a couple of shots of it for the book, which was rapidly sorting itself out in her head. They should be on their way to Glasgow and then on to the north-west. All she had wanted was information out of Chip and his obvious interest in her was beginning to make her feel ashamed. Maybe they could cut Tom's party and return today. Once Chip had gone back to his office she'd discuss it with Herk.

Finally, they turned left off the highway at a discreet Cerigo sign and along a curving, gravelled track flanked by giant cacti and aloes. The long, one-storey wood and glass reception building looked an expensive architectural item. On both sides the grounds stretched out along the cliffs, with a dozen whitewashed hacienda-style villas almost hidden behind lush bougainvillea and plumbago tumbling over pergola dividers. More LA than Henry Miller country, Tire thought sourly, putting on her brightest smile for the tall figure in black jeans and white shirt coming out to greet them.

Chip introduced him as Emilio, the manager, kissed her warmly on both cheeks before she could stop him, made his excuses and left, saying he'd see her at the party. A syrupy stream of a welcome, compliments and then sales talk followed as Emilio waved his bronzed arms around, exposing more of his tanned chest, and constantly put on and took off his sunglasses. Herk, standing with an impressive array of cameras round his neck, said he would wander off to take photographs, avoiding those areas that were occupied by guests.

A dreary hour followed until Tire was almost screaming with boredom and irritation at the inconsequential trivia that poured out almost non-stop as they walked round the property. She had clipped her mini tape recorder on her shirt blouse to give the illusion that his pearls of wisdom were being saved for posterity, leaving it switched off. Butting in only twice, she learned he had never met Stone senior, although he very much hoped to rectify that soon. And he had met Harman Stone once, since he had only been manager for two weeks, having come up from LA.

Mercifully, two sets of new guests arrived when she was on the verge of being very rude. Concerned that she had not seen Herk in a while she went off to look for him. On her second circuit she was beginning to get more anxious. He was nowhere to be seen or heard. Leaning against a rail as the ground fell straight down to the sea, she clenched her jaw and looked down the hundred-foot drop to the rocks and water below. Nothing was visible on the shoreline although there were several adjoining buildings halfway down the cliff edge, with a track leading to them. Damn. Had she missed that bit of the guided tour? She racked her brains. Hot tubs, sulphur springs. That was it.

A discreet sign hidden behind tumbling passion flowers pointed to a boardwalk, overhung with green ferns, which led down stone steps and sloping gravel stages towards the baths. At the entrance was a rope bearing the notice 'closed till 3 pm for cleaning'. She stepped over it carefully, listening intently. Only the waves and the squawking of seabirds broke the silence.

She tiptoed quietly through the lavish changing rooms, grateful she had remembered to put on canvas deck shoes. Through a small gym, the door to the hot tubs stood open. For no reason she could later recall she picked up a ladies' pink dumbbell from a shelf, which weighed heavily in her hand and walked towards the door.

The open deck had three huge, stone-encased, hot tubs. The furthest two were empty. The third and nearest tub was partially obscured by the half-open door and beside it she could see a camera strap lying on the ground. She pulled the door back slightly to see Herk's body almost completely submerged with only half of his face showing, his eyes closed. Trails of blood were bubbling across the surface.

A tall man stepped out from the corner, holding a long-handled brush, and for an instant she thought she had gone mad. He leered at her, exposing broken front teeth and said in broken English: 'Anjep. I thought you would come looking for him. Hah.'

Anger overtook fear and without pausing to think she hurled the dumbbell at him, which caught him under the chin and snapped his head back. It wasn't heavy enough to do him major damage, but it threw him off balance and as he staggered to regain his footing he tripped over the pole of the brush, falling back against the iron barrier. He was tall enough for the rail to catch him just below his centre of gravity so she ran across, grabbed the brush end and pushed him over. Then she stood in appalled silence until a hoarse voice said: 'Well, that makes it twice I owe you, then.'

Collapsing onto her knees beside the hot tub, she held Herk's face in her hands and bent her head to touch his forehead, tears streaming down her face. Sniffing furiously, she croaked with an anguished squeal: 'That man?' He was the one you killed in Spain.'

'His bloody twin brother, so he told me. Now help me out of here. The sulphur's beginning to get to me.'

A luxurious towel was put to good use cleaning his cuts, which he insisted were superficial, and drying him off. She tried to shut her ears as he went off into a bathroom to force himself to throw up the sulphurous water in his stomach. Handing him a bottle of mineral water, which he drank gratefully, she said: 'What now? I reckon we should scarper home.'

'Nope,' he answered shortly. 'We act as if nothing has happened and continue as planned. With luck the tide'll take him out.'

Passing a mirror she caught side of her sheet-white face and haunted eyes circled in dark pools of flesh.

'That easy?'

'It's that simple,' he said evenly. 'Just put it to the back of your mind and forget it for now.'

The towels were thrown into huge laundry baskets, except for the one smeared in Herk's blood, which he tucked under his arm. He collected his cameras and picked up a mobile phone lying beside them and set the hot tub to empty before they started up the path. Tire was trembling so much he had to grab her elbow to keep her steady. At the top he listened intently and looked around. A hushed calm lay like a blanket over the property.

Nudging Tire onto a small path that ran through a rockery garden shaded by ornamental trees that blocked the view from the rest of the property, Herk stopped at a huge stone dolmen and whispered: 'Stay here.' Within thirty minutes he was back, wearing a baseball hat that covered his wet hair and most of his cuts, and carrying a floppy sunhat that he rammed onto her head, pulling down the brim. 'Lipstick on,' he instructed, so she fumbled in her bag and put a fuschia smear round her mouth. He then tucked his arm into hers and they walked to the jeep, parked a hundred yards away.

There was only one exit road so they could not avoid passing the reception building. 'Chin up and smile,' he hissed at her. Luckily, Emilio was standing beside a white Cadillac, with an obsequious smile on his face, as the two oversized occupants in shorts and Hawaiian shirts emerged.

Tire managed a friendly wave and a blown kiss, then put her hand over her mouth as they drove round the first bend and out of sight, trying to suppress the urge to throw up.

How she got through the rest of that day she never knew. Herk insisted they lunch at the café at Nepenthe and act normally. They sat at the far end of a long bench table full of animated, chattering tourists. Tire kept her head firmly turned away, looking out over the oak and cypress-strewn land that fell away to the brilliant blue sea below, stretching miles along the cliffs and coastline into the distance. She barely touched the goat's cheese salad that appeared in front of her and heaved slightly at the sight of Herk tucking into bacon and scrambled eggs.

After a second cup of coffee, she was still shaking but managed to fill him in on the conversation with Chip from the night before and the phone call with Wally Strang. Munching his way through a piece of blueberry crumble, he said: 'So you're intent on going up to face Stone then? In Wester Ross? I thought you said we'd cut and run after this trip if it got too big to handle.'

'I don't know, Herk, I don't know,' she said irritably, clenching her fist. 'But he has to be stopped. He just burnt some people to death trying to get Jimmy Black. Anyway, I did promise to go to Glasgow. So let's go one step at a time.' Wrapping her arms round her shivering body, she added weakly: 'I can't face this party tonight.'

'No choice,' he answered shortly, pulling across a plate of mixed cheeses and insisting she at least ate some bread.

A sense of impending doom enveloped her on the short drive back to their residence. Dread of what she'd done and dread of the consequences if the police found out blotted out fear of repercussions from Stone. Herk had sensibly managed to leave no time for her to brood so she showered, dried her hair and threw on her black velvet pants and gold satin top, doubled up her make-up to hide her pallor and went down.

The party was in full swing under flower-festooned pergolas with lights blazing and a band playing by the pool's edge. The film's stars and cast were obvious from their slim profiles and casual, high-fashion outfits, while the crew came in all shapes and sizes in jeans and shirts. A few middle-aged men stood out awkwardly in evening dress, clearly the financiers. It all passed in front of her as one giant blur. Clinging on to Herk's arm, she nodded to a small table in a corner almost in the shrubbery furthest from the music. To her relief, Chip Nathon was talking animatedly to a middle-aged blonde in a slinky blue dress and she slid further behind the bush, hoping to avoid his notice.

Two glasses of champagne made her head swim, but helped to take her mind off the afternoon's horror. Eventually, Chip came across with his companion and sat down. He smiled embarrassedly at Tire, introducing Maggie as a friend from San Francisco who had turned up unexpectedly.

He looked conspiratorially at Tire, lowered his voice and said: 'Another development.' He nodded knowingly at her. 'There was an accident at Cerigo this afternoon. A worker fell onto the rocks. Concussed, broken leg, maybe spinal injury. They only found him about 3 pm and airlifted him out.' He tapped the side of his nose. 'There's bad luck hanging over that outfit, I tell you. My Maybelle always said once the ball starts rolling, it doesn't stop.'

'You don't say,' Herk murmured, pouring out more champagne.

'And,' Chip added, still whispering, 'I was speaking to Harman again. He said his old man had cut off all contact from his own office. Everyone. Won't talk. The boy is seriously getting the wind up. This smells like bankruptcy to me. I've seen it before and it's never a pretty sight.'

The band struck up Chaka Khan's 'Ain't Nobody' and Maggie tugged at Chip's sleeve, forcing him to his feet. 'It's our number, honey. It's too sweet of them to play it. C'mon.' His colour reddened and he avoided Tire's eye, as he was pulled onto the dance floor to be clasped firmly to the blue dress.

'Thank Christ for that,' Tire said burying her face in her hands, then sat up with a sniff to finger off any mascara that was running. 'I didn't kill him. Jesus, what a relief. But he might talk.'

'Nah. That kind of fall. Head injury. He might never remember. Luckily he'd put his mobile phone on a shelf before he beat me up. I took it and sent a text just after we arrived at Nepenthe, so that puts us in the clear.' He grinned.

She resisted an urge to throw her arms round him and slumped back in her chair, trying to ignore the singer's hopes for eternal love wailing out across the terrace.

CHAPTER 46

The dilapidated curtains in the back bedroom let whorls and streaks of grey light penetrate through the decaying fabric. Curled up on his side and covered by a duvet, Jimmy traced the random trails and patterns as they drifted aimlessly across the dusty wall whose paper was torn loose in places. Maybe he should leave Elly, he thought. Go away somewhere on his own where he wouldn't bring danger to her or anyone around him. The prospect of being separated tore at his heart, but he couldn't see any other option. Or perhaps take his own life. It was him the man was after, not her. Then she'd be safe. Tears slid down his face.

Climbing quietly out of bed, he collected his clothes and went into the kitchen to dress without disturbing her. A cup of tea revived his spirits, but the decision was hardening in his mind. He had no idea how or where but it was the only solution. Maybe he could disappear below those floating leaves in the pond, down into the mud. Drinking turpentine would be too messy and take too long.

Until recently he had rarely reflected on the life he had been forced to lead. Each day had been accepted with unthinking resignation. Taking control of his life, even in the act of ending it, would have required a sense of power he had never possessed. He remembered back to the good moments playing secretly with Lachie, meeting Elly on brief occasions behind the laundry outhouse. The long years of harsh desolation accepted at the time as the norm, perhaps his due, he tried to blank out. Now, just as he and Elly might find happiness and security, it was all being destroyed.

His anger surged then quailed, like a candle flame guttering in the breeze. It stayed alight long enough for him to make a further resolution. Before he went, he'd finish the painting of the path where his mother had died. That would be his revenge. His voice from beyond the grave, speaking the truth. Even if no one heard or understood, he would have stood up for her. It was the best he could do.

A noisy altercation on the street below did not disturb his concentration as he mixed paint on his palette and started to fill in the blank on the canvas. He knew he would not have time to do it properly since the paint should be left to dry between coats, but he pushed on regardless, adding thick layers of red in a spreading puddle.

Heavy footsteps were clattering up the tenement stairs as Elly came through, a coat over her nightdress, to bring him another cup of tea. She looked doubtfully at his efforts and then tutted irritably as a fist hammered on the door. A voice shouted: 'It's Dorry. Open up.'

The massive figure, who had brought them fish and chips the night before, lumbered in, his face red and sweating, his denim jacket ripped down one sleeve. He held a mobile phone in one beefy, calloused hand, pressed a button and handed it to Jimmy.

'Wally here,' the voice bellowed out of the phone, making Jimmy jump. 'You're to come with Dorry and stay with Ricky at his house beside me. You'll be safer there.' The phone went dead.

'I'm not leaving my painting,' Jimmy said fiercely, tears in his eyes.

'It's horrible,' Elly responded with equal force.

'Get your coat.' Dorry's roar was accompanied by a ferocious glare. 'We'll sort all that out later.'

Despite both their protestations, Jimmy stubbornly insisted on bringing the painting with him, holding the wet side away from him, with a plastic bag in the other hand, containing brushes, palette, paint tubes and turpentine. He told Elly to sit in the front passenger seat of the muddy pick-up truck that Dorry pointed to, looking around suspiciously as he did so. Jimmy sat in the back, holding the canvas upright. The smell of oil paint caused Dorry to curse under his breath and open all the windows on the twenty-minute drive out to Milngavie.

The barrier and interior gate swung open to a bleep command. They climbed out and Dorry pointed to the far side of Ricky's house, while he spoke in a low growl into his mobile. They walked hesitantly round the stone terrace, past the luminous blue pots to the open kitchen windows. Wally nodded curtly as he passed them. Inside, Ricky was sitting with his heavily bandaged ankle tucked under his seat. He managed a strained, though cheerful, smile and waved at them to sit down. Elly looked at him expectantly, but he shrugged silently and splayed his hands in an apologetic gesture.

A waft of cigar smoke preceded Wally's return. All three stared at him apprehensively. He sniffed, put a polished, tan brogue on the strut of a stool and looked down the table across to the far window. 'Right. Here's where we're at. Another two bojos tried to get you this morning.'

Elly gave a low shriek while Jimmy blanched and opened his mouth to speak.

'Later,' Wally admonished him with a sharp look. 'Dorry's boys got them. One's foreign, the others a local low-life. Which is good.' He drew heavily on his cigar. 'Because the Glasgow lad'll crack sooner, since he knows my reputation.' He smiled thinly. 'In addition, there's a writer who seems to know about your man.' He nodded to Jimmy. 'And she's coming day after tomorrow.'

The words came out of Jimmy propelled by a rising desperation: 'I need to go away. Disappear. Elly can stay here.'

'No,' cried Elly and Wally in unison.

The clack-clack of Wally's lighter on the polished table echoed round the stainless steel kitchen units. 'Trouble was, I couldn't persuade the police to write you off as dead in that fire. Joe tried, but the fire service wouldn't play ball. And the polis had your new address, so someone must have blabbed. Anyways, all to the good since we got the bastards. Once they talk we'll know more.'

Jimmy half-stood up and looked at him with mute anguish, which earned him a hostile glare, so he sat down again.

'Remember, son, it isn't just you that needs avenging. I have my nephew to think about. This woman that's coming sounds as if she knows a fair amount, even though she was dancing around on the phone.'

He issued more instructions about staying put, announced both houses were on lockdown and that Dorry was in charge and left. Jimmy laid his head on his arms on the table and wept.

CHAPTER 47

A brilliant azure sky bathed the trip from Big Sur to San Francisco next morning. Ten hours later, heavy grey cloud greeted the plane's arrival in London. Tire's body was exhausted, her nerves jangled, but her internal motor had kicked in. Her ability to switch onto adrenaline when all else failed would keep her running. Herk's silence was ominous, but she ignored it as they grabbed a taxi for a dash back to the Soho apartment to collect warm, waterproof clothes and back to the airport again.

Glasgow was drenched in a steady downpour when they touched down late in the afternoon. She glanced at Herk as they climbed into the small Ford saloon he'd suggested hiring. His blank expression suggested a soldierly obedience. The car indicated an urban-only trip.

Finally, she said: 'Wester Ross?'

'Fly to Inverness, pick up a Range Rover,' he replied curtly, then tapped a finger on the wheel. 'That's supposing you won't be argued out of it.' He didn't sound hopeful.

Having phoned Wally Strang to get the address, they set off along the motorway, through the Clyde Tunnel and onto the maze of traffic lights at Anniesland Cross. Crossing a canal, they surged away from red sandstone tenements into suburban Glasgow, with prim bungalows one side of the dual carriageway and rolling green fields on the other. The sedate grey mansions of Bearsden gave way to open countryside skirting round the secluded backwaters of Milngavie.

The GPS led them through a series of turnings till they reached a gated cul-de-sac with Hunter Close inscribed on a flashy blue and gilt board. The rectangular barrier slid back as they drew up and Herk pointed to a camera flashing red at them. The high, grilled gates, with arrowhead spikes, of the first of two entrances inside, glided open. A gravel drive led up to a large house barely visible behind high shrubbery and trees.

'The front entrance seems well enough protected,' said Herk, looking at the high, stone, perimeter wall topped with rolls of barbed wire.

Tire surveyed the large whitewashed villa, which had a top-heavy, cluttered feel, with windows bulging out from the first floor and a witches' cone tower planted incongruously off-centre on the roof. The window frames were painted in the same brilliant hard blue as two giant pots, either side of the steps, and the walls adjoining the front door. Several sculptures were dotted around the grass; stone abstracts and a bent metal frame painted in shrieking red and yellow. A Mediterranean folly, she thought, shivering in the damp Scottish air.

A swarthy young man with improbably blonde hair and an apron over his purple trousers and shirt, reeking of cologne, stood in the doorway. Herk blanched slightly when the lavender fragrance enveloped him and walked behind Tire into the marble-floored hall.

The sitting room was vast and high-ceilinged, with several seating areas decked out in sharp reds and blues. Ricky Marinello was leaning against the wall of the far window corner, which was decked out with ultra-modern, pristine white wing chairs sitting on a scarlet geometric rug, its swirls repeating up the wall in two giant motifs.

The heavy glass top of the coffee table in the centre was perched precariously on what looked like a giant strand of tagliatelle shaped out of beige metal. Waving them to sit down, he hobbled painfully to the nearest seat and sank down with a sigh. He leant over to find a bottle of wine in a cooling bucket on the floor.

'Only white wine in here, I'm afraid,' he remarked with forced cheerfulness, pouring into two empty glasses and topping up his own. 'Just impossible to get red wine or beer out of that fabric if it's spilt.'

'I'd believe that,' Herk remarked sagely, trying to keep his elbows away from the chair arms.

The atmosphere was tense and expectant. Ricky bit his lip and fiddled with his wine glass, clearly waiting. Exhaustion and jet lag flowed over Tire, making her suppress an urge to yawn.

A clatter at the door brought Herk to his feet and a skitter of claws on the polished parquet provoked a squeal from Ricky. 'Not in here, Wally, I beg you. Butch, get away from that chair now!'

His voice crescendoed as a large Rottweiler skidded and splayed across the polished surface, landing beside Tire and rubbing his head enthusiastically into her arm. Unable to stop herself she giggled, running her free hand through his fur and then buried her face down his back.

'We'll have our drinks in the conservatory. These seats are not fit to sit in.' The burly figure clad in a loud, beige check suit gave a cursory look at Tire, a more hostile one at Herk and marched off to a door at the far end with the dog click-clacking obediently after him.

'He does this deliberately, damn him,' Ricky hissed. 'Just so he can smoke his bloody cigars.'

The Victorian-style sun room at the back of the house had iron struts between the glass panes and scrolled in half-circles above the double doors to the garden. Wally sank into the largest black rattan armchair, having first tossed four cushions onto the floor and pointed to his side, where the dog immediately sank down and put his enormous head between his paws.

'I'll have a glass of red, Ricky.' He lit a cigar, inhaling in short puffs till he was satisfied it was alight. His beady eyes flickered between Tire and Herk: hard, appraising. He's exerting control, she thought, getting everyone off balance. She waited, risking a glance at Herk, who was looking absent-mindedly out of the window.

'Right,' he said harshly. 'I want to know what you know.'

Over the next five minutes, Tire filled him in with the background details about the Stones, the deaths that might be connected with them and the disappearance of Louis, Harman's stepbrother. She skipped the illegal drugs and Wrighton, and mentioned their own near miss in Spain and the cryptic message on the mobile about LN and Jimmy Black.

'Aye, they've made two attempts to get him this week. That fire at his flat and another go at his studio. Luckily my boys got them both.'

Rain started to pitter-patter on the conservatory roof, then to sheet down, casting a grey pall over the garden. The increasingly resonant thuds on the glass swamped the conversation. Wally stubbed out the chewed stump of his cigar in the gold ceramic ashtray on the table beside him and lit another. Then just as suddenly the rain eased off and a thin light spread across the glistening grass outside.

'Now, how come you got away?' he said, jabbing a stubby finger at Herk, who smiled grimly and didn't respond. Tire flinched and stared at her glass.

After a pause, Herk said steadily: 'They had unfortunate accidents. All three of them.'

'Did it to themselves, you mean? Good for you.' Wally nodded approvingly, then frowned. 'What do you mean three? I thought you said two.'

'Another in California. But he's not dead, just badly injured,' said Tire reluctantly, her eyes downcast. Keen to get off the topic, she said: 'You mentioned on the phone your nephew had been killed?'

'Aye, Jimmy Black,' Wally said grimly. 'He swapped names with...' he waved his cigar in the air, 'this Jimmy, when they were in the Hall and got bumped off when he came out. Mistaken identity.' His rumble of disapproval brought the Rottweiler to its feet, the massive black head level with his shoulder issuing a supportive growl. He added grimly: 'And they made more of a mistake than they knew, tangling with me.' He shook his head exasperatedly. 'If I'd just known. I'd have looked after him when he came out. Bunch of real no-hopers on that side of the family.' He cleared his throat with a bark. 'But family is family. And I'll have the bastards who did this. Now who is...?'

Tire interrupted, saying there was also a journalist investigating the Stones who had been killed in a car crash up north.

Wally leant back, screwing up his face in disbelief. 'Christ, worse than the fucking mafia. Bodies all over the joint. Who are these guys?'

'The son is a wide boy, sells illegal drugs and god knows what else. The father is a saint. Helps lonely old-age pensioners, funds Alzheimer's research. Friends in high places. One of the untouchable ones.' She held his gaze steadily.

Wally looked as if he was going to spit on the floor. 'They're always the fucking worst, the charity mingers. Got black souls, my ma always used to say, and she wasn't wrong.' He blew a smoke ring across the room, watching it disintegrate as it reached the damp glass.

The measured thud of heavy feet preceded the arrival of a hulking figure, well over six feet and veering towards twenty stone, dressed in scruffy jeans and sheepskin jacket. He stopped just outside the open doors, cast a hard look at Herk and extended a hand smeared with dried blood.

'Sorted him, boss,' he grunted.

'The Glasgow lad, what did he say?' Wally turned, his eyes intent. When no answer was forthcoming apart from a slight twitch of the massive bald head, he stood up and moved outside.

'That's Dorry.' Ricky leant forward confidentially, offering Tire a bowl of nuts and lowering his voice. 'He lives next door and is in charge of security.' He grinned. 'Do you know how he got his name?' He paused expectantly. 'The dormouse. Isn't that great? He's the size of a pantechnicon.'

'What does Wally do?' Herk asked, propping a desert boot across one knee.

'Best not to ask,' was the whispered reply. 'He's in construction and… other things.' Ricky lifted an eyebrow knowingly and winked. 'I loathed him at the beginning, but I've got used to him and he knows about protection.'

'For sure.' Herk cast a doubtful glance out of the door.

After a muttered conversation Wally returned, sat down with a thump on the chair and waved his empty glass at Tire. She stifled a grin and moved across with the bottle. His musky cologne, with a hint of leather overlaid with cigar smoke, reminded her for a moment of Chip Nathon. With luck, the slinky blue dress would be keeping his miseries and her conscience at bay.

Putting a ruddy hand thoughtfully on the Rottweiler's head and teasing his fur, he said: 'The lad admitted he'd done the first fire in Dowancross Street with the foreign geezer, called him Janski. And they tried to do the second fire at the studio, which is when Dorry got them. He said they were short-handed, which is why he'd been hauled in. Evidently two brothers headed security for this outfit and one was killed in Spain.' He smiled unpleasantly at Herk. 'Another's in the States. And if I remember right,' he said looking sharply at Tire, 'he's out of action?' She nodded weakly.

He stretched his leg, tapping his polished shoe against the metal table support. 'Seemed to be some sort of desperation about this, he was told. They'd screwed up before and the boss wasn't pleased. But…' he paused for effect, 'useful thing to know there were only four guys doing the dirty work. From Eastern Europe somewhere. So now they're all accounted for. The one we've got can stay where he is. He's not going any place till I find out if he was the one who killed my nephew.'

Tire felt the relief ripple down her spine and glanced at Herk, who was sitting upright and stony-faced.

'Can you find out who exactly they were taking orders from?' she said. 'Was it Paul or Harman Stone?'

Wally eased himself out of the seat and nodded. 'Might take a while. The local lad didn't know and the Janski one is close-mouthed. Dorry'll lean on him, but he can't do too much damage since the polis will have to get him at some point.'

'Are you not staying for supper, Wally?' Ricky asked cautiously.

'Nah, wife's got company the night,' Wally said shortly. 'But before I go we need a plan of action here. What comes next?' His eyes moved glacially round the group, stopping on Herk. 'Getting the guy who did it is one thing. Getting the boss who ordered it is another. You reckon it's the son?'

A steady drip-drip of water from the creepers up the side of the house onto the glass roof filled the silence. Tire stared out into the garden, unable to clear the fog in her head, wondering when she could get some sleep. Herk sat looking blank, avoiding Wally's glare.

There was a hesitant knock on the inside door and Tire looked round to see a slight, grey-haired man in an incongruously large painter's smock, standing waiting on the threshold. The Rottweiler's tail thumped enthusiastically on the floor. Wally beckoned him in and Tire moved along the couch to let him sit next to her, with the dog on its haunches in front of them, happily licking at his hand.

Taking a deep breath, she said: 'You're Jimmy.' His grey eyes crinkled into a shy smile. 'You get on well with Butch,' she added, instantly feeling stupid, but it was the first thing that came to her mind. He bent forward to lay his forehead on the dog's head and tickled it under its chin.

'Aye, we used to have a Mastiff when I was little, all black but kind of like him.'

Butch almost purred with pleasure at the attention. An impatient tap on the glass table from Wally's heavy signet ring earned a disapproving cough from Ricky, who shifted in his chair and said: 'Jimmy has been remembering more and more about his early days, which is great; well, most of it anyway.'

A wave of sympathy for the crumpled figure now looking desolate beside her made her pause. Another clack and a stronger foot tap. She found her phone and, keeping it tilted away from Jimmy, she flicked through photographs until she found one of a younger Paul Stone. Putting a hand on his arm she said kindly: 'You're sure you want to do this?' He nodded dumbly.

His gasp of terror when he saw it as he shrank away and buried his face in his hands reverberated through her chest. She laid the phone on the table and leant across to put an arm round him and whispered urgently: 'He's nearly finished and he can't harm you anymore.'

'You reckon?' Wally's foot clamped down onto the floor, his body tense and his expression sceptical.

'He's the main protection for his son and he's gone to ground at a shooting lodge in Wester Ross,' she replied with vigour, 'with no security.'

'Like a cornered rat,' he said with relish, picking a flake of cigar paper off his lip.

'Or a wounded panther,' Herk answered sourly.

'Ah well, just as well you're going with her, then.' Wally extended his mouth to show his stained teeth in a sarcastic grimace.

An anguished 'No' from Jimmy made Butch flinch. 'I won't have anyone else put at risk because of me. There's already two dead.' His eyes flickered between Herk and Tire in agitation. 'If he's done for, why don't you just leave him... to rot.'

She took one of his trembling hands and said determinedly: 'Because I think his son had one of my friends killed and there's a man in prison who shouldn't be there.' Herk let out an exasperated sigh, so she added with a tentative glance at him: 'And I'd like some photographs of the charity icon at his last stand.'

'Then you can push him off the edge of a cliff like the others. Works for me,' Wally remarked cheerfully, standing up. 'Sorry I can't be of help to you. Different country up there. I got no contacts.' He clapped Herk hard on the shoulder as he passed his chair. 'Good luck, son.'

He paused at the door. 'If you're stuck, give me a bell and I'll send Dorry and a couple of the lads up in my chopper.' Butch reluctantly drew himself away from Jimmy and trotted after him.

Needing fresh air to shake her head into gear, Tire stood up and said she would walk round the garden. Jimmy was bent over in the corner of the couch holding his arms across his chest, his head bowed, so she suggested he come along to tell her about the sculptures on the lawn. Once down the steps to the terrace, she looked back and saw Herk on his mobile.

Studying the bronze headless torso of the woman seemed to revive Jimmy's spirits and he talked eloquently about the sculptor's intentions as his eyes roamed over the massive thighs and pendulous breasts. She glanced up to see Herk still engaged in conversation. Moving across to the male nude, Jimmy became more animated, talking of the classical tradition of naturalistic figures, at one point taking a paint-stained rag out of his pocket to wipe some bird shit off the statue's leg. Tire tried to drag her mind away from an image of Jin's naked body standing at her bedroom window, his long sinewy legs reaching up into a neat butt and triangling up to broad shoulders. She warmed at the thought, then instantly felt a clutch of dread, remembering where he was.

After twenty minutes they turned for the house and Jimmy pointed out the intense blue pots and paintwork that Ricky had copied from Yves St Laurent's Marrakech garden. She grinned and said they probably looked better in the stronger southern sunlight than in Glasgow drizzle. His lips twitched.

Herk snapped his mobile shut as they climbed the steps. She looked at him and said: 'Long conversation.'

'Sorting out a four-wheel drive for Inverness,' he said abruptly, chewing his lip and sighing. 'There doesn't seem much argument about it.'

'I could go on my own,' she said unconvincingly, which earned her a withering grunt.

There were left on their own while Jimmy went off to change and Ricky to supervise dinner.

'What exactly do you expect to get out of this jaunt up north?' Herk said dourly, pouring himself another glass of wine.

She shifted uneasily from one foot to the other, searching for the right words, considered sitting down, then decided walking would keep her awake. 'Look,' she said, pacing up to the far end of the conservatory, flicking the leaves of a tall fern, then striding back, explaining it to herself as much as to him, 'Pa Stone may well throw himself off a cliff, though I'd doubt it. He's beyond stubborn, reinforced steel for a backbone. We just don't have enough evidence against Harman at the moment. I need to drag something out of him and...' she raised a hand to stop him interrupting, 'it needs a dramatic photograph. Newspapers will take a flyer, hedged round with ifs and buts, if they have a decent image.'

'I thought you were going to write a book,' he said, shaking his head doubtfully.

'Books take time. We need to get Greengate out of prison before his heart keels over. A Sunday splash first to launch the story will get publishers hungrier, bring in some cash and I'll have time to sort out the detail of the Stone and Wrighton finances later.'

'Well, if you say so, but I'm no arty photographer. Reconnaissance was my game.'

'You'll do fine,' she said giving him a reassuring smile, then sagging into a chair. Blowing out her cheeks with tiredness, she added quietly: 'I keep apologising for dragging you into this. But I just don't see an alternative.'

The dinner summons came, which turned out to be just the three of them, since Elly was under the weather in bed and Jimmy insisted on staying with her. A heartening lasagne sat in a ceramic oven dish in the centre of the kitchen table, with first helpings already on plates and glasses of red wine poured. They ate in silence, with Ricky forking his food around nervously, putting the occasional lump into his mouth.

Eventually, he said in a hoarse whisper: 'Not my kind of thing this. Violence gives me the total heebie-jeebies.' He looked down the kitchen, bending forward slightly to check no one was listening. 'What I haven't told Jimmy yet,' he said in a rush, 'is that my cousin in Italy, he's a lawyer, thinks he's tracked down the will of Jimmy's mother, Alessia Neroni. I thought I'd wait to see what's in it before I let him know.'

Tire's tiredness disappeared. 'That's useful to know,' she said, fingering her wine glass. 'And he couldn't trace the son after her death?'

'No, he disappeared and the house was sold. Oddly enough, my family come from the same area in Umbria, so it wasn't that difficult.'

Noting down the details of the lawyer, she felt her excitement rising. It was all coming together, the jigsaw of the Stone family history. The pieces he'd kept separate from his public image. The polished, charming, altruistic Stone was only the tip of the iceberg. She knew his origins. His treatment of his stepson alone would nail him and there was enough circumstantial evidence of incriminating deaths to drag him into a major scandal. With him skewered, his son's activities would come under scrutiny.

She stared out into the blackness beyond the window, only the waving shadows of trees visible in the faint moonlight. Was she getting too hooked into Paul Stone? There would certainly be a colourful piece in him. But he might know nothing about his son's involvement in Erica's death, or the illegal drugs. Perhaps her loathing for society luminaries was distracting her.

Exhaustion was making it difficult for her to focus. But she knew the decision to go north to face Paul Stone had been made. Her gut said he had to be the way into Harman and it was vital to get to him before he imploded. Herk's reluctance worried her. It wouldn't be lack of courage, but she trusted his instincts, which were clearly waving a red flag. Still, needs must. They were on a roll and stopping now was not an option.

CHAPTER 48

The Inverness plane shuddered in the cross-winds, dropped abruptly several times in the turbulence, then stabilised again. A few passengers, clinging to their armrests, looked terrified. The rest, mainly businessmen, continued to read their papers or tablets, with unconcern. The hostesses swished along the aisle, removing coffee cups and orange juice.

Tire's rising tension had little to do with fear of flying since she'd long ago in her travelling career given up worrying about crashing. Only one flight, years back, in a ramshackle Cessna with Jin, escaping out of Ethiopia with a drunk pilot, had ever seriously frightened her.

She had woken up to a text from Chip Nathon saying Harman had been sent a cryptic message from his father saying goodbye. This levitated her out of bed in a panic. Shit. He couldn't suicide or disappear before she'd got to him. Getting him to confess what he knew would be a stretch, but she needed the photographs and an interview of sorts as background.

A quiet snore beside her indicated Herk was power-napping. He only came to as the plane was taxiing along the runway.

'I remember this when it was a wooden shack,' he remarked, looking round the new, high-ceilinged, aluminium arrivals hall. 'They used to weigh you with your luggage. Quite upset the ladies, as I recollect.' He grinned, asked her for a hundred pounds and left her to wait for their bags – they contained walking boots and heavy outdoor jackets, which had been too bulky to travel in the cabin.

Fifteen minutes later they were on their way in a battered, mud-spattered Range Rover. 'One in every airport, have you?' she murmured and got no response.

The solid steel girders of the Kessock Bridge sped the A9 traffic over the Beauly Firth and on to the turnoff for the A835 for Ullapool. He had not asked her what the plan was, merely requested the address of the shooting lodge to set the GPS. The fertile farmlands of the Black Isle came as a surprise since she'd been mentally gearing up for the bleaker coast further north, although the dark sprawling ridge of Ben Wyvis in the distance struck a chord.

'That's known as the Hill of Terror,' Herk said, pointing a finger. 'Don't know why. Dead easy walk up.'

'You've climbed here?' she said, surprised.

He nodded. 'My ma's uncle was a great climber, all over the world. He retired up here and I came up a couple of times.'

She looked questioningly at him, pleased to have a distraction. 'He wasn't from Glasgow, then?'

'Oh yeah. Shipyards at Clydebank. When there was work. He was much older than my grandfather, born in the 1920s. The lads used to escape out into the country, live off the land, well, poach to be honest, and taught themselves to climb. World class, some of them, later on.'

'You were fond of him?'

'Fond?' He gave a short laugh. 'Nah, he was a hard man. You didn't want to get on the wrong side of him, I tell you. But he taught me a lot.' He cocked his head. 'He came out of nothing and made something of his life with no help from anyone. I respected him.'

The crop fields gave way to birch woodland as they headed for Garve, a small, neat village straddling the road north, with whitewashed cottages sitting demurely behind low stone walls.

What am I going to do? what am I going to do? The voice was back inside her head, nagging at her like a fractious child. Jin had often accused her of winging it, flying into risky situations and assuming her quick wits and guardian angel would produce a result and an exit strategy. Why hadn't Jin texted her? Lord knows where he was. But there wasn't enough space in her head to worry about him as well. What she needed now was focus. The main danger she foresaw was that Paul Stone would not be there, or would blank her. She needed to prise some tangible information out of him.

Climbing up into open high land of Glascarnoch, the landscape became more familiar and less populated. Empty hillsides were covered with low-growing tufts of heather, with blackish peat bog in places and the occasional fence. The loch shone an icy blue below the snow-streaked top of Ben Dearg as they skirted round the tip. Down past a spectacular gorge, her stomach sank with the terrain. Ullapool came and went, with more white-walled, slate-roofed houses flashing past. The road narrowed to a single track. Her chest was tight.

'Well, has all that thinking produced a plan, then?' Herk's voice pulled her back to the present.

'I assume he'll know who we are?' she said, scraping a fingernail against her front teeth.

'Depends on how much the security guys share with him. The one in California had our photos on his phone, which is how he cottoned on.'

'So likely. No sense in dreaming up a cover story.' She stared out of the window, momentarily distracted as Stac Polliadh came into view, rising up to a ragged ridge of bare rock. 'Have you climbed that? It's my favourite mountain.'

He gave her an exasperated glance. 'Focus. Yes, and Cul Beg that's around somewhere.'

She scratched her forehead, then sat up straight. 'Appeal to his arrogance. He wants to be remembered. They all do.'

'Doesn't sound likely.'

'Think about it. He may not know everything Harman has been up to, but he's played the world for a fool for decades. No sense in going quietly into the night. It'll be his revenge before he dies, to let everyone know just how much he suckered them.'

Herk braked sharply and reversed fifty yards into a passing place as an ancient Land Rover bounced towards them. A ruddy-faced driver in a flat cap gave them a cheery wave. Herk checked his mobile and reset the GPS before moving on.

'No reception here. Just as well that came through earlier,' he muttered. 'Coordinates, I mean. Easier than road directions. GPS was never designed for wildernesses like this.'

She considered making a caustic remark about Speedy Charlie manning the base station, but decided against it.

A right turn with a walkers' sign for Stac Grianach led along an even narrower road, winding upwards through open country, with sparse grass struggling to maintain a foothold in the poor soil. Two isolated cottages a mile apart sat in the lee of the hill, sheltered from the wind, with only a few scraggy sheep for company. A dark hulk of mountain loomed in the distance like a giant prehistoric fossil.

As the road dipped down into a valley with an elongated loch ahead, a substantial house came into view. A carved wooden sign announced Suairceas Lodge. The solid sandstone building rose two storeys, topped with a profusion of slate-topped gables over each set of windows, round all four sides. It was a complex rather than a home.

They drove up to the front on a wide, gravelled path and parked with the Range Rover's nose pointing to the exit. Herk scrambled out first and pulled out a capacious, multi-pocketed waxed jacket from the back. Tire stretched her legs cautiously, feeling sick. Then, glancing at Herk to see if he was ready, she marched towards the front door. It opened before she could pull the antique bell rod. A tall figure, with pure white hair, in an immaculate tweed suit, gave her a sardonic look and turned on his heel. He said over his shoulder: 'You're persistent. I'll give you that.'

They followed him across the tartan-carpeted hall with heavy panelling and oil paintings of stags on the wall. The sitting room overlooking the loch was furnished like a gentleman's club, with a surfeit of green leather armchairs, more tartan and one wall dedicated to stuffed stag's heads and curiously unreal fish mounted on varnished plaques. A slow, orchestral melody was playing that she couldn't place.

He stood with his back to them and said: 'I would offer you tea, but I have sent the staff away. What do you want?'

'I want to tell your story,' she replied, hoping her voice sounded more robust than she felt.

'Tcheuch,' he said, half-laughing and half-coughing. 'Many people have tried in the past and have failed. What makes you think you'll be different?'

He turned towards her, holding onto the polished shutter on the edge of the window and she could see deep crevasses on his face, down each side of his aquiline nose. His eyes, the colour of dark agate, were glittering but sunk in wasted flesh. His cheeks, flushed in places, were sallow in others.

Moving out of his eye line, she sat down on the edge of a leather sofa facing the window and, when his attention moved to Herk, switched on the tape recorder clipped in her top pocket. Without bothering to ask, she lit a cigarette and contemplated him.

'You're dying,' she said, 'and broke. You've fooled the world for a long time. I thought you'd like to set the record straight before you go.'

'Why should I talk to you?' He gave her a scathing look, moved to the nearest armchair and sat down with a sharp intake of breath. 'You know nothing,' he spat out. 'A flim-flam writer with a murderer for a father.' Her heart froze and she swallowed. Her eyes held his gaze as her brain kicked into gear. Two can play at that game, she thought.

'You were born in Arles-sur-Tech to a mentally unstable mother, a prostitute, and an unknown father,' she said flatly.

He half-rose out of his seat and fell back, his face twisted.

'You were brought up in a Pyrenees mountain village, then Barcelona, then there's a blank until you stepped self-created into a stellar career, stepping over a few bodies on the way. And you never abandoned your mother.' She smiled icily. 'Some might say you deserve credit for having pulled yourself up from nothing.'

'You,' he barked, waving a bony finger at Herk. 'A brandy. That cupboard.' He sat awkwardly, half-slumped, protecting his stomach.

Two goblets, each with an inch of amber cognac, were laid on the table between them. She nursed the glass balloon between her hands and took a sip. Stone leant forward with difficulty, extending a thin, heavily veined hand to grasp the glass. He took several sips while she waited.

'Your mother?' she prompted after a few minutes.

'She saved my life,' he said harshly, avoiding her eye. 'She did what was necessary to feed us.' He sighed. 'Then she went mad. Well, maybe she always was mad. But she was all I had. I owed her.'

'Your father?'

He gave a snort. 'Who knows? Arab, French, Spanish. Could have been any of dozens. I never thought to pursue the matter.'

His shoulders were drawn inward and one knee trembled, causing his foot to twitch. The solid granite ashtray on the table appeared to fascinate him. Then his gaze roamed aimlessly round the wall of stuffed trophies. The music came to a lingering, mournful finish. The silence hung suspended, with only the querulous wail of a curlew battling the wind outside. Another rougher cry could have been a stonechat.

Richard Strauss, she thought triumphantly, 'Metamorphosis', that's it. In memoriam of Germany's defeat. What was she doing, letting her mind wander? The oldest trick in the book was to look beaten and ill. He was bluffing. Pinning her eyes on his lowered face, she willed him to look at her. Finally he looked up, tightening his lips into a faint smile, and waved his empty glass at Herk. He made a beckoning gesture to continue her questions so she plunged in.

'The drug research? One drug to destroy the memory of your past and the other to extend your life indefinitely.'

'Neatly put, my dear,' he replied, his heavy-lidded eyes impenetrable. He breathed in hoarsely. 'Though not strictly accurate on all counts. Immortality was never my aim. I just wanted my mother to be sane. But she moved from madness into dementia, so I never had a sensible conversation with her.'

'What did you want to ask her?' Tire leant back taking another sip, the brandy running warmly down her throat, trying to think how to work Harman into the conversation.

'Why she put me through… everything she put me through. She could have given me away. Instead she perverted me. Brothel, asylum. I had to be very strong to survive all that. But it haunts me and I wanted rid of it before I died.'

'You tried the drug yourself?' she said.

He shook his head. 'No, the results from the guinea pigs we tested on were not satisfactory. There were damaging side effects.'

'Children, you mean?' she snapped.

He shrugged and pouted. 'They were derelicts from broken homes, abusive parents. Worth nothing. They got a holiday out of it.'

Don't let anger cloud your judgement, she told herself, digging her nails into the palm of one hand. His arrogance and indifference made her want to physically attack him. Instead, she said quietly: 'And Louis, your stepson?'

He made a dismissive gesture. 'Spoiled brat. His mother doted on him. I was just getting on my feet financially then. I couldn't let a child wreck it.'

'Why did you kill her?'

His eyebrows lifted in surprise. 'She was getting troublesome about money. She called me tessoro at the beginning but she didn't mean it. Just Italian gush and then she defied me once too often. I slapped her too hard and she feel onto a stone path. So I had her body dropped into a lake nearby where she used to swim.'

'Poor bitch,' she replied with feeling, putting down her glass before she broke the stem. 'So you grabbed what you wanted and condemned little Louis to a worse childhood than yours.'

A short laugh rasped across the table. 'You are too sentimental, my dear. I wonder you've got this far,' he said with a sneer. 'I could have got rid of him as well. He had a chance.' The dark eyes reminded her of a cockroach: pitiless, sly, alien.

Aware that she was getting tired from the sparring match that was the subtext to his confession, and wary of his motives, she forced herself to ask: 'And Erica Smythson?'

He laughed out loud, 'Oh, no. You're not pinning that on me. Have a barrister murdered in central London? Whatever you might think of me, I'm not stupid.' His mocking smile indicated he'd scored a point. Her jaw tightened.

'But Jack Greengate is innocent?' she prompted, unwilling to let go the advantage.

He cleared his throat, hesitated and looked at his feet before saying with a disinterested shrug: 'Possibly. I really don't know anything there.' His jaw muscles tensed, marking a hard line up his sunken cheeks. Her eyes never left his face as she followed his twitches and edginess. Finally, he shook his head: 'Your friend's death was someone else entirely.'

'Who?' she said, her throat tight.

The eyelids hung heavily, half-masking his basilisk stare that slid over her, deflecting any interaction. One knee started to tremble again and his attention wandered upward to a stag's head with fourteen-point antlers spread out in a majestic arc.

'Tell me,' she hissed, unnerved by the prospect that all her chasing around had been after the wrong people. He started to look bored, so she racked her brains to find an oblique way in. All she could see in her mind was Harman in the orange jacket.

'He doesn't take after you, your son? Not cast from the same mould.'

He leant forward to take a cigarette from her packet on the table. His bony hand made her shrink back. He lit it, had another sip of brandy and gave a cold chuckle.

'Oh, how wrong you are. He couldn't be more so. He's my mother's son.'

'You're brothers?' she said, startled.

He ran his tongue round the inside of his teeth and hesitated, then said roughly: 'Yes, and he's my son.'

Her stomach curdled and she stopped breathing for a moment. He watched her discomfort with a flicker of a smile. Then he said: 'Not quite what you think. I provided the... wherewithal, and she was inseminated. She was in her late forties then, but she was obsessed with having another child. To be honest, I never thought she'd get pregnant, let alone have it grow up. She went completely mad after that. He never knew and I sent him abroad to school.'

That was a curve ball, she thought, sitting back stunned. Not only revolting, but an indication he was as bad, if not worse than Harman.

'You know he's selling these memory drugs, illegally, on the darknet with Rupert Wrighton?'

'And what if I do? They have made considerable sums of money; well, my son has. I no longer have any need for money given my limited time left, otherwise I would have demanded my share.' He gave a cynical laugh.

He was being much more open than she had expected. Surprisingly so, for a man who had gone to such lengths to bury his past, and always exerted maximum control. What was he up to? He took pleasure in pulling other people's strings so why was he laying it all out on a plate for her? An uncomfortable chill crept up through her belly. He was playing her, she was sure of it, giving with one hand what he intended to take away with the other.

'If you will excuse me, I must go to lie down.' His voice had subsided to a tired croak, and he wiped one hand against the sweat drops on his forehead, before standing up with an effort. Tire rose to move away from him, putting a chair between them. As he walked stiffly to the door, holding onto the wall for support, she said: 'You know who had Erica killed?' Then she cursed herself for sounding as if she was pleading.

He paused without turning round and replied, sighing: 'I have a name somewhere. The lawyers dug out some information which meant nothing to me. But it is in other papers at the keep I am renovating. If I am well enough tomorrow I can look it out. It isn't far. We can talk then.'

There was the sound of footsteps, a door shutting, then silence. Herk had a look of watchful suspicion on his face and she shot a questioning glance his way.

'I don't like this at all,' she said.

'Me neither. All too pat. Let's go.'

They stepped out into the hall and the door clicked shut behind them. Herk suddenly held up his hand, as a faint crackling from the alcove beside the front door increased in volume, until there was a swoosh of flame on a line across the carpet, searing up to the stone ceiling canopy, blocking their exit.

'Fucking booby trap. C'mon,' he said, grabbing her arm.

They tried several doors, all of them locked including the one they had been in. The smoke was becoming unbearable when she finally found one open door at the back, through to a butler's pantry that led to worn stone stairs down to the servants' quarters. At the bottom there was a long dismal corridor with locked doors down one side. A faint glow of daylight came through an open door at the far end beside curved stone stairs leading upwards. They ran towards it and into a long, narrow room, which had small, slit, grilled windows at the end, only to turn rapidly when the door slammed shut behind them.

Stone's voice was muffled by the solid oak between them. 'Enjoy your confession, my dear. The staff will let you out.' His laugh echoed up the winding stairs.

The room was bare apart from an ancient wooden table against one wall, standing on giant flagstones. Herk walked across to the door and sniffed the lock. He said calmly: 'He's doused that in petrol and something else, so shooting the lock out won't be sensible. Whole thing could blow up.' He turned round. 'And even if I could get the bars off these windows, they're too small to get through.'

Sagging against the table, she said weakly: 'He said he'd sent the staff away. It could be weeks before anyone turns up.'

Herk methodically scanned the floor, walls, ceiling. She followed his gaze until she was dizzy.

'Trouble with these old houses,' he said, 'they're built to last.' He sniffed and added: 'But there's always a weak spot somewhere.'

'You're sure? Prisons don't have weak spots. They used to wall people in till they starved. Immurement, it's called. Vestal virgins in Roman times who misbehaved...'

'Would you stop blethering?' he snapped. 'And help me drag the table over there. There's a damp patch on the ceiling above the door. It might have rotted what's above.'

With the table in place, he started hammering on the edge of a cracked flagstone with his heel, trying to break off a sliver. She watched for a moment and asked: 'Wouldn't a knife be easier?

He shook his head. 'I've only got a combat knife. It needs something blunt to scrape away the plaster.'

With a grin, she handed him her Swiss Army knife. He took it without comment and stood listening. Only when there was the faint sound of a car driving away did he climb onto the table. After half an hour's scraping, he was coughing and covered in grime and white dust and there was a gaping hole in the ceiling.

It took another four hours of chiselling and banging, with the knife and a chunk of stone she had managed to prise loose from the floor, before he broke through plaster and brick to rotten timber planks. He found a strong enough handhold on a stone ledge to swing up one foot to batter the wooden struts into the adjoining room. The light was fading fast, so he demanded a torch from his jacket, before hauling himself up into the gap, and through with a thud onto the floor next door. She heard a door open and his steps receded into the distance.

Pulling her Barbour tightly round her, she shivered in the darkness, aware that she was frozen through. She smoked a cigarette down to the filter before he returned. There was a scrape of furniture moving and his head appeared.

'Put that damn thing out. Away from the door, it's flammable,' he said. He then scrambled back to give her a hefty push on her bottom to get her up to the hole and through.

'Upstairs is damp,' he whispered as he joined her. 'He must have turned the sprinklers on as soon as we were locked in. Bastard. Bit of a mess, mind you. He clearly didn't care what happened to the house.'

'Or us,' she replied with feeling.

He gave a short laugh. 'Oh aye, he did. Just the wrong sort of caring. Let's get out of here.'

The long stone corridor with dull green walls led into a vast kitchen with barred windows and a sturdy outside door, strapped with metal flanges. There was no key.

'I'm afraid it's the coal hole,' he beamed, opening a cabinet door beside the range, and starting to haul solid fuel logs out onto the floor. After ten minutes, he had cleared enough space to wriggle through and kick open the lid of the outside log box.

'See, what'd I tell you?' he said as he pulled her through. 'There's always a weak spot.'

Out in the fresh air she breathed deeply, leaning against the wall for support. The night sky was pitch black, apart from a few stars twinkling in gaps of cloud. A tawny owl broke the silence, its call echoing round the hills skirting the valley. Another wailing wheeze in the distance made her frown in concentration.

'That's odd,' she said.

'What?' Herk looked concerned.

She chuckled and put an arm round his shoulders. 'Nothing ominous. It's a shearwater, I think. But strange to find them inland. They're normally island or cliff birds.'

The owl 'kewicked' loudly again, close at hand. 'That's a female,' she said. 'Different call to the tu-whit tu-whoo of the male.'

'Fancy,' he said, pulling her towards the front of the house. He took off his jacket and crawled under the Range Rover with his torch to check the underside. Once satisfied, he climbed in and started it. The engine noise shattered the stillness and the headlights tongued an enormous beam of white across the darkness. Tire shivered involuntarily, then felt foolish. Stone would be long gone.

'Now, tell me,' he said, turning left out of the lodge gates onto the single-track road.

'I've no idea what we do next?' she said, hunching her shoulders.

'Oh, that. Nah. Wait till we've eaten. I think better on a full stomach. Those birds?'

In spite of herself she broke down into giggles as the pent-up tension of the past few hours let loose. Gasping for breath and wiping the tears streaming down her face, she said: 'Herk, you're incorrigible. Do you think the birds'll tell us what to do next.'

'Nah, I'm just interested, that's all,' he replied equably. 'They've been right so far, as has your astrology. I like to keep the whole picture in mind.'

'You mean the alternative universe? The one that's on a parallel track to the real one?' She blew her nose, hooted quietly and settled back into her seat. 'Owls are birds of wisdom and of Athena, the warrior goddess.'

'Well, that makes sense. And the other?'

'Shearwaters?' She sighed. 'Souls of the damned and the voice of the devil.'

'Oh, cheery then.' He braked suddenly to avoid a sheep on the road.

She sat lost in thought, remembering childhood nights spent on the cliffs watching the Manx Shearwaters coming back into the burrows to feed their young. Their asthmatic croaks as they approached land had never sounded satanic to her. More comforting and familiar, as she lay wrapped up in a sleeping bag in a crevasse sheltered from the wind, welcoming the fluttering of their wings.

***

They turned left onto the coastal track with not a car or human habitation to be seen. Fifteen miles further along the twisting, constantly rising and falling road, the small isolated hotel she had booked was a welcome sight, its lights flaring out from a glass-walled front room across a stony beach.

The owners, dressed casually in jeans and identical checked shirts, a slim wife and tubby husband, were standing together behind a reception desk as they went in and introduced themselves as Maggie and Donnie. They were unfazed by the lateness of their guests, but insisted they eat immediately.

Tire marched straight for the table beside the fire in the empty dining room and sat gratefully warming her hands as the logs sent flames leaping up the chimney. The car heater had been on, but she was still chilled through. Herk refused to discuss plans until he had eaten his fill of an entire basket of homemade bread with vegetable soup and a sizeable plate of haddock and chips, followed by sponge covered in syrup and cream. Coffee and a malt whisky arrived as he was polishing off cheese and biscuits.

The walls of the dining room were covered in watercolours of mountain and sea scenes so Tire passed the time chatting to Donnie, who had served their meal, about local artists and her childhood holidays on the islands. After a while he pulled up a chair and joined them in a whisky. Taking a deep breath, she said: 'Do you happen to know Paul Stone from Suairceas Lodge?'

He looked at her doubtfully, gave a non-committal smile and said: 'Not really.' After a pause, he added: 'He's not much liked locally. Odd man from all accounts. Not too friendly.'

Herk choked on a cracker and Tire leant across to thump him on the back. Another round of whisky was poured from the bottle sitting on the adjoining table.

'He's doing up another property, I gather,' she said.

'Ach. Daft as a brush, some of these foreigners.' Donnie tapped a stubby finger to his head. 'It's north of Stoer Lighthouse on the cliffs. A half-ruined keep built to withstand invaders three centuries ago. Lord alone knows what he wants with that. More money than sense. My wife's cousin Neil did some building work and there are a couple of rooms habitable. Who would know why? There's not a decent track up to it. They had a terrible job getting materials in. Then he just fired him, with the job only a quarter done.'

Herk stared grimly at the fire. Tire drummed her fingers on the tablecloth, wondering what Stone's obsession with a historic fort was. He was hardly the type to opt for a hermit's death.

'Neil never found out why he wanted it?' she asked.

Donnie cocked one ear to the door, where his wife's cough was summoning him. Heaving his bulk up from the chair, he said: 'To be honest, he thought he was going wrong in the head. He called him the Earl of Hell.'

They sat contemplating the fire and their whisky glasses until the bottle was nearly finished. Neither raised the subject of tomorrow.

CHAPTER 49

A cacophony of birds calls eased Tire into the morning. Refusing to think about what came next, she lay on her back and ticked them off in her head. The noisy peep-peeps of the red-legged oystercatchers were easy. An agitated, black-capped tern kee-yahing almost drowned out the low, rasping croak of a shag, no doubt standing poised on a shore-side rock. Suddenly there was pandemonium, as herring gulls arrived with squealing catcalls and raucous laughter to plunder for spoils.

Sunshine filtered through the floral curtains, bathing the room in a comforting glow. Deciding not to decide for five minutes, she wrapped the quilt round her, padded barefoot across the floor to pull back the curtains, and tucked herself onto the window seat, to survey the stony beach outside. The sea slapped lazily against the grey boulders and pebbles on the beach, heaving a weighty blanket of brown kelp on the surface as the waves rolled forward and slid back. The rhythm of the tide always calmed her down, a reminder of a constant world that rolled on undistracted. A black guillemot, with a splash of white, bobbed on the water just offshore beside several white eider ducks with dark heads.

A knock on the door interrupted her reverie. She called 'yeah', and Herk came in carrying two mugs of coffee. He sat down on a small armchair and looked questioningly at her.

She chewed a fingernail and stared at the sea and sighed. 'You reckon we've pushed our luck too far? Three near misses,' she said.

He scratched his ear and gave a neutral grunt.

'Oh, dammit,' she said, jumping to her feet and starting to pace up and down the small room, with the quilt draped down to her feet. 'We've come this far and I need to know who had Erica killed. I can't give up now.' She looked beseechingly at him.

'Well, that's the decision then,' he said evenly. 'We leave in an hour. You'd best move if you want breakfast. You'll need your walking boots.'

A blustery Atlantic wind had got up by the time she dressed and made it to the dining room, tossing up foamy waves and smashing them against the shore. Herk was munching through a full fry-up of bacon, eggs, black pudding and potato scones. She winced. Donnie brought her scrambled eggs and coffee, hovered for a moment and then sat down. His bushy grey eyebrows were pulled together in a frown, forming a continuous shaggy mass.

'I assume you're going to see Mr Stone at his keep?' he asked cautiously. 'Not my business, of course,' he said putting a reddened hand onto the table and drumming his fingers. 'But I phoned the wife's cousin this morning, Neil, and he said to watch your step. He said he had been instructed to install a couple of things that worried him.'

'What?' Herk's head shot up and he stopped chewing.

'A metal grill that would block the room nearest the cliff off completely. It was fixed below floor level, so you'd never get it open if you were inside. Like a medieval prison, he said. He had to get a blacksmith in Perthshire to construct it in iron. There was also a trapdoor through the floor at the window which overhangs the drop; that opened directly onto the rocks below.'

'Instant rubbish disposal,' Tire murmured.

'This is on the floor above the room he has as an office. So I would watch your step. Neil said there were times he looked completely mad. The devil shone through his eyes, was how he put it. That was when he asked why he was putting these things in. He doesn't like being questioned.'

The windows rattled in the sea breeze and the oystercatchers' alarm calls were ratcheting up as gulls swooped down.

'I don't suppose you know anything about a journalist, Davey Campbell, who was killed in a car crash near Lochinver, eight years ago?' she asked, pushing the rest of her scrambled eggs to one side.

There was a pause as he looked thoughtfully at her, then he nodded. 'Yes. He was up here asking questions.' He scrunched a napkin in one hand before continuing in a rushed whisper: 'None of this is certain. But the local policeman, he's the brother of the postmistress in Ullapool, had his suspicions that it was not an accident. And one of Mr Stone's jeeps was taken to Aberdeen to be mended shortly after that. Why would he do that? It's nearly four hours away. There's a perfectly good body repair shop in Inverness. That only came to light months later, when a mechanic from there came home to visit his aunt.'

They took their leave half an hour later, promising to phone in after they had seen Stone, to reassure Donnie they had got out safely. A low mist hung over Loch Vatachan as they skirted round it, grey merging into the dull russet of the bracken and sombre green of the coarse grass on the flat land surrounding it. Round a bend on the single-track road, another loch sat glacially still, its chrome surface reflecting the rain clouds above. Mountain peaks jutted out of the horizon like watchful sentinels. Across the River Polly, a meandering stream that took its name from the giant pimple that was Stac Pollaidh behind, were scattered crofts hinting at a village. The remote hamlet of Invercraig came and went without leaving an impression.

'We're just winging this, are we?' Herk's question pulled her away from her concentration on the scenery.

'I dunno. Doesn't feel good,' she muttered. 'I can't leave it. Yet I feel we're being sucked into a spider's web.'

'Yup.'

'OK,' she said firmly, as much to herself as to Herk, folding her hands primly on her lap. 'Bare minimum, we need photographs. Just rattle as many away as you can. We can tidy them up later.'

'There are some from yesterday,' he said. 'Taken on a button camera in the house, not great, but passable.'

'Great,' she said, giving him an amused and surprised glance.

'And,' he said with emphasis, 'I suggest we don't put a foot inside this time.'

'Agreed.'

Her attention was caught by the distinctive soaring crag of Suilven, its steep scarred sides rising to a long, peaked and rounded ridge. A majestic island of prehistoric sandstone rising out of a tawny surround, relic of an ancient battle for supremacy between the volcanic core and the land itself. She missed his sceptical shrug at her assurance.

By the time they reached Stoer Lighthouse on the cliffs above the entrance to the Minch, the tension in the car was rising. The clouds had lifted, deepening the blue of the sea, although the wind was still strong, sending muscular ripples of water far out towards the horizon. Twenty minutes later they turned left off the single-track road onto an even narrower, unsurfaced trail. It headed out towards the furthermost point of the peninsula. A padlocked gate barred their way, with a prominent 'Private' sign on it. To her surprise he reversed a hundred yards down the track and parked in a dip behind a clutch of boulders.

The keep was not visible because of the rise of the land, although Herk was convinced they were in the right place. He gestured to her to put on boots and jacket while he collected two cameras from a bag in the boot. One he hung round his neck and the other went into a capacious pocket. At his insistence they did not return to the gate, but walked eastwards keeping the fence in sight until they reached the land's end. Only then did he climb over, reaching back to give her a hand.

There was half a mile of rough grass, heather and some black peaty holes between them and a crumbling rectangular tower with narrow slit windows that was now in view. It was built onto the cliff edge, rising up a hundred feet straight out of the natural stone into a manmade fortress. The roof had partly disappeared but one section nearest the sea had been re-slated.

The wind was gusting strongly and they had to bend into it to make headway. There was no cover, so Herk kept a watchful eye on the keep although there was no sign of life or any parked vehicles.

The terrain was heavy going, with clumps of heather giving way to swampy bog in places, with no sheep tracks to make it easier. Tire was concentrating on her feet, trying not to think about what was ahead. The westerly blast was obliterating all sounds, so she did not hear the swoosh behind her just before she was sent flying into the ground by a hefty dunt on her shoulder. Herk swore and ducked down beside her. A huge, heavy-headed, brown bird with flashes of white striped on its wing tips was circling round a hundred yards away to make another pass over them. She clutched onto him.

'It's a great skua. We must be near its nest.'

'It's the size of a bleeding eagle,' he hissed in her ear.

'Not quite,' she chortled, not clear why she was so amused. 'You need a walking stick and a hat. Wave it above your head and it'll get bamboozled.'

She bent her head as the bird came flying low over them, its powerful wings drumming through the air. Once it had skimmed over them again she moved her position to get out of a damp patch and glanced up at the keep. Herk was searching around for stones and pulling at clumps of vegetation for ammunition.

'Christ. Look. He's there.' She pointed to the highest point in the tower where it was open to the elements. A figure in a long, loose, white shirt was standing facing out to sea, his arms raised. His hair was dishevelled, standing out in clumps and being whirled by the strong breeze. Herk, now lying on his front, put up his binoculars.

'There's blood on his robe,' he said. At that point Stone turned. There was an extensive red stain extending from below his throat to his knees. Herk handed her the binoculars and started clicking away with his camera. For several moments her journalistic brain was awestruck at the dramatic image. Stone turned to stare directly ahead to the mountains beyond, impervious to their presence.

The skua prepared for another divebomb, so Herk rolled over and threw a hefty clod of heather that caught its underside and sent it veering out to sea. He hauled her to her feet and said: 'C'mon, the fence and then stick close to the walls.' They ran for the building, losing sight of Stone on top.

Leaning against the rough stone walls, sheltered from the sea blast, Tire became aware of music thrumming out of the slit window way above their heads. It was playing at full volume: shrill, dissonant, with a wailing soprano soaring above clashing brass. Herk looked at her with an eyebrow raised.

She thought for a moment and said: "Elektra', Richard Strauss.'

He shook his head in exasperation. 'Not that. What next?'

'He's gone completely crazed, maybe dying.' She chewed her bottom lip.

'Or he's staged it all to entice us in,' he answered shortly.

Before she could answer he pulled out a small handgun from a back pocket, checked it and then indicated she should follow him. Round the side of the tower, up some broken steps, the heavy oak door, strapped and studded in iron, was ajar. The music gushed down the worn circular stairs ahead of them like a river in spate, bubbling and frothing, searing at their ears as the singer raged at high pitch.

They crept round and round the spiral steps upwards, until a landing opened out with a room to their left, its glassed, slit windows looking out to the Atlantic. There was a desk, a few books on a shelf and a single bed with rumpled, blood-stained sheets and a duvet on it. Herk walked across and turned off the stereo, which brought a blissful silence. They waited. Five minutes passed. Then a faint thud of footsteps came down from above. Paul Stone stood at the door, his hair on end, his face and hands bloodless and blue in contrast to his smeared shirt. His sunken eyes were glittering, constantly shifting their focus.

'You will have to forgive my appearance. My condition induces nosebleeds,' he said, waving a hand across his chest, not looking directly at either of them. 'You got out,' he remarked. 'Pity. Anton set up the fire trap for me some time ago for such an exigency.' A sardonic smile crossed his face. 'I thought there might have been a pleasing symmetry in you dying imprisoned like your father.'

Tire blinked, feeling her chest pinch with a stab of anger. 'And you thought you'd meet your end to the strains of your mad mother,' she snapped, pointing to the stereo.

He gave an unpleasant laugh. 'The curse of the House of Atreus,' he said. 'It does have a certain resonance, I would have to admit.'

Herk was edging towards the door and Stone, although he showed no signs of moving.

'Erica Smythson?' Tire said steadily. 'You said you had the name here.'

'And you believe everything you're told, do you?' he sneered, putting a hand up to support himself on the doorframe.

A sickly sweet, fruity smell mixed with stale sweat wafted off him, making her want to gag. She tried not to breathe in and said: 'You lied to me yesterday?'

A wooden chair scraped on the stone floor as he sat down heavily. 'She was proving to be a nuisance. If she had been successful in getting Greengate off, it would have opened a can of worms that threatened my reputation. He had found out about the Mexican drug facility. My son had carelessly left papers lying around. He framed him in the most asinine way possible. I could not believe the police fell for it. And I had pressure brought to bear on Greengate to plead guilty to protect his son.'

'So why lie yesterday?'

A skeletal hand, with bulging purple veins, ran through his wispy hair. The expression on his face was, for the first time, tinged with embarrassment. 'I needed to give my son time to escape. He left for South America last night.'

Hell and damnation. He raised a hand.

'You can save your energy trying to get him extradited. He has several ailments due to his unusual birth. He won't make old bones.'

'Inbreeding, you mean?'

'Call it as you please. It won't affect me. He has enough money to live well for a couple of years, which might be as long as he has.' His eyes wandered over to the single bed in the corner and his shoulders drooped. She needed more.

'Wrighton? He had nothing to do with Erica's death?'

'That fool? He's capable of organising nothing. He couldn't even protect himself against my son, who has taken his money and left him with some very angry friends whose investments have also disappeared into thin air.'

'How did you persuade Erica to come to Hammersmith in the early hours?' she said quietly, digging her nails into her hand to keep her anger under control.

He moved across to sit heavily on the chair in front of the desk and hung his head, breathing heavily. 'Easy,' he wheezed. 'I knew she was having an affair with the lawyer Crumley so I got him drunk and then told one of my aides to phone her and request help for him. She never hesitated, stupid fool. He blacked out and remembered nothing of that evening.'

'Which of your thugs was driving?' she pressed on.

Another short cackle. 'You won't get him. He died in Spain ten days back. Anton. He was a bastard like me, from Romania originally, brought up in a Russian orphanage.' His elbow, leaning on the table, was pressing hard to keep him upright.

Muffled squawks and squeals from the colony of seabirds, nesting on the cliff below and occasionally flitting past the window, penetrated through the thick glass. The buffeting of the wind was growing stronger. She lit a cigarette, ignoring his irritated cough, and said: 'Was it all worth it? Scrabbling just to get to the top of the dung heap?'

'Scrabbling?' he said faintly, still managing to sound dismissive.

'You must have been desperate to be taken as an equal, mixing with the great and the good. Or was it all a game so you could laugh at them? The ones you suckered with your charitable piety.'

His trembling had turned into spasmodic shivering and his face was ashen grey. She reached down onto the bed and pulled up a rug and threw it across him. He tugged at it ineffectually, but managed finally to wrap it round himself.

'You think too much,' he said, looking abstractedly into the corner of the room. 'Motives are never as clear-cut as you imagine. I needed to survive and keep my mother safe. That took money. I discovered how easy it was and everything else followed. I never expected to get this far. With my kind of childhood you are surprised when you get through each day.'

Not that different from the Mexican Sanchez, she thought. Living like a hyena.

His exhaustion was beginning to pull her down so she moved further down the wall away from him, closer to Herk, taking a few deep breaths to clear her head. 'What do you think your elite friends will say when they find out about you?'

He levered himself to his feet and walked unsteadily to the door without looking at her, saying over his shoulder: 'I won't be here to care, will I?' Gesturing to Herk to get out of his way, he moved out of the doorway and started to climb slowly up the next spiral of stairs.

After five steps, he stopped and said over his shoulder: 'My influential friends in government won't let you tell my story, you know. Too damaging for them and you have no real proof. They'll smear you, put pressure on newspaper proprietors. You might manage a conspiracy website. You'll see. My reputation will remain intact.' He laughed roughly then, three steps later, added: 'Turn the music on as you leave.'

Herk pulled her arm, muttering: 'That's the best advice I've heard. This place could be booby-trapped. C'mon.'

He picked up the remote control and switched 'Elektra' back on, loosing the vengeful howls and shrieks of the singer to pulsate against the stone walls. Tire, unnerved by Stone's jibe of no evidence, tugged at the locked drawers on the desk. She pulled out her pocket knife and levered it in the crack until the wood split, but nothing budged. Herk pushed her aside, pulled a chisel from a trouser pocket, jammed it into the gap she had created and smashed down on it with a clenched fist. The front of the top drawer came away, exposing documents, several leather-bound pads and three flash memory sticks. She grabbed a canvas travel bag lying in the corner and shovelled the contents in, then kicked the lower drawers hard until they came free. A laptop was in one. The other was full of pills, which she left.

Down the worn stairs, pursued by the soprano's violent screams and the crescendoing clamour of an anguished orchestral score, they exited quickly and ran towards the rough track to the right of the building. The music mercifully faded as they moved further away. Resisting a temptation to turn round, Tire followed Herk to the first rise in the ground as the trail bent round a huge boulder.

They lay down behind it, panting for breath. She clutched the bag to her chest as if it was a child in need of protection. Herk tugged at his ears, as if to clear an annoying blockage, and raised his head above the massive chunk of granite. Resting his camera on the top and adjusting the focus, he started clicking.

Stone was back on the ruined roof, still wrapped in the blanket, facing away from them out to sea. The wind tugged at his white hair, standing it up in spikes and creating a ghostly aura round his head. The music bellowed and moaned, merging into the sea birds' calls, to create a babel of piercing cries.

A flash of brown to her right pulled her gaze away and she saw the skua heading for the figure on the tower. Its five-foot wing span skimmed it effortlessly up and through the broken wall on the nearside. It dragged its claws across his head, pitching him forward, then continued out to sea to circle round for another attack. He stumbled forward into a higher portion of the wall, holding a hand to his stomach, bent forward, obviously in pain. After a moment he disappeared out of sight, then re-emerged, holding onto the top stone with one hand and with a handgun in the other. As the skua came close he held the gun over his head and fired. Feathers went flying.

'Bastard,' she muttered.

But the bird managed to gain height and sheered off to the far end of the cliff edge, where it landed and shook itself vigorously, dislodging a few more feathers. Stone then raised the gun to his head and fired again. He crumpled out of sight. The singer ground relentlessly on.

'He's gone,' remarked Herk in a matter-of-fact voice. 'Now let's go.'

'Do you not think?'

'No, I don't. The police can sort all that out. And we should get to the car before that damned crater comes circling back round.' As she looked across, the skua gave a few experimental hops and then, satisfied all was in working order, took off over the cliff edge in the other direction. The mêlée of the opera, and the din of sea birds disturbed by the shots, followed them back to the Range Rover.

She threw the bag into the back and collapsed against the door, lighting a cigarette with difficulty in the wind, feeling wrung out.

'Inverness?' she asked.

'Lunch,' he answered firmly. 'I'll text Donnie when we get reception and tell him to stand by.'

The wind was gusting up to force six as they passed Stoer Lighthouse, breakers crashing against outlying rocks and the cliff base, forming a wide waist of churning white water. Was it really all over? She couldn't quite believe how much he had admitted and on tape and he was dead.

Her head was whirring into list-making gear, planning what came next in pulling information together, sorting out a newspaper contract and then a book after that.

'Now I have three questions,' Herk said, slowing down to allow several sheep to cross the road. 'Two only need brief answers.'

She laughed, snuggling back into her seat. 'Fire away.'

'One, that skewer. And two, that curse of Atreus he was talking about.'

The heater was beginning to relax her and Herk's chatter, which she half-suspected was to distract her, was welcome.

'Great skuas are pirates, the locals call them bonxies. They steal other birds' food and sometimes kill the birds themselves to eat. They're predators, but very protective of their young.'

He nodded. 'Aye, for sure. The curse?'

Sighing heavily, she looked out at the mountain looming on the horizon and said slowly: 'Long story from Greek mythology.'

'Make it brief,' he said, tapping a short message into his mobile phone.

'Revenge really, in a nutshell. Each generation of the Atreus family hates the one before. Granddaddy boiled and ate some of his kids. Pa killed a daughter to bring him good luck, then Mother killed him. This opera…'

'Godawful screeching racket,' he interrupted.

'… is the daughter Elektra wanting her mother dead.'

The afternoon sun, forcing itself through gaps in the scudding clouds, shone flickering beams on patches of purple heather and russet bracken, drawing colour out of the bleak landscape. A grouse flew low over the moor, disturbed by their passing.

'Aye, well, I can see why it's a curse. They never get their feet free. Like him.' He jerked his head backwards.

She stretched out a leg, tapping her boot on the footrest. 'I was wondering about that. In the original Aeschylus play, it was the son, Orestes, who saw Ma off and then went mad. Maybe the screech just reminded her of him and his hatred of… her, I suppose, and the world in general. That's probably what drove him on. Hate is a great motivator.' She sighed. 'I suppose I'll have to disentangle his motives.'

'That's the other question,' he said swiftly, his face brightening as the small hotel came into view. 'Will his friends be able to stop you?'

'There is not a snowball's chance in hell,' she said fiercely, as they drew up. 'There'll be two days' fulsome compliments in the press when news of his death gets out. Like Robert Maxwell, who was the greatest guy on earth until all the shit emerged. Or Jimmy Savile. Then the vultures will come out to pick over the carrion. They can't stop it nowadays.'

'I know, I know. With you swooping down for first bite?' he said, grinning.

'Vultures have a holy mission to keep the world clean,' she said, nudging him on the arm with her elbow.

CHAPTER 50

Donnie was standing on the front step to welcome them with a broad smile on his face and ushered them straight into the dining room. Maggie brought through piping-hot scotch broth and homemade bread, while he listened to Herk's brief description of seeing and photographing Stone shoot himself on top of the tower.

'Good riddance,' he said, pouring himself a whisky. Then he looked at Herk, raised one shaggy eyebrow and said with a knowing wink: 'I don't suppose you want to be held up by the police for days. Let me phone Callum direct and he might come himself. He never liked the man, so he won't fuss about why you were there.'

After finishing the soup, Tire refused the stew that was offered and went upstairs to make phone calls, leaving Herk to cope with Callum, who had promised to turn up in an hour. Twilight was casting deep shadows across the surging waves, obscuring the line between land and sea, with the faint glow of a moon behind clouds above the next headland. Standing at the window, she dialled Ricky's mobile and wondered how Jimmy would react to the news of his stepfather's death. He answered instantly, then asked her to wait as he moved to another room.

'Your news first,' he said, obviously pent up with excitement. 'We wondered where you'd got to. Jimmy was getting worried.'

'Stone's dead,' she said unceremoniously. 'Shot himself.'

'Wow, that's great. Jimmy will be so relieved.' He sighed dramatically and added: 'And all the rest of us, Wally too.'

With a wince, she remembered she had not asked Stone who had killed Wally's nephew. A bat flitted across the road, a black shape barely visible against the darkness, followed by two others.

'Let me tell you my news.' The voice on the other end of the phone was lowered so she had to strain to hear.

'My cousin Lorenzo in Viterbo, he finally found out about Jimmy's mother. It was reported as an accident when she fell into Lake Bolsena from the high rocks. He also got hold of her will. She left everything to Jimmy. House and money. Nothing to the stepfather. So he's going to claim it back for him, which will be a lot easier now he's dead. I haven't told Jimmy yet.'

'Ah,' she said cautiously, 'that might be a problem. I think Paul Stone was broke.'

'Oh, drat. That would be a bitch. I had my eye on a nice cottage for him with a double garage that would make a studio.'

Promising she would find out about Stone's finances and help by getting Jimmy's claim pushed hard, she said she and Herk would come down to Glasgow tomorrow.

'He's sticking to Jimmy as a name, rather than Louis?' she asked.

'Yes. Says he can't go back now. Too late. And he is quite stubborn.' He sighed and said: 'See you.'

She swithered about phoning her agent and decided that sorting out the bag of Stone's papers and trying to get into his laptop was a priority. An hour later she was little the wiser, having waded through copious financial statements. They could go to Russell, although she had found Stone's and his mother's birth certificates and all his marriage certificates, which would be useful. The laptop password defeated her so it would have to wait till London to be handed over to a hacker she knew.

Summoned downstairs, she was glad to take a break and answered the policeman's questions briefly. A burly, ruddy-faced figure with his jacket unbuttoned and his tie loosened, he stood by a crackling fire with a whisky in his hand smiling benignly at her. He said one young policeman had been to the keep to confirm that Stone was dead and was standing guard. But they had not sent the ambulance out to the keep or visited it himself since it was dark and therefore dangerous. The morning would do, he assured her. He had looked at Herk's photograph. She noted the singular. Obviously, Mr Stone had been disturbed in his mind and that was all there was to it. He would report with the evidence to the Procurator Fiscal, who would most likely not take it any further.

The evening drifted by in a haze of good-humoured bantering from the men and too much alcohol. Tire sat detached from it, her mind racing and her panic rising about not knowing what outlet to aim for with her information. She tried to calm down by reminding herself that no one else had access to all the papers, the knowledge about his past and the deaths that had followed him in his rise to prominence. It was his 'you'll see' comment that kept bugging her. Had he set up barriers in advance against her publishing what she had found out?

Late next morning, having been released by the police and taken their farewells of Donnie and Maggie with promises to return, they headed for Inverness airport. An hour later they left the Range Rover in the long-term car park with the key dropped into a box. Inside the terminal, the departure board indicated a delay in their plane to Glasgow due to a tardy incoming flight. They checked in their luggage and collected a coffee to drink outside.

Huddling against the sleek grey sides of the building with a sharp easterly blowing, Tire could feel her adrenaline pumping despite her hangover, with her to-do list growing ever longer.

'Good morning.' The well-bred voice made her jump. She turned into the wind to see Jake Harrister standing with a coffee in his hand.

'What are you doing here?' she said.

He sipped at his coffee, smiled thinly and replied: 'I understand our erstwhile acquaintance is dead.'

'And you just happened to be up here on holiday, did you?' she said slowly.

He laid his paper mug on a metal plate on the wall, tugged at the cuffs of his tweed jacket and surveyed his polished shoes, then said crisply: 'We were informed by the local police last night since he had connections to important people within the government. So he is on an alert list My brief is to ensure his body is returned to London discreetly.' He looked over her shoulder into the distance and added flatly: 'To minimise any adverse publicity.'

'Who are we and who the hell do you work for?' She took a step towards him, waving her cigarette irritably, which left a shower of sparks as a gust eddied round the terminal.

He sighed and studied the ground again. 'I work for Her Majesty's government.' He paused. 'As you well know, in a lowly capacity.'

Her eyes, glittering with hostility, never left his face. 'And?' she demanded.

The tannoy gave out the call for their boarding so Herk lifted his bag. Harrister put up a warning hand, an inscrutable expression on his face. Looking her directly in the face, he said: 'I don't suppose there's any possibility of me persuading you not to go into print.'

'No,' she said, vehemently.

'You realise if you go ahead I cannot help you find out about your father. Indeed, I won't be in touch with you again. My position would not allow it.'

'Not career-friendly, you mean,' she spat back. 'You know exactly what an asshole Stone was and you're trying to buy my fucking silence for your godawful superiors. What kind of jerk are you?' She was breathing heavily, oblivious to Herk tugging at her sleeve.

Harrister gave a tight-lipped smile and said: 'It's the way of the world, I'm afraid.'

'Yours maybe. Not mine,' she responded. 'And what about Greengate? You're just going to let him rot in prison?'

The second call for boarding wheezed out above their heads. He ran a hand down his coat lapel and said in precise, professional tones: 'I have my instructions. If you insist on going ahead, that is your choice. We do not live in a dictatorship.' She gave a sarcastic snort as he added in a tone could have been mildly threatening: 'Though you may not find it that easy. He was very well respected.'

They stood looking at each other, her eyes sparkling with dislike and his coolly detached. Then he said quietly: 'You know Harman, the son, has disappeared to South America? He's been moving money out for a while. So you won't track him down in a hurry.'

The final boarding call came so she bent down, lifted up her bag, which contained Stone's laptop and documents, and gave Harrister a contemptuous look. As she brushed past him, she thought she heard him quietly say: 'Good luck.' Was that ironic, she wondered, or a genuine off-the-record sentiment?

'By the way,' he called from behind her, 'I gather the police think Paul Stone destroyed all his records and threw them into the sea. His office was wrecked and empty when they got there.'

CHAPTER 51

In Glasgow, Tire, mindful they had a plane to catch to London in three hours, rattled through Stone's confession, their imprisonment in the house and the finale at the fort on the cliffs. At the end she paused, looked at her knees and said quietly to Wally: 'I'm sorry, I didn't ask which of his goons killed your nephew.'

Wally waved a magnanimous hand. 'Don't you worry your head about that. The one Dorry leant on.' He smiled grimly. 'Janski. He coughed before we handed him over to the polis. He's up for torching Jimmy and Elly's flat. He won't be out in a hurry since that old biddy died in the fire.'

There was an audible whimper from the far end of the conservatory, then Elly's knitting needles continued clicking faster.

He blew a perfect smoke ring and turned to smile broadly at Herk. 'He said it was Anton, the one you did away with in Spain. So honour is done and I owe you, pal.' He nodded approvingly.

Tire winced and said anxiously: 'I don't think we want to admit to that.'

'What do you take me for?' Wally asked, shaking his head in disbelief. 'It was an accident. We all know that. But the right people will know what kind of accident. So my reputation is safe.'

'He didn't happen to mention who bumped off the journalist Davey up north?' she asked.

'Aye, Anton and his brother, Ilic. He's the one you knocked off in the States, isn't he? Doubt you'll get him on that. Too long ago.'

'No,' she said. 'Just tying up loose ends.' Turning to Ricky, who had been sitting listening intently, she said: 'What about Jimmy? There'll be a horrendous mess with Stone's finances if he really was bust and some big guys will be bullying for first dibs at whatever is left. Bankers and the like.'

'Scum,' rumbled Wally. 'Worse than fucking criminals, most of them.'

'I'll let you know when my accountant has run through the figures. I've got most of Stone's info here.' She patted her travel bag. 'Tell your cousin that at least two statues from Italy went to the resort in Spain. The alabaster ones that Jimmy painted.'

Ricky ran a finger along the crease in his trousers and smiled uncertainly. 'Sure. Maybe you can talk directly to Lorenzo. All that high finance is beyond me.' He looked disconsolate. 'I had just so hoped he would get a decent lump sum out of it to buy a place of their own.'

'There's no worries on that score,' Wally interrupted. 'He's keeping my nephew's name so I've kind of adopted him. There's a property of mine in Glasgow, off Queen Margaret Drive, overlooking the river and the Botanic Gardens that would suit him.' He turned to smile at Elly, who kept her head down. 'It's on the top floor so there's good light and enough space for a big studio as well as living accommodation. And walking distance to the shops.'

'That is very kind of you.' Elly's voice was trembling. She laid down her knitting and came across to perch uncomfortably on the edge of the sofa. Holding a handkerchief to her nose, she said: 'Jimmy doesn't want any fuss. He just wants to live quietly and do his paintings. And Dr Donaghue says he has to take it slowly. It's all been quite a shock.' She stood up awkwardly and smiled apologetically to Tire. 'He really is very grateful. But he just can't show it at the moment.' She shuffled quietly into the corridor leading to the kitchen.

Ricky waited till she was out of earshot and whispered: 'The psychiatrist came here to visit Jimmy. Nice man, very kind and sensible. He said we shouldn't expect too much of him, given what he went through in that dreadful place for most of his life. And he's got that dreadful woman Birch, his colleague, off Jimmy's back. Elly said she was quite useful, but she was only interested in boosting her career with a juicy story for her thesis..'

'Ach, Jimmy's strong as an ox,' Wally growled. 'I've known guys come out after decades in the slammer and they were like zombies, less wits than that potted fern there. Jimmy's going to be OK. He's got support now and Tiresa here will sort out the money end with your cousin, and I'll fill in for the meantime. No problem.'

He stood up, waving his cigar at her, his other stubby hand resting on the head of the Rottweiler, which had risen in unison. Herk was given a warm nod of approval by the dog before it walked out onto the terrace heading for home, followed by a lumbering Dorry.

They took their leave of Jimmy, who was dabbing blue furiously on the canvas, seemingly oblivious to their presence. On impulse, sensing his tension, Tire walked forward and held his arm with the paintbrush from behind to prevent any mishaps and hugged him. 'It'll be OK, you'll see,' she whispered. As she reached the step up into the house, Jimmy cleared his throat and said hesitantly: 'What would you like me to paint for you?'

She thought for a moment and said with a grin: 'Do you paint birds? Herk would like that.'

The rush-hour traffic was building as their cab headed for Glasgow airport. A crash near the Clyde Tunnel threatened to delay them further. They just managed to get their luggage checked in before the flight closed and were through the departure gate straight onto the plane. Despite a howling baby in the row behind, Tire spent a fruitful eighty minutes transferring Herk's photographs onto her laptop and updating her list of urgent tasks for when she hit her apartment. She had already texted Russell telling him to expect a deluge of scanned documents and sent a further text to her hacker to turn up after nine to get into Stone's computer.

A strategy was also coming together about how to circumvent any dirty tricks by Stone's influential friends. Don't go in cold. It was too big and shocking a story. Create a context. A small story here, another there, preferably on foreign media sites, not under her name. The internet would join the dots and start to spin interest up to centrifugal force: what an old rock singer boyfriend had called 'howl round', as amplifiers picked up echo sound and doubled and tripled the effect. At that point, the UK media would be begging for information. Then she could step in.

Once she had Paul Stone cleared off her schedule, she'd turn her attention to her father's story. Damn St Clair for dying before he could tell her what he knew. And double damn Harrister for using it to threaten her into silence. Nothing was going to shut her up and she'd find out for herself if he refused to help. A project for the future. She filed it away.

Only when they had landed, collected their luggage and were stowed in a taxi did she notice that Herk, leaning against the armrest and staring out of his window, had been unusually silent.

'What's up?'

'Nothing.'

'Yes, there is.' She kicked his boot with her toe. 'Spill.'

'No big deal. I was just pondering on my options for what comes next.' He wrinkled his nose. 'Suppose I could always go back and stay with Ma.'

A great gale of laughter bubbled out of her before she could stop it. 'Give me a break,' she gasped. 'And do what? Help her polish the family medals?'

He attempted to look affronted and failed, giving a small chuckle. 'I dunno. OK?'

'Herk, I don't know how to put this to you.' She took his hand in hers, holding it firmly as he tensed. Leaning across, she kissed him lightly on the cheek and whispered in his ear: 'Those photographs of yours. The disgraced philanthropist meeting his maker on the top of a ruined tower in a scene of unimaginable drama. They're iconic.' She moved back to her side of the seat, her eyes sparkling. 'Have you any idea how much money you are going to make from them? Never mind the thirty per cent you'll get from anything I earn from the Stone saga.'

His look of wary disbelief brought on another bout of giggles. His boots were wrapped tightly round one another and his hands were clasped with the thumbs pressed together as he absorbed what she'd said. His eyes were narrowed as if he feared he was the butt of a joke.

Taking pity on him, she grinned and said: 'You'll be able to get yourself a nice little pad in Camden near your Dying Duck barmaid and help out Speedy Charlie, until you decide on your next career move.'

He sat nonplussed and eventually said, gruffly, fixing his eyes on the back of the cabbie's head: 'One – you're no organising me. Two – you shouldn't count chickens. Three – I'm not taking money from your writing.'

'Oh yes you are. I couldn't have done it without you. It was a team effort. And its thirty per cent of net, minus agent fee and expenses. Plus a hundred per cent for your photographs.'

The argument raged until they arrived in Soho, with neither of them budging.

Outside the apartment, she was fishing in her bag for the key when Herk pulled her back, his ear against the door. An irregular thumping was drawing closer, then a clatter, a muffled curse and then the door was thrown open. A dishevelled, broad-shouldered figure leant against the frame, one leg in plaster up to the knee with a slit jean leg flapping round it and a crutch lying halfway down the hall behind him.

Jin was back. Tire's eyes widened and she hoped the expression on her face was delighted, which was partly true.

'Your lousy stars came early,' he grunted, giving her an amused look, his hooded eyes dancing between delight and irritation. 'Fell down the goddamn aircraft steps in Hamburg on the way back.'

Believe it if you like, she thought to herself, giving him a hug as he wobbled on his cast. Guarantee it happened somewhere else. She sighed.

Just her luck. Desperate as she was to see Jin, this was not a good time. Why couldn't her life schedule itself more sensibly?

'Right,' she said, resolutely. 'Work first. Jin, you help Herk with his photographs and send them off to your agent to hold, till I say go. I must get stuff sent out.'

Later that night, lying beside Jin in bed, having made love gently and drifting into an exhausted sleep, she wrapped her leg round his cast and sighed contentedly. He understood a crazy lifestyle. He'd cope. For as long as he was here.

EPILOGUE

Paul Stone's death by suicide, when suffering from advanced leukaemia, was announced two days after he shot himself. The obituaries applauded his charitable efforts to alleviate the suffering of others and his devotion to his mother. Several MPs, lawyers and business leaders spoke warmly of their personal experience of his charm and compassion.

A week later, the media pendulum started to swing and cracks appeared in the Paul Stone story. Questions were asked about the origins of his wealth on internet forums. The fissures widened, with a savage attack on his financial dealings in the US press led by an ex-business associate, Chip Nathon. A story followed in the German media about his son's mysterious disappearance, with comments by a disgruntled holidaymaker. Rupert Wrighton was named as a business associate. A Scottish tabloid revealed exclusively that ex-Dunlothian Hall painter Jimmy Black was Stone's stepson.

Within a month, a six-page exclusive in a UK Sunday newspaper under the byline T.A. Thane laid bare the progression of Pol Pedra's life from inauspicious beginnings, through two name changes, two dead, wealthy wives, an abandoned and defrauded stepson, several circumstantial deaths, a mad mother, a son who was also a brother, illegal drug testing on children, high social status and ultimate financial failure. Photographs by Herk Calder. The headline read, 'By the Light of a Lie'.

Barrister Sebastian Crumley successfully appealed the conviction of Jack Greengate for the murder of his wife on the basis of new evidence from Paul Stone's former bodyguards in prison in Scotland and the USA. Lorenzo Marinello, an Italian lawyer, reclaimed a small part of Louis Neroni's lost inheritance after lengthy arguments with other creditors, and emerged with half a million pounds and two alabaster statues.

A biography of Paul Stone was being rushed out for publication in six months' time.

ACKNOWLEDGEMENTS

Thanks to playwright Shaun McCarthy whose inspiring approach to drama gave me the impetus and tools to switch to fiction. And to Chris Wakling of Curtis Brown Creative, who gave me the heart and confidence to finish the first draft. James Pusey of The Literary Consultancy was invaluable with constructive comments and encouragement when my morale was flagging. Plus the CBC gang who stayed together online as we supported each other through the soul-destroying and hair-tearing process of crafting our perfectly-tuned pitches and synopses for agents. Any mistakes, needless to say, are entirely owned by me.

Hina Pandya picked me up off the floor when I was ready to jettison the project altogether with a million marketing plans. Louise Bolotin was a wonderful proof and continuity editor. And James of Spiffing Covers produced exactly the design that was needed.

Last but not least, thanks to Turtur, a turbo-charged Weimaraner, who kept me healthy, dragging me away from my writing desk for snake-hunting forays in the vineyards twice a day.

27504486R00149

Printed in Great Britain
by Amazon